**The Urbana Free Library**

To renew materials call
217-367-4057

Tor Books by J. A. Pitts

*Black Blade Blues*

# Honeyed Words

## J. A. Pitts

TOR®

A Tom Doherty Associates Book

NEW YORK

HONEYED WORDS

Copyright © 2011 by John A. Pitts

A Tor Book
Published by Tom Doherty Associates, LLC
175 Fifth Avenue
New York, NY 10010

www.tor-forge.com

Tor® is a registered trademark of Tom Doherty Associates, LLC.

Library of Congress Cataloging-in-Publication Data

Pitts, J. A.
Honeyed words / J. A. Pitts.—1st ed.
p. cm.
ISBN 978-0-7653-2468-9 (hardcover)
ISBN 978-0-7653-2907-3 (trade paperback)
I. Title.
PS3616.I917H66 2011
813'.6—dc22
2011013443

First Edition: July 2011

Printed in the United States of America

0  9  8  7  6  5  4  3  2  1

I'd like to dedicate this book to two of my oldest friends—
Lucien (Lou) Cerwin and Alan Burstein.

Alan and I were roommates straight out of high school.
For living with me, he very likely deserves a Purple Heart.
Alan did a stint in the Navy, and ended up an engineer in
the private sector.

Lou has been a supporter of my dreams since the day we
met all the way back into the seventh grade. He's always had
a sharp mind and a flair for speaking it loud and proud.
While we may not always agree on politics, I know he's in
my corner, no matter what. Lou retired from the Navy recently.

I'd like to thank both of these guys for the service they've
done for our country. It isn't everyone who can dedicate a
significant portion of their lives so we can enjoy the freedoms
we have grown accustomed to.

Both of these guys flew to Seattle for my book launch and
have gone way above and beyond in the support and promo-
tion of my writing. My life is richer for having them in it.

# Acknowledgments

Here we are at my second published novel. Between the day job and everything else life tosses my way, I'm thankful that I have such a wonderful group of folks who support me in my endeavors.

First and foremost, of course, I need to thank my family—Kathy Pitts, my awesome wife and partner. By the time you folks read this book, we'll be celebrating our twenty-second wedding anniversary. My son, Patrick Pitts, who's become an adult when I wasn't looking. I love all the help you give me in brainstorming the story. You are excellent. And my youngest, Emily Pitts. What a wonderful young woman you've grown to be. Thanks for the humor and the constant hugs. They make the day-to-day existence so sweet. Thanks for everything you do.

The fine folks at my day job have been very supportive. It's wonderful to have so many people excited for all this. I'd like to call out Linda Ingram especially, for being so optimistic and wonderful about the books.

There are those who are quieter, supporting me day-for-day with their loyalty and friendship. These folks are hard to come by, and should never want for acknowledgment. My buddy Allan Rousselle has been that kind of friend. He's a damn fine writer in his own right. He has a quick wit and keen insight into story. Thanks for all the help.

The first reader crew from True Martial Arts and beyond has returned with a passion: Dan and Jen Berg (and baby Elizabeth), Owen and Chelsea Wessling, and Toby Goan. I must also mention three very dedicated friends: Deb Kerekes, who's read even my earliest dregs, as well as Rob Scott and Alecia Bolton. And I mustn't forget some awesome authors: Brenda Cooper and Shannon Page. You've all influenced not just my novel, but my life, and I'm richer for the lot.

Once again, I want to thank my agent, Cameron McClure. I think Cameron's influence on my work is excellent, but her impact on my growth as a writer, especially on the business side of things, is immeasurable. Thanks a ton.

The crew at Tor is astounding. My editors, Claire Eddy and Kristin Sevick; the art director, Irene Gallo, who always does superb work; and the whole support crew who remain nameless to me (I'll meet them all someday) and yet they produce a wonderful product that just happens to contain my words. Thank you all for helping me see Sarah to a public viewing.

This is my second book with a Dan Dos Santos cover. I love the way Dan has with Sarah and the feel he has for capturing the essence of the story. The man has talent.

Finally, I'd like to thank all the readers, reviewers, and bloggers who found my book worth their time to discuss and promote. I truly appreciate the tweets and e-mails I get. It's an amazing thing to find that the stories from my psyche have resonated with so many of you.

# Honeyed Words

# One

Jimmy Cornett, the leader of Black Briar, paced the length of the room, eleven long strides before turning and making the return trip. In his left hand he carried a highball glass with three fingers of Glenlivet single-malt scotch but had not taken the first sip.

His world had gotten a helluva lot more complicated these last six months. Running the farm and Black Briar was full-time work. He loved the reenactment and the swordplay, but until this spring, that's what it had been: play. When the dragon attacked the farm with choppers full of trolls and giants, the thin veneer of it all slid right off the cracker.

His sister, Katie, had a better handle on it all. He'd always discounted her beliefs, nodding and patting her on the head. But they were definitely the children of their parents, and the secret world of dragons and myth should not have come as such a surprise to him. Of course, they had been rather vague on the whole "dragons will attack your farm in helicopters" aspect of it all.

He felt a tightening in his chest as he thought back to the battle just a few months earlier. Black Briar had been prepared, sort of. They'd trained for the various reenactment wars around the country. They were good, a well-considered mercenary house on the fringes of the stalwart Society kingdoms. While the Society of

Creative Anachronism did things right, down to the linen shirts and hand-sewn boots, real steel weapons and man-to-man combat, nothing prepared them for fifteen-feet-tall giants, hordes of trolls, and a fucking dragon.

They may have come through okay, if not for that damn drake. Killed his best riders: Susan and Maggie. Mangled Maggie and burned Susan to the ground. So many fallen that long black night.

His wife, Deidre, still wasn't home from the rehab center where she'd been recovering from the injuries she'd sustained. There was a damn good chance she'd never walk again.

Sarah had kept the dragon busy, let him rescue Deidre after the giants had broken through their defenses. But part of him blamed Sarah for all of this going down the way it had. Sure, she didn't really understand that the sword she had reforged was the legendary Gram. Hell, only Katie had thought it possible, and even he'd laughed at her. It wasn't until the dragon had kidnapped his baby sister, along with Sarah's blacksmith master, Julie Hendrickson, that Jimmy had accepted the truth. All the crazy shit his parents had told him. All the history and stories were really true.

Didn't mean he had to like it.

And he wasn't alone. He had friends—friends who knew the truth about the world.

Stuart and Gunther sat on either side of a small table, each ensconced in a large leather wingback chair. They hadn't waited and were sipping their scotch while Jimmy gathered his thoughts.

The room was filled with cabinets and display cases, bookshelves and weapons racks, which held a smattering of items: swords, tomes, scrolls, cups, necklaces, and trinkets. The northern wall was dominated by a huge world map.

Jimmy's grandparents had commissioned the map from dwarven artisans in the early twentieth century, but it was based on a much older one, only known by rumor and hearsay. Each continent was laid out in meticulous detail. Political demarcations were absent, but geographical locations were noted in abundance. Remarkable about the map were the tiny lights that glowed from spots on every continent. Most were major cities; they'd figured those out early on. Some were obviously deep in ancient mountain ranges, and two were mysteriously in the middle of an ocean—one in the Atlantic and one in what is now called the Sea of Japan.

These lights, these pinpoints glowing in the shadows of the room, represented the dragons that ruled the world. Jimmy had first seen the map when he was nine. He remembered that day like many children remember the day they learn Santa Claus isn't real or that their parents are human and fallible. He didn't understand the ramifications of this knowledge at first, not even after his parents had disappeared. It took Sarah, Gram, and that damn dragon, Jean-Paul Duchamp, for the truth of the world to finally become clear.

He'd been in his room in a tent made from blankets, pillows, and a couple of ski poles. He had his flashlight and was reading comic books way past his bedtime. It was late, close to midnight, when he heard a commotion outside. An odd warbling sound echoed through the house. Jimmy scrambled out of the tent and jerked the bedroom door open. Katie was screaming, and his father was rushing toward the front door, pulling a leather harness across his shoulders and settling a long sword into the attached sheath.

"Dad?" Jimmy called. His father paused at the door, his face grim. "Go help your mother," he said, then turned without even waiting to see if he complied. The front screen slammed with a bang that startled him.

He turned to the sounds of Katie's cries. His mother came down the hallway carrying his screaming two-year-old sister in her arms.

"Come on, Jim. Hurry." She waved at him, cradling Katie to her chest.

At the end, near the library, there was an open panel, one he'd never noticed before. She sat Katie on the ground. "Take her hand," she said to him, holding out her own. Katie loved Jimmy, and leaned into him, quieting.

"Don't make any noise," his mother said before kissing him quickly on the forehead. "I'll come get you when it's safe. Go down the stairs. We won't be able to hear Katie there."

"But, Mom. What's going on?" He was horrified. They'd never acted like this. "Where's Dad going?"

She knelt down and cupped her hand against his cheek. "He's going to protect us," she said. "I need to go help him. Can you be strong for me, James?"

When she called him James, he knew it was serious. He swallowed hard and nodded. "I'll keep Katie safe."

She smiled at him, which filled him with warmth. "You are brave and strong."

"Me, too," Katie piped up.

Their mother smiled worriedly and kissed her on the cheek. "Yes, popkin. You are brave and true. Now, go." She shooed them onto the dark landing. "Just go to the first bend. It's seventy-three steps. You'll be safe there."

The door shut with a quiet click. Jimmy pulled the penlight from his pocket and strained to see down into the void.

"Come on," he whispered.

"It's dark," Katie whined. "I don't like it."

"We'll be safe." He squeezed her hand as they crept down into the unknown.

He counted the seventy-three steps and stopped at the first bend. He sat down, his back against the wall, and pulled Katie into his lap. She snuggled up against him and whimpered quietly.

"I'm gonna turn the light off," he said, stroking her hair. "Save the batteries."

"I want Momma."

"She'll be back soon," he said and clicked off the light.

As his eyes adjusted, he could make out a glow coming from below.

"Pretty," Katie said, slipping from his lap.

"Katie, wait." She scooted down the stairs on her bottom, one riser at a time, and he followed, holding his breath. Where the stairs ended they found a room full of treasures, lit by the glowing dragon lights.

He'd found out later that a group of refugees from Vancouver had stumbled onto the farm, harried and wounded, triggering some sort of alarm. His father had come to the strangers' aid, helping fight off a giant and getting mostly dwarves, along with a few humans, into the barn before the sun rose.

It was later, days after this incident, that his father had accompanied him down to the bunker and explained to his son the meaning of the map.

It held hundreds of lights. Some glowed brightly, while others flickered and waned. Only one had grown dark in recent memory. Jimmy pulled his thoughts back to the present and paused in his pacing. He dragged his finger along the bottom frame of the map and stared upward. The map rose from just three feet off the ground to near the ceiling, putting the light for Vancouver out of his reach.

Gunther and Stuart had the best view of the map, sitting a dozen feet away, against the opposite wall. The first time they'd seen the map, three days after Jimmy received the news of his parents' disappearance, they had commented on how much the map reminded them of the night sky.

"So damn many," Stuart growled when no one had spoken.

"The bastards feed off us like maggots. It's about time we began to do something about it."

Gunther winced and sipped his scotch.

Jimmy turned, his face flushed with anger. "And what do you propose?" he said, sweeping his right arm to encompass the entire map. "Do you honestly think they'd sit idly by while we . . ." He paused, struggling to keep his anger in check. "We can't just hunt them down. This isn't the Middle Ages. They're practically immortal, have learned to adapt in ways we can only guess at. They don't even look like dragons most of the time. They control multinational corporations and some entire countries, for god's sake. Hell, I wouldn't put it past one of them to use nukes if push came to shove." He looked between the two men, feeling the desperation crawling in his belly. "Most of us don't even know they exist. Can you imagine what the common man would think if he learned we weren't at the top of the food chain?"

Gunther sat his glass on the table, took up his cane, and struggled to his feet. They watched him, saying nothing. The vivid memory of Gunther being smashed to the ground by a giant's cudgel was still too fresh in their minds.

"You overestimate their power," Gunther said, stepping toward the map and pointing at Vancouver with the head of his cane. "They've ruled us for so long that we've forgotten ourselves."

"Amen," Stuart said from his seat. He'd worn his anger on his vest since the spring. Since they'd lost so many friends in the battle with the dragon, Duchamp, and his minions.

Gunther nodded. "We were part of an event that has not happened in written history. Not since St. George have we even heard rumors of a human destroying one of them. Now one of our very own has stepped into legend."

Jimmy flicked his hand toward Gunther and barked, "Bah. We were lucky."

"Were we?" Stuart yelped. "We lost twenty-seven good people. You think that's lucky?"

Gunther leaned on his cane with both hands firmly covering the worked bull's-head handle. "I grieve as you do," he said, turning to his friend. "But this is nothing compared to the wholesale slaughter in the Dark Ages. Entire villages wasted, broad swathes of countryside slaughtered in the great migration."

Stuart growled low in his throat. "So says your order," he finally voiced. "There's proof of the Black Plague, you know."

Gunther sighed and glanced at Jimmy.

"Plague, famine, war, and worse," Jimmy said, his voice even. "My father explained it to me as well. One does not discount the existence of the other."

"We've read all the notes Jim's parents left us and have researched on our own over the last thirteen years," Gunther offered. "Nothing prepared us for Sarah."

They fell silent at that. Jimmy turned, facing the map, his eyes falling on Iceland, the last place anyone had seen his parents. Gunther watched the two of them—friends and compatriots—slowly turning his head from one man to the other, waiting for the thunderheads that had been brewing for weeks.

"Deidre will be home soon," he said. Jimmy nodded once and took a deep drink.

"About damn time," Stuart said. "Black Briar is too quiet without her around to keep us all in line."

Jimmy snorted a quiet laugh. "She's worried no one needs her."

Stuart leaned back into the thick leather chair, his anger visibly fading. "Tell her that we miss her and that if she doesn't get back here soon, we're gonna let Gunther start using her kitchen."

Then it was Gunther's turn to laugh. "I will not risk that woman's wrath," he said. "I'll go up against giants and dragons, but Deidre scares the hell out of me."

Jimmy nodded once, a smile on his face for the first time in a long while. "She is my light and my life."

Each man lapsed into quiet contemplation, sipping his scotch. The anger in the room had finally begun to dissipate.

After a few minutes, Gunther shuffled back to his chair and sat down with a grunt. "But we need to discuss Sarah," he said. "We have to figure out who she is."

They each nodded but said nothing, waiting for the other to bring up the subject of the fiery smith.

Jimmy's phone buzzed with an incoming text message. "In case you were wondering," he said, shaking his head, "Katie and Sarah are at the Blain crossing into Canada. Katie says they will be in Vancouver in just under an hour." He paused, glancing up quickly.

"What?" Stuart asked.

"Well," Jimmy said, clearing his throat. "She also says that Sarah is hot."

They all laughed.

Jimmy slipped his phone into his pocket. "That sister of mine sure can pick 'em."

"Aye," Gunther agreed. "First Melanie, now Sarah."

"Oh, she's dated more than those two," Jimmy said, running both hands through his hair. "Drove me and Deidre crazy in high school. The drama and the angst of teenage love."

Stuart picked up the crystal decanter and poured himself another scotch. "Love ain't nothing but drama and angst," he said. "Been burned myself one time too many."

"I've been lucky," Jimmy said. "Deidre is the best thing that ever happened to me."

"Hear, hear," Gunther said, raising his glass.

Jimmy retrieved his glass and stepped toward them. Stuart stood, and the three of them held their glasses high.

"To the women in our lives," Gunther said, clinking his glass against first Stuart's, and then Jimmy's. "May they always find their way home to us."

They drank, draining their glasses. Stuart lowered his glass and performed the sign of the cross. After a moment, they set their glasses on the table and Stuart picked up the decanter once again.

"Now, about Sarah," he said, pouring a strong dash into each glass. "Who is this girl? What do we really know about her?"

Jimmy went back to pacing, but Gunther stepped over to the map, following a series of lights that filled Central Europe like a cluster of stars.

"Maybe she's one of the two ancient lines of gods—Æsir, Odin's crew, maybe, or one of the older lot, the Vanir," Stuart suggested.

"Doubtful," Jimmy said, striding to a case and pulling down a sheaf of papers. "According to the records my father uncovered in Reykjavík, the dragons have a covenant to kill all of them on sight."

"Sure," Stuart said. "But how do we know when we find one of the elder gods? Can the wyrms really tell the difference?"

"According to Markús Magnússon," Jimmy said, pulling a page from the middle of the stack and setting the rest down on a glass case filled with golden armbands and torques, "in 1288, the last known of the Vanir had been killed by a young dragon in Düsseldorf. She was only an infant, but he describes her as a glowing child, with hair like spun gold and a laugh that would quiet the meanest heart."

"Who does he think she was?" Stuart asked.

"Freya . . . ," Gunther replied, not turning from the map, ". . . is the last we know to be reborn. The dragons have feared their return for as long as the monks and scribes have kept hidden records."

Jimmy and Stuart exchanged a glance.

"My order," Gunther continued, "kept records of each Æsir or

Vanir that was reborn, and their inevitable demise at the tooth and claw of one of the drakes."

"And," Jimmy continued, placing the parchment back on the pile with the others, "Sarah has met at least two dragons in her life, and neither of them thought she was an elder god returned to exact her vengeance."

"Well," Gunther said with a grim chuckle. "We don't know what Jean-Paul Duchamp believed, may his carcass rot in hell."

"True enough," Jimmy said. "But this Frederick Sawyer in Portland has seen her on multiple occasions, and all he's tried to do is invest in that movie company she works with . . . oh, and buy the sword."

The three of them looked to the left, to the black blade that hung from a coatrack by the blood-encrusted leather rigging Sarah had worn into battle with the dragon.

"I think that is the key," Gunther said, turning from the map and limping toward the sword. "This blade is the crux of things."

"Gram," Stuart breathed. "How did she come by it, much less wield it?"

"Katie says she bought it at an auction a few years ago. Some estate sale where the original owners had both died. Kids were selling off everything since they lived in Florida."

"Quite the coincidence there, Jim. Don't you think?" Stuart asked.

Gunther stood in front of the coatrack and examined the sword. "Völsung," he pronounced finally.

"Why not?" Jimmy asked. "Hell, we have giants and trolls, witches and dragons. Why can't my sister's girlfriend be of the lineage of a defunct German tribe purported to be descended from Odin himself?"

"Holy cats," Stuart said, scrubbing his face with his meaty hands. "Sigurd's great, great, great, et cetera granddaughter?"

"The sword sought her out," Gunther said. "How else can you explain it? And you know she claims to have met Odin himself."

"Katie confirmed that," Jimmy said. "Said he'd been haunting her place for years. She thought he was a harmless beggar."

Gunther turned to face them. "Beggar perhaps, but if he's Odin . . . How the hell did he get this old without the dragons killing him again?"

"Good point." Jimmy rummaged around the bookcases for another bit of history. They waited while he pulled down a large dusty tome and opened the leather binding. "There are records of the dragons killing the gods over the years. I've counted six times Odin has been reborn. Three times for Thor . . ." He turned a page, drawing his finger down the thin, spidery script. "Loki is mentioned half a dozen times."

"Okay, let me get this straight." Stuart stood to stare at the great map. "The dragons have been in charge of things since before man figured out how to write, and you're saying not only did they miss Gram when they were collecting all the trinkets from the elder gods, but they missed Odin being reborn?"

"I believe that is a valid assumption," Jimmy agreed.

"You realize," Stuart added, "if they missed Odin, then our Sarah could well be one of the elder gods, reborn."

They considered it for a moment, contemplating.

Gunther shrugged, turning to face Jimmy. "Either way, then maybe it's time to poke our heads out of this turtle shell and see who of your parents' secret society have survived in the intervening years."

Jimmy nodded slowly. "I'll look into it."

"Good," Gunther said. "Would be nice to get some experienced help."

Stuart reached out and poked Gram in the sheath, setting it to swinging in short, reducing arcs. "They are scholars and scribes," he said. "They watch. What we need is someone who isn't afraid to take action. Why else collect all this?" He turned to encompass the room. "There are a lot of weapons in here."

Weapons hadn't stopped the dragon from snatching Katie—hadn't kept Deidre whole, or even kept his parents from disappearing. But his father wielded a blade. He'd seen it once. Perhaps there was a place for more than waiting.

"Our weapons held up well against the giants," Jimmy said.

"Dwarven made," Stuart added. "For the cost, they should have."

Jimmy took down his sword, a long thin blade that had tasted the blood of giants and trolls. "The axe needs to be repaired," he said, pointing to the great double-bladed weapon Stuart had used in the battle months earlier.

"My blade is barely scathed," Gunther grumbled.

"Aye, no nicks on the blade, but more than enough on the warrior." Stuart smiled up at his large friend. "I'm just happy you live to whine about it."

Gunther growled. "A few more weeks of physical therapy and I'll be good as new. Hip is doing much better."

"We cannot fight them openly," Jimmy warned. "The witch, Qindra, and therefore her dragon mistress, Nidhogg, knows about Black Briar."

The other two men frowned, losing the jovial banter.

"We need to proceed cautiously. Find my father's contact and see who of the old crew is alive."

"And in the meantime?" Stuart asked.

"In the meantime," Gunther said, "we keep a close eye on our little berserker blacksmith and try and keep her out of trouble."

For a moment, they stared at one another, and then they burst out laughing.

# Two

I followed Katie into the Generalissimo on Granville. The sign over the marquee read Sold Out, and the fire marshall's sign said the place held 1,500 people. Great, I thought. Fifteen hundred screaming filking fans. Maybe this was hell after all.

Katie tugged my hand as the line snaked between velvet ropes. Katie skipped with every other step, totally loving this. Ari Sveinsson. Who knew the little pisher would be a huge singing sensation? Hell, the last time I'd seen him, he'd been trying to schtup one of the tavern wenches at the same ren faire where I'd met Katie. Now the waif had grown up to be a hunk, with a voice that made girls' panties fall off.

I squeezed Katie's hand when the line slowed, and she leaned in to kiss me. "This is so great," she said.

I shrugged, embarrassed. The public displays of affection were getting more commonplace, but I still had moments of total freakitude. Don't get me wrong, I was coming to grips with the relationship, and we had been building it back slowly, after the events of the spring. While she still hadn't gone into details about what happened to her and Julie after Jean-Paul kidnapped them, I know she cried when she thought I wasn't looking. She was hurting more than she wanted me to see, but I loved her. How could I not see?

"I just hope I don't want to kill myself when he starts singing."

Katie laughed, flashing a smile that sent my heart fluttering. "He sings divinely," she said. "And he's hella cute, too."

Two college girls in front of us squealed and began ranting about how hot Ari was. It was pretty annoying.

We followed a group of older women once the line split into two: one line for fast entry, the other to check IDs and wrap glowing plastic bracelets around the wrists of anyone who wanted to buy alcohol. Most of the patrons were underage, so they didn't bother to try but rushed into the club.

Once we were ensconced in alcohol-friendly shackles, we grabbed a side table and flagged down a waitress. In the middle of the club, the dance floor was clear of tables and chairs, allowing a standing-room-only crowd. I would've considered it a mosh pit, but that didn't jibe with the phrase—*filk concert.*

"Dear Odin, or whomever is listening," I whispered as the waitress walked toward the long bar in the back. "Please, no Simon and Garfunkel."

The drinks arrived before the opening act started. I demolished my Long Island iced tea just as the mandolin and Autoharp began the opening strains of Zeppelin's "The Battle of Evermore."

Katie squealed and grabbed my arm, shaking me. I could barely make out what she said over the screaming crowd, but my guess is, "Told you so."

So, in general, The Harpers did not suck. Reminded me of a cross between Flogging Molly, Jethro Tull, and the Hammer of the Gods—Led Zeppelin.

The alcohol even loosened my shoulders. By the time I'd finished my second Long Island iced tea, The Harpers had polished off a great set—ending with the lead string player rocking a seven-minute version of "Going to California" with a twin-neck lute.

"Did you see that?" Katie asked as the house lights came up enough for everyone to find the restrooms and the bar. "Did you see what he was playing?"

"Lute of some kind," I said as I stood and stretched.

"Chitarrone," she said, practically bouncing. "That is the coolest."

I smiled. Double-necked lute. Never knew what would make Katie excited.

Katie went to the bar to refresh our drinks, and I excused myself to go to the LGR—little girls' room—as my mother always said. Once Katie was in the crowd at the bar I diverted to my real goal and went to find Wenceslas. I'd bought the tickets from him, and he'd promised to get me passes for the after-party. It was the icing on the cake for Katie's birthday.

I veered away from the stupidly long line to the women's restroom and walked up to a muscular man who was striking out with a young coed.

What a schmuck. Let the girl go pee first, geez. Figures I'd find him trolling the bathroom line. "Jesus, Wenceslas. Little early to be hitting on the teenagers, ain't it?"

He turned around and squinted at me. We went way back, ren faires and jousting tourneys. Guy was good on a horse. Good enough with women when he wasn't wasted. Unfortunately, he didn't look like he was feeling any pain at this point.

"Beauhall," he shouted, holding his thick arms out as if I'd hug him. "My favorite blacksmith."

I stood my ground and let him stumble forward. *This is for Katie*, I reminded myself as he grabbed me in a sloppy bear hug. When he lifted me off my feet I seriously considered kneecapping him.

Of course his hug went on too long, so I pushed him back to arms' length and put on my best smile. "You said I could find you easy enough," I said. "But I didn't expect you to be waiting for me in the bathroom line."

He laughed, too loud and forced. "Can't stay away from my fans."

Several of the women looked around, giving me a pitying look, shaking their heads.

"Thought Ari was the family superstar," I said loud enough for the women to hear.

"Aye, my kid brother is doing okay," he said, flexing his biceps at the slowly churning bathroom line. "But I'm twice the man he is."

I tried really hard not to roll my eyes, but some of the women seemed to look at him a second time. He wasn't a bad-looking guy, but was a little off the obnoxious scale. Good to see he hadn't changed in the last few years.

"You got my passes?" I asked as he started to move toward the line again, forgetting me in his drunken state.

"Passes?" he asked, looking my way. "Beauhall?"

I glanced around, looking for anyone with the hanging badges of the staff or roadies. "Yeah, big guy," I said, pulling him to the side, away from the women, and lowering my voice. "You promised me passes to the after-party to go along with the concert tickets."

"Oh, did I?" he said, swinging around to look past me to the coeds who seemed to keep his attention. "I'd thought to use them to score tonight."

Several of the women and one guy were watching us, giving Wenceslas the once-over. "Oh, I think a big strong hunk like yourself wouldn't need those to score with this crowd."

He chuckled, giving me a one-armed hug. "You always had a thing for me, didn't you, Beauhall?"

I tried not to grimace. "How's Pericles?" I asked, trying to divert his one-track mind. "Those new shoes holding up?"

Gotta give him some credit. Man loved his horse. "Aye," he bellowed. "Pericles is a proud papa now. Virile like his master."

I knew all that, having just shod the horse a couple of weeks earlier. Wenceslas had him out to stud at the moment. Starting his own herd of jousting horses. Smart guy, really. When he got enough blood to his brain that wasn't soaked in alcohol.

"So, passes?" I asked, holding out my hand. "Then you can go back to scouting this evening's conquest."

"I like your thinking," he said, fishing a couple of laminated passes from his back pocket. "My silly-ass brother wants me to pull in lots of groupies for the party, so pretend to like him, will ya?"

I slipped the passes into my back pocket and patted him on the arm. "Sure thing, big guy. Be careful out there."

He leered at me and stumbled back toward the line. He was going to make someone very happy later, or pass out trying.

Of course there was no line to the men's room.

I looked around, didn't see any security guards, and slipped into the men's room. One guy stood at the urinal but didn't notice as I stepped into a stall. No sense letting all that plumbing go to waste.

By the time I finished, the men's room was crowded with women. Guess I broke the ice. Made sense. I bet there were only a couple dozen guys in the whole club tonight, including the bands, roadies, and security guards.

When I got back to the table, Katie was talking with a couple at the next table. They were both con-folk—dressed for a pageant. Damn fine costume work; not an amateur stitch to be seen. Katie introduced Carol and Paul, who hailed from Surrey and were erotica writers. We exchanged pleasantries, and then settled down as the house lights flickered. Nearly time for the main act.

Katie sipped a glass of wine, and I took a quick gulp of my third

Long Island. "Katie?" I asked, touching the side of her face. "I have a surprise for you."

She set her drink on the table and scootched her chair around to face me. "I love surprises."

"Close your eyes and hold out your hands."

I stared at her, studying the way her nose crinkled as she scrunched her eyes closed. God, she was beautiful. I so needed this moment, this chance to give her some joy. The last few months had been hard.

Katie kept her pain buried deep, side by side with her fear. She woke crying some nights but allowed me to hold her, and her nightmares had begun to go away. She kept her shields tighter these days, more brittle.

It killed me to see her spirit so fragile. Doubly so because it was partly my fault.

The last five months have been a struggle, that's for sure. But Katie has been a trooper through the whole thing. Teaching me to knit alone should get her the Nobel Prize. But she kept her own stuff bottled up—always cheerful, but distant. I could see the haunt in her eyes, the pain and the fear—that more than anything kept the pain alive. I couldn't fix her. Didn't even know where to begin. While I rescued her from the dragon, I hadn't found a way to free her soul. Not yet anyway, but I was working on it.

I could see Paul and Carol watching, so I pulled the passes out. "Hold your hands out," I said. Katie leaned forward, groping my breasts and giggling. Carol laughed, and I swatted Katie's hands. "Be nice."

"This is the best birthday ever," she said.

I placed the two plastic cards into her hands, and she opened her eyes.

I never saw her move. One second her eyes got as big as headlights: the next she was in my lap, arms around my neck, kissing me like a porn star.

Paul wolf-whistled as I wrapped my arms around Katie and kissed her back. After a moment, she broke the kiss, nuzzled my ear, and whispered, "You are so getting laid later."

Maybe this filking thing wasn't so bad after all.

# Three

THE CONCERT DIDN'T SUCK. THAT'S ALL I KEPT REPEATING to myself as Ari performed. The boy had a voice like an angel, even if he dressed like Jack Sparrow's gay hairdresser. Despite the paisley trousers and the wide-cuffed pirate shirt that was opened to his navel, or maybe because of them, the crowd was in lust with this boy. He did nothing for me, but hell, he could belt out tunes and give Robert Plant a run for his money. He did some covers— sure, Zeppelin, Grand Funk, some old blues stuff—but his filk stuff, the fantasy lyrics with known tunes, or the original stuff really had the crowd wowed.

The last echoes of Ari's voice were barely fading when the house lights came up and Katie went into overdrive.

"Can we go now?" Katie asked, bouncing in her seat. "Can we? Huh? Huh?"

I laughed, feeling a little twitchy. "You'd better remember who you came here with." I didn't mean to be jealous, but there was something inside me that began to wake up and take notice.

She leaned into me, planting a sloppy kiss on my lips, and grabbed my hand. "Come on," she said, pulling me out of my chair. "Let's go party."

The house lights were a little too bright, and I was a little buzzed from the drinks, but it had been a couple of hours. Most of it had burned off.

Katie had drunk more than I had, but she was solid on her feet. Actually, once the crowd was pushing toward the exits and we'd managed to slip upstream toward the back of the club, she began to dance. I loved to watch her move. I stayed back a few paces, watching her spin once, her arms outflung. But when she stumbled, I was there in an instant. I caught her before she fell to the ground, swung her around, and pulled her to me.

She looked into my eyes, and I saw the mischievous look I'd learned to love and dread. "Nice catch," she said, kissing me on the nose.

We walked the rest of the way down the service ramp toward the two large bouncers who didn't look like they were having a good time. That and the forty or fifty young girls in corsets, spandex, or, in one case, surgical gauze caused me to slow down. "There has to be a different entrance."

Katie looked around for a moment, and then straightened up. "No way. We're running the gauntlet."

"Could be a little crazy," I said.

"But we have these," she said, waving the passes in front of me. "None can stand before such might."

I bowed to her, spreading my arms out with a flourish. "As you wish, milady."

She giggled and grabbed me by the arm, nearly dragging me off my feet. "Besides, I can hide behind you."

"That's great." I plucked the passes out of her hand and turned toward the crowd. Katie grabbed the waistband of my jeans and followed behind me real close as I began to work my way through to the bouncers. "Pardon me, coming through, excuse me, dreadfully sorry . . ."

One very large woman turned to block us, one hand on her hip and the other aimed at me with her working finger out. "Now see here, sistah," she slurred. "We gotta right to be here."

"Yes," Katie said from behind me. "Ari told us to look for you. Said if we saw you to let him know."

The woman was twice as wide as me, with her hair teased into some sort of eighties-psycho-cheerleader pomp with streaks of purple and gold.

"You know Ari?" she asked, her anger melting to awe. "Can you get me in? I'm supposed to marry him."

I felt my face stretching as I craned around to look at Katie—seriously?

"Said he loved me at the show in Cleveland."

"I'm sure," I muttered.

"We'll tell him you're out here," Katie said, pushing me from behind. "Once we get inside."

The woman looked at us, debating, but the combination of desperation and alcohol won out. She swung around like a barn door, pushing several other girls out of the way. "Let 'em through," she bellowed. "They're gonna talk to Ari for me."

I shuffle-stepped forward, aware of all the eyes on us, hungry eyes, full of need and . . . one of the young goth girls didn't look quite right. There was something about the way her eyes were glinting, the tilt of her jaw, the way her hair covered her ears.

"I think she's an elf," Katie said, following my gaze. "But why would real elves be waiting in line?"

I handed the passes to the bouncers, who ushered us past the velvet ropes. Once we were on the other side, I looked back. "You sure?" I asked. "Real elves?"

Katie craned her neck to the side, trying to see through the milling crowd. "I've never met an elf. Maybe we should go talk to her."

The bouncers gave us a look. Crossing back over to the milling crowd may be a bad idea. "You sure you want to be late for the party?"

I could tell she was torn. She glanced down the hall toward the party, then back at the crowd.

The girl was gone. I'd been watching her, watching us. Just glanced away a second and she'd vanished.

"She's gone," I said. "Maybe next time."

Katie pouted a few seconds and threw her arms up. "What can you do? Let's go party." She sauntered off, turning the corner as the ramp continued downward while I got a pair of lanyards for the passes and slipped one over my neck. I hurried to catch up with Katie. Were there real elves? How the hell did I know? I needed a guidebook to my own damn world after I reforged Gram.

I staggered, a sharp pain in my left calf. Gram! I had been avoiding her, keeping my mind on other things, but she was out there, sleeping. *Soon*, she whispered in my dreams. *Soon we hunt again.*

I leaned against the wall for a minute, rubbing my leg and trying to breathe.

I pushed off the wall and turned the corner. Katie stood leaning against the silver push bar of a small door, impatiently waiting.

I walked up to her and placed the lanyard over her neck, and then I bent in and kissed her. "You ready?" I asked.

"You bet your ass," she said, pushing her hip into the bar. A cacophony of party sounds blasted outward.

She slid her arm in mine as we waded into the debauchery.

There were people everywhere. Most were drinking tall glasses of some blue concoction and smoking. The room hung heavy with the mixed odors of sweat, cloves, pot, and alcohol.

Women lay around on beanbag chairs, couches, and long divans, while topless waiters and waitresses carried drinks around. No checking IDs here. I'd say half the patrons didn't have the telltale wristbands that allowed them to drink during the show.

I grabbed a beer from one of the many coolers that lined one wall, and Katie snagged a glass of wine from one of the buxom lasses. We walked around, Katie sipping her wine and obviously searching for Ari, me drinking my longneck and watching.

The place felt like a trap. I was on edge and couldn't pinpoint a threat. There was a lot of groping going on. No one paid any attention to the raunch going on around us, and I tried not to be judgmental. The room was a lot bigger than I thought it would be, because as we neared the end, we could see it turned to the left and continued back on itself, a larger room divided down the middle with huge rolling walls.

The party on the other side was a lot less Caligula. Ari held court on the far end, surrounded by girls ranging in age from high school to college. The folks from The Harpers sat in two clumps along the left wall, and other small groups stood around talking. Katie, brazen as you please, cut through the crowded room like a shark. I could barely keep up with her as she made a beeline toward Ari.

He noticed her approach but feigned disinterest. It was obvious he was deliberately looking away. I caught his brief wide-eyed stare. Didn't blame him, really. She was hella cute, but a little conservatively dressed compared to most of the women in the room.

"Ari Sveinsson," she snapped in her best schoolteacher voice.

Ari's head jerked around, his mouth agape.

"I see you haven't learned anything in the last few years?"

I was puzzled; hell, everyone was puzzled. I sidled up to Katie and whispered, "Hey, babe. What are you doing exactly?"

Ari rose, shedding girls like Poseidon climbing out of the surf. "Well, well. If it isn't the Sheriff of Not-Getting-Any."

The crowd oohed and aahed as Ari stood in front of Katie with his hands on his hips.

"Droll," Katie said. "Got a fine set of pipes on you, I'll grant you that," she said. She stepped forward and poked him in the chest. "But there's a young woman out in the club who thinks you promised to marry her."

Ari flushed, and the people in the inner circle there tittered behind their hands. "Oh, dear lord, not again." He slapped his left palm against his forehead. "I've never spoken to her directly."

"So you know her?"

One of the roadies in the back called out, "Not as well as she'd like him to."

The crowd laughed again.

"I was singing at a club in Cleveland, and I talk to the audience about the songs. You saw it tonight."

I stood back, not wanting to interrupt whatever this was turning into.

"I sang one of the ballads, and she thought I was singing to her."

Katie walked around him, eyeing him up and down. "She seemed pretty insistent."

"I swear. It's like she was mesmerized, but I never touched her."

Katie looked at me over his shoulder and winked. "Okay, I'll let it go this time." She walked around to the front of him, her arms crossed and her face set in a very stern expression. She leaned in and whispered something that no one but Ari heard.

"Right," he said. "Can we get back to the party?"

Katie stepped forward and hugged him, to his obvious surprise. Several of the seated women rose up, their hackles raised. "Been too long, you snot," she said, pushing him back to the crowd. "Try not to break too many hearts."

What the hell?

"Who's your hot friend there?" he asked, stepping back toward Katie and looking me up and down.

Katie watched me, a smirk on her face. "You don't remember Sarah?"

Ari glanced at her, then back at me. "I think I'd remember a hottie like her. She's stacked."

Katie choked back a laugh and I felt my blood rising. "Last time I saw you," I said, stepping forward into his personal space, "you were having trouble holding your pants up after Gwendolyn left you hanging in a horse trailer."

He squinted, pushing his face forward and looking up toward my eyes for the first time. "Did my brother sleep with you?"

This sent Katie into full-blown laughter. I wanted to pound them both.

"Never mind," I said, turning away. "You aren't worth my time."

He jumped a little skip into the air, waving his hands around. "Right," he said, shaking his head. "You're that dyke blacksmith."

Katie stopped laughing.

A red haze fell across everything as I moved at him. I reached for Gram, ready to fight him, and then I realized I didn't have the sword. Instead I grabbed him by the front of his silly-ass pirate shirt. I pulled him close, leaning in to whisper into his face.

"You need to learn some manners."

Time shifted back to normal, and someone behind Ari shrieked.

Suddenly, two very large, hairy, tattooed men were scrambling toward me.

"Whoa there, boys," a voice called from behind me. Everyone paused and looked over to Cassidy Stone, the lead singer of The Harpers. "Everybody needs to just calm down."

The crowd mellowed at his words. I could feel the power of it washing over me. The wall of anger that had flashed into existence receded at his words. Freaky.

"Let him go," the singer said, his voice mellow and sweet. "I'm sure he didn't mean nothing by it."

I glanced at Stone and gave a half shrug, pushing Ari away from me and into the arms of one of the bouncers.

"You okay there, son?" Cassidy asked, not looking too particularly concerned. His Scottish accent gave me a bit of a shiver. That's when I realized Cassidy was on the far side of thirty.

"What the hell's your malfunction?" Ari yelped, his dulcet tones lost in a moment of panic and fear. "You got no right . . ." The roadies took another step toward me, and I stepped back into a fighting stance.

"Oh, Ari," Katie said, walking over to me and looping her arm into mine, wrecking my stance, but settling down the crowing voices in my head. "Didn't you ever get the hint? I wouldn't sleep with you at the faires, and neither would Sarah. It's not just because we prefer girls." She leaned in and kissed me full on the mouth. As her tongue danced across mine, the battle voices began to slip into nothingness.

The crowd buzzed for a moment—or maybe it was just the way she held the sides of my face as she kissed me—then she let me go and spun back to the crowd.

"But as cute as you are, you are still a clueless prick."

No one moved for a moment; then someone began to laugh. Then one of the roadies joined in. Soon everyone else was laughing and coming to Ari's aid, offering him beer, wine, clove cigarettes, and several kisses.

Thus distracted, he slunk back to his web of groupies, and I stepped back to face Cassidy Stone.

"Thank you," I said. "Didn't mean to pop off like that."

Cassidy shrugged. "Boy needs to be taken down a peg or two if he wants to survive this game."

I nodded once and stuck out my hand. "Sarah Beauhall."

He wore a band of gold on his left bicep. Detailed work there, carved and shaped with precision. I'd like to talk to the goldsmith who made that one.

He gripped my hand. "Cassidy Aloysius Stone, at your service."

We shook. His grip was strong and his hands calloused from years of playing guitar, lute, and Autoharp.

"Oooh, nice name," Katie said. "Means famous warrior."

"Aye," Cassidy said, taking her hand in his, kissing the back of it, and bowing. "A beauty who knows the origins of ancient names and can best young Ari there is a friend to be cherished."

Katie seemed to melt. "He's cute," she said, hanging onto my arm. "For an oldster."

Cassidy laughed, grabbed us each by one arm, and marched us over to his party. He introduced us to the rest of the band, and before you knew it, Katie had a bottle of mead and a twelve-string guitar. I sat behind her, one hand on the small of her back, while she launched into a round of drinking songs.

I hung with them for an hour, maybe two. Not really sure. The alcohol buzz and the general windowless, smoky haze sorta killed any real sense of time. When they showed no chance of slowing down, I excused myself to find a bathroom.

Katie stopped playing midchord, her hand over the strings and a worried look on her face. "Where are you going?"

"Bathroom," I whispered to her, leaning against her shoulder. "You keep playing."

A moment of panic flashed across her face. She glanced around, taking in the room, the people, the party. "Be careful," she said.

I placed my hand on her shoulder. "I'll be okay," I promised. "You keep playing. I'll be back before you know it. Just need a spot of fresh air."

She leaned her cheek against my hand. "Don't be gone long."

I kissed her and squeezed the hand over the fret of the twelve-string. "Sing something raunchy," I whispered. "I'll be back in two shakes."

She smiled at that and nodded.

I glanced over at Cassidy, who'd watched the scene carefully. "I'll watch over her," he said to me.

I nodded and took off. It was just the bathroom.

The room turned around one more corner, and I found a couple of roadies doing coke near an exit. One of them pointed out the washrooms, and I left them to their drugs. The room was fairly crowded, but I managed to do what I needed to do without resorting to the men's lavatory.

I wandered the party after that, grabbing another beer and listening to snippets of conversation. Seems that since I'd killed Jean-Paul, Vancouver had undergone some sort of renaissance. Crime was flourishing—prostitution, drugs, gambling, all sorts of vice— but the city was friendlier, less seedy. The new guy in charge was apparently the self-proclaimed King of Vancouver. Unlike Jean-Paul, who got his demands met using charm, wit, and torture, this guy only demanded profits and loyalty. Pretty much he left his people alone to do their business.

I bet he had an easier time retaining employees than Jean-Paul. I'd seen how he treated his close and personals when he got angry. I couldn't imagine what doing business with him had been like.

Just thinking of Duchamp made my right hand hurt. I clenched and unclenched my fist a few times, working out the kinks. You could barely see the scarring, and I had a good eighty percent usage of that hand again. The knitting was helping, much to my chagrin. The pain still haunted me though. Ghost pain, the doctor said, but I woke shaking some nights with visions of my wrist burned down to the bone by dragon fire.

There was this one moment, however, when I was sure the witch, Qindra, had visited me in the hospital. I distinctly recall her chanting, the smell of whiskey, and a blue fog that rolled from her mouth and doused the fire in my arm like calm, cool water.

As I wandered back, I could see Katie was having the time of her life. She was holding her own with The Harpers. Ari had disappeared with a couple of his girls. Good riddance, I thought. He reminded me too much of our main actor over at Flight Test—JJ Montgomery. Decent actor, but a shit when it came to women.

What made some men such pigs? Sex was important, and pretty obsessing at times, but to crawl all over all those women while the others were there watching—what was the point, beyond narcissism?

And what was with the women? Why would they allow themselves to be used like that? I knew I was still fighting through the prudish ways instilled in me by my Ma and Da, but as much as I disagreed with Da particularly, I think he was right on one thing: You need to treat each other with respect. He thought there were two standards, which I didn't agree with. You didn't just respect women, especially because they were weaker or some such. You respected all people—allowed them their individual rights, without stringing them along, filling them with false hope.

Like that girl outside waiting to get into a party she'll never see in her lifetime.

I needed some air. Things were suddenly too stuffy. I thought about making my way over to Katie, telling her where I was going, but the noise had reached a point where I couldn't think, and the memories were thick with pain.

I went back to the coke roadies and chatted them up, told them I needed some air. They introduced me to Pablo, the bouncer at the back door, let him know I was "one cool chick."

Whatever.

# Four

THE GREAT HALL SWALLOWED THE QUIET NOISES OF THE children as they scampered about doing their duties. The house had settled back into a routine—as much as could be expected after the last rage had taken so many of the favorites.

Qindra sat at tea with her mistress worrying over Nidhogg's growing weakness. "What is it you wish, Mother?"

Nidhogg placed her teacup on the saucer daintily. "I like not these rumors of the King of Vancouver."

*Is that all?* "Surely that is beneath your station," Qindra said, keeping her eyes downcast. "You are grieving."

Nidhogg slammed her fist on the table, sending teapot and cup dancing, spilling tea. "Do not mollycoddle me, child. I am fully aware of what goes on within my own domain."

"Yes, mistress." She could not risk her raging again. "Vancouver is in flux, but it will not sink into chaos."

"I cannot tolerate one of the Reaver's brood moving in. It would unsettle things."

That would be unpleasant. The wild ones wished to rule openly—break the compact, and the chattel be damned. Luckily they were in the minority, and kept that way by the high council.

"Perhaps you should claim it as your own," Qindra finally said.

"Until a suitable caretaker can be determined. None would dare question your right."

Nidhogg considered a moment, the gleam in her eye as bright as ever. "Intriguing thought. Or, perhaps we should watch this King of Vancouver, secretly support his claim on the city, if for no other reason than to thwart that jackanapes, Frederick Sawyer."

Qindra smiled. "You are quick in the game of thrones," she proffered. "I will make some subtle inquiries."

Nidhogg nodded and then took up her teacup as if nothing untoward had occurred. "You are invaluable," she said. "Your mother would have been proud."

Luckily the teacup covered her reaction. Qindra took a quiet sip and let the thought of her mother's broken body fade from her mind. How many had Nidhogg destroyed in her rages? How many lost to the madness?

"I thank you for your kind words."

They sipped their tea in quiet solitude. The very house itself seemed to hold its breath. Around the great hall, the others remained motionless, frozen in their tasks. Only their breathing gave them away as living beings.

Nidhogg sat her cup aside, drew a long stuttering breath, and whimpered. "The blood," she whispered. "I cannot rid the air of its stench."

Qindra sat her teacup down, slid to the floor, and folded her hands on her mistress's knee. "Come away with me, only for a drive. Leave this house and breathe the fresh air."

Nidhogg stroked Qindra's hair with her gnarled hand. "You are as a daughter to me, fair one. But I cannot leave here, as you well know. It is unseemly for me to be seen out in the world of whisperers and spies."

*Paranoia*, Qindra thought. She bowed her head, setting her cheek on her hands.

"You have not lain your head upon my lap in many a year," Nidhogg whispered. After a moment, she began to croon a ragged tune.

Qindra recognized it. A lovely ballad she remembered her mother singing, back before she fell to Nidhogg's madness. "I love that song," she said. "I miss you singing."

Nidhogg stopped stroking her hair but kept her hand on Qindra's head. "I am old," she said as if this were a new discovery. "And I fear my own mind ofttimes."

"Hush, now." Qindra started to raise her head, but Nidhogg held her firmly in place, her strength suddenly manifest.

"'Ware, child," Nidhogg said, her voice clear and crisp. "It is I who am the mistress, you the servant."

Qindra tried to relax, let her muscles grow limp. "I meant no disrespect, mistress."

"I am rid of sleep these nights," Nidhogg went on as if Qindra had not spoken. "Death haunts my dreams—death and decay."

Qindra looked around the room as best she could. The newly appointed Eyes sat clutching her book, her face painted with nausea and fear.

*Fear, you should*, Qindra thought. *Your predecessor died screaming at that very spot.*

"The wheel is broken," Nidhogg continued. "The world has grown ill. I can taste the black blood. Dark magic is upon my land."

*Dark magic? Wheel?* Qindra's mind raced. She'd noticed nothing. Mayhap it was time to change her focus from the young smith, Beauhall, and seek out this new obsession that unsettled her mistress.

"The dead," Nidhogg wailed. "The dead will give me no peace."

Several of the smaller children began to cry, nearly silently, but loudly enough for Qindra's ears.

Nidhogg held her there for a very long time. Qindra began to ache from the awkward position. "Shall I quiet the dead, Mother?" she finally asked.

Nidhogg said nothing immediately; then she began to hum another song, one Qindra did not recognize—full of dissonance and discord. After several minutes, she pulled her hand from Qindra's head.

Quindra slid to the floor, barely daring to breathe.

Nidhogg kept singing as she reached beside her chair and pulled out her knitting. She began to croak out words in the ancient tongue.

Only the words *regret* and *decay* were clear to Qindra's mind. A song of loss and mourning.

Qindra lay on the ground at her mistress's feet until the most ancient of dragons dropped her knitting to her lap and filled the great hall with her quiet snores.

Only then did Qindra crawl away, not even rising to her knees until she'd reached the great doors to the main house. Only then did she rise, brush off her dressing gown, and look back at her mistress.

"Leave her," she said quietly to the room. "Return to your rooms and say your prayers this evening."

She did not wait to see if they complied but opened the doors and swept out into the hall.

The wheel is broken, blood haunts my mistress, and the dark magic is upon the land. Ill tidings and damnable luck.

She returned to her room, to her scryings and her runes. There would be little sleep in this house this evening, of that she was sure.

# Five

It was chilly out there after being in the crowded party. It was around two in the morning, and I could see my breath. Fall was strange in the Pacific Northwest. Seventies in the day and low forties at night. I hugged my arms and walked out across the gravel toward the two large tour buses.

I didn't have any particular reason; they were just the only two things out there. Past them across a dozen feet of scrub was a service road with no traffic. It was pretty quiet, actually—a nice change from the overwhelming drone of the party. I stopped at the first tour bus, leaned back against it, and closed my eyes, letting my body relax and drawing in breaths of clear night air.

The cold made me think of flying. I'd ridden the Valkyrie's winged horse and chased the dragon through the thick clouds as the morning sun broke over the horizon. I could almost feel the cold wet of the clouds as we soared across the mountains. Of course, the final battle had been filled with pain and heat. Burning, roasting, charring flame. My right hand spasmed and I bolted up from the side of the bus, remembered smoke burning my eyes—blistering my lungs.

I leaned forward, hands on knees, and tried to breathe. The cool air felt good going into my body, and the smoke and fire were just vivid memories. After a minute I heard a noise around the side of the bus. It sounded like someone moaning. My mind clicked over into hyperawareness, and I rolled onto the balls of my feet, knees slightly bent, my hands in tight fists.

I listened closely and heard a shuffling and another moan. I edged around the bus and peered around, ready to kick someone's ass.

What I saw through the open door of the bus, instead of a bad guy, troll, or mugger, was Ari doing the nasty with two of the groupies.

I pulled my head back, hoping they hadn't seen me. Not that I thought they'd have seen a flying saucer if it landed in the scrub alongside the road.

Two girls and one guy screwing on the stairs inside the bus. He was living the dream. The Red Sonja–looking chick had her face buried in the crotch of the petite girl with tattoos, piercings, and green hair. The rock star was doing Red from behind. I couldn't be sure they even noticed Ari. At least the girls were really into each other. He'd be out of the picture soon enough.

I had no desire to watch that, so I quietly made my way back around the other bus, letting the night air clear my head. I only closed my eyes for a second, when I heard someone stumbling toward me. It was the tall girl with red flowing hair and a skimpy skirt that until about two minutes ago was hiked up over her ass. She stopped at the front of the bus, leaned one arm against the grill, bent nearly double, and vomited.

Jesus, but she sounded like she was going to hack up her spleen. I came toward her. "Hey, you okay?"

She wiped her hand across her mouth and spit. "I need a drink."

Yeah, she needed more booze. "Sure you wouldn't like to go back inside and freshen up?"

She stood up, rearranged her breasts inside her shirt, and smoothed the latex skirt down over her upper thighs. "Good idea," she said, pulling her hair back off her face. I didn't have the heart to tell her she'd gotten vomit in her hair. Where was her girlfriend? Wasn't it her job to hold her hair while she barfed?

The redhead stepped away from the bus and began a rather crooked path back toward the club. I watched her for a moment, debating whether or not I should help her or if she was going to fall down.

That's when the screaming started. Okay, I can totally understand drunk chicks getting laid by C-list celebrities, and even the joy of doing something you know you shouldn't oughta, but nobody screamed like that unless they were afraid or in pain.

I ran back around the bus in time to see the other girl on her knees in the parking lot, her head thrown back and another scream about to erupt from her. Halfway across the scrub to the service road, three guys were dragging Ari away.

They had a bag over his head and his paisley pantaloons bunched around his ankles, but he was fighting—kicking and yelling for all he was worth. But they were big. I sprinted forward, clipping the nearest guy in the back of the leg and sending him crashing to the ground. He dropped the leg he'd been holding, and the other two guys stumbled as Ari's weight hit the ground.

I grabbed the second guy, spinning him around and landing a solid roundhouse into his breadbasket. It was liking hitting a steer. He dropped Ari's left arm and stumbled back, holding his midsection. The last guy dropped Ari and lunged at me. Damn, I wish I had Gram. I could hear her in my head, crying for battle. The fog flooded my brain and I launched myself into the mêlée.

By this time, the first guy was on his feet and swinging a wild punch at my head. I danced back and kicked the guy I'd punched, sending him over onto his back, where he sat up, shaking his head once before falling onto his back.

The guy I hadn't touched yet rushed me, wrapping his arms

around me and driving me backward. I stumbled and we both went ass-over-teakettle. As soon as we hit, his shoulder against my chest, I used our combined momentum to flip him over by thrusting upward with my hips and legs. He flew over my head and landed with a grunt.

It hurt like a bitch, and made breathing hard for a minute. I struggled up onto my elbows just as the guy I'd clipped first dove on top of me. He did not appreciate me raising my knees, but I didn't want his huge bulk squashing me into the gravel like a bug. He felt it as I torqued to the left and let his weight carry him off me. He would be catching his breath for a minute, I hoped, as I scrambled to my feet.

Two sorta down. I turned around. The guy next to Ari was not really moving. The guy I'd flipped over my head was rising, but not moving too fast, and the third guy rolled onto his stomach before rising up onto his hands and knees.

The girl continued to scream. I hoped she or the redhead would get the roadies or bouncers to lend a hand.

Ari was trying to stand, but his hands were tied behind his back and a gunnysack still covered his head. In addition, his pants were around his ankles, exposing him in a way most men would not want. Fear is not kind in certain situations.

"Hang on, Sinatra. I'll get you." I stumbled over to him, keeping out of reach of the guy nearest him who still had not moved. Maybe I'd really hurt him. I had Ari sitting up, glancing back at the other two.

"Gotta get you back to the party, big guy," I said, yanking Ari to his feet. I debated on taking the sack off his head first, but I figured he'd want a chance to cover his wilting manhood. I got as far as steadying Ari and was reaching for the sack when the guy on the ground lunged over and grabbed me by the ankles. So, okay.

Lesson learned. Dude was faking it. I hit the ground hard. My jaw snapped shut, rattling my teeth as my chin led the way.

I was seeing stars, one of the girls was screaming, Ari was swearing, and someone kicked me in the ribs. The blow was hard enough to roll me over. One of the attackers landed on my chest with both knees, grabbing me by the throat. He was cutting off the blood to my brain. I only had a couple of seconds before I blacked out.

I bucked, kicking my legs out, while I pounded his arms with my own. Man, he was freaking strong. "Don't," I squeaked out as my eyes filled with stars.

The screamer must have decided to play. She hit the guy with a purse the size of a St. Bernard. I rolled over, gasping for air and rubbing my neck. The girl squatted down beside me. "You okay?"

She looked like hell. Her makeup had not been good before the drinking and fucking. Now, with the tears, it was like a mime had been murdered.

I nodded, and she helped me sit up. The guy beat me to my feet and stumbled toward the service road as a large white van came screaming toward us.

"Damn," I choked out and pointed. The two other guys had a very limp Ari between them and were dragging him toward the van. The third guy reached them just as someone threw open the van door, and they tossed Ari inside.

Screaming Girl helped me to my feet. I took two steps toward the van and realized I'd never catch them.

"We'd better go back and get help," I said. Okay, my windpipe hadn't been crushed exactly, but I'd wager I'd have a bruise the size of a ham.

Face it, I'd mostly gotten my ass kicked. Those three guys were big. I'd gotten in a few blows they'd remember come morning, but they'd snatched Ari, and I hadn't stopped them.

"I'm Brianna," the screamer said to me as we made our way back toward the club. "Why'd they take Ari?"

Damn good question. Did he schtup someone's wife or daughter? Lord knows. I'm sure the police would figure it out.

When we got near the club, Pablo and the coke roadies were rushing out to gather us up.

Brianna relayed what happened with quick, precise sentences. She didn't cry once. The roadies assumed I'd been out partying with Ari and didn't ask me anything. Brianna's story was good enough. Pablo pulled out a cell phone and called the Mounties while we spread the word of Ari's kidnapping.

People scrambled, dumping booze and drugs, gathering stray bits of clothing, and generally making themselves and the club presentable. It's like they'd done this before. By the time we heard the first siren, the place could've passed for an AA meeting.

I collapsed next to Katie and let her fuss over me. Brianna was queen of the ball, telling and retelling the story. Once the police arrived, I let her tell her part first. They questioned me, asked if I needed an ambulance, et cetera. I told them I just wanted to get back to our hotel. After an hour of information gathering and promises to remain in touch—even after we went back to Seattle— they let us go.

Sleep was the only thing I wanted. I was bone tired, and starting to hurt in some very unfortunate places. I hoped I hadn't pulled a muscle in my back. That would totally suck.

Cassidy and his partner Katherine hustled us into a cab, slipping the driver some money and telling him to take us to our hotel. He leaned into the back window and kissed Katie on the cheek. "Daren't you fret now," he said, trilling his R's with gusto. "We'll check in with you afore too long."

Katie patted his hand and he stepped back, slipping his arm around Katherine's waist and waving at us as we pulled away.

"What was that all about?" I asked, laying my head on Katie's lap.

"He wants to talk music," she said, stroking my hair. "That and Ari, of course."

Of course. I dozed most of the way uptown.

Katie undressed me, gave me a couple of ibuprofen, and tucked me into bed. Not exactly how I'd hoped to be spending the first night in the hotel, but at that moment I couldn't keep my eyes open even to watch Katie undress.

# Six

KATIE WOKE UP FAR TOO EARLY FOR THE NIGHT THEY'D HAD. The clock said it was ten, which meant she'd gotten about seven hours' sleep. With all the wine, and the smoke, and then, my god . . . Ari. She sat on the edge of the bed and held her head in her hands.

Coffee . . . she needed about a gallon to kick-start her brain. Sarah would want the same. She pulled on her sneakers, grabbed her wallet, and headed down to the coffee shop.

Twenty minutes later she'd gotten back with two large coffees, each with a couple extra shots of espresso and enough chocolate to sate a romance writer's' convention. Sarah wouldn't eat anything right away, so she hadn't bothered with the stale donuts.

Sarah was sprawled across the bed, facedown with one arm hanging off the edge and her left leg exposed up to the subtle curve of her ass. Katie leaned over the bed and traced her hand in the air, just above Sarah's leg, debating on waking her. It had been a long time since they'd been intimate.

When she thought of it, she got sorta tight inside. Katie took a deep breath and let her eyes travel back down to stare at the runes burned into Sarah's calf. She'd memorized them, seeing them in her mind's eye as she fell asleep some nights. Something in them called to her, warning her, perhaps, of darkness and pain.

The hours she and Julie had been held captive by the dragon

and his minions haunted her, but she wasn't going to let the bastard win. Sarah killed him; his thugs were scattered and killed by Black Briar; and they'd come home, battered but whole.

Julie was much worse off, she assured herself. With the physical therapy and all.

She stepped away from the bed when she realized that her heart was racing and her vision blurred. Sarah stirred, and Katie thought again about just touching her, seeing what happened. Making out at the concert had been awesome. Why was she freezing up now? The anxiety crested over Katie, giving her a moment of blind panic, then her breathing started to calm.

Sarah loved her. She'd proved it. Katie wanted her, wanted to make love to her, to feel her naked body against her own, taste her . . .

But not now. Not this moment. Katie backed away from the bed and took her coffee to the desk. She watched Sarah sleep while her computer booted. *Something had to change*, Katie thought. She needed to work through the fear.

The first drink of her own coffee went down like a mouthful of sweet lava. It would have to cool down, unless she wanted to lose the ability to ever taste again. She cruised several Internet sites, letting her subconscious drift, slowly introducing the cooling coffee into her system while letting her brain slip into neutral. By the time she got around to opening her e-mail, the caffeine and sugar had hit her bloodstream like a shot of lightning.

She had mail from Deidre. Her sister-in-law had been home for a couple days between the hospital and the rehab facility. She was learning to operate without the use of her legs and was progressing well.

Katie hadn't talked to Jimmy much in the last few months, between his anger toward Sarah and his blaming her for the dragon attack, and the fact she had finally realized the depth of Jimmy's deception. He'd known about the dwarves, known of the dragons, and had kept most of that from her. Oh, he'd given her little crumbs, enough to fill her schoolgirl fantasies, but he hadn't trusted her with the whole truth.

She wasn't sure she was ready to forgive him for that. Not yet.

But Deidre. She had really taken over when her mom and dad had disappeared, helping Jimmy look after her, being more a friend than just a surrogate mother. She loved Deidre dearly.

She called Deidre. It would be good to catch up. Maybe get a little of the anxiety out in the open. Deidre always knew what to say to help Katie find her path. It was one of her many gifts.

She spent the next fifteen minutes chatting with Deidre, trading information about the nursing facility and the concert. The news of Ari was quite a shock. They spoke about Ari's attempts to sleep with any woman associated with ren faires and how he seemed to have hit the easy-chick lotto . . . right up until he got snatched. Once she heard how Sarah had tried to break up the kidnapping and gotten smacked around for her trouble, Deidre grew more serious. The battle was still vivid in everyone's mind, Deidre's especially.

And of course she took Jimmy's side of things. Not totally, but Katie wasn't feeling too generous when it came to her big brother these days. They finally collapsed into exhausted silence. Deidre just didn't have the stamina these days, and Katie was out of sorts. Ari's kidnapping had triggered a resurgence of the trauma she'd been working to bury for months. And it was giving her a headache.

After they'd said their good-byes, Katie popped a couple of ibuprofen and went back to the computer.

She sipped her coffee and trolled through the rest of the local news highlights, landing on an article that caused her to sit up, gulping hot coffee, and nearly choking. Some kid had been found killed out near the industrial area north of Stanley Park. The photograph showed a sign taped to his chest. The reporter was puzzled, but Katie knew exactly what it meant.

"Sarah?" she cried, her voice rising into panic. "Holy shit, wake up and come see this."

She stood up so fast she flipped the chair over backward. Sarah raised her head from beneath the blankets, mumbling something incoherent.

"Come on," Katie said, peeling the blankets off Sarah. "Get up, already. Somebody's murdered a dwarf."

# Seven

KATIE RIPPED THE BLANKETS OFF ME, PULLING ME FROM AN exhausted sleep.

"What?" I asked. My mouth tasted like Muppet roadkill. I rubbed my eyes and rolled over onto my back.

I lay there, arms splayed to the sides for a moment, letting the AC wash over me. The blankets had gotten too hot and I needed to cool down.

"Get up. You're not gonna believe this." She bounced on one side of the bed, jostling me uncomfortably.

I cracked my eyes open and stared at her. She was up and dressed, and far, far too bouncy. And . . . I looked down toward my toes . . . I was naked—definite disadvantage.

I rolled over, catching her by surprise, and pulled her on top of me. Then I rolled us both over and landed on top with her hands pinned to the sides of her head. I'd show her for being bouncy in the morning.

She laughed, which was a good sign, because I hadn't had as much to drink as she had, and I felt awful.

"Get off," she grunted, wiggling her hips to try and dislodge me. "I gotta show you something."

I leaned down and kissed her. "Only fair—I seem to have shown you everything."

Her eyes held something. Hesitancy? She shuddered, and then pushed her head upward, kissing me again. We spent the next little while like that, making out and, well, you know. It wasn't until I tried to undress her that she stopped me.

"Wait," she said. "One, you smell like an ashtray, and two . . ." She pushed my arm off her chest and rolled to a sitting position. "I need to show you something."

I sat back, pouting a little, and leaned back against the headboard while she grabbed her laptop and handed it to me. "I saw this while you were sleeping." She pointed to a picture on the screen.

I clicked on the picture to expand it and saw a dead kid taped to a basketball pole. The sign taped to his chest read: DRAGON FRIEND.

That caught my attention. "Holy shit," I breathed, sitting bolt upright and placing the laptop on the bed between my knees. "I think that's a dwarf."

"Right," Katie said, handing me a coffee. "Not as hot as it was forty minutes ago, but there's enough sugar in there to stop your heart."

I sipped the coffee and read the article. Gang activity in the area last night. Eyewitness at the crack house across the street saw a couple of guys getting the crap kicked out of them well after midnight.

I immediately thought of the only dwarf I knew—Rolph. He'd been the one to point out the truth of Gram and helped me reforge her, back before I learned of the dragons. His was a tormented life, being the last to forge the blade and doing it badly, cursing him to a life of misery and regret.

One of the things I remembered most vividly was his constant fear of the rising sun. Shitty way to die. I didn't know much about dwarves, other than their connection to smithing and such, but the fact that exposure to sunlight killed them had been pretty high on his list of important facts.

"Poor bastard," I said, leaning back against the pillows. "I need to talk to Rolph, find out how a dwarf kid would be labeled a dragon friend." Then I needed to ask why that was a killing offense all of a sudden. Just how much had changed up here since I'd killed Jean-Paul? That King of Vancouver I'd heard about last night. Did he really hate dragons enough to kill kids? What was the connection? And the guys who snatched Ari last night, they were dwarves I thought.

Katie closed the lid on the computer and stroked my thigh. "You think there's a connection with Ari?"

I placed my hand on hers and squeezed. "Good possibility. Let's see what Rolph knows." I kissed her quickly, then rolled off the bed and grabbed my dirty jeans off the floor. I fished around for my cell phone and saw the battery was dead. You'd think I would remember to plug it in every now and again.

The charger should have been in my computer bag along with my passport, but it didn't seem to be around.

Katie just rolled her eyes at me. "It's probably on your counter next to a half-empty cottage cheese container."

"Not funny," I said, frowning at her. "Ever since Julie moved in, she won't let me leave things lying around. She even makes me do dishes."

Katie smiled. "Oh, the horror."

"Hey, I have a busy life."

Katie just smiled and shook her head. "How's she doing?"

I shrugged. "Doctor says she's healing fine. The physical therapy is going okay, but she won't talk about what happened when . . ." I hesitated, not wanting to send Katie into a funk.

"When we got kidnapped?"

I nodded. "Yeah."

"Give her some time," she said. "Maybe she's talking to someone else."

"I hope so. Maybe Mrs. Sorenson, the cabbage lady in the next apartment."

"She's sweet. When is Julie going back to work?"

I shrugged. Couldn't even get Julie to talk about it. "Good question. Not soon enough, in my book. I think she'd benefit from getting out, seeing our regulars. Swinging a hammer and dealing with horses."

"I bet that would be therapeutic."

"I'll bring it up again when we get home. Can't make her do anything, though."

Katie smiled. "No, I imagine not. Not like getting you to wash the dishes."

"Touché."

But, I still needed to call Rolph. "Let's stop and buy a new charger," I suggested. "Rolph's number is in my phone."

"You should just upgrade your phone," Katie offered. "I'd let you use my charger, but it doesn't convert to older-than-sin."

I squinted at her. She was always so damn funny. "I think I'll shower," I said instead. "You can stay out here and be miss smart-ass if you want, or you could join me."

She looked at me for a second, checked that the door was locked, and began taking off her clothes. The hotel wasn't the Ritz or anything, but the shower was pretty large. I set the water to a hard spray and turned it all the way to hot. I wanted to breathe in the steam. It felt like my lungs were full of sludge from last night. The mirror covered the wall behind the vanity, so I could get a good look at the bruises that were forming on my neck. Just below my left breast, a large one had already begun to darken. Likely a boot. I'd be pretty mottled by the end of the day. I was already stiff. The shower would help work out the kinks.

I heard muffled voices and looked around. Sounded like *naked* and *nipples*. I stepped into the door. "You say something?"

Katie was just pulling her sweatshirt over her head. "What?" she asked.

The television wasn't on. She shimmied out of her sweatpants and began to unhook her bra.

"I thought I heard you say something."

She shrugged, stepping out of her panties, and strode across the room to me. "Must have been the television next door. Wasn't me."

She pushed me back into the bathroom, shut the door, and climbed into the shower. She squeaked, before turning the water cooler. "Damn, Beauhall, you trying to kill me?"

"No ma'am," I said, climbing in after her.

I thought I heard someone else a couple of other times, but I was pretty distracted there for a while.

We washed each other, slowly. Getting to know the curves and lines again after far too long. Her face clouded for a moment, then relaxed into a look of bliss as I ran my hands over her breasts. Her nipples grew stiff under my palms, so I bent my head down to take the left one in my mouth, tracing the areola with my tongue.

She brought her hands to the back of my head, gasping.

I moved my hand down her back, cupping her ass, allowing my fingers to slide between her cheeks while I drew my other hand down across her belly, strumming my fingers down the small patch of hair, parting her for the first time in months.

She stiffened against me, paralyzed for a moment, and then moaned, nearly falling. I caught her, wrapping my left arm around her waist and continuing to stroke her, bringing forth short, sharp gasps of pleasure.

I moved from one breast to another, lathing each, before trailing across her chest to the other nipple, nipping and suckling in turn.

Sooner than I expected she shuddered against me, whimpering and hugging my head against her chest as the orgasm spasmed through her. I held her, holding my hand against her, allowing her to grind against the heel of my palm.

After a few moments, she pulled my head up and kissed me. I could taste the tears that ran down her face.

"I love you," she mumbled, over and over again, covering my face with kisses.

Then it was her turn to kiss her way down my neck, finding the spot at the base that made my toes curl. That one spot, just above the artery there where, with the right combination of teeth, lips, and tongue, I lose the ability to stand upright.

Luckily, I could lean into the corner of the shower as she kissed her way down my body, and the world disappeared in an explosion of pleasure.

Afterward, as we were getting dressed, I realized I was short a bra. Not something you just lose in a hotel room, right? We looked under the beds and everything, but no luck.

"I remember you undressing me last night," I said. "But things are pretty fuzzy."

"I put it on the dresser there," she said. I walked over, catching my reflection in the mirror. There was no bra on, under, or behind. "Damn, and I liked that one, too."

Katie was shoving dirty clothes into the dresser and closing up the suitcases. "I'm sure it will turn up," she said. "Let's go get some food."

I rifled through my suitcase, pulling out another bra, along with jeans, T-shirt, and underwear. "With the amount of smoke in the air last night, maybe we should just burn what we were wearing anyway."

We dressed, tidied up the room, and checked the essentials. Money, wallet, purse (for Katie), and tourist map. Oh, and Katie had a very cool digital camera. At the last minute, I added my knitting to my pack. It was damn annoying, but I needed the exercise with the right hand. It had healed up great after the battle with the dragon, but I was not getting the dexterity back as fast as I'd hoped. Yes, I'm stubborn, but knitting seemed so—grandma.

Katie said if I got good enough I could knit her a nightie. Always nice to have a goal.

Vancouver was in so much trouble. We were going to eat, shop, and explore the city into submission. I've been shopping with Katie. It was a distinct possibility. Should be a good day. Except for the dead dwarf kid, Ari missing, and my bruises blooming, the morning had started nicely, and I was feeling pretty relaxed, considering.

# Eight

WE PROWLED THE GASTOWN–STEAM CLOCK DISTRICT—A touristy section of Vancouver down on the waterfront. Katie loved the huge steam-powered grandfather clock, and I relaxed, watching all the people wandering around, laughing and having a good time.

My throat hurt, and I was stiff all over, but I didn't want to be a wet blanket on Katie's birthday. It's not everyday you turn twenty-five—quarter of a century. I remembered it like it was yesterday. I'd be twenty-seven soon and I felt damn old.

The shops were cool. I loved the one that sold Persian rugs, and Katie almost tried on a kilt. She decided that being descended from some French guy shouldn't be cause not to wear a tartan. The price decided it in the end. She just couldn't justify spending that kind of coin on a wool skirt. I picked up a cell phone charger from a little kiosk near the steam clock.

We wandered west and stopped at the train station to check out this really cool statue of an angel reaching toward heaven with one arm. A dead soldier draped over her other arm, face upward toward heaven. It was pretty moving.

The plaque read:

TO COMMEMORATE THOSE IN THE SERVICE OF THE CANADIAN PACIFIC RAILWAY COMPANY WHO, AT THE CALL OF KING AND

COUNTRY, LEFT ALL THAT WAS DEAR TO THEM, ENDURED
HARDSHIP, FACED DANGER AND FINALLY PASSED OUT OF SIGHT
OF MEN BY THE PATH OF DUTY AND SELF SACRIFICE, GIVING
UP THEIR OWN LIVES THAT OTHERS MIGHT LIVE IN FREEDOM.
LET THOSE WHO COME AFTER SEE TO IT THAT THEIR NAMES
BE NOT FORGOTTEN.

1914–1918    1939–1945

"That's what we should do at Black Briar," I said, suddenly very determined. "We should erect a monument. Like they used to do in the olden days, you know, like the Vikings."

Katie held my hand and leaned her head into my shoulder, staring at the statue. "That is very sweet," she said quietly.

We stood on the sidewalk for a long time, lost in thought. I'm not sure what Katie was thinking, but I could not get the last moments of Susan and Maggie out of my head. That kind of love, that determination and dedication . . . I hoped I had that someday. Oh, I was sure I loved Katie, but we were newbs with all this. Maybe we'd grow into that strong a bond, and I was keeping my fingers crossed, but it didn't come along very often in life. I kept my arm around her after that. It was a big step for me, being out in public and all, but it felt right.

Past the train station, we watched a cruise ship launch. It must have been a common occurrence, because there was no one on the dock, so Katie and I waved at them as they left, hooting and hollering along with the cruise folk. Seemed to make them happy, and I know it helped my spirits.

We watched the ship until we lost sight of it, then we stopped at a nearby deli, ordered an instant picnic, and hiked over to Stanley Park.

I wanted to walk over to Second Beach before we ate, but Katie

insisted we stop and pay our respects to Robert Burns. His statue
was at the entrance, so we didn't have to go out of our way. We
spent ten minutes admiring the wide array of bird droppings and
little notes people leave at these sorts of places, and then we made
our way through the wooded area toward the water.

Second Beach is stunning. We found a fallen tree and spread
out our foodage. I was starved and dove into my sandwich without
much thought to conversation. Katie ate more sparingly, picking
her food apart and watching the water. Once I'd knocked off most
of a pastrami on rye I leaned back against the tree and pulled out
my knitting. Knit one, pearl three. It was a pain.

After I finished two rows, Katie sighed.

"What's on your mind, hon?"

She looked over at me and smiled. "This is just nice, you and
me, alone."

There were a dozen people on the beach below us, but I took
her meaning. "Yeah, parts of this weekend have been great."

We sat enjoying being in each other's space.

"I wish you'd just move in with me," she said finally. "It would
be easier."

I dropped my knitting into my lap and turned my head to look
at her. She was so earnest.

"I've been thinking about it," I told her. "You know that. I just
can't leave Julie right now. She's got nothing at the moment. I
can't abandon her after all she's been through."

She kept smiling, but I thought it was a little more brittle than
before. "She's a grown woman, Sarah. She doesn't need a nursemaid."

I shrugged. The guilt was enormous. I'd brought the dragon
down on her. It was my fault the sword was reforged. If I hadn't
acted, she'd still have her home and her forge. I had to make amends.
Had to see her safe.

I shrugged again. "What else am I supposed to do, Katie? I owe her."

She reached over and touched my cheek. "Guilt is a terrible weight to bear."

"It's only until she can get back on her feet," I promised. "We can talk about it in a few months, okay?"

"Sure," she conceded. "Just makes it hard to have any quality alone time at your place with Aunt Bea always hanging around."

That made me smile. "I'll see if I can arrange for her to seek more outside interests."

Katie finished her sandwich then. I loved her, but she was persistent when she wanted something. I guessed I should have been happy since she was the one who pursued me. I'd never have had the nerve to hit on her.

"I wonder who would want to snatch Ari like that?" she asked after we packed away the lunch leavings.

"Good question," I said. "Could be ransom, I guess, or unrequited love, that sort of thing."

"Dwarves snatched him," a voice said from behind us.

I dropped my knitting and spun around, placing my weight on my right knee, planting my left foot firmly on the ground under me.

There was a girl standing behind me, and she looked familiar. I'd seen her at the party, in the line waiting with the rest of those who were just not cool enough.

She had thin features, almost pinched, with a long, narrow face and ears that were not exactly pointed, but definitely elongated. She was dressed in dark clothes, and her eyes were lined with black. Her lips were fiery red, and her fingernails matched.

Katie was on her feet, watching the woods behind the girl.

"Who's with you?" she asked firmly.

"It's just me and Gletts," the girl said. "I'm Skella." She kept her hands crossed over her skinny chest. "You're that blacksmith, aren't you?"

I stood, confused. "I'm *a* blacksmith, yes. But how would you know that?"

She smiled, turning her face from gaunt goth chick into that of a fairly pretty young woman. "You killed the dragon, that bastard Duchamp."

"Whoa," Katie said, stepping away from the edge of the woods and looking around. "Who are you again?"

Gletts stepped out of the brush. He was a male version of Skella, a skinny kid in clothes too big for him. "We shouldn't be talking to her," he said to Skella. "She ain't our friend."

"Shush, you," Skella said, pushing him away. He stutter-stepped to the side, but didn't go very far. "I know all about you," she said, facing us squarely. "We got word pretty quick up here. Not everyday one of the wyrms gets taken down."

"Ha," Gletts laughed. "Not everyday for true. Not never in my reckoning."

"We just wanted to say thank you," Skella said. "We heard you were roaming these parts. Glad you decided to visit us here in the park."

"You live here?" I asked.

"A few of us, yes," she answered. "Most of our kin were driven off by the dragon years ago, but us and ours have hung on here. Kept to ourselves, you know?"

I understood perfectly well. "What have you heard about a dwarf boy that got killed out near . . ."

"Dragon friend," Gletts interrupted me. Then he spat.

Katie spat, too, making a warding sign. Gletts smiled at that, kindred spirits.

"He was delivering a message from the dragon in Portland," Skella said. "Courier only, but the King of Vancouver saw fit to make an example of him."

"Lousy way to die," Gletts said, the anger raw in his voice. "You'd think with you killing one of them, they'd think twice before they tried to push anyone else around."

"Meaning?" Okay, I thought I grokked his meaning, but wanted to be sure.

"Sawyer, trying to weasel his way into the Vancouver area," Skella said.

Gletts laughed. "Old Nidhogg between us and him, he's out of his pickled brain."

I almost laughed. This skinny kid, full of piss and vinegar, talking about one of the dragons like he was some cranky neighbor. Kid had balls. No coward, this one. "I've met him," I said.

They both turned to me, eyes level, expressions flat.

"He ain't Duchamp, that's for damn sure," Gletts said. "But he's a dragon, just like the rest of 'em. Right awful bastards, the lot."

Skella nodded, but was looking from me to Katie, as if she was trying to decide something.

They looked like nice enough kids—well, Elvish kids at least. Hell, they could be twice my age for all I knew. Not sure they got enough food, though. Worn looking, and a little on the thin side. I wondered if maybe they were homeless. Lot of that going around.

"You hungry?" I asked, remembering the potato salad and second sandwiches in the pack. "You look like you've missed a few meals."

"We could eat," Gletts said, his eyes eager. "Never turn away hospitality."

"This is our place," Skella said. Her voice and body language was all about caution. "We should be offering them something."

Katie smiled and picked up the pack to hand out food.

"It does appear," I said, "that you have offered us leave of your home, and some interesting information."

Skella eyed the sandwich Katie brought out of the pack. "That's true. Maybe we could share a meal with you."

And so we did. They ate every last crumb we had with us, and would've eaten more.

They gave us a lot of information, like how this mystery guy calling himself the King of Vancouver had been consolidating all of Jean-Paul's holdings. "It's like he knows where all the bodies are buried," Gletts said after he'd licked his fingers clean. "Making peace with the gangs and all. City is getting quiet again after weeks of street fighting."

Skella let Gletts talk, as he seemed to relish the intrigue and violence. When he'd finally run down, she looked over at me and took her turn.

"Dwarves took your singer friend. We heard about it."

"Why'd they snatch him?" Katie asked.

Skella shrugged. "Not sure. I just know there are lots of new folks, fey and not, that have been flocking here. The King is claiming Vancouver as a free port. No dragons or their ilk allowed. If he thinks you may be working for one of them, he has you rubbed out."

"So, these dwarves," I continued. "They're new to town then?"

"No, been here longer than we have, or so Gran says."

I thought a few minutes. Rolph probably had information on them, being a dwarf himself. Hell, they could be family for all I knew. Not sure I totally trusted him, not after last year when he tried to take Gram away from me. To be fair though, I was trying to give it to the dragon Duchamp at the time. In my defense, I was exchanging it for Katie and Julie. It was a big mess, but it worked okay in the end. I killed the dragon, saved the girl, and liberated this fair city. Not bad, if I do say so myself. And I couldn't really blame Rolph. He served the sword before all else. He'd be outraged to know I'd let Jimmy keep Gram hidden at Black Briar. I wasn't even sure myself why I hadn't gone and taken her from him. Well, beyond cowardice, I guess.

I'd give Rolph a call and see what he knew.

# Nine

Jimmy stood in the bank vault, hidden behind the curtain with his father's safety-deposit box. Inside were a few important papers and three small clay figurines: Odin, Thor, and a Valkyrie. Each stood on a round pedestal about two inches across. There were initials carved on the bottom of each.

He picked up the Valkyrie and studied the way the carvings wound around the base in an unbroken chain, including the stylized figure of a dragon biting its own tail.

He pulled a bandana out of his pocket, wrapped the Valkyrie in it, and set it on the floor. With a quick motion, he stomped his boot down, shattering the statue with a dull thunk.

"Everything okay in there?" the guard asked from the other side of the curtain.

"Fine," Jimmy said, bending down to pick up the bandana. He unwrapped the shattered clay statue and pulled the pieces apart. Inside the base was a ring with a green gemstone. A sigil was carved in the stone, sort of a fanciful *S* or *F*. Inside the body of the Valkyrie was a thinly scrolled sheet of paper. He unrolled it. It was in code, but one he had a passing familiarity with. Here was his contact. Jimmy placed the ring inside the watch pocket in his jeans and tucked the paper in his shirt pocket. He placed the bandana-wrapped pottery shards inside the safety-deposit box.

Before he closed the lid, he slid his fingers over a small journal inside. His mother had been working on it when his parents disappeared. He didn't have enough knowledge to decipher the markings, and the one time he'd tried, he'd nearly killed himself. His mother knew magic and wards. There was something in the way the journal was protected that had caused him to collapse into seizures. If Deidre hadn't been home, he may have died. He'd hidden the journal here, but one day, he'd have to decipher its secrets. Somewhere in there were the answers to his family's origins; he knew it.

With a sigh, he shut the safety-deposit box and stepped out from behind the curtain.

The guard replaced the box and Jimmy took the key.

Now to decipher the note from his father and see if he could contact this secret member of his father's cabal.

# Ten

Skella and Gletts showed us around Stanley Park. Skella was eager to show us the *Girl in a Wetsuit* statue out on the shore, said it was based on one of the Vanir—the oldest race of gods, older than Odin and his crew— the Æsir. This beautiful maiden swam these waters as either a young maiden or a powerful salmon. Legend had it she was murdered by one of the Æsir— likely Loki, the trickster. Rumor was she had a great trove of treasure hidden somewhere in one of the many coves along the coast and Loki coveted her gold.

Katie said it was likely he coveted her treasure all right, but doubted it was anything more than the cove between her legs.

Gletts laughed at this, losing the last of his aloofness. Skella found the thought disturbing and ushered us farther around the park.

We spent the entire afternoon with the two goth kids—elves, I had to remember— and ended up having a grand time. Turned out Gletts had a wicked sense of humor, and Skella's sweet laugh seemed to make him swell with pride.

At one point, as Skella and I discussed the history of the area, Gletts wove two flowered necklaces for us. I laughed, of course.

"Sorry, dude. Really not me," but I put it in my pack all the same. Skella looked upset, and Gletts hurt, but Katie made a big deal about putting it on, and that seemed to make them somewhat happier.

Near sundown, we ended back at the park entrance. A mother and her two children sat on a bench along the far side of the square. The younger child was eating ice cream, but the older boy, about eleven, was facing away from his family, fervently working a Rubik's Cube. Gletts leaned against the great statue of Robert Burns watching them while Skella hugged us both.

"Come back anytime," she said sweetly. "It has been our honor having you in our home."

Gletts grunted, whether in agreement or not, I couldn't tell. "Have your people always lived here?" I asked.

"As far back as we remember," Skella offered.

"Not Gran," Gletts said, pushing himself off the statue. "She remembers Alfheim, our true home."

Skella looked a little sad at that and shrugged. "True enough, but what can you do?"

"Why can't you go back to Alfheim?" Katie asked.

Gletts laughed. "Because we're idiots," he barked. "We can't find the way."

"We once traveled through Asgard," Skella said. "But when the wyrms destroyed the Vanir back in the beginning of time, they broke the rainbow bridge, and that way has been closed to us ever since."

Katie's eyes were as huge as headlights. "Broke the bridge?" she whispered.

"Boo hoo," Gletts said. "They were fools—"

Skella shot him a withering look, which caused him to blanch.

"—leastwise, that's what Gran always says." He shrugged and went back to leaning on the statue.

Not a new argument, I supposed. But one where the sides had long been established.

"They were arrogant, yes. Allowed themselves to be duped. Loki played no small part in their undoing, and his reward was a slow death."

"Loki was killed?" Katie asked.

"Where have you been?" Gletts asked, obviously disgusted. "If they were around, do you think they'd let the dragons run the show?"

Suddenly I remembered a dream—Odin crucified to a tree, imploring me to find the others, his children and his people.

"The dragons killed all the gods?" I asked, fearing what the answer was.

"Yes, obviously," Gletts said.

"Maybe not so obviously," Skella said, patting me on the arm. "You must be new at this."

This caused Katie to laugh. "Gods, dragons, giants, elves—"

Gletts bowed at that last.

"—yeah, I'd say we are new to most of this."

"I think they are not all dead," I said quietly, hoping not to unbalance the world. "I believe one of them lives."

"Not possible," Gletts said. "The wyrms kill any that are reborn. They've killed whole villages, burned whole towns, on the rumor that one of the elder gods has been reborn."

*Interesting*, I thought. Were the dragons slipping? Arrogance brought down the elder gods. Could history be repeating itself with the dragons?

"And if I told you I met one of them?"

Skella reached forward and grabbed my arm. "You speak true?"

"He vanished," Katie said, watching me.

I nodded. Woden, the one-eyed god, had ridden in the back of my poor dead hatchback at one time. I'd saved him from attack by two brutish giants, and he had blessed or cursed me, depending on your outlook.

I lifted the hair off my face and leaned forward so Skella could see the runes buried in my hairline. "He touched me, brought fire to my mind."

Gletts hovered over Skella's shoulder as she peered at my forehead. "Blessed mother," she whispered. "We are doomed."

Before we knew what had happened, they both turned and ran across the concrete. The moment their feet were on grass once again, they faded, disappeared.

"What the hell?" Katie blurted out, running to the lawn. "They just vanished."

"Aye," I said, not bothering to move. "This may have been a huge mistake."

She walked back toward me, puzzlement written on her face. "What happened?"

"Not sure whose side they are on, after all," I said, picking up my pack.

"But they seemed to really hate the dragons."

I shrugged. "That was pretty abrupt."

She watched the tree line, thinking. "Maybe we should head back to the hotel. They mentioned Ari was snatched by dwarves, but they never really said how they knew."

"True," I said, slipping my arm around her waist and steering us toward a taxi stand just outside the park. "If they are in cahoots with the dwarves, and they think we are trucking with elder gods, maybe we are working to cross-purposes."

"None of that makes any sense."

I looked at her. "We just spent the better part of a day with two elf kids dolled up in goth clothing. We discussed dragons, shapeshifting elder gods, and dwarves. Why would the possibility of them knowing about the dwarves because they were helping them be that far a stretch?"

"Elves hate dwarves . . . all the literature says so."

I looked at her. "By all the literature, you don't mean *The Lord of the Rings* and *Dungeons and Dragons*, do you?"

She smacked me on the shoulder, which I deserved. "Elves are children of the light. Dwarves, children of the night."

Which brought my mind back to that poor dwarf kid, murdered for trucking with dragons.

The cab ride was mercifully mundane. Katie lay her head against my shoulder and closed her eyes. She'd been up earlier than me, and we'd had a pretty long day of hiking around. It had been a decent enough day, but I wanted to get back to the hotel and get ready for dinner. We were going for Indian food. Katie wanted something spicy; I was sure I could find something to like. They'd have chicken, right? and bread?

Back in the room, Katie flopped down on the bed, mumbling something about a nap. I thought maybe she'd want to snuggle, but she crashed hard. I turned on the television with the volume low and plugged in my cell phone. The battery was good and dead. After I was sure Katie was not going to wake up, I stripped out of my clothes and padded into the shower.

By the time I was finished, Katie was snoring. Not like her, but it was a strange bed and she didn't look like she was completely comfortable. It was still fairly early, so I wrapped my nakedness in a fluffy hotel robe, turned off the television, and checked on the phone. One bar of battery, good enough. I powered it up, and it immediately began buzzing with messages and missed calls.

Two of them, to be precise. I put on my headset and checked the messages—one from Julie and one from Rolph.

Julie's message was to wish Katie a happy birthday, and to remind me to be home in time to work on Monday. "Yes Mom," I muttered as I deleted the message. I had to be in Cle Elum bright and early to help Frank Rodriguez. Like I'd shirk work.

The second message was short. "Smith, this is Rolph. I need to discuss events of late. Please return my call."

He was chatty.

I brought up his number on the speed dial, picked up my pack, and went back into the bathroom. I sat on the toilet and propped one foot up on the side of the tub, then shook the bottle of nail polish I'd picked up for this trip—a deep red called Bimbo Limbo. I was going to paint my toenails. I hadn't done that since college. No one who knew me would ever know, besides Katie; she was in for a serious surprise.

By the time I had the bottle shaken and opened, Rolph answered.

"Hey, Rolph, it's me, Sarah." I leaned over and dabbed a wide red swath over the nail on the big toe on my left foot. Very bright.

"Ah, smith," he said, sounding relieved. "I'm afraid we are once again faced with hard tasks ahead."

I dipped the brush back into the tiny glass jar, taking care not to knock it from the edge of the sink. Great. Now what?

"I know you already have word of the skald's kidnapping."

"Yeah," I said, dragging the brush carefully over the nail again. "Katie and I were there. I fought with the bunch of them—bastards."

"Impressive," he said. "I know of the scoundrels. I am surprised they let you live."

"I can hold my own in a fight," I said, piqued. "I give as good as I get."

He chuckled. "I meant no disrespect. You are as fiery as ever."

More psychoanalysis. From a dwarf, no less. "What's on your mind, Rolph? What do you know about the guys who snatched Ari?"

"One moment," he said. He covered the phone, speaking to his girlfriend, Juanita. She'd rescued him after the dragon battle, got him to shelter before the rising sun. They'd met on the *Elvis Versus the Goblins* movie shoot. We were surprised she threw JJ over for Rolph, but love works in mysterious ways.

The next two nails were easier, smaller. In fact, they were so small the polish smeared a teensy bit onto the skin around the third toe. I wiped it off with a thumbnail, getting most of it.

Catching a low mumble from behind me, I turned in time to see movement in the mirror. I put the brush back in the bottle and stood up, glancing out into the room, stepping lightly so I didn't smear the polish on the three painted toes. Katie was still sleeping. I'd have to wake her soon or she'd sleep through the night. The mirror was still pretty steamed up, so maybe I'd only caught a glimpse of myself moving around.

I heard a faint voice ask, "Is she naked?"

"Who's there with you?" I asked Rolph. The sound was distorted for a moment before he came back to the phone. "Only Juanita and I, why?"

"Which one of you asked if I was naked?"

He laughed. "Neither of us."

"I heard someone ask 'Is she naked?'"

I looked around. As I turned my head, I again thought I saw something in the mirror. Holy shit. I leaned forward and wiped the mirror with the back of my hand. I bet they have a peephole in here. The mirror was on the sidewall, however. The one that backed to the rest of the room.

"I'm afraid you have lost me, smith."

"Can we meet in person?" I asked him, feeling strange.

"Perhaps that would be best," he said. "Juanita suggests we meet for dinner on your way back home."

"Excellent."

I walked back out into the room and wrote the name and address of the restaurant on a hotel notepad.

I plugged the cell phone back into the charger and looked over at Katie. Maybe we should bag dinner. She looked like she was good to sleep through the night.

Katie's suitcase sat open on the chair by the window. On top she'd laid out her frilly underthings. I traced my hands down the white silk camisole. She was such a girl. Her blouse and skirt were hanging in the closet; the top was a short black number with very thin straps. Nice. I'd never seen this outfit. It could be new for the weekend. I never even thought of doing that, buying something new, pretty . . .

I glanced over at my own suitcase. Things were jammed in there with no thought to keeping pleats straight or preventing un-necessary wrinkles—just not on my radar. I dropped the robe, grabbed her things still on their hangers, and walked to the mir-ror over the dresser.

I held the clothes up, checking how I'd look in them. It was startling. Totally not something I'd ever wear, dear god. And these would never fit me, much too small. And I couldn't pull off a skirt—all that shaving, and waxing, primping . . . the underwear alone would kill me.

But I had to admit it wasn't that bad. Wouldn't the world be stunned to see me all shorn and spiffy. I glanced over at Katie, sleeping curled up in her sweats. Would she like it if I femmed up? I didn't want her to change, and I couldn't imagine she'd want me to, either. But what if?

It was complicated. I didn't want to fall into stereotype here. If I decided to shave my legs and put on a skirt one day, I'd like it to be on my terms and not cause the world to shift on its axis.

As I turned, the tattoos on my calf came into view. Who was I kidding, the world had already tilted damn near off its axis. I had tattoos erupt through the skin on my calf just from reforging and handling a magic sword. I'd killed a dragon and rescued an elder god. Hell, I'd even been kissed by a Valkyrie.

That was a moment that takes your breath away.

Guiltily, I returned her outfit to the closet, turned off the lights, and slipped into bed with her. Maybe we just needed the night to recover. It had been a rough couple of days.

Besides, my head swam with the whirl of roles and expectations. I just wanted to be me.

# Eleven

I WOKE EARLY—LIKE 4 A.M.—AND GOT DRESSED IN THE DARK. Katie's soft breathing told me she still slept. She was going to be pissed she slept through her birthday dinner, but I didn't have the heart to wake her. Or maybe I was just being selfish and scared.

Once I had my sweats and sneakers on, I grabbed my running pack and wrote out a quick note. A run would do me good. I felt tight, wound up. Kicking out a few miles would change that.

Ninety minutes later, my muscles were humming, and the endorphins were kicking in. I love the way I feel after a run. Wish I could remember to do it more often.

Katie was still asleep when I got back to the room. I'd shower first, and then wake her.

I stripped down and saw the open bottle of nail polish on the vanity. Of course . . . I glanced down. Three toes on one foot painted, the rest naked. Figured I couldn't concentrate long enough to finish one foot.

Waste of eight bucks. The bottle made a forlorn thud as I dropped it into the trashcan. That's what I got for trying to be someone I'm not.

After a quick shower, I puttered around the room, making noise while I packed, hoping to wake her. After a few minutes I got a wet washcloth and wiped her face with it, and she slept on. I stripped

the bed and jostled her, tickled her, poked, and prodded . . .
nothing.

Someone in the room next door was having an argument, and
for some reason it was giving me a headache. Thoughts of ambu-
lances and emergency rooms began to dance in my head. I dug
around in my pack, thinking I had some ibuprofen, and managed
to stab myself with something. I pulled my hand out of my pack
quickly and stuck the offending finger in my mouth. What did I
have that was sharp? And why did my finger taste funny? I turned
my pack upside down. There, in the midst of my assorted shit, was
the flowered necklace the elves had given me. As the room grew
fuzzy, I saw there were thorns on those vines.

I realized two things as I fell over backward. First: my finger
was good and numb, likely an effect of whatever the flowers
were—and of course, Katie still had on the necklace. I hadn't taken
it off her.

Second, Skella and Gletts were standing in our dresser mirror,
watching us. It didn't make any sense at first, them standing there.
I know they weren't in the room with us, so the only plausible
answer was that they were in the mirror. Crazy making, I know.

As I hit the floor it got even more surreal.

Gletts stepped through the mirror. "I thought she'd never pick
up that necklace," he said, very put out.

Bastard.

"Don't hurt them," Skella said, sounding freaked. "See if she
has it so we can fix this."

They didn't realize something. I could feel my body succumbing to whatever poison was on the flowers, but my mind remained
clear. I tried to sit up, struggling to rise, and somehow snapped
out of my body. It was like back in the bar all those months ago.
One second I had lost control of my body, the next I was floating
outside myself—I'd gone astral again.

Gletts was rummaging through the dresser and closets. I quietly floated upward, hovering to the left of the mirror, where Skella couldn't see me. If I wasn't so pissed at them, and afraid for what was about to happen, I might think the whole thing was freaking awesome.

"I can't find it," Gletts growled, throwing Katie's birthday outfit to the floor as he ransacked the closet. "Why wouldn't she have it with her?"

Skella pressed against the mirror from her side. I could see the side of her face and a room behind her. It looked rough-hewn, cut stone and timbers. There were a scattering of tables, cauldrons, and assorted tools: hammers, saws, and the like. A huge fire roared in the center of the room, and on the far wall, chained upside down, was Ari. "What the hell?"

Skella snapped her head around, saw me, and shrieked. "Gletts, she's awake!"

Gletts spun around, saw my body lying on the floor, and looked over at Skella, confused. "She hasn't moved."

"I heard something," she said, looking around, apparently not seeing me.

I reached out, my hand passing through the mirror like it was a doorway, and touched the side of Skella's face. She shrieked and fell backward, knocking over a table covered in beakers and glass jars.

Gletts whirled around, running toward the mirror. He had no problem seeing me.

"How?" he asked, pausing long enough for me to lunge forward and tackle him. "Get off," he cried as we tumbled to the ground.

Since I could feel both Gletts and Skella, I assumed they somehow lived in both states—astral and physical. I didn't get to enjoy the effects of gravity, however. Should've remembered that from last time.

Gletts punched me in the side—which I felt—and scrambled away on all fours.

I tried to follow him, but I seemed to be partially stuck in the desk chair. Problem with being in spirit form—interaction with objects in the real world were not as you might expect. It was odd to see one of the wooden rungs stuck partway through my thigh. It took a second to pull myself away from the chair, and while I was delayed, Gletts dove into the mirror.

"Sonuvabitch," I growled, floating off the floor once more. I sorta swam over to the mirror, determined to follow him, when Skella's face appeared. She was crying. I stuck my head into the mirror, and she placed her hand on my head, pushing me back gently.

"I'm sorry," she whispered, glancing back over her shoulder. "We were going to remove the necklaces." She pursed her lips, almost pouting as she thought to say something else.

"What're you on about there?" a gruff voice called from across the cavern. I could see three large men dropping tools and shrugging out of cloaks. Dwarves.

Skella swung back around to face me. "The poison will wear off in about six hours. Get out of Vancouver."

I fell back, unable to grasp her hand. She mumbled something, waved her hands, and the mirror fogged for a moment, then returned to showing me the room.

Great, we'd been poisoned by the elves and I was out of my body again. Now what could I do?

# Twelve

Six hours, for fuck's sake. It took every single second of six hours for the poison to wear off. I floated around, unable to push my way into any of the mirrors, which sucked. I couldn't even knit, as much as I loathed doing so.

One thing I had, though, was time to think. Jimmy had some answering to do. He had knowledge I didn't. Was he aware of the elves? This whole mirror thing was way out of my realm of reality. I'd been lazy, not confronting him—scared, frankly, to push things. I couldn't face him, not with the massacre in the spring. Hell, I'd even let him hide Gram. What was I thinking? Gram was a part of me now, an integral tug on my psyche. When things settled down—when I got the job front rolling again—I'd do something about it. Yep, definitely, just as soon as I fixed a few other things in my life.

Who was I kidding? If I waited around for things to settle down, I'd die without any answers. What I needed to do was change my direction. Maybe hit Jimmy head-on? I needed to just go out to Black Briar and face the music. This was some spooky shit. A year ago, I didn't know dragons existed. Today, I found out that a couple of elves could travel into my room through mirrors and poison me in a way that leaves me helpless for hours. Talk about the ultimate roofie. I hate to think what they could've done to us. What a dangerous fucking world.

Once the effects began to ebb, I found myself pulled back to my body. Not like I was doing any good out here anyway. Well, keeping watch was a good thing, right? I couldn't even pick up a book or turn on the television. There were some serious drawbacks to all this.

I woke with my head pounding and desperately thirsty around three in the afternoon. Not sure why no one had rousted us from the hotel. I'd be checking that.

I rose, stumbled into the bathroom, and vomited into the toilet. The porcelain felt good against my forehead—cool. After a moment, I pulled myself to my feet and turned back to the room. The mirrors were normal, and the room was trashed. Katie's skirt and blouse lay crumpled where Gletts had thrown it, bastard. He did not want to run into me again anytime soon.

Katie was still out, which scared me. She'd had that necklace on for a long time. Using a thick washcloth, I held onto the necklace with one hand and snipped the vine with a pair of scissors Katie kept in her pack.

Red welts circled her neck where the thorns had pierced her. The numbing effect must have been quicker with her, since she hadn't complained when she put the necklace on, but I'd fallen to the poison much faster than she had.

Once I had the necklace cut, I gently lifted her head and pulled the vile thing away. I placed it and mine in a plastic bag and set it in the ice bucket. I'd dispose of those later.

I washed Katie's neck and checked her for a pulse. Her heartbeat was strong. I called down to the front desk, and they said we had the room for one more night. Said we'd called down the night before and asked to extend. Guess it was a good thing, considering. I'd bet it was Skella. Good service on the hotel's part, though.

I ordered room service and went around picking things up while I waited for food. What had they been looking for? They didn't steal anything, passed up the cash I had, credit cards, laptop . . . Could this be about Gram? What else did I have that a couple young elves may want?

And Skella didn't act like someone who wanted to hurt us. She looked chagrined, like maybe they'd been forced to do this. And what of Ari? They were underground it seemed—caves somewhere? But he was alive. I'd seen him move. He didn't look comfortable by any means, but he lived all the same.

Right at six hours after I cut the necklace off her, Katie began to stir. She woke moaning and groggy at first, then threw up all over the place. I held her until she stopped, then helped her into the shower to clean up.

"Weird dreams," she said as she stuck her head under the spray.

She opened her mouth and let the water run over her face for a very long time.

I stripped the bed and called down to housekeeping to explain that Katie had the flu and that we'd be checking out soon. They said they'd clean up after we left. I put a twenty on the desk with a note thanking the staff for such good service.

I put on my Bluetooth and called Rolph and Juanita. I explained it all to him as best I could and apologized about missing dinner.

"I have heard rumors of the mirror children," he said, after I'd run down. "I only know them from children's tales, but I would think they could only traverse into places they'd previously been."

"Why's that?" I asked.

"The stories I heard as a child said they would come into your home and take little things, trinkets and such, or in a worst case steal your child."

"Damn," I said. "Stealing babies?"

"If they are somehow mixed up with the taking of your singer friend," he continued, "they are in league with some distant relations of mine. I will dig around, see what I can uncover."

"We're going home," I told him. "This weekend has totally gotten out of hand."

"Good idea," he offered. "I will contact you. In the meantime, I would ask about the safety of a certain artifact."

Smooth . . . "She's in a safe place," I said, not caring to go into details. "I don't think there is any chance your mirror children can find her, but I'll double-check when I get home."

"Good," he said. "Good to know you are on top of the important things." He paused for a long moment, perhaps discussing something with Juanita. "It is good to see you coming around. The world is dangerous and unpredictable."

"That's a big duh!"

Most of the clothes had been in our packs, but there was no way I'd gotten things back into Katie's correctly. She was a meticulous packer. When I packed, I just shoved things in until I could barely zip it up. She was coordinated.

She left the towels crumpled on the bathroom floor and walked out into the room, naked . . . of course. I don't know why I hadn't thought of it before, but I quickly grabbed all the towels and used them to cover the mirrors in the room. This was going to be difficult.

I explained what had happened as I covered the mirrors. She dumped her pack out onto the floor and fished out the delicates she wanted. I tried not to get too angry in the retelling. She helped by, you know . . . being there.

She put on the new outfit as I wound down and watched her.

"They didn't feel foul," she said as she straightened her skirt. "Seemed likeable enough."

I sat on the edge of the bed, hands hanging down between my knees. "It's weird," I agreed. "Gletts was pretty damn cavalier about the whole thing, but he is a boy. Skella seemed upset about it all."

Katie set about repacking her suitcase and watching me. "Too bad we missed last night." She sighed.

"We'll celebrate next weekend," I promised. "I'll cook." I smiled real big, shoving my hair out of my eyes.

This brought a laugh. "Seriously, like without a microwave or boxed dinner?"

I rolled my eyes. "Of course. I've survived this long, haven't I?"

She winked at me and zipped up her bag. "Let's get out of here. I'm feeling claustrophobic. Maybe you can buy me a burger on the way home."

"Deal!"

We'd been driving about twenty minutes when Katie turned down the radio and placed her hand on my knee.

"So, um . . . when did you paint your toenails?"

I looked at her for a second, smiling sheepishly. "Whilst you were poisoned and unconscious."

She nodded once, and we listened to road noise for a few minutes. "Might want to paint them all," she said. At least she was smiling.

That's what I'd heard when I was painting my toes. *Is she naked?* indeed. That had to be Gletts, the little pisher.

All this new magic—elves and more dwarves. And the King of Vancouver, whoever the hell he was. There was some serious insanity up here.

I was just glad to be heading home. I had to get to Cle Elum by seven tomorrow morning. Time to earn back some of the money we'd just spent on the weekend.

As far as romantic getaways are concerned, I think the weekend broke even. Too much violence for my taste, but there were parts that were nice.

Seriously.

# Thirteen

WE SWITCHED CARS AT MY PLACE. I REALLY WANTED TO BURY my head under some blankets for a few hours, but she was wired.

"You could come to my place," she said, grabbing me around the waist as I pulled her luggage out of my trunk.

It was tempting. I liked the way her hands felt on my stomach as she wormed them under my shirt. But I had to work in the morning. And I felt like I could sleep for days.

"Not tonight," I said, turning to catch her hands in mine before she got too far. "Work tomorrow."

"Me, too," she said. "You can go to work from my place in the morning."

I kissed her, but pulled back before it got too passionate. "You are pretty damn persuasive," I said, stepping away. "But I should really check in on Julie."

Katie crossed her arms and harrumphed. "Bother," she said, putting on a semiserious pout. "She's a grown woman, Sarah. She doesn't need you mothering her."

I looked at her, then cupped her chin in my left hand and kissed her on the nose. "You know why. Maybe we can go out again this week."

For a moment, I thought she was going to stamp her foot, but then she yawned.

"Go home, hon."

She shook her head at me, and then stifled another yawn. "Okay, you win."

We walked to her car, loaded the trunk, and said our good-byes.

I watched her drive away. When she was out of sight, I grabbed my kit and sloughed my way upstairs.

The hallway smelled like boiled cabbage. My neighbor, Mrs. Sorenson, seemed to have a mission to spread the joy of boiled cabbage and fat cats to any neighbor who would stand still. She was actually very cool.

Julie had gotten to know her over the last few weeks. I think it was good for both of them. Mr. Sorenson had passed before I moved in. She was pretty lonely.

I opened the door to the apartment and lumbered inside. I dropped my bags by the dining-room table, stepped into the kitchen, and opened the fridge. There was still some milk and a few other things that were likely part of Julie's food hoard. I sniffed the milk just to make sure it was not spoiled. I had a track record for letting things go bad in my fridge.

At least I was using a glass these days. Then, if the milk had gotten chunky, I could tell as I poured it. Before, when I drank straight from the carton, I was occasionally surprised.

The milk was cold and very satisfying. When I was rinsing the glass, Julie walked in from the bedroom. Only one of those, so I slept on the pullout couch. Not as comfortable as my bed, but she was the one recovering.

"I was wondering when you'd get home," she said, rubbing her eyes.

I glanced at the clock. It was just after one.

"Sorry if I woke you," I said, pulling out a chair and sitting down at the table. "Been a helluva weekend."

She smiled at me and pulled out another chair. It hurt me to watch her leverage herself into it in such a dainty and fragile way.

"Did Katie have a good birthday?"

"Well . . ." I must've grimaced a little, because she got that concerned-boss look on her face and leaned forward, placing her elbows on the table. "Trouble?"

"You might say that." I ran my left hand through my hair. "You see any news this weekend?"

"Ah," she said, sitting back in the chair. "I was afraid you might have gotten mixed up in that singer's disappearance."

"You don't know the half of it."

I spent the next half an hour filling her in on the whole thing. We'd shared many stories over the last few months, including all the gory details of the dragon, giants, Woden / Odin / Joe . . . the whole nine yards.

She had good reason to believe, having been snatched by the very dragon I managed to kill. But, like me, she was just learning all the strange details of our overly complicated world.

"I'm sure the local authorities can handle the kidnapping," she said. "Rolph has contacts in the community, right?"

"Aye," I agreed. I yawned large enough for my jaw to hurt. "I really need to get some sleep."

"Right," she said, pushing herself up from the table and sorta hopping to a solid stance. "Work in the morning."

She didn't look at me as she said it, but I knew what was written on her face. This was killing her day by day. She needed to get back out there, smell horses, feel the hammer. Julie was mentor, master, parent, and friend, all rolled into one. She was the best damn blacksmith I knew, and if I was very lucky, I'd be a lot like her when I grew up.

"Want to go over to Cle Elum with me tomorrow?" I asked,

hopeful. A day with Frank would replenish her flagging self-esteem. He thought she was something special.

"PT in the morning," she said, her shoulders slumping. "I swear that woman is trying to kill me."

I smiled. "I'm sure it's helping." The physical therapy was taking longer than the doctors had originally planned. The surgery had done a good job putting all the pieces back together after the dragon had smashed her right femur, but with the steel rod, pins, screws, and new hip, she was struggling.

"Oh," she said as she limped across the room, leaning on her cane, "Jennifer called. Wanted to remind you about the Flight Test meeting tomorrow night."

Crap. I'd forgotten with all the craziness. I was a stakeholder in the movie studio I worked for—Flight Test, Ltd. Frederick Sawyer, the dragon in Portland, had purchased a twenty-five-percent stake but had to give it up when the Seattle dragon, Nidhogg, caught him meddling in her domain. She gave me half of his share and had kept the rest for herself. Twelve and a half percent was damn good.

*Elvis Versus the Goblins* was in distribution and had hit a couple of film festivals. I'd bet we were going to get good news. Besides, the crew was itching to start the next project.

"Yeah, okay. I'll be sure to make it."

She waved over her head and shut the bedroom door.

I hated that I couldn't fix her. I'm a maker, as she is. We transform the bones of the earth, iron and steel, into useful objects. Watching her suffer made me feel useless.

I flipped the couch cushions onto the floor and pulled out the bed. The bills on my desk were getting pretty deep, I noticed, as I shimmied out of my jeans. I'd need to pay them soon. Maybe Tuesday. A quick brush left my mouth minty and clean. I wasn't sure why that seemed so important as I climbed into the bed, but it distinctly did not taste like the powder from those flowers.

I sat bolt upright in bed. Damn it. Mirrors. I crawled out of bed and took down the mirror in the hall. It fit nicely behind the couch, with the reflective, elf-displaying side facing the wall. That should confuse anyone who cared to look. I draped a towel over the vanity mirror and pulled the bathroom door shut, just in case.

It was nearly two before I turned out the light. Work was going to come damn early.

# Fourteen

FREDERICK SAWYER PACED OUTSIDE ROOM 100 OF THE MULT-nomah County building. The halls bustled with bureaucrats, law enforcement, and common citizens, who were starting their work-week with the usual apathy he expected from thralls.

The planning commission was due to begin within the next half hour, and Frederick was here to determine why his project continued to be delayed. This delay had gone on for over four months and was costing him hundreds of thousands of dollars in lost wages and revenues.

Delays of this sort were not uncommon, but this smelled of interference and meddling beyond the simple need of bureaucrats to create further bureaucracy.

Frederick was not one to let the rage take him, even when faced with an obstacle that could cost him a large sum of money. There were others of his kind that would hunt down those who offended them, shred their bodies with tooth and talon, burn the remains to ash, and scatter the dust to the winds with the beat of their mighty wings.

His breathing was a little too hard, he realized. Perhaps the pseudo-metaphor was a bit too close to the truth. The drones on the planning commission did not make the laws. It was just their job to implement the will of the state and federal authorities, as well as the Multnomah commissioners.

His pride still stung from that incident in Seattle over the movie studio. It galled him that his investment of time and money would be in Nidhogg's hands. Rumor had it part of it went to that smith, Beauhall. She was an interesting one. He smiled. He'd be keeping an eye on her and her clan, that's for sure. Perhaps the investment would bear fruit of a different flavor. There was always his influence over the young actor Montgomery. His loyalty was easily maintained. He may not have an open hand in the movie studio, but he had his claw on the pulse, so to speak.

Now, if he just could get his hands on that bloody sword. That was a trifle worth his estimable time—an echo in the ether that set his teeth on edge.

But back to the business at hand. This office park was costing him a fortune with every delay. The commission was sympathetic to his plight, as his design followed the density plans, as well as provided green space and a dedicated place for the county to use for social services—mainly homeless services. Frederick knew where his bread was buttered. Toss the bureaucrats a few crumbs and they would follow you to hell.

He only just noticed how the rest of the visitors and participants of the commission had drifted from him, giving him a wide berth. *Has my anger grown so obvious?* he thought.

From the back of the milling crowd, Frederick caught sight of his able servant, Mr. Philips. The dapper man traversed the throng with quiet aplomb.

Frederick stopped his pacing, straightened his collar and cuffs, and crossed his hands behind his back. "Mr. Philips," he said, once the man had breached the final cadre of government officials. "I hope you bear me good news."

Mr. Philips did not betray his emotional state, but he never had. Frederick had no wish to play poker with the man. Stone cold to a fault, that fellow.

"I'm afraid I have some unfortunate news," Mr. Philips said, stopping before his master and pulling a small notepad from his breast pocket.

Frederick waited, not wanting to appear too impatient or draw the attention of any of the nearby individuals.

"First," Mr. Philips said, making a small check on his notepad with a short pencil, "the problem with the construction seems to be the state of our major contractor's insurance."

Frederick kept his face impassive, but he could feel the heat rising in him again. "Insurance?" he asked quietly.

"Yes, sir," Mr. Philips said. "It seems the company in charge of overseeing the construction of Duchamp Office Park has suffered from a revocation of their liability insurance. Something about lost paperwork and inadequate documentation." He looked at Frederick, his face as calm as a monk's.

"I see," Frederick said, tasting the words in his mouth as if they were mothballs. "And may I assume that a mutual acquaintance of ours holds said insurance policies?"

Mr. Philips nodded. "Indeed. The underwriter for those policies is none other than her grace, Nidhogg."

Frederick grimaced. "I think she has left grace in the dust of time," he said, the bitterness thick on his tongue. "She is a spiteful cur who has lived past her time."

"I'm sure you are quite correct," Mr. Philips said. "Be that as it may. She is the reason this project has been delayed."

Frederick felt his nails cutting into his palms. This would mean more groveling to the most ancient of dragons . . . the cow . . . and her pet witch, Qindra. He ground his teeth and took a deep breath. "Set up a conference call with Qindra at her convenience, if you please."

"Very good, sir," Mr. Philips said, handing Frederick a business card. "She will speak with you this evening at six. She can be reached at the number on the back."

*This is why you serve me*, Frederick thought, allowing a feeling of control to slip back over his anger. "You are efficient as always, Mr. Philips."

"I live to serve," his thrall said, bowing at the waist, more of a nod, really, than a full bow. "As for the other problem . . ."

Frederick's smile vanished as soon as it had blossomed on his face. "Not another?"

"I'm afraid so," Mr. Philips said, opening a manila folder and handing Frederick a five-by-seven color photo. "The dwarf lad you sent to Vancouver was found secured to a basketball pole and forced to watch the sunrise."

Frederick winced. "Ugly way to die."

"Indeed," Mr. Philips said, handing over a second photo. "The sign he wore is clearly a warning."

"Dragon friend," Frederick read. "Do you suppose this King of Vancouver even heard the message young Bartleby was sent to deliver?"

"His name was Bömburr, sir."

Frederick looked at him, confused. "Pardon?"

"The dwarf lad. His family has served you for generations. His name was Bömburr. He left behind a mother and three younger sisters. His father was killed serving you several years ago in that mission to Belarus."

Belarus . . . ? Frederick thought back. Something about a business deal with that dragon in Minsk.

"They serve the wheel," he said, waving his hand to dismiss Mr. Philips's comment. "I am not ready to give in just yet."

"Of course," Mr. Philips said. "I assume you wish to send another emissary?"

"Hmmm . . ." Frederick tapped his chin with one long finger. "We've lost three. I'd hoped the dwarf would appeal to the King's sensibilities after he killed the last two."

"Quite erratic," Mr. Philips said.

"Must I go myself?" Frederick asked. "I do not like this King and his unwillingness to open clear lines of communication."

"Perhaps he dislikes dealing with those of power."

Frustration flooded Frederick, a flash of heat and anger. "Does he understand whom he trifles with?"

The people in the hallway shuffled away, their faces averted.

Mr. Philips was an intelligent man, savvy in the ways of politics and finance. He served Frederick with knowledge and insight no other had been able to display in all Frederick's centuries of life. "It is obvious he is a charismatic leader who has no love lost for your attempts to reach out to him."

"Vancouver must not be an enemy. Another of my kind cannot be allowed a firm foothold," Frederick said with a growl. "I am too close to expanding my holdings. Nidhogg will not last the decade, and I will crush her resistance before long. No other dragon shall have Vancouver as long as I have blood in my veins."

"This King, at least, does not seem to be a dragon," Mr. Philips stated.

Frederick paused. The statement was true. "He clearly is not human, but that leaves us with the question of just what sort of creature he is. It is obvious from the warning sign displayed on young Barnabas that someone other than one of the ruling class has assumed power over the city and its environs."

"A likely supposition," Mr. Philips agreed. "But, as he has expressed a vivid disinterest in negotiating with your kind, I believe, perhaps, we should consider letting things lie."

Frederick gazed at him a moment, shocked by the tact. "Do nothing?"

Mr. Philips nodded slightly. "There are other ways to influence this King, do you not agree?"

In the game of thrones, Frederick was no novice. His servant's suggestion had merit. "Excellent, Mr. Philips. I believe you have the right of it. We shall bide our time, see how this King settles into his new kingdom."

Mr. Philips bowed again, this time a full sweep, the top of his head carefully presented to Frederick in a sign of both respect and submission. "As you wish."

Frederick smiled. An able servant indeed. How valuable one such as he had proved.

"Now, let us assuage the consternation of our fine commissioners. Let them know that we have everything under control and will be back on track by the week's end."

Mr. Philips looked at Frederick, his eyebrows high.

"Nidhogg will release the block," Frederick added. "Qindra will demand some punishment for my transgressions, I am heartily sure. But, it has never been beyond me to grovel to meet the greater goal."

"But of course," Mr. Philips said.

Frederick opened his briefcase and placed the manila folder with the pictures of young Bradley's demise inside. Horrible way to end a life. He would use this to leverage the dwarven community against this usurper in Vancouver. Waste not, want not.

# Fifteen

CRAZY QUILT FARM WASN'T MUCH OF A FARM THESE DAYS. Mrs. LeBlanc ran a quilt store, holding bees, keeping the community stocked in fabric and gossip. Mr. LeBlanc was a retired real estate agent who loved horses. He had seven, and three ponies that he took around to little kid's' parties. It was a quiet retirement for him, and something he loved.

Today we'd work all his stock. It would take the greater part of the day. We set up shop near the front field and got Frank's rig set up for working shoes.

I walked the horses around, letting Frank see how they moved. He knew horses like most people knew their own hands. Each one needed a little something different. As he watched me lead them around, he'd talk out loud, observing things like limping or difference in gait.

We managed to get the ponies and three horses done before lunch. That left the three high-steppers and one Belgian for afterward. I pulled out a couple of sandwiches, a bag of carrots, and two bottles of water. Frank's lunch consisted of an apple and a bottle of vitamin-fortified water. "Watching my weight," he informed me. He didn't turn down half my second sandwich, however.

Frank was old school. Loved the art of blacksmithing more than the business side. Julie told me how the old German masters would hand an apprentice a block of iron and a key. The block of iron was to be reduced to the same key as the one the apprentice held, by just filing the metal. Once that key had been created, the apprentice was assumed to be a journeyman.

Frank added a twist on that—made his apprentices cast a bell of a certain note. They could pick and choose as they saw fit, but before Frank would let them go on, they had to add a bell to his elaborate collection, which hung along the ceiling of his smithy.

Quirky, but something I could understand. He said it was tradition, that it linked the student and master. Built a reputation to carry on the journey. That's how Frank was. Legend and lore are an integral part of a blacksmith's life.

"A smith has to know the history of things," he said. "Take this anvil, for example. It once belonged to the Bellingham International Railroad."

"Never heard of them."

"Small outfit, only twenty or thirty miles of track, crossed the border to Canada from Bellingham."

Odd bit of knowledge. I'm sure it was important to him, though. "Interesting," I said.

Now it was Frank's turn to laugh. "Right, pretty trivial, but it's important to know the history of our possessions." He reached back to his toolbox and pulled out a three-pound hammer. "Like this beauty," he said, handing it to me. "Fellow that owned this before me was named Peabody. Made little ornate dragons to be placed around in people's gardens."

I stiffened when he said dragon. Reflex, I imagine, but I had a chill that did not go with the heat of the day.

"You got something against dragons?" he asked, watching me out of the corner of his eye.

My alarms were going off. Suddenly I wasn't so sure how much I knew about Frank Rodriguez. Did he work for Nidhogg, or

Sawyer? Just because I was only learning about the oversociety didn't mean others were as willfully ignorant as I was.

"Not a fan of the mythos," I said, hoping I didn't squeak. "I prefer my fire in the forge, not spread out over the countryside."

"Good," he said, drinking the last of his water. "Their lot has a bad reputation."

I watched him as he hopped off his truck and gathered up the trash. "Someone I think you should meet," he said, not looking at me.

I slid off the truck gate and dusted off my jeans. "Yeah? A friend of yours?"

He shrugged. "Julie will be needing a new smithy if she's gonna get back on her feet."

This threw me. "Sure."

"She can't rebuild on that land, you realize."

What? "Um . . . I'm not following."

"Better let my friend, Anezka, give you all the details," he said. "She's the one who understands the hoodoo. Let's just say that the way it burned . . ." He brushed his hands, three broad swipes against one another and flung his hands outward, as if he were pushing away some energy. "She's particular about strangers, though. I'll have to work out the logistics with her before I introduce you."

"Afraid I'll embarrass the grown-ups?" I asked.

He smiled sheepishly. "Something like that. Let's finish up here, and I'll get a hold of Anezka in the next couple of days."

The rest of the afternoon crawled by. The four horses that were left were big boys; the Belgian topped fifteen hands high. He wasn't too happy about being handled by me, either. Took all my best coaxing to get him to walk around enough for Frank to make his assessment.

Maybe it was how agitated I was. The end of that lunch conversation had me on edge, and I guess the horses could feel it. Frank kept looking at me funny, like I was going to sprout wings.

We settled up with the LeBlancs and headed back over the pass. Frank didn't talk much on the way home, like he was chewing on something and he wasn't too fond of the flavor.

I fell asleep. One second I was watching the trees and the river flow by, the next I heard him put the truck into park and the noise of the drive stopped.

He nudged my shoulder. "Come on, sleepyhead."

I wiped my face and opened the truck door. In a few minutes I had my gear transferred back over to the Taurus and was standing in the smithy with Frank. He was filling out paperwork, and I picked up a broom to sweep. Yolanda came in just then, and smiled at me like a movie star.

I'd only met her once, but she was a stunner. Even over fifty, she radiated joy. Frank and Yolanda have been married since before dirt, and they had been through a world of crap from the community, especially in the early days. Yolanda was dark, a mix of Native American and African that mingled in a look of both strength and beauty. If she were young today, she'd have her pick of men, but when she graduated in the late seventies, the world was not too keen on interracial marriages.

"Glad to see you sweeping up," she said. "Does a body good to keep things neat and tidy."

I nodded. "Yes ma'am. Helps me settle my thoughts. Let's me know the work day's done once things are in order."

Frank came out and kissed his wife, then the two of them looked at me, arm in arm. "You good with waiting 'til the end of the week to get paid?"

"Sure," I said. "Julie paid me weekly."

"Good," he said. "As for tomorrow, why don't you just meet me out at the Circle Q? That way you can save yourself a trip over the pass."

"Thanks," I said.

"Maybe you can sleep in," Yolanda said. "You look like you are about to fall over."

"Rough weekend," I said, smiling. "Was in Vancouver for my girlfriend's birthday."

I froze. Holy crap, had I said that out loud? I felt a flush spring up over my chest and neck.

Yolanda laughed. "Well, I'm sure the two of you had a good time," she said. "I remember me and Frank spending some late nights in Vancouver."

"Hush, you," he said, squeezing her closer to him. "Don't tell tales like that."

Yolanda winked at me.

"Well . . ." I wasn't going to stop blushing anytime soon. But they hadn't said anything about my use of the word *girlfriend*. Maybe Julie had told them. "I'll see you tomorrow, then."

Frank nodded, and I walked to the door.

"Drive careful," Yolanda called.

"Youngsters," Frank said as I closed the door. I could hear them both laughing as I walked away.

Okay. That didn't hurt. Maybe they just didn't have a problem with me dating a girl. Maybe they didn't figure it was any of their business. Katie and her old girlfriend, Doctor Melanie, kept telling me that most folks didn't care one way or another. Still, it was hard to convince myself of that.

By the time I'd gotten off I-90 and onto the surface streets of Bellevue, even I thought I was being a dumbass.

# Sixteen

I ARRIVED AT CARL'S PLACE IN SHORELINE A FEW MINUTES early. I was a little anxious to meet his parents. They lived in a nice neighborhood—quiet and homey. The squeals of laughing children echoed through the streets as I walked up to the porch. It was a good sound, comforting.

Carl met me at the door, Jennifer on his arm.

"Hey, girlfriend," Jennifer said, hugging me.

Carl shook my hand. "Good to see you, Beauhall. Have a nice break?"

We'd finished the last of the Elvis movie just after I got out of the hospital. The edits were done a couple of months later, and the movie had been out and about.

"Doing okay," I said. "Miss the studio and the crazy hours."

"I'm sure," Carl said, guiding me around the house.

Everyone was in the family room: JJ and Clyde and one of the camera guys were in the middle of a game of nine ball, while Cherie (JJ's remaining bimbo) sat on the edge of a couch having a conversation with Carl's mom.

Carl's dad stood behind a bar, drawing a tall draft beer from the built-in tap. Qindra, the witch, sat at the bar in a nice, respectable business suit. As far as I could tell she was totally normal tonight, no glowing jewelry, no obvious signs of magic.

"Welcome to our board," Carl said, sweeping the room with his arm. "We call this the meet-and-greet portion of tonight's festivities."

Jennifer slid out from Carl's other arm and walked around to me, taking me by the hand. "Let's go to the little girl's room, shall we?"

I looked from her to Carl, who was as perplexed as I was. "Um . . . sure. Why not?"

We circled back and walked to the end of the hall. The bathroom was done up in seashells, pale blues, and whites. It was lovely and looked like something my mother would have done.

"What's up?" I asked, not really wanting to watch Jennifer pee.

"We haven't had a chance to talk in a while," she said with a funny look on her face. "And I just needed to tell someone."

Oh, lord. Was I getting laid off again? I hadn't worked in five months as it was.

"Well," she said, fidgeting. "Carl and I have decided to take things up a notch."

She grabbed the edge of the counter, turned away from me, and pulled her pants down over her left hip, exposing an awesome Celtic tattoo. The knot work twined around in thin black lines, forming an intricate heart.

I leaned forward to get a better look. "Holy crap, Jennifer."

Something in Latin filled a narrow, rippling banner that crossed the lower portion of the heart. The colors were vivid—mainly green, but there were reds and yellows also.

"Isn't it beautiful?" she asked, grinning like a cat. "Carl will die if he knows I showed you."

For a moment, I flashed back to a nightmare where I'd branded Jennifer, Carl, and the whole movie crew with the mark of NI-DHOGG. The coincidence was unnerving.

"What spurred this?" I asked, straightening up.

She turned, buckling her pants. "I saw the ones on your calf, and it's been in my mind."

Yikes. Not like I planned to inspire body art or anything. Especially since I didn't get a vote on the markings. I had Odin and Gram to thank for those lovely things. "What's the line in Latin?"

"Amor et Ecstasis—Love and Ecstasy. We got them the day after we . . . you know." She turned beet red.

"Hot damn, Jennifer," I said high-fiving her. She was quite pleased.

"Do not tell Carl I told you we've slept together, okay?"

I smiled. "Sure thing." I glanced over to the mirror, considering the possibilities of eavesdropping elves, gave it my best go-to-hell look, then plunged on. "So, you know," I wiggled my eyebrows at her. "How was it?"

"Sarah," she squealed, slapping me on the shoulder. I swear it was like junior high. She lowered her eyelids and her voice seemed to drop an octave. "It was amazing," she said. "Magical."

"Awesome. Tell me it wasn't here with his mom and dad in the house."

She made a face. "Dear god, no. With all the noise?" She quickly covered her mouth, like she'd said too much. "Never mind. No. It was at my apartment."

"About damn time," I said. "How's he feel about the whole thing?"

She shrugged, smiling from ear to ear. "It's like we're in high school," she said. "Every spare moment in the last two months, we've been ripping each other's clothes off. It's been wild."

I thought back to Saturday with Katie. "I can't imagine Carl being wild."

She winked at me. "You have no idea."

Now I was feeling all mushy and romantic . . . and a little turned on. I'd definitely need to call Katie tomorrow.

We rejoined the rest and things got rolling. Never been to a board meeting. Can't say as I ever want to go again. Sure, we learned that *Elvis Versus the Goblins* was making money, and our next movie had a budget in the low millions, but damn. If the pie hadn't been so good, I can't say it was worth being in the same room with JJ all that time.

After the meeting broke, I hustled out of there as fast as I could. Almost made a clean getaway, too.

"Beauhall," Qindra called to me.

I stopped and turned back. She hurried toward me, clutching her briefcase in one hand and her heels in another. Speed over fashion. I was moving pretty fast.

"What's up?" I asked, giving her the stink eye. I didn't trust her as far as I could throw her. She worked for the enemy.

"You seem to be well." She paused, watching me. "I've been thinking about you lately. What's new?"

This was a tad bizarre.

"Not much new," I said with a shrug. "Just living my life."

She smiled. "Good to hear."

We stood there a second, eyeing one another.

"I could use a drink," she said. "Would you like to join me?"

I thought a moment, trying to skip over the derogatory remarks and the smart-ass responses that immediately sprang to my mind.

"I . . . uh . . ." I was confused. "Why?"

"Fair question," she said. "I thought we could discuss current events, catch up on the ramifications of what has transpired over the last six to nine months."

I squinted at her. "I'm not sure we would see eye to eye on most things." I preferred being honest, if a little blunt.

"I also think we could discuss your tendency to lose control, act out."

Couldn't get much blunter than that.

"I can help you," she said. "I think."

I thought to myself just how she would know about how out of control I had been feeling lately and then decided that it was better to engage with the enemy on neutral ground in order to get information. "What the hell," I said. "Not like I have anything else to do besides sleep."

She described a pub just over a couple of blocks away in a strip mall and headed back to her car.

I was really going to have drinks with her. She'd healed me at the farm, and there was a good chance she did more later, but that time in the hospital was pretty fuzzy.

So far she or her mistress hadn't taken any action against Jimmy and Black Briar, so maybe we were in the clear. Not like I was going to be best friends with her or anything, but sometimes it paid to have your enemies close.

# Seventeen

THE DIRTY OLIVE WAS UNREMARKABLE AS PUBS GO, BURIED in a strip mall next to the highway. I give it credit that there were no pickup trucks parked out front.

I pulled into a slot in the middle of the parking lot, across from a rent-to-own place. Qindra pulled in beside me in a subdued gray-and-black ragtop Miata. Very stylish, in a cute girl way.

She didn't close the top. "Not worth it," she said. "Besides, no one messes with my ride."

"If you say so."

She smiled at me, flashing a set of perfect teeth, and nodded to the bar. "Best damn martinis in the city. If you like that sort of thing."

"I'm more of a beer gal," I said, following her in.

The place wasn't smoky, since that was illegal these days, but it stank of old cigarettes and sour beer. Not a bar in the world that didn't have that amazing underlying stench. On top of that, however, was a wicked odor of cooked beef and something sweet and tart. I couldn't place the smell, but my stomach told me I'd had enough to eat at Carl's.

We stopped at the bar, ordered our drinks, and took them to the back. Place was nearly empty. An older couple, forties maybe, sat at the bar hitting on each other halfheartedly.

Near the door to the kitchen an old Asian woman sat nursing a cup of coffee. She had on a stained apron, likely the cook. She didn't look at us as we walked past her.

We dropped our drinks on a table. Beer for me, and a dirty martini for Qindra—extra olives. She smiled at me, pulling the olives off the skewer with her teeth.

"You play darts?" she asked.

There were three boards along the back wall.

"I'm sure I can manage it," I said.

"Good," she said, walking back to the bar.

I took a sip of my microbrew and watched her as the bartender handed her two sets of darts. Real things, it turned out, metal tips.

I think I'd thrown darts at a cousin's as a kid. Not a real memorable experience. Ended in someone crying, bleeding, things broken, whuppings all around.

"It's easy," Qindra said to me. "You hold the dart by the barrel like this." She held one up so I could see. "The vanes here, or fletching, help stabilize it in flight."

"Yeah, I get the general concept."

"Cool."

We threw three games. She kept some sort of score, apparently, and I ended up buying the second round of drinks.

I think she hustled me, but it held my attention.

Too many rules for my liking. Something about hitting certain sections of the board, not just the bull's-eye. I thought it was all about the center. Go figure.

"You totally suck," she said, walking back to our table. "Stick to blacksmithing."

She was smiling and laughing as she said it, so I didn't get mad. Mostly.

"Good plan," I said, pulling my chair around backward and

sitting in it with my chest against the tall back. "Besides the darts and the olives . . . just why are we here?"

"I think we have more in common than you may think," she said.

I couldn't pick out the genetic features in her face, but she was damn pretty. Knew it, too. She wasn't exactly arrogant about it, but she used her looks as naturally as breathing.

Not really in my league. I glanced down at my boots and jeans, then over at her expensive suit and very nice heels.

"If you want to talk to me about your religion, or want me to sell some form of soap product as a member of your club, I'm really not interested."

She shook her head. "Always the smart-ass, huh, Sarah?"

I shrugged. "Can't fight nature."

She just smiled at that and waited, like she was expecting something from me, but I didn't call this little meeting. Really only one reason I could figure we were here, so why not jump into the deep end of the pool? "Why is Nidhogg interested in little ole me?"

"Interesting." Qindra took a healthy drink of her second martini, keeping her eyes on me. When she set the glass on the table, she toyed with it, wetting her finger and running it around the lip of the glass.

"I know you have trouble controlling your anger," she said finally. "I'm not sure if this is something new for you, or what?" She looked at me, expecting an answer.

"I've been a hothead most of my life," I said truthfully. Da would agree.

"I thought perhaps it had something to do with that sword you made."

I took a long sip of my beer. "I make lots of swords. You may want to be more specific."

She sighed. "There is really only one blade we can be discussing."

She leveled her gaze at me. "Something Jean-Paul was willing to break compact over. A blade that Frederick Sawyer was willing to play his hand for . . ." She paused, watching me for a reaction. "It is not beyond their kind to covet something, to desire it above all other things."

"Yeah. You work for some charming people."

She held up one finger. "I am beholden to only Nidhogg."

Great. Like that was different. "Fine, you and the oldest dragon of them all. I feel so much better."

"You are too young to understand," she said, dismissing my comment. "You were not raised to serve them, as I was."

Raised to serve them? Was that any different from what Da did? Raising me to serve his dear and fluffy lord? But I had free will, after all. Didn't Qindra?

"My mother served Nidhogg before me," she said. "As did her mother's sister. It does not always follow the parent, but it does follow the blood."

"Follow the blood? Servitude?"

She shook her head. "No. Not exactly. We all serve someone, in some way. Surely you understand that much about the world."

"There may be those to whom I allow my allegiance," I said. "Friends, family, country, that sort of thing. But I don't serve baby killers."

"Always with the drama, eh Sarah?" She leaned back in her chair and crossed her legs. "You share a lot in common with them. There is a light inside you that reminds me of them in a way."

"I'm no dragon," I said. *Right? How could I be?*

She laughed. "Of course not. They are rare and powerful, but they are not so easily hidden to those who watch for such."

Those who watch? Did Nidhogg fear another dragon in her territory? Was that why she was so quick to stick it to Sawyer? Beyond the tit-for-tat politics of rival predators, maybe there was more here.

"No, you are not one of the scaled ones." She was openly curious. "Nor do I believe you are one of the elder gods, returned to set my mistress afright."

I was impressed, frankly. She was talking to me as if I was in the know—one of the in-crowd.

"Maybe," I said, "I'm just a blacksmith who happens to have been in the wrong place at the right time."

"Perhaps."

Just *perhaps*. I didn't like the level of scrutiny she was giving me. Hell, at this point I wasn't sure why I had come here at all. As a matter of fact, this whole thing was starting to stink like bad cheese. I'm not the same as them.

"You serve them; you are complicit in their crimes."

She nodded once. "Alas, you are correct. I have many crimes to atone for," she said. "Things you would find unsettling in your immature view of the world."

"Immature?"

"Oh, Sarah. You understand *immature:* childish, churlish, infantile." Her grin was Cheshire in magnitude.

Now she was just pissing me off. I sat back, trying to keep the anger tamped down, making ready to stand. "Thanks for the dart lesson." I said through gritted teeth. I stood and walked around the table, counting slowly in my head.

She was testing me. Looking for a weakness, a chink in my armor. I was really in no mood to play.

"How's Katie?" she asked.

I whirled around, slammed one hand onto the table, and leaned into her personal space. "None of your fucking business." She didn't even flinch.

"I think something happened to you when you fixed that blade," she said. "I know somehow you found a sword that had been broken and fixed it. My mistress had several bad nights around that time. Around the time you met the dwarf, Rolph Brokkrson. Around the time that Frederick Sawyer became entangled in Flight Test and the same time that Jean-Paul began nosing around Seattle looking for something that upset my mistress."

Her breath smelled of gin and olives, but it wasn't exactly unpleasant. We were practically nose to nose, and I could feel my pulse pounding in my ears.

I looked into her eyes, saw how startlingly clear they were, and pulled back, letting my anger ebb.

"I thought you were going to kiss me for a moment," she said, standing up. "I think your passions run high, and you do not know why."

What the hell?

She opened her purse and took out a card. "I think you need therapy," she said. "But if you want to talk about anything, give me a call. I may not be as awful a person as you have painted in your head."

She grabbed my hand and placed the card in the palm. I watched her face as she dragged her manicured nails across my palm.

"There are things in this world you should know," she said. "Dragons are not the worst thing that has happened to the world. Maybe, if you delved into the history of things, you would understand that perhaps they are the lesser of two evils."

"They kill people, eat them, ruin lives, and dominate people," I said, crushing the card in my fist. "They hunt us and manipulate us, keeping us like herd animals, branded and culled for their individual needs."

She slipped the strap of her purse over her shoulder and shook her head slowly. "Sarah. It is a small price to pay for the lives most of us live."

"Death before tyranny," I said. "Better to die free than live in their shadow."

"Willful ignorance is unbecoming in someone such as you," she said. "There are those out there, cloistered groups, who study the world as it truly is. They know the depredation of dragons, and they chronicle the comings and goings of forces greater than either of us have ever known."

She was pretty damn powerful as far as I was concerned. I'd seen her blow up a helicopter by scratching a painted rune off one of her fingernails, releasing the stored magic. And I'd felt her voice in my head, blocking the berserker in me.

"And I should find one of these groups and learn the truth?"

"Yes," she said, smiling again. "You should. I believe your friends may have an inkling where to start."

I studied her for deception, watched her face for malice or contempt. But there was none there. She was a blank slate.

"I honestly mean you no ill will," she said quietly. "You are a wild card, Sarah Jane Beauhall. A powerful woman who cannot understand her place in the world."

She had me there. "Life's a bitch; then you die."

She smiled. "Not always," she said, letting the smile slip from her face. "Maybe that has been the greatest sin."

"I'm sorry, what?"

She looked at me, considering. "There is a thought that perhaps the wheel is broken."

A shock ran through me. Odin had said those words to me, spoken them to me in a dream.

"What wheel? Why is it broken?"

"Perhaps it has been hubris after all," she said, her eyes unfocused.

I'm not even sure she was talking to me anymore.

"There are those who believe with the wheel broken, our world will drown in decay. I believe this is what haunts my mistress. I am afraid this is our downfall."

"But, what wheel? Is this something we can fix?"

She focused on me again. "It is something to consider," she said, letting the smile return to her face. "Perhaps that is your calling, my friend. Is it possible it is you who will right the wheel?"

"Me? I can barely take care of myself."

She shrugged. "You have been granted knowledge few hold. I believe that you are someone with extraordinary gifts. Even if you do not see them."

"Gifts?" I asked. "I didn't want any of this. The price has been too high."

She patted me on the arm. "It is often those who have greatness thrust upon them who protest the loudest. Not all gifts have strings, Sarah. Not all causes are equal. Take care."

She strode away then, not looking back. She was impressive, that one. Sexy as hell, all the right parts in the right places, but she exuded power like no one I'd met.

I grubbed around in my pocket, pulled out a five, and dropped it on the table. She'd already left a twenty without my seeing her put it down, but I wasn't letting her cover my portion.

The night was black by the time I headed to my car. My head was swimming. Part of me liked Qindra. She was fun to hang out with, funny, smart, and definitely easy on the eyes. But, I had to keep reminding myself: she was the mouth of Nidhogg. People died at her command.

Or so I assumed. Hell, I only knew Frederick Sawyer and Jean-Paul, and them only at a cursory level. Maybe Nidhogg wasn't like the others. Maybe the female dragons were benevolent. The male dragons were right bastards so far, but we humans weren't all alike by any means.

I drove home, thinking of how little I really knew about any of this. I needed someone with better intelligence. Katie would tell me anything, but she didn't seem to have all the accurate facts.

Jimmy, likely. He, Stuart, and Gunther had those weapons they wanted hidden from the dragons. I guess it was time I pushed them for some answers. Any second now. Yep, I'm gonna jump right on that.

Or, I'd keep finding ways to avoid them. That was the more likely scenario for now.

# Eighteen

Jimmy, Gunther, and Stuart huddled in the bunker, working at a table under the dragon map. Gunther tucked a jeweler's monocle against his eye and examined the etched sigil on the stone. Jimmy and Stuart looked on, each having had their turn at the ring previously.

"It is hard to decipher," he agreed. "It is definitely a monogram of some sort, identifying the family this gem belonged to." He picked up the ring and held it up to the light, eschewing the monocle. "The fire does dance in it, though."

Stuart sat back, rubbing his eyes. "Definitely dwarven. Probably magic in some form."

"Possible," Jimmy said, standing. "I'm not sure if I'm supposed to use this to contact someone, hide it, use it for payment, or what?"

Gunther set the ring down and smiled at the two of them. "No use speculating. What you really need to do is decipher the note that accompanied it. Speculation rarely bears sweet fruit."

Stuart grunted, but didn't disagree.

Jimmy walked to a tall cabinet and pulled out a small wooden writing desk, placing it on the table between them. "I've been working on this," he said. "I believe it is a cross between the Aquincum cipher found in the notes of Marcus Aurelius and a mathematical skip pattern involving a key I can't determine."

The three of them studied the page. "I could see if I can get some time on the Cray over at the university," Stuart offered. "Translate it from the Latin and then work the numeric transposition?"

"Worth a shot," Gunther said. "Save us getting lucky."

Jimmy sighed. "This shouldn't be so hard."

Gunther laughed. "Jim. If it was easy, it would be pretty damn useless as a code, don't you think?"

"But if my father wrote the code, he didn't need to decipher it. Who was this meant for?"

"You, of course," Stuart said, slapping the table. "I bet the key is some combination of your social security number, birthday, or something. He had to know you'd need help one day, after he was gone."

Jimmy looked at Stuart, his eyebrows high on his forehead. "Birthday? Soc number? Seriously?" He leaned in toward Gunther and whispered loudly for effect. "Remind me to visit his computer at work."

Gunther grinned.

"Hardy, har, har," Stuart said, shaking his head back and forth. "I just meant it would probably be something personal to you, ya know? Something he said or did that would trigger a recollection."

"Wait," Jimmy cried. He pounded up the stairs, whooping.

"I guess he knows what it is," Gunther said, grinning.

"Ya think?"

After a few minutes, Jimmy came strolling down the stairs, flipping through an old Boy Scouts manual. In the margins on the page with constellations, there was a note scribbled in his own childish hand.

"Dad and I were out camping, around the time Katie was born. I'd complained that she was gonna chew up my toys, and generally make my life miserable."

The twins smirked at him.

"Anyway, he took me out and taught me to find the North Star. Said it was critical to understand how to find your way in the wilderness. We found the North Star, and he showed me how to determine our longitude and latitude that night. I wrote it in the margins. He told me it would save my life someday."

"Even with that, this is not going to be easy," Stuart said, looking at the paper. "Could take us weeks."

"That's been hidden away for years," Gunther said. "No reason to rush now. We'll just take our time and do it right."

"What about the other two statues?" Jimmy asked. "Maybe I should break into those, too. See what we find."

Gunther studied him a moment. "You handled each of them, right?"

Jimmy nodded.

"And this is the one you picked, the one that spoke to you in the moment."

"Sure."

"Did your father leave you instructions to these?"

"Just this." He got up and pulled a small cigar box off a tall cabinet. He set it on the table in front of them and opened the lid. Inside were odds and ends: marbles, jacks, two magnets, and a broken yo-yo. Taped to the inside of the box was a handwritten note.

"He told me that if I ever got into trouble to look to my treasures." He took up the marbles and rolled them in one hand. The scritch of glass scraping on glass drove a chill through the room. "When they went missing in Iceland, I was at college, but this was still in my room, hidden under my bed. I hadn't thought about it for years, but he knew it was there, knew I'd find it when I needed it."

Stuart slid the box around and read the note aloud.

"IN GREAT MOMENTS OF FEAR AND LOSS, WE TURN TO OUR
TOTEMS, OUR RELICS, TO SEEK ANSWERS FROM THE UNAN-
SWERABLE. TO SEEK THOSE WHO HAVE GONE BEFORE, AND
UNRAVEL THE MYSTERIES THAT PLAGUE OUR DREAMS."

"I got the safe-deposit key when they read the will," Jimmy
said, scrubbing his face. "Their lawyer had had it in his possession
since the time I first saw this map." Jimmy pointed to the dragon
map that dominated the room. "He knew then that I'd have to
seek answers when they'd gone beyond our reach."

"So, why the Valkyrie?" Gunther asked. "Why not the statues
of Odin or Thor?"

"Back to Sarah," Jimmy said quietly. "She told us how they'd
come to take Susan and Maggie to Valhalla."

The three men sat quietly, wrapped in thought.

"Makes sense," Stuart said, wiping his eyes. "Still haunts my
dreams."

"Aye," Gunther agreed. "Old One-Eye has proved a rascal, for
sure, but the Valkyrie seem the logical choice, all things considered."

"My gut tells me to start here," Jimmy said, sure of his decision.
"I think we need to figure this out, before we risk the other two
statues."

Gunther dragged his finger on the table, spinning the ring in a
lazy circle. "This may not lead us to someone your father knows,"
he offered. "It may be something you need to protect yourself.
Some magic to balance that set against you."

"That seems more likely," Stuart said, straightening his shoulders. "Or maybe something you need to protect."

Gunther clapped Stuart on the shoulder, smiling at his friend.
"Aye, that smells right. The Orders were as likely to hide artifacts
as secrets."

Jimmy reached across the table and took up the ring, holding it in his open palm. "Maybe I'm supposed to wear it."

Stuart and Gunther both lunged at him, slapping their hands over his. They shared a quick glance, laughing.

"Better to understand it first," Gunther said. "May not be for you. May be for Katie."

"Aye," Stuart said with a grunt. "Or it may be cursed. Just handling the ring could be sending out all kinds of woo-woo vibes."

They all three looked toward the stairs.

"Best to keep it down here, then." Jimmy set the ring in the cigar box, rolled the marbles back inside, and closed the lid. "On to the code, then."

Gunther drummed his fingers on the table. "We do this, there's no going back; you know that. You can't unlearn the secrets you unravel."

"True," Jimmy said. "But we don't have to take action. We can bide our time further, if we need."

Stuart looked up. "Not bloody likely. That ship sailed when Sarah killed the dragon."

# Nineteen

I met Frank at the Circle Q the next morning. I'd had about seven hours of sleep: better than my average. I pulled up to the front barn, right next to Frank's truck, and got out. He was having a conversation with Mary, the farm owner. I have to admit, my stomach was a little tweaky. I hadn't been out here since the dustup with Jack and Steve, two of her old hands. That night of drunken excess was not something I liked to think about, but the fight and near rape were fairly vivid in my memory. I know Jack and Steve had moved on, but it was like I expected to see their ghosts.

I guess it was my own ghost I was more afraid of at that moment. Some memories were better left to die a quiet death.

Mary was cordial and left us to our work. Only five horses today, but that would be a good chunk of change. We'd work this farm for most of the week as she had a big herd.

We broke for lunch, each lost in our own thoughts, and finished up around two in the afternoon. I wasn't complaining; I could definitely use a little free time after the whirlwind events of the past few days.

Frank talked with Mary as I finished packing my gear. I walked down the long aisle of the barn, making sure each of the horses we'd worked with were settled in their stalls securely. Dotting the i's, crossing the t's.

Mary nodded to me as I walked up.

"I'll be sure to pass on your concern to Julie," Frank said solemnly.

"Is there a problem?" I asked. I hoped that we weren't dwelling on the crap that happened in the spring.

Mary looked at me, and her face softened. "Just business," she said.

"I hope it doesn't have anything to do with me," I replied. I knew it was self-centered, but I couldn't stand it if Julie lost a customer because of something I'd done.

"If I had a problem with you," Mary said, her gaze steady and serious, "I wouldn't let you near my animals."

Frank watched me, curious.

"Well, with Steve and Jack bugging out on you . . ." Maybe I should've let it go, but I had to get this stuff in the open.

"Look," Mary said, using her best boss voice. "My employees are my business. I understand this is a small community, and rumors get around, but I'd thank you to not go spreading tales."

Woah . . . what the hell was that?

"I'm sure she meant no offense," Frank said, stepping in.

"None at all," I said, shocked. "I'm sorry. I didn't mean to be disrespectful."

She glared at me a minute, then shook her head. "Ain't that important," she said, obviously holding on to some level of anger. "They didn't steal from me, if that's what you're thinking. They just left me without notice. Luckily, the foaling season was over."

"I could come help out, if you need." It seemed to be the right thing to say.

She looked from me to Frank, then back again. "I could use someone who ain't afraid of hard work, and the smell."

Frank chuckled at that.

"We're done early today," I said. "Could take the next couple of hours and muck stalls if that's what you need."

"Deal," Mary said, shaking my hand. "You know the routine?"

"Yes, ma'am," I said, feeling better than I had all day. Hard work didn't bother me. Having people thinking poorly of me was much worse than a little smell and sore muscles. Besides, I felt like I owed her.

Frank had me walk to his truck. "She says folks are talking that maybe Julie's fire wasn't an accident."

I looked at him like he was speaking Klingon. "What?"

"Not really my business," he said, obviously wanting my take on the whole thing. "Some folks think it's suspicious that Julie gets hurt, her place gets burned down, then them boys skedaddle off to Oklahoma without as much as a how-do-you-do."

My head was spinning. "Who's saying things?" This made no sense. "Someone's claiming that Jack and Steve did that to her, burned her out and ran off?"

He shrugged. "I know Julie has her reasons for keeping things under wraps, but the fire's suspicious, and those two aren't exactly Boy Scouts. Bartender over at the Triple Nickel says they got rough with a gal the night before, thought it might have been a triangle thing between Julie and them two boys."

I sat on the gate of his truck, my heart hammering. What the hell? Julie and I don't look anything alike. How could folks mix the two of us up? But then again, rumormongers don't need facts.

"That's not how it went down," I said to Frank. "Julie went out with Jack a time or two, but he showed his colors soon enough."

"Not really my business," he said. But it was obvious we'd all just made it our business. "That's what I was discussing with Ms. Campbell when you came up. Not sure what you think you had in the mess, but she likes you and Julie and didn't want to see either of you getting a bad reputation in this business. Horse folks talk."

I nodded. "Aye, and blacksmiths."

He just grunted and opened his truck door. "Was nice of you to offer to help her out. She'll be okay, but folks see you covering for her, helping out, will go a long way to quieting the more reasonable of the lot."

"Thanks," I said, sliding my hands into my pockets.

Frank smiled at me, started his truck, and pulled around to the side of the barn. I watched him as he waved. Soon all I saw was a cloud of dust.

People are crazy. Julie was as good as they get. If I ever found out who started those rumors, I'd give them a knuckle sandwich.

I wrapped up just after five. Not a bad job for only three hours. Mary was impressed.

"Make sure you tell Julie I asked after her," she said as I was washing up. "Jack said something to the effect that she'd been a big reason for him and Steve bugging out."

"Ain't true," I said, suddenly defensive again. "Julie is as right and honest as anyone I know. If anything, he was fleeing his own guilt."

She watched me for a second, appraising me. "I'm glad you speak up for her. Says a lot about a person to have folks defending them." She glanced at her feet, trying to say something hard, I reckoned. "I heard a few things that I didn't give any credence to." She looked back up at me. "Wasn't about Julie."

I froze, my heart a rock in my chest. "About that . . ." I started, but she held up a hand, interrupting me.

"Some men talk about things they shouldn't," she said firmly. It was like she was trying to tell me something with her eyes, saying something that she couldn't put words to.

I nodded, swallowing hard. "Sometimes good people say things when they're angry. Act in ways they wouldn't normally."

This woman had class. Hardworking, and stout. Her face had

lines that spoke of hardships and joy. The eyes were the true mirror, and they held no judgment.

"Even the good Lord had his moments of doubt and pain. I'd say we are all due a little forgiveness."

Relief washed through me. Before I realized it I was crying. Quietly at first, but she stepped in and drew me to her, hugging me despite the filth and sweat.

It didn't last long, just a brief thunderstorm in an otherwise quiet day. I felt like a hundred pounds of pain had been lifted from my head.

"Sometimes men make the world hard," she said, holding me out at arm's length. "It don't help us to add to it."

I wiped my face and smiled at her. "Thank you."

"You hear of anyone who is looking for work," she said, moving us back into a business mode, "you let me know. They gotta be good with horses, and not afraid of hard work."

"I'll let you know."

She waved at me as I climbed back into the car and pulled down the long drive. Mary Campbell was damn fine people. Took her kind to keep the world from spinning out of control.

Which, of course, made me think of the dragons.

The conversation with Qindra kept playing in my head. What would the world be like without the dragons running things? And how much did they really control?

# Twenty

JULIE WASN'T HOME WHEN I PULLED IN AROUND SIX THIRTY. I jumped in the shower quick, and then grabbed a beer from the fridge. I sat in the armchair, holding the cold bottle to my forehead, and debated on what I should do with my evening.

I could clean house, but Julie had started doing that more and more. Gave her something to do, and I think with the sudden appearance of flower vases with doilies under them she was making herself at home. About damn time.

Of course, I was beginning to not recognize my apartment. I hadn't lost a goldfish in months, and the fridge had real food in it, and nothing was covered in mold. It was like being invaded by house elves. And not the kind that spy at you in the shower.

The stack of bills on my desk wasn't getting any smaller, so I figured that was the right thing to do with my evening. I hated it, but they weren't gonna pay themselves.

I fired up my online checking and began slitting open envelopes. The stack never seemed to grow any shorter. The student loans were the hardest to take, but I ground my teeth and plunged ahead. Mary said she'd pay me at the end of the week for mucking stalls, and I'd get to do it at least one more day this week. Frank would pay me for the horse work, and then I'd be flush again.

Sorta.

The one thing I liked about online banking was that I could postdate the payments, and they'd go out in a few days. Better than skating checks like I did in college.

With figuring the hours I'd work for Mary, and my cut of the farrier money, I had enough to cover all my bills, fill up the car a couple of times, and buy some groceries. The damn Taurus drank more gas than my old Civic ever had, so that was putting a crimp in my budget. But the movie thing would kick in again in the next couple of weeks and I'd have that revenue stream.

I was checking my budget forecasts and thinking how I couldn't even pay my rent at this point. Crap. Back to Top Ramen.

Maybe I'd have to slide my insurance check. Hate to go without coverage. I flipped through the envelopes on my desk. This weekend was spendy, but the credit card allowed a very minimal payment.

I put my head in my hands and felt the headache coming on. There was another option, of course. Right in my desk drawer, a large parachute fraught with uncomfortable attachments and an unfortunate amount of spilt blood. I slid the drawer open and looked in at the check Frederick Sawyer had sent me for the sword.

Fifty thousand dollars. It would be so damn easy to put that in the bank. I could get a new car. But I didn't want to be beholden to Sawyer, even this slightly. Of course, I had my stake in Flight Test from him, more or less. But that was wergild, earned with blood and sweat. He lost it on the field of battle, reparations for the hornet's nest he'd stirred up.

I know Nidhogg pressured Frederick into giving up most of his stake, taking some for herself, but who understood politics, especially among dragons? Hell, as far as I knew, they could even be related. Not that many of them out there, in the grand scheme of things, right? Surely they were all related somehow.

I closed the drawer, hiding the check once again, and rubbed my eyes. Tomorrow I'd see if Mary needed any work on the weekend as well. Extra hours would help. One of these days I'd start an honest-to-goodness savings account. When and if I ever had enough to save.

I went and got a drink of water. Balance in the checking was pretty low, but I wasn't getting evicted today. Just needed to make a few things late so I could pay the rent. Then catch up over time, leapfrogging my way fiscally.

My cell rang. It was Katie.

"Hey, hon," I said, feeling a moment's lightening of my mood. "How was your day?"

"Great!" she screamed into the phone. "I bought a new car."

I felt a twitch in my left eye. Goodie.

"Don't be mad or anything," she said. "But I want to come pick you up and take you to dinner. Show off the car."

I let my head fall into my open palm, thinking. Her old car was new, before the dragon torched it. Of course her insurance was going to replace it. Me, my little car had been paid off for years. Barely enough insurance to tow the damn thing.

"Sure," I said. "Just wrapping up a few things."

"Good," she said, practically squealing with excitement. "I'm outside your apartment building right now."

Of course she was. I smiled, letting a little of her joy infect me. What the hell. I needed to eat, and seeing her would be nice.

"Okay, I'll be right down."

I grabbed a light jacket and wrote a note for Julie. No reason for her to worry. Dinner out would be nice. Talking over the stuff out at the Circle Q would be good.

I stopped and grabbed my mail before I jetted off. More bills, lucky me. I trudged back up the stairs, flipping through the huge stack of envelopes. There was a bunch addressed to Julie. Apparently her friends had finally gotten word that she was staying with me. There were half a dozen cards and only two bills. I'd have to look at them later.

At the bottom of the stack was a card with my name on it. I held it up, saw the kittens-and-crosses motif on the envelope, and immediately flipped it into the garbage. Mom had been using the same stationery ever since I could remember. I didn't have time for her usual preachy bullshit.

The bills went onto the desk, and I was out the door. I was looking forward to seeing Katie.

# Twenty-one

KATIE HAD GOTTEN A NEW MIATA—STUNNER. IT SEEMED everyone owned one. She wanted to surprise me with the fact that she got the midnight blue, instead of her usual red. "You can even drive it," she'd said.

I'd given her the stink eye, like I'd be seen driving such a chick car.

She punched me, the harlot.

Dinner was brief, Mexican down the street, but the conversation was excellent.

She'd been exchanging e-mails with Cassidy Stone of The Harpers. He wanted her to jam with them again sometime. She was so damn cute about it. With Ari out of the picture, their tour had come to a crashing halt, so they were back home in Boston trying to figure out what they were going to do next.

By the time I dragged myself back up the stairs to my apartment, the earlier trauma had been wiped away. Damn, that girl had a way of turning my head round and round.

With her kiss still lingering on my lips, I jogged up the stairs three at a time. I was feeling springy. Julie wasn't home but I could tell she'd been there, since the cards I'd left stacked on the counter were opened and displayed around the dining-room table. That's something my mother would have done.

Well, Mom would have stacked them across the top of the television first, but the leftovers would be on the dining-room table.

I was getting a glass of water when Julie came in. She walked across the room with just her cane. I watched her, making sure she was okay, admiring the way she didn't fight it but let things happen at the pace they needed to work.

"Evening," she said, approaching me.

"Been out, I see."

"Mrs. Sorenson is teaching me the finer points of gin rummy." Julie settled into a chair across from me and leaned her cane against the table. "How'd it go out at the Circle Q?"

I watched her for a second. I was fairly sure that Frank would have called her already. Was she fishing for different news? Looking to see how I handled things? Or maybe Frank hadn't called.

I shrugged. "You heard Steve and Jack took off, leaving her high and dry?"

Julie just nodded, her lips a tight white line across her face.

"Well, I stayed after we finished up with the five horses today, and I mucked stalls."

"Really?" She seemed genuinely surprised.

"She needed the help, and I need the money." Same story as always, I thought.

"About that," she said and pointed to my computer. On the screen was my accounting software, open with a big fat negative number in the pending column. "Couldn't help but notice," she said, not showing a second of remorse.

"I'll be okay," I said. "Not like this is new for me. I've had plenty of thin times."

She shook her head. "You are a stubborn one. Not that I'm much better." She dragged her fingers through her hair, pulling it back off her face. "You know I have some money coming in, Sarah. Disability and insurance."

"No way," I said. "You need to save that to rebuild the smithy."

A little smile flickered across her face. "Stubborn as a mule and as optimistic as Susie Sunshine some days." She reached over and put her hand on mine, squeezing it. "You let me stay here, ornery girl. Least I can do is kick in for some of the utilities and such."

I glanced over at the computer. Wouldn't take much to get me back in the black, to be honest. A few hundred a month would be a huge help. Then, maybe I'd quit thinking about that damn check.

"Not too much," I said, feeling a little chagrined. "Just enough to cover the gap until the movie money kicks in again."

"We'll see how it goes," she said, pulling a check out of her shirt pocket. "Here's for half the utilities and rent—"

I started to rise, a protest fully formed on my lips, but she pulled me back down by the hand she held, forcing the check in it with the other.

"—not asking your permission," she said. "Last I checked, I'm the one teaching you things. Isn't that the arrangement?"

I sat back down, resigned. I could really use the money, but I owed her, damn it.

"Okay, just for a little while," I said. "But I'm banking any extra for the smithy myself."

"It's your money," she said, smiling. "Do what you think's best."

I sat back, looking at her. She had a way with the world that I both feared and admired. I hoped I had my act together as much as she did when I was her age.

"Now, tell me about Ms. Campbell," she said, crossing her hands in front of her on the table.

I told her how the day went, explaining that Frank was gonna call her, and even got around to talking about the rumors, and the semiconfession I'd given.

She just nodded, pretty grim at the thought of her peers talking smack about her, but glad that Ms. Campbell had our collective back.

"She's a good one, that Mary Campbell," she said, smacking the table when I was done. "If you end up working for her on Saturday, maybe I'll go out with you, spend some time with her, have some tea and chat about things."

It was good to have that particular part of my past out in the open. My heart felt lighter.

"One more thing," Julie said.

I scowled at her; I could tell by the way she looked at me. I could be downright petulant when I tried. "Can't we just leave this on a good note?"

She smiled and pulled an envelope out of her pocket, sliding it across the table to me.

I didn't touch it, fearing it would bite me. It was the envelope from Mom.

"I threw that in the trash," I said, feeling the heat on my neck.

"Missed," she said. "Found it on the floor beside the can. Sorry." She looked like she was, honestly. "With all the other cards, I thought it was one of mine; just figured it had fallen to the floor. Wasn't until I'd opened it with the others and began to read it did I realize it was for you."

She watched me, expecting something from me. I had been very clear with her how I felt about my parents. Can't say she ever really approved, but she'd respected my position.

"I don't need another preachy lecture about the sins of my life, or how much I've disappointed them."

"I read the letter," she said, staring directly into my eyes. "Has your mother ever once said she was disappointed in you?"

"She doesn't have to say it," I said defensively. "You should know how easy it is to make your opinions clear to those around you. You don't always tell me when I'm screwing up, but I get the message loud and clear."

Julie laughed at that. "Lord, girl, if only that were so. You are the most stubborn person I've ever met. There have been moments when I thought the only way to get through your thick skull was to crack it open with a hammer."

I scowled at her. She didn't look like she was busting my chops, but she wasn't lying.

"I can be defensive," I agreed. "But you've got no clue what it was like growing up with those folks!"

She sighed, a tired, deep sigh that felt part sympathy and part lecture. "Sarah. How old is your sister?"

"Megan?"

"Do you have another?"

I thought about it. I hadn't been home in five years, so I guessed it was possible. But I doubted they were writing me to tell me they'd had another baby, not at their age.

"Megan would be almost seventeen." Damn, really? I did the math in my head. She was ten years younger than me—no, wait. I counted back. Twelve. "She's fifteen."

Julie patted the card and letter in front of me. "You might read that. I didn't see a lecture in there."

"Doubtful," I said honestly.

"Well, I don't have your background for reading into family dynamics, but she mentions Megan."

"Megan was a good kid, but I haven't seen her since she was ten. She probably doesn't remember me." That wasn't exactly a stellar argument, I knew. "I love the kid," I went on. "Hell, she looked up to me as far back as I can remember. I was always finding her in my room, digging through my stuff, pretending to be me when she didn't know I was looking."

"I'm not surprised," Julie said.

I plowed on. "And I left her there, of course. Not like I had any business looking after her; I can barely keep myself out of the poorhouse."

"Sarah, she's not yours to raise," Julie said quietly.

I didn't slow down, just rambled. "Besides, Mom would look out for her, shield her from the crazy. Of course, she'd done such a quality job with me."

Julie let me run down, watching my face. I hated when she did that. It was like she was peeling my face away to look deep inside me.

"From what I can tell," she said, "you turned out to be a helluva woman. Can't say they did too bad a job." She leaned against the table, leveraging herself up. "I'm going to bed. Big day of PT tomorrow."

I gave her a feeble wave. "Night, boss."

The path to the bedroom had been cleared just after she'd moved in. I ditched the beanbag chair and moved the coffee table over in front of the stereo so she could walk back and forth without much chance of running into things.

Made me think about my own life, and how I managed to run into every bitty bit between here and there. I waited until she'd closed the door, drained my glass of water, and set it on the envelope. I just couldn't face that tonight. I wasn't sure I'd be able to face it ever.

I went into the living room, opened the hide-a-bed, and got ready for sleep. Tomorrow would be a long day.

# Twenty-two

I TOSSED AND TURNED FOR A GOOD HOUR. I KEPT THINKING about Megan and the way she looked up to me, how she wanted so much to please me when we talked on the phone. When I'd gone away to college it had about killed her. Now, I'd gone and given her up as bad rubbish.

Five years. I'd thought about her in that time, off and on, but had never mustered enough gumption to call her. Not like talking to Ma or Da on the phone would hurt or anything. Besides, I could call when he was at work. Gave me even odds she'd answer the phone.

But I was a coward. I'd left her to the world I hated so much. Not like she was my daughter or anything, and they weren't beating her. I just couldn't take their politics and their attitudes. Too much hatred and fear for my tastes.

And if that wasn't abuse enough, whom was I fooling? Don't need to beat a body to break 'em.

I got up, knowing I'd never sleep at this rate. I grabbed the glass off the envelope, filled it with water, and sat down.

Julie had slit the envelope open with a knife—there was no ragged edge. I tipped the envelope to the side, and a small card poked out. It slid out easy enough, another piece of Ma's stationery.

I'd gotten that set for her when I was eleven. That was sixteen years ago. Surely she'd gone through it all by now?

But then, whom did she have to write to? Her parents were both gone, and she was an only child. Da never kept us anywhere long enough to make any friends, up until we landed out in Crescent Ridge. Anyone she knew there, she knew through church, and she didn't need to write them letters. She saw them three days a week.

Last I heard, she'd been homeschooling Megan. Poor kid.

I picked up the card and a picture fell out. It was Megan, taken when she wasn't expecting it.

She was leaning against the family pickup truck with her arms crossed and a sullen look on her face. She looked just like me, at least body language–wise.

What shocked me the most, however, was that her hair was short. Well, short by Da's standards. When I was her age, I could sit on my hair, it was so long. One of the reasons I shaved my head when I got to college.

Megan's hair was shoulder length, but there was a wide purple streak across her bangs. Cutting her hair and dying it? Brave girl. And the skirt she wore was scandalously close to her knees. And . . . sure enough, she was sporting combat boots.

Our dear father must have gone out of his mind. Maybe things at my place had changed more than I'd imagined possible. But not too much. She had the look of someone who rarely saw anything outside her own head. I recognized the look, that far-off stare, wishing you were somewhere else . . . were someone else.

Megan was beautiful, that much I saw. She'd gotten more of Ma than I had, where I had more of Da. She was probably beating the boys away with a stick.

And winning a might more at home than I ever had.

I stared at the picture for a few minutes, then flipped open the card. Inside were a few handwritten sentences.

*Thinking of you. Wish you'd call or come by.*

There was a letter inside. One page only, covered in tight script I recognized as Ma's.

*Dearest Sarah,*
*    I pray every day that you will find it in your heart to come home to us, even just to visit. Your father and I miss you fiercely.*

I put the letter down and rubbed my temples. Da only missed controlling me.

*    Marybeth asked after you just this week. You know she's had her third child. Boy this time. Gabriel is pleased, of course. He had been fearing being overwhelmed with women.*

Gabriel had been a tall boy, gangly and shy. My father thought the world of him, hoped I would have married him. I didn't mind Gabe, but I knew I wasn't going to make no preacher man's wife, or any man's wife, for that matter. Gabe was a deacon at sixteen and was preaching once a month by the time I'd gone off to college.

Marybeth had been my best friend since we moved to Crescent Ridge. First girl I ever kissed. I hoped she and Gabe were happy together.

*    Megan is having some trouble with a couple of the boys at church. She punched the older Abernathy boy, said he was getting handsy. She reminds me so much of you it hurts to look at her sometimes. I miss talking to you. You remember when you couldn't sleep? How*

*we'd get out the cookies and milk and talk the night away? You had some pretty big dreams back then. I miss your dreams.*

I was crying by then, damn it.

*I'm losing her, Sarah. Like I lost you, only worse. She blames us for driving you away. Says hateful things from time to time, which I can forgive, but she's a whole different kind of trouble. Your father and I agreed to let her go over to the public school this year, though it worries me. I fear she'll take up with some of those heathen boys, and get into Lord knows what kind of trouble.*

"Heathen boys" were any boy, as far as I could tell. Leastways, boys that weren't Gabe, if I remembered correctly. That was one thing they never questioned. I had no interest in boys, heathen or otherwise. Ma always said I was a good girl. If she only knew the truth.

*She's not talking to your father or I at the moment. Calls it a strike. She tried a hunger strike a while back, went seventeen days without eating, but we put a stop to that. Now she just won't talk to us.*

*Last thing she said was that she hates me and wishes she'd run away with you. I'm at my wit's end, Sarah. She worships you even more so since you've been gone. Built up this hero image of you, making up all sorts of adventures and such to explain why you've never come home. Five birthdays, five Christmases and Thanksgivings. Plays and soccer games . . . Yes, did I tell you she's playing soccer. Your father about exploded, but I saw how much it meant to her, so I put my foot down.*

That was a rare occasion. I'd have liked to have seen that.

*Anyway, I don't want to lecture, but I think you've been mighty selfish. I can see you are still mad at your father and me, but Megan didn't do anything but love you.*

*Won't you come see her?*

*I pray you read this, though you've never answered a single letter I've written in the last five years. Maybe the good Lord will see this one through.*

> *Christ first among all things,*
> *Momma*

Damn, damn, damn.

I couldn't help it. I cut out the light, crawled into bed, and cried myself to sleep.

# Twenty-three

SKELLA KEPT THE MIRROR OPEN AS THE DWARVES TRUDGED back from their night's foray. Three had been to Memphis, which had been extremely dangerous, but they'd insisted it had to be done.

Gletts argued with the leader of the dwarven clan, an old man named Krevag, trying to explain again why the idea of selling the potions to the dragons was foolhardy.

He was not winning.

Kraken and Bruden, the two most adept at blood magic, laughed, calling Gletts a coward and a fool. Skella wanted to defend him, but she needed to keep the ways open, keep the eaters at bay.

Finally, when the final party returned from Dublin, she closed the mirror and collapsed with exhaustion. Distance had no meaning when traveling the ways, but the shields and protections needed to keep it safe were taxing.

"We should kill the bard and take all the blood at once," Bruden bellowed, seeming to reach the end of his rope.

"Nay, brother," Kraken mewled, oily and soft. "Let us continue to bleed the lad, taking our drips and spinning an empire."

Krevag barked with laughter. "You believe the lies of that deranged whelp of Duchamp's, that necromancer he fancies himself.

What proof do you have that these potions will work as you describe?"

Kraken cast his languid gaze at Krevag. "You are venerable, old man, but these are not the days of old. We do not fear the dragons. We will rise above them, casting them into the shadows, where they belong."

*Fools*, Skella thought. *Drunk on dreams of glory.*

"What if we refuse to help you any longer?" Skella said, rising to her feet. "What if we leave you in the ways for the eaters to hunt down and consume?"

"Skella, no," Gletts said, stepping between her and Bruden, who acted as if he'd strike the young elf girl. "She doesn't mean it," he said, spreading his hands and looking at Krevag. "We will help you, as is our bargain."

"I think we need a new bargain," Kraken said, nodding at Bruden. "What think you, brother? Perhaps these whelps need a bit of motivation."

He spun, clipping Gletts in the side of the head with his large fist.

Skella shouted and ran, but Bruden ran her down, tripping her feet, sending her sprawling.

"'Ware," Krevag shouted. "If you harm them, you will break compact with their kin."

"The compact be damned," Bruden said, kicking Skella in the chest. "It's time we put the whole lot under lock and key. See how you like threatening us then," he yelled, kicking her again.

Skella held her hands over her face, trying to ward off the blows that fell on her like hammers. After the third blow, she blacked out.

# Twenty-four

I went down to Katie's on Sunday. We had lunch and talked. I told her about the letter, showed her the picture.

"Wow," Katie said, studying the photograph. "She looks just like you."

"Yeah, right."

"Seriously," she said, handing it back to me. "No one would doubt you were sisters. She even has your sullen look down."

I glared at her a couple of seconds, then looked down at the picture. She was much prettier than I ever was.

Maybe it was because Katie learned more about Megan and what I was going through with the letter that we talked for a couple of hours. She finally opened up about what happened to her and Julie when Duchamp snatched them in May.

"I had gone to the smithy to look for you, and was talking with Julie when the dragon attacked. He didn't even bother to see who was there, just flamed the place and sent in trolls to ransack everything. They took the safe with all your swords and smacked me around."

She paused, remembering. I knew it was painful, but she needed to get it out. I sat, watching her, willing strength to her.

"Julie fought them." She had a feral grin at that. "Took down one of the trolls, before we were overwhelmed."

"We'd been pounded on pretty hard. I blacked out a while, and woke up in a van. Next we were dragged onto a helicopter and flown out to cabins on the edge of Lost Lake."

That's where I fought Jean-Paul at the end, where I finally killed him. He'd been hiding out there. If I'd known that, I would've waited until he burned them all down before challenging him.

"Duchamp had a young man there, crazy bastard. He made one of the giants break Julie's leg, just so he could taste her pain."

I held her, her back pressed into me, snuggling.

"Jean-Paul wouldn't let him touch me," she said, shuddering. "He beat me, humiliated me in front of the others." She stopped, pushing away, turning to face me. "But he never raped me, no matter what he said."

I reached out and touched her face, tracing the tears. "It's over."

I felt a ball of pain vaporize at that. I'd feared the worst.

In the end, she'd fought him so much that he just knocked her around and left her in disgust.

If I hadn't shown up at the movie shoot, she was sure things would have gotten even uglier. The young man, whom she could not describe, had tortured Julie, then decided to give us both over to the giants and trolls to play with for a while.

Then the call came in to trade us for the sword. That's when things stopped being quite so ugly.

She cried as she told me everything, kept her face down, choking out the words when the emotion was too strong. There was rage there, anger and hurt.

I held her as she wailed, let her purge the poison that had been laying dormant inside her for so long, then rocked her when she calmed.

I had a moment of melancholy—bittersweet and heavy—wishing I'd been faster, done more to stop all that from occurring, but she sensed it.

"Don't you dare sink back into that," she said, her voice raw. "I needed you strong, needed you whole so I could finally share this. Please don't fall back into the trap of what if. Just hold me and tell me everything's going to be okay."

What could I do? I loved her, damn it. Heart and soul. How had I ever lived before her? "Of course," I said, my throat aching from wanting to cry. "We are going to be more than okay. I promise: we're safe."

And she lay in my lap and cried.

We spent the rest of the afternoon tangled in her bed. I held her while she cried, then held on for dear life as we made love. She needed the release, needed to purge the pain, override it with the good and whole.

We spent hours that way, raging and making love with reckless abandon. I led, coaxing her to release over and over until she found her confidence, taking control and driving me to my own climaxes. Finally we just couldn't take any more, and we let exhaustion take us down into sleep.

Hours later I headed back to my place. I know the fight with the dragon had been hard, had cost all of us more than we'd ever imagined, but I think it would begin to fade now. We'd purged some demons today, conquered them with sex and love. I was feeling wrung out, but happy.

Frank had called and left a message with Julie. He had some things to take care of in Cle Elum this week. Just as well. Mary didn't really have any more work for us over at the Circle Q. We'd need to move on to other farms, and Frank really wasn't open to driving farther afield.

Which, it seems, was why he thought maybe I should drive out to Chumstick and visit Anezka. Chumstick was way the fuck out there, frankly—north and a lot east of Seattle—out Highway 2 over Stevens Pass up beyond Leavenworth. Anezka had offered to help out with some of Julie's regulars. I'd never met her before, so I thought it would be interesting. Frank had said she thought differently about smithing—mentioned she had some funny notions about Julie's smithy burning the way it did. I couldn't wait to pick her brain on all this. Made me a little anxious, even. Like thinking about the first day of school.

Julie didn't know her much either, just that she was an artist these days. She'd given up farrier work and only did commissioned iron work for gates, railings, and such. High-end work, with lots of flair.

Seemed like somebody I could learn a thing or two from. Would be good to expand my circle of contacts, too, expand out beyond my comfort zone.

And speaking of comfort zone. There was something I decided I needed to do.

I waited until after Julie had gone to bed before I acted. It's not like I'd forgotten what happened in Vancouver. Hell, Ari was still missing. But the elves, Skella and Gletts, there was something funky going on with them. They could've killed us, but they hadn't. Neither Katie nor I had suffered any long-term consequences of the poisoning, and Skella had told me how long the poison would last. Fair and foul. I needed more information there.

I pulled the mirror out from behind the couch.

I propped it against the coffee table and sat in front of it, cross-legged with a hammer at my left side. I watched for three hours, willing Skella or Gletts to make an appearance. I had my iPod on, listening to Stiff Little Fingers and thinking about how the elves could've been wrapped up in Ari's kidnapping.

They didn't appear. Not sure why I thought they'd show up at my mental urging.

When it became apparent they weren't coming, I went to plan B. I rummaged through the bathroom for one of Katie's old lipsticks.

It was a dark blue. I remember the night she'd worn it, all dolled up in a punk-rock outfit, hair teased like a metal groupie. We'd gone to a party, friends and new lovers. I'd been a total wreck, but we'd ended up having a blast.

I took the lipstick into the living room and wrote on the mirror, marking each letter precisely and, of course, backward.

*We need to talk. Promise to play nice.*

I made sure the mirror was back behind the couch, tight up against the wall before I went to bed. They weren't coming into my house without my permission.

Maybe they'd show up tomorrow night. I was looking forward to the possibilities. If they talked to me, I'd probably lose the urge to punch them.

It could happen.

# Twenty-five

BESIDES THE FACT THAT MORNINGS SUCK IN GENERAL, I WAS excited to be heading over to Chumstick. One, I'd never been there, and two, it would be cool to meet another blacksmith. Especially one who had a whole different approach. She was an artist, made a living with her creativity and her hammers. Not like farrier work. I was good at it—don't get me wrong. I loved working with horses, but there was something a little wild about making art with fire and steel.

The drive was long, but the morning was beautiful so I didn't mind. Gold Bar loomed just ahead once I got onto Highway 2, and I thought of Black Briar. I needed to get out there, make some peace, even if only in my own head. I missed Stuart and Gunther, the whole crew, the living and the dead.

And Jimmy and I would need to come to terms here soon. I was falling deeper and deeper for Katie, and if that was going to be a permanent thing (was that even an option?), then he and I needed to fix this gulf between us. And hell, I needed more information than he'd given. Answers to questions I didn't even know how to ask. And he had Gram. I realize I'd been hiding from her as much as anything. That sword scared me—compelled me in ways I had nightmares about. Maybe that was the real reason I'd been avoiding Black Briar so adamantly. To do otherwise was to take up the

sword again. I was afraid of what would happen the next time she
and I found ourselves driven to a cause.

But I didn't need to worry about that today. I waved in Black
Briar's general direction as I cruised through Gold Bar and settled into the slog over the mountains. Stevens Pass is scarier than
Snoqualmie Pass—more twists and turns and the road isn't nearly
as wide. I loved the view, though. The mountains felt closer, the
rock more exposed and raw. I could feel the earth's bones here, old
and weary.

I cruised through Leavenworth, a quaint Bavarian-style village
that served really only as a tourist trap. I'm sure it was cool enough
to live there, but they really pimped themselves out to the kitschy
traveler.

The cute shops and flowered clock were nice enough, but I
wasn't so much impressed. The town felt sad to me, living in the
shadow of the mountains. I think I'd go crazy living here. I'd bet
this was dwarf territory, though. Felt right.

Not that the locals would know anything about it. Most of us
went about our days never understanding that there was another
world under the surface, one fraught with peril beyond the imagi-
nations of many of us.

Once I cut north and headed to Chumstick, things opened up
a little more, giving the impression you could breathe. It wasn't
a very long drive once I cleared Leavenworth, and Chumstick
wasn't big at all. I'm not even sure how it got to be a town, it was
so small. But that's how we roll up here.

Anezka's place was easy enough to spot. She had a very cool
archway over her driveway, a cross between Herman Munster and
Roy Rogers. Tall and Gothic, with a cowboy flair.

I parked across the street from her place; the gravel along the
road was wider there, like it was meant for parking. There was no
traffic this far out, but something made me approach the street

cautiously. I had that feeling like there was something dangerous just out of sight. I checked around. Nothing in the road, nothing coming across the field opposite the rambling spread.

I sized the place up before crossing the road—three buildings interconnected with roofs and shared walls. The first one was obviously a house, and the second was a carport/corral/junkyard. To the far right was Anezka's workshop. I could hear someone working behind the house—the sound of someone cutting metal echoed across the yard.

Stepping into the road took a bit of effort. By the time I'd stepped off the blacktop and up to the arch toward the forge, it was like pushing through a thickening in the air, a membrane of some ilk.

Her place was protected. It came to me as I stepped under the arch. The runes on my calf and scalp began to tingle, a crazy burning itch. Once I was on her property, however, it faded. That was something I'd be asking about.

Several metal sculptures dotted the ragged yard between the house and the road. They were almost whimsical, all twisty and windswept.

"Nice," I said aloud as I ran my hand along one particular piece. It reminded me of the winged horse Meyja in a rather abstract way. I'd borrowed her from the Valkyrie, Gunnr, for the price of a kiss, to chase after that evil bastard Jean-Paul in the spring. Winged horse to follow a dragon. It had been magical.

That's how the sculpture felt: magical. Not woo-woo magic like Qindra did, but artistically awesome. The way the metal swirled around a central focal point gave the impression of a flying creature descending in great loops. This didn't feel like dragon, either. Nothing predatory. It was peaceful, with several pieces burnished to reflect the sky overhead.

The sound of the cutting torch stopped suddenly, and I turned toward the shop. A tall figure came out, pulling off a thick pair of welding gloves. I hoped it was Anezka, but whoever it was, they were freaking me out a little. The welding mask, with the expected blackened window in the faceplate, was a stylized warrior's mask, with very strong hints of a sun god—Mayan maybe, or Aztec—visceral. Flames of shaped steel flared out in a delicate aura, creating the illusion that the helmet was bigger than it actually was. It looked damn heavy.

I straightened up and faced her squarely, my shoulders dropped and relaxed. I let a smile slide onto my face, but didn't grin, no teeth baring here. Greeting a stranger in the most basic, evolutionary sense. As she flipped the mask up to expose her face I would not have been surprised to see an alien, or a monster. The tension was palpable.

But no, just a woman. Rather plain, honestly—blocky features and short, chopped hair, more to avoid heat than any style, I'd guess. She had a stern look but held out her hand.

I took it without hesitating. Her grip was strong and rough. Lots of manual labor in those hands, anger as well, I could feel. Anger and I were close friends. Here was a kindred spirit.

"I'm Sarah," I started . . .

"Anezka," she said at the same time. We both smiled, and her face brightened several shades toward pretty.

"Frank said you'd be here by seven."

I glanced at my watch: eight fifteen.

"He wasn't specific when he texted me," I said, feeling like I'd gotten off to a bad start.

She nodded once and turned back to the forge, motioning for me to follow her. "We start work at seven around here. Better to get up early so we can siesta in the afternoon."

"Siesta?" I asked. She didn't look Hispanic, but with the mask . . . "You from south of the border?"

She stopped and looked back at me. "Father was Czech and mother was grade-A American mutt. Don't mean I can't nap in the heat of the day."

Not like I needed to step into a second faux pas this early in the day. "Sorry, I didn't mean any disrespect."

She rolled her eyes and started back toward the forge. "Frank said you were awkward."

Great. Lovely. "Anything else he warned you about me?"

She stopped and smiled again, placing a hand on her hip and looking me straight in the eye. "He said you were a damn good farrier, but were defensive and prone to moping around."

This was not how I imagined my day starting. I knew if I said what was on my mind, I'd just confirm everything. Not like any of it was untrue.

"Fair enough," I said, walking around her toward the forge. "Nice place you've got here."

She laughed quietly and followed me, walking around the open-air shop. The southern and northern walls were brick and mortar, but the western and eastern walls only came up a couple of feet. The rest consisted of large shutters that were lifted upward and supported with a long pole. They became awnings, and the smithy was open to the world. She had the eastern wall open, facing the road, but the shutters in the back were down. Back there was where she'd been cutting steel.

Pretty slick setup. Didn't hold in the heat during summer, and if the shutters were lowered, they would keep out the elements in rough weather.

Along the wall farthest from the house, she had a set of four lockers, a couple of long worktables, and three thick-bodied mannequins.

Somebody made armor here; I'd bet my last dollar on it. Useful skill to know. Armor was tricky business and very expensive.

In the center of the building three anvils faced the road, so when she worked, she could see who was coming and going. Her tools were on two long racks, one on either side of where she'd stand with enough room to walk between them and the anvils.

Behind her, she had two forges. One was a full-on brick forge, with a bellows and everything . . . real nineteenth century. In front of that, she had a couple of propane tanks and a small forge, where she could heat up smaller pieces without using much fuel. Overall, the place was designed very economically for a single smith. Well, the brick forge would take two to operate. Odd.

No room here for another smith, the layout said. I looked around to the worktable along the far wall and some other odds and ends. She'd rearranged the place not so long ago. The wooden floor was grooved from the pacing back and forth, smoothed and polished from treading feet. I placed my hand on one of the rough-hewn support posts and tried to breathe in the place. I had the distinct impression that at some point in the past, this place had been set up for two or more smiths. It had that feeling.

Not my business unless she offered, and I wasn't comfortable asking. Besides, we needed to get a game plan together. "Which farms are we hitting today?" I asked, hoping I was nonchalant. Some of the smaller ones would be needing their animals tended now, if not sooner.

"None," she said, walking out behind the forge to where she had been cutting steel with a torch. I had to duck to get through the heavy timber doorframe but let out a long, low whistle when I raised my head and got a look at the back of the place.

There were sculptures everywhere. She had an acre or more out back, which ran away to scrub and rock on the other side of a split-rail fence.

The statues were huge. There were several full-sized warriors, each wielding sword and shield. They were arrayed in a three-point inverted wedge, allowing an opportunity to flank the dragon they were facing.

And what a dragon it was—holy crap. Thirty feet long from nose to tail. The angle of the shoulders told me the wings, when added, would be swept back, which didn't make a lot of sense. The dragon was on all four legs—one of the taloned front feet rested on a smashed warrior in full plate armor. No facial features to render, I guessed.

The tail was in the wrong position, though, trailing back for stability. Wasted weapon. The tail should be whipping around toward one of the warriors.

Trust me on this one.

It was like a giant diorama—and it wasn't finished. The dragon was missing a good third of its scales, and the wings were not complete. One of the upright warriors was missing an arm. There were two fallen warriors splayed on the ground with their armor rent open. They had no heads. I expected they'd be needing heads somewhere in the scene, attached or no.

I looked from the scene back to Anezka, who was watching me.

"Christ on a crutch," I said, shaking my head. "How much time do you have into this?"

She shrugged, but I could see a smile touch the edge of her lips. "Three years," she said. "I hope to finish it and ship the whole damn thing down to Burning Man next year."

"Beautiful work," I said, meaning it. The dragon looked like it had been built up from a significant support structure, with each scale that covered the body hand shaped and welded onto the underlying structure with a crazy amount of precision.

"This looks like it took you a damn long time just to design and map out. How do you keep the individual scales in the correct order?"

"Computer design, actually," she said, pointing toward the

house. "I was in industrial design for a while, before I decided to get out of the crazy, bat-shit world of corporate America and join the world of the living."

She and I were going to get along just fine.

"I want to finish the piece I'm working on," she said, turning away from the dragon scene. "I thought you could help me out, see how the day goes. That way we could feel each other out and see if we can work together."

I shrugged. "Seems fair. But if we are going to consider hitting the Triple Loop Ranch tomorrow, we'll need to give them a call to set something up."

"Of course. Let's see how things go this morning. We can always call them after lunch."

I followed her to the smithy. She handed me a welding apron and a sturdy pair of gloves. They had chain between a layer of cloth and an overlay of thick leather. Very protective in case you needed to catch a swinging sword. She was used to some pretty wild work, I had the feeling.

We headed outside and around to the back of the carport. My job was to hold stuff, mainly. I stood and stared at the huge sheet of steel she had supported by a block and tackle. There were two hoists back there, and it was clear that their original use was to pull out engines. Right now, she had the steel held upward by several lengths of chain wrapped around it, but it rested on the ground.

The steel was easily an inch thick, five feet wide and eight feet tall. I did the math in my head—roughly a ton. I wouldn't want that falling on me. Crazy for her to be working like this alone. Too damn dangerous.

She spent the first hour cutting out several square pieces of steel from the greater piece. Not from the side or anything, but directly from the middle, like windows. I couldn't really tell what she was going for. Had me curious, but she was keeping her vision to herself for now. All I know is, bracing a large sheet of steel while someone else cuts it with a torch is pretty tiring.

After we finished, we rolled the engine hoist into the yard, and then brought in the fallen warrior with the missing arm.

Anezka walked to one of the lockers in the back and pulled the arm out of a large laundry bag. Odd place to store an arm, but it wasn't my smithy.

"What happened to the arm?" I asked.

"Raccoons, bad weld, gravity . . ." She shrugged.

Well, that was definitive. She was odd, this Anezka.

It didn't take too long to weld it into place. She was meticulous and very precise. I paid close attention to her work, watching her maneuver the tip of the flame to get the most precise cuts and heat the metal for a good, even weld. Welding was as much art as science, and she had a steady hand and a very good eye.

By the time we had the warrior back under the baleful eye of the dragon, it was nearly eleven.

"Lunch?" she asked, taking her gloves off and dropping them on a worktable next to her warrior welding mask.

"Sure," I said, setting my plain, unadorned welding mask on the table next to hers. "I could definitely eat."

"Burgers, sushi, or breakfast?" she asked, pulling the apron over her head and throwing the neck loop over the nearest mannequin. I did the same with mine, onto a second mannequin, and rubbed my head with both hands. My scalp was itching and my legs were twinging. Magic in the area?

"Burgers are good," I said, looking around.

"You okay?" she asked, watching me with a funny look.

I shrugged. "Got a chill."

She laughed.

I caught her glancing behind me to the left, back near the old forge with the bellows. No idea what she was seeing, but it was kind of creepy. I held my hands up and twisted back and forth a couple of times, stretching out my back and glancing behind me. I didn't see anything, but something had caught her attention.

"Want I should drive?" I asked.

"You'll have to," she said, clapping me on the shoulder. "I don't have a license."

Odd again. How'd she get groceries, supplies?

Lunch was going to be interesting. I had about a million questions.

"Can I use your bathroom?" I asked.

"Sure," she said, escorting me to the house, through the carport. "Inside on the left, just down the hall."

The house was spare: old seventies-style kitchen, mustard yellow appliances, and hideous green shag in the living room.

I found the bathroom easily enough, but when I shut off the water from washing my hands, I could hear her arguing with someone. I craned my head at the window but couldn't quite see to the smithy.

There was no car in the drive, and no one else had parked out on the street. I let the screen door shut a little hard so she knew I was coming and walked across the carport to the smithy.

She sat on the worktable, swinging her legs, a satchel in her lap.

There was no one else in the smithy.

"I thought I heard you talking to someone," I said, looking around.

She looked at me quizzically. "I do that sometimes," she said, hopping off the table and walking toward my car. I shuffled around the row of anvils to catch up to her.

"You argue with yourself?"

"It's a long story. Let's get some grub."

I unlocked the car with the fob and hustled around to the

driver's side. She was already in and buckled by the time I got the driver's-side door opened.

"Kelly makes the best burgers in Leavenworth," she said, as if nothing strange was happening. "Will be good to see her; I don't get into town much."

"Good to know," I said, adjusting the mirrors.

I gasped. Skella was there, her face behind mine, like she was in the backseat. She held one finger in front of her lips and winked.

"You okay?" Anezka asked.

"Fine," I said, jamming the key into the ignition. "Just a cautious driver."

I glared at Skella who mouthed *sorry* and then held up a piece of slate. There were words written there, awkwardly and with misshapen letters. Hard to write backward.

"Tonight, midnight," it said; then she was gone.

I pulled out into the road, making a U-turn back toward Leavenworth.

Damn, my life was strange. Okay, I'd asked for a meet, but jebus, how'd she find me in my freaking car mirror? Had she been in the Taurus? Rolph said he thought they could only use mirrors they'd seen before. Maybe it wasn't the mirror. Maybe it was whom they wanted to see.

# Twenty-six

WE PARKED IN A GRAVEL LOT BEHIND A STRIP OF KNICKKNACK stores. The crowds were light, it being Monday, I guessed. The restaurant was down a flight of stairs to the basement. The girl behind the pie case who took our orders was young and cheerful. I was surprised there was no one else in the place.

We ordered monster burgers, curly fries, and sodas. Everything was huge, geared for the ever-expanding tourist. I ate half my burger, but Anezka plowed through hers like she hadn't eaten in a month.

While she ate, I looked around the place. Exposed beams were painted in rainbow colors and each one was covered in dollar bills. Apparently someone wrote a compliment on a bill and left it for a tip decades ago, and the tourists have kept up the tradition. Very oddly sweet in a capitalist-driven sort of way.

I picked at my fries, and Anezka ordered bread pudding. It was huge. Watching her eat all that food made me a little queasy.

The television on the wall was showing a golf tournament with the sound turned off. I was vegging while she wolfed her food down, trying not to look at her.

She belched loudly and licked the remaining icing off her fork. "You know," she said, dragging her tongue along the tines of the fork, "you don't look like a dragon slayer."

The runes on my scalp flared to life, and I dove to one side as she lunged across the table, stabbing at me with the fork. The thunk of the metal striking the bench seat rang loudly as I rolled away.

What the hell? I scrambled out from under the table on all fours, rolling to my feet as Anezka fell into the bench seat I'd just vacated. I looked around for a weapon of some sort as I backed away. There were no other customers, and the girl who ran the counter was nowhere in sight.

I dodged back along the middle row of booths and around to the aisle close to the bathrooms. There was only one way out, up the narrow stairs, and I didn't see anything I could use as a weapon.

Anezka sprang up from the booth, only it wasn't Anezka. Her face peeled back, shredded and tattered, as the mouth opened like a hinged garbage can, lined with teeth.

"What the hell are you?" I shouted, dancing to the side as the creature shook like a dog shedding water. The flesh and clothing that had been Anezka sloughed off, splattering the surrounding tables and chairs with wet, oozing shards.

I darted toward the stairs, and the monster lunged that way. It stood about four feet tall, covered in fine red scales. The skin of its face was stretched tight over its skull, giving it the creepy look of a desiccated corpse. The ears were little nubs on either side of its face and the nose was two slits over the cavernous mouth.

It was a scaled eating machine, all gristle and bone. It swiped a taloned claw forward—the blackened claws sliced through a wooden beam easily a foot thick.

"You are too soft to slay one of the great ones," it said. Flames flared across its scalp, dying out in the next second.

"Friend of yours?" I asked, sliding across a table and launching a bottle of ketchup at the freak show.

It caught the bottle in its gaping maw, cackling gleefully. I rolled across the next bench and grabbed two more bottles of ketchup as the sound of grinding glass echoed through the place.

"It's been so long since I've eaten this well," the critter said, belching again. "I wonder what you'll taste like?"

More flames danced along its arms and legs. As I watched, it seemed to grow.

Fire creature; eats a lot. Fuel makes fires bigger . . . crap!

I needed something to put out fires. There was a fire extinguisher on the stairway coming down, and probably one in the kitchen, but I didn't want to get cut off back there. I'd likely find a knife, but with those scales and talons, I didn't want to risk it.

Food was the key for the moment. Not that I needed it getting any bigger, but I also didn't want to get tagged. "Hey, ugly . . . catch." I tossed the second bottle of ketchup, and it jumped, snatching the bottle from the air.

I ran for the stairs, kicking a display of chips behind me and tossing the third bottle of ketchup back by the soda fountain.

It didn't take the bait but leapt over one table and across a counter, then swung around a support post, flying straight at me. I fell back onto the table, which groaned and sagged under my weight.

No table dancing here.

I twisted around. The lump in my back proved to be the salt and pepper shakers, small glass jobbies, solid and heavy. I threw those as hard as I could at the eating machine and crawled over the bench. It ate both in one gulp as it flew across the room at me, landing on taloned feet and hands, smashing the table I'd just broken to the ground.

I scampered to the staircase, stopping to grab the fire extinguisher from the wall; then I turned and backed slowly up the stairs. The beastie was coughing and retching at the bottom of the stairs, hacking up gouts of flame and something that could've been blood, but was likely ketchup.

"Hope you like cold," I said, pulling the pin from the extinguisher and squeezing the trigger.

Foam shot out of the nozzle, spraying the bottom of the stairs before I got my aim down. I worked the spray over the damn thing as it sputtered and flamed.

It shrieked, dancing backward, falling over the chip rack. I followed it down a few steps, keeping the spray on it until the extinguisher ran dry.

It flopped around on the floor, its limbs flailing about, smashing the glass pie case and splintering a long wooden bench, but finally quit moving. I stepped onto the bottom landing and swung the extinguisher into the creature's skull with all my strength, smashing it with a wet crunch.

It kicked once, then stopped moving.

I stumbled backward, sitting down on the stairs, where I watched its one taloned foot, ready to fly up the stairs if it moved. I doubted that it was getting up again, not with the way I'd just smashed its skull like that, but hell, I hadn't expected Anezka to turn into a damn . . . "Fire goblin?" I asked the air.

"Kobold," a voice said behind me. I whirled; Anezka stood at the top of the stairs. She had a motorcycle helmet in her hand and a long steel pry bar in the other. "I see you managed okay."

"What the hell is going on?" I yelled, climbing to my feet and storming up the stairs. "Is this some kind of fucking game with you?"

She held the helmet and pry bar up between us in a purely defensive stance. "Sorry about that."

Sorry? I blinked. "Sorry, like gee, didn't mean to borrow your best shoes, or gee, sorry I spilled my beer on your rug. Are you fucking insane?"

Laughter, sweet and rich, was not what I expected. Crazy, maniacal ranting, high-pitched tittering before an irrational soliloquy about some universal wrong or other, but not the warm, welcoming noise that rolled up from her.

"I apologize for his behavior," she said, smiling. "I hope you can find it in your heart to forgive me. But I needed to be sure—test your mettle. I don't have time for brittle iron or delicate flowers."

Delicate flowers? Was she drunk? "Fuck that," I growled, stepping toward her.

She backed up to the doorway, and I noticed the sign had been turned around to CLOSED.

"You okay up there, Anezka?" the serving girl called from downstairs.

"Yeah, Kelly. We're good."

I gaped at her. This was beyond weird. "I'll pay for the damages," she called down.

"Gonna be a helluva mess to clean up," the girl said, coming around to the bottom of the stairs. She was drying her hands on a rag. "This your kobold?"

"Yeah," she said. "Sorry about that."

The girl shrugged. "Gram taught me enough about them. I'll call her and we'll clean up. Glad you didn't try this on the weekend. We'll be closed a day or two as it is just to get the cleanup done."

"I'll send over some fireweed to help keep the fire under control," Anezka said, not taking her eyes off me. "He'll fade in an hour or so. Tell your gram I owe her."

The girl shrugged. "Gram says you and she go way back, Seið-kona."

I looked back at Anezka . . . Didn't *Seið-kona* mean witch—like Qindra? I guess it was possible.

"Not quite," Anezka said with a chuckle. "Tell her to come out for tea."

"She'll like that." Kelly turned to the busted pie case. "All my morning baking gone to waste." She waved the rag over the top of her head and went back into the restaurant proper, stepping over the body of the kobold.

It had begun to deflate, like a sagging beach ball. What the hell was going on?

"I'll tell you what," Anezka said. "Why don't we get a drink, something strong, and I'll fill you in on all the details."

Fuck that. I slammed the fire extinguisher on the stair beside me and stalked up the stairs. If she was there when I got there, I was going through her.

She backed up, letting me have access to the door and watched as I stormed off. She didn't stop me, just let me get all the way to my car.

"I had to see if you could handle yourself," she called after me.

I stopped with my hand on the door of the Taurus and flipped her off, got in my car, and pulled out, slinging gravel as my tires spun. I'd made it around to the back of the big hotel complex when I thought of Frank and Julie.

Frank trusted her, but said she was strange, had strange ideas. Julie needed the help.

And what had she said about fireweed keeping the fire under control in the burger place? Damn it. I hated needing answers.

I drove around the block. When I got back, she was sitting on a small dirt bike, helmet on, and waiting. She nodded at me and pulled out onto the main road. I shook my head and followed her, swearing under my breath. I must be out of my mind.

# Twenty-seven

I sat in Anezka's living room, nursing a cold beer and scowling.

"My father was a blacksmith from the old country," she said. "He met my mother when he fled the Nazis during World War Two."

"Must be pretty old," I said.

"They were seven when they met," she said. "My mother had been visiting Italy with her parents, and they took my father with them when they left the country. He didn't know where his parents were, but he had the family seal." She pointed to a disk covered in runes and other markings suspended from a chain hanging in a shadow box above her fireplace.

"He'd been an apprentice at his father's forge before the Nazis came. His father pressed that amulet in his hands and bade him flee. The Nazis were looking for artifacts, any item of power to get their hands on."

"So they worked for the dragons then?"

Anezka laughed. "On the contrary. There had been no dragons in Czechoslovakia for generations. Most of the region had been unclaimed by any of the drakes for centuries. That was one of the reasons for the Hundred Years War."

I wasn't a history major. Europe was always in one war or another.

"Anyway," she said, waving her hand, "when I came of age, I became an apprentice in my father's shop, learning the intricacies of flame and steel. It wasn't until I was eleven that I took the amulet down from the mantel and found our family's secret."

She walked to the fireplace and opened the shadow box carefully, taking out the amulet. "This is ancient," she said. "Passed down from smith to smith, for longer than memory."

I watched her—her face was reverent. There was no greed, no hunger in that look.

She turned to me and held out the amulet.

I didn't even hesitate. My hand was out before my mind acknowledged it. There was something at my core that recognized that amulet.

The metal was heavier than it looked. The chain was an alloy, much younger, and hadn't tarnished. I recognized two of the runes: Othala and Kenaz. The first meant ancient obligation and protection. The second meant fire, passion, creativity, knowledge. Kenaz was imprinted on my left calf and on my sword.

"And this lets you call the kobolds?" I asked, letting its weight settle into my palm.

"Just one, and I don't call him. He just shows up whether I like it or not."

She sat on the chair opposite me and picked up her beer, taking a long draft.

"Sucks," I said. "Sorry I killed him."

She laughed. "He's not from here. He'll re-form in a few hours. This has happened before, although never quite as flamboyantly."

"The way he ate," I said, shuddering. "And all those teeth. He'd have had me for dessert."

"Not beyond possibility," she said, her eyes twinkling. "Although the plan was to see how you handled yourself."

"Nice," I said, feeling the heat return. Anger is fire, no two ways about it. The amulet in my hand began to glow slightly as my anger surged.

Interesting.

"He can be pretty helpful," she said. "If I thought things were going to get out of hand, I wouldn't have sent you to Kelly's place." She looked up at me, a half smile on her face. "Didn't figure on him getting so aggressive."

"He wanted to kill me," I said flatly.

She studied her beer a moment longer, scratching a fingernail through the label. "Perhaps." There was a far-off look in her eyes, as if she were remembering other incidents, other tests.

"It is not beyond his capacity," she said finally. "He also protects the forge. He has claimed it as his territory, his and mine."

"But would he really have killed me?" I asked, sitting up straighter in my seat.

She thought a long moment. "I'll ask him when he gets back. But you have to understand. He's old. Like a couple of centuries old, and there has been no dragon slayer as far back as I've ever heard. Kobolds are kindred to dragons, brothers of the scale, or so he claims."

Makes a sort of twisted sense, I guess. Scales, flame. I could see the connection.

"But when I killed Jean-Paul he didn't just melt away like your little buddy."

"No, true," she said. She walked across the room, her bare feet whispering across the carpet. Once she'd retrieved another pair of beers, she returned, handing me a fresh one.

I took it. It was only three in the afternoon, but it was one of those days.

"Anyway," she continued, sitting back in her large cushy chair and slipping her feet under her bum, "he's from the land of fire. As far as I can tell it's another dimension. Dragons are born here, in our world."

The beer cap dug into my palm as I twisted it off. I took a long pull, letting the rich flavor of chocolate and hops hit the back of my throat. I usually preferred something lighter, but the porter she offered definitely had a kick.

"Okay, so you have this kobold, like a familiar, that helps out around here?"

She nodded. "He sleeps in the brick forge."

Of course he did. How silly of me to not make the connection earlier. "So what now? I proved I could kill him with condiments and foam. Where's that leave us?"

She took a long draw on her beer and belched loudly, not unlike her kobold friend. "I say we call some of the farms and set up some time to work them. Line up farms for the whole week."

I had to think about it for a minute. Was I comfortable around her? It all came back to Julie in the end. I needed to keep her safe, keep her customers happy for when she got back on her feet.

"Okay," I said. "Excellent." I got up, set my beer down on the glass and worked-iron coffee table, and fished my keys out of my jeans. "I'll get my pack from the car."

"Good, bathroom break," she said, hopping up from the chair.

I made it to the door when I realized I had the amulet in my hand. It had taken on my body temperature and somehow I'd forgotten I held it. The glow had mellowed out now that I wasn't angry, but it had a distinct strobing pulse that matched my heartbeat. Creepy.

I turned and Anezka was just closing the bathroom door. I looked down at the amulet in my hand. No way I was taking that out of the house. I crossed to the fireplace and opened the shadow box. The glass front opened with a touch and I looped the chain back over the peg. Once the door was closed again with a quiet snick, the amulet stopped pulsing.

Besides, it was obviously another test.

The disk's markings showed in the palm of my hand. As I watched, they began to fade. Nothing permanent, thank goodness, but I had the sickening feeling it wanted to meld into my body.

By the time I was back in with my laptop, Anezka had changed into a pair of shorts and an oversized T-shirt advertising some biker bar in California.

While my computer booted, I sat back in the chair I'd been using and drank more of my beer.

I glanced over at the helmet she had sitting on her bookcase. "How do you like riding a motorcycle?" I asked.

"Not much of one," she said with a snort. "I think my blender has more horsepower than that little rice burner."

"Dirt bike?"

"Yeah. Good enough to get me back and forth to town. I don't need to go far."

"I haven't ridden one since I was a kid," I said. Back in . . . what? The early nineties? "My cousins had dirt bikes. I got to ride them one weekend while my folks were off to some couples' encounter group."

She took a sip of her beer and watched me.

"My Da flipped out. Not proper for a girl, or so he said."

There was something in her eyes, at that. Some mischief or other I couldn't peg. "How you like that Taurus?" she asked finally.

"Hate it, but it's temporary, until I can afford something better. My car was smashed the night I fought the dragon."

"Heard rumors," she said, watching my face. "Read between the lines and such. Not much got out, but we knew. Those of us who care about such things."

She wanted me to confirm details, answer questions. I wasn't ready for that, not with her. Killing Jean-Paul was not news to her, but details—who was involved, how had it gone down, et cetera . . . that I was not ready to dig into.

"Did someone else work here?" I asked, changing the subject. "I noticed the forge had once been set up for a second smith." Not too worried about rudeness at this point, and the beer had loosened up my internal editor.

"Different story," she said with a deep sigh. "I don't know you well, but considering how today has gone . . ." She shrugged. "My last lover decided to go back to his wife."

There were no tears in her eyes, not that it surprised me.

"Oh, I knew about her, if that's what you were wondering. Hell, she and I were lovers." She watched me for a reaction.

I just sipped my beer and waited. I read enough articles in *The Stranger* to know about alternative lifestyles.

A smile flirted with the right side of her mouth, and she pressed onward. "Polyamory is a difficult arrangement. We'd met at Burning Man a few years ago, hit it off, and formed a triad."

"Sounds like work to me."

"Not really work so much as scheduling. It suited us for the first two years. I loved them both, but Flora didn't like living here. Claimed the mountains and the rain kept her depressed. She wanted to go back to the desert. Justin hung out another six months, but in the end he was only interested in learning smithing skills."

"So, he was the second smith?"

"Yep."

"How'd your kobold buddy like him?"

"Hated him, frankly." She rose from her chair and crossed over to the credenza. After rifling through a pile of papers, she pulled out a picture and walked over to me, dropping it onto my keyboard. The three of them were lounging, totally naked, under what looked like Stonehenge.

"Nice," I said, handing the picture back. "Naked in England."

"Oregon, actually. There's a replica there."

Flora and Justin were in their thirties, maybe. About a decade younger than Anezka seemed to be.

"I fell in love with Flora first," she said, staring at the picture. "She was doing crazy chainsaw carving in nothing but a thong, a leather apron, and leather work gloves."

"Sounds dangerous."

Anezka smiled. "Wicked, more like it. Girl rocked my world. But Justin, oh my. He was smoking. Had a power to him that just made your panties fall off."

I didn't get the feeling it would take that much with Anezka.

"They were into some bizarre shit," she went on. "He'd done taxidermy at one point, and their trailer was full of stuffed animals. Weird stuff. After a while, it started to creep Flora right out. When they moved up here, he started getting even darker, and she took to carving all the exposed beams and such with the scenes from her nightmares."

There was a look there, in her eyes. A yearning and, maybe, a hint of fear.

"So, Justin was a creep?"

She shrugged. "Creepy, at least, but good in the sack."

"And he picked you over Flora?"

"Other way around."

"Meaning?"

"Flora picked me over him. Only when he wouldn't leave, she decided I should pack the whole thing in and follow her. She was pretty angry that last night, said some harsh things about Justin and how much he'd become a sick fuck." There was definitely pain in her eyes. Loss, sorrow.

"Why didn't you go with her?" I asked.

"This is my place," she said, somewhat indignantly. "I wasn't abandoning my life because some art chick got her panties in a bunch."

She looked down at the picture for a long while, and then dropped it on the coffee table. "Anyhoo . . . Bub hated Justin particularly. Flora he didn't give two shits about."

"Bub? That the kobold?"

"Yeah, short for Beelzebub, like the demon?"

Duh. That was a name I recognized from Da and his particular brand of crazy. "Cute."

"Justin took me for several thousand dollars, a truck that was in his name, but I'd been making the payments." Her voice was getting bitter. "And several different moulds we'd built to make some pretty intricate cast-iron pieces."

"Sorry to hear it."

For a moment, I thought maybe she was going to throw her now-empty beer bottle across the room, but she kept her cool and let out a stuttering breath.

"His stuff, technically," she said angrily. "Bastard. My work, my designs, but we made the moulds together and I let him have them. Of course, I thought he was coming back. Still could, I suppose; he was here in the spring."

"So now it's just you and Bub rattling around the old place?"

"Which is why I'm looking forward to working with you for a few weeks. Hell, if you're interested I'll even sell you Justin's old bike."

Man, I hated that damn Taurus. "Well, I can't really see getting around on a dirt bike."

She laughed, loudly, nearly choking with the ferocity of it.

When she calmed down she got up and motioned me to follow her out to the carport. I leaned against the doorway with my arms crossed over my chest as she began moving boxes, two doors, and a slew of odds and ends to unbury what was quickly becoming a motorcycle. Once she'd dug deep enough she whipped off a large tarp to reveal a Ducati 998.

Damn, that was one hot bike.

"She needs work," Anezka said, turning to me with a flourish. "But she ran the last time I had her unburied." She walked over to a tall cabinet and began rummaging through coffee cans of various doodads: bolts, nuts, nails. After a minute she produced a key and walked back to the bike.

The moment was anticlimactic. She turned the key and nothing happened.

"Probably the battery," I said.

"Yeah. I haven't started it in six months or more."

She pulled the tarp over the bike, and we walked back into the house.

"Bastard left the papers here and everything," she said with an evil grin on her face. "I'll sell it to you for three hundred dollars."

I eyed her, looking for a catch. "No idea what that runs for normally, but I would bet you a dollar that three hundred is dirt cheap."

You ever have one of those moments where you connect with a person, get them on a deep-down level? There was a flash, and suddenly I understood. She didn't give a shit about the bike; she just wanted to hurt Justin, even if she never saw him again.

"You could work it off here, helping me work on the installation."

It would be cool, learning new things, sculpting, creating art. "You sure?"

"He loved this bike," she said. "I want to see the look on his face if he ever saunters back in here, sweet-talking and looking for a booty call."

My left eye twitched at that. Booty call? Really? But I let her go; she was on a roll.

"Think about it," she said. I could tell the idea was really working her. "Imagine cruising over the mountains with that powerful

Italian bastard vibrating between your thighs. It would be like riding an orgasm."

I snorted. Seriously? She didn't really notice in her fevered state.

"I think this is a stellar idea," she said with a quick nod.

"I have a friend who's familiar with bikes," I said. "Let me talk to him, maybe get him to come out and look at it. Would that be okay?"

"Yeah, great!" This had her more animated than I'd seen her.

"You'll like Gunther," I said. "He rides a Harley and owns his own jazz store in Seattle."

She tightened her mouth into a not-frown and nodded her head, in that *interesting news* sort of way.

"Is he gay?"

"Nope."

"Excellent. See if he'll come out."

We went back into the house, and I spent the next hour calling around to the farms we normally worked. I lined up the Triple Loop Ranch for tomorrow and Broken Switch Farm for Thursday and Friday. That would make Julie happy, and we'd get a good amount of shoeing in.

Monday we'd do more work here at Anezka's place and I'd learn more of her world. It would be fun. But I wanted to clear it with Julie. Learning from another master was cool, but I didn't want her to feel like I was cheating on her.

As I was packing up my laptop, I thought back to the amulet that now hung in the shadow box.

"Make sure Bub is fine with me coming back," I said. "If he's not, I'll just meet you out at the farm."

"Fair enough," she said. "I'm sure he'll have a whole new respect for you."

*Yeah*, I thought. *Or fry me while I'm not watching.*

"Wait," I said as I realized the flaw in the plan. "We need a truck, gear, anvil . . . Can't get our gear out on that dirt bike of yours."

"I have a truck," she said. "Don't worry about it. I'll just meet you at the farm. Leave me the address and I'll look it up online."

I wrote down the address —"I thought you didn't have a license" —and handed it to her.

She shrugged. "Not your worry, is it?"

"I guess not."

As I was crossing the perennially empty road to the Taurus, my cell phone buzzed. It was a text from Jennifer. They wanted me to swing by the studio tonight.

Glad I got this before I was back in Bellevue or, worse, at Katie's in Kent.

I texted her back, threw my gear in the car, and waved at the house.

Anezka stood on the porch, gave me a head nod, and walked into the house to await the return of her demon lover. Okay, maybe not lover, but they definitely had a bizarre relationship.

There was one lonely woman. I hoped we got along over the next few days. So far it had been an ignominious beginning.

# Twenty-eight

I called Katie and gave her the quick and dirty about my day. She was sympathetic, and we agreed to get together for dinner on Wednesday. Would be good to compare notes.

She agreed that I should have Gunther look at the bike. Better to engage an expert, she said. Funny girl.

I showed up in Everett much earlier than normal, and the security guard was just setting up his card tables. Carl had kept him on even after Frederick had stopped coming up and taking such a heavy hand in the day-to-day running of the studio. Nathan was a good guy. He'd forgiven me for my transgressions back in the spring, and I was getting to like the guy. Always quick with a smile and a kind word. Ex-military, Jennifer told me, and single. But too damn young for Anezka, and I sure wasn't looking.

"Evening, Ms. Beauhall," Nathan called as I walked up the stairs. "Looks like we're getting back into the swing of things around here."

I stopped at his little table and signed in. I thought it was a waste of time, but it made him and Carl happy.

"About damn time, if you ask me," I said cheerfully. "Nothing like starting a new movie to disrupt the sleep patterns."

He smiled and nodded. "Just glad to be getting a steady paycheck," he said. "Temping just isn't cutting it."

"Well, I'm glad you're around," I said honestly. "Back in the day, we'd walk out of here in the wee hours of the morning. Never knew when some freak was going to jump you."

"Hey, about that." He held up a clipboard with several newspaper articles attached. "I read how you tried to stop that singer from being kidnapped up in Vancouver."

I rolled my eyes. "Wrong place, right time."

"You betcha," he said seriously. "After what you did in the spring, saving all those people from that burning barn."

Was that awe painting his face . . . maybe the beginnings of hero worship? I punched him lightly in the arm. "Dude, you were in Afghanistan. You're a hero. I'm just lucky."

Now he blushed and stepped back. "Maybe," he said. "Still, I'm pretty impressed that you'd just mix it up with creeps like that."

"You're sweet," I said with a smile. "Maybe Carl should give us both a raise for being too cool for his studio."

"Right . . . not."

He was flustered.

"Well, can't keep them waiting."

He waved as I opened the doors. Definitely nice to be someplace I was appreciated.

I walked into the studio, letting it wash over me. I had high expectations.

There on soundstage 1, Carl and Jennifer were obviously blocking a scene. Jennifer was on the ground holding a roll of tape, and Carl was taking exaggerated strides across the floor and counting aloud.

". . . three . . . and four."

Jennifer tore the tape with her teeth and marked where Carl now stood.

"Hello," I called.

"Hey, Beauhall," Carl called, stepping toward me, holding his hand out to shake. "Glad to have you back on set."

I stepped forward and took his hand, giving it a firm shake. "Good to be back, boss."

He swelled a little at this, put his arm around Jennifer, and smiled at me. "My two best girls . . ."

Jennifer nudged him with her hip, and his smile faltered.

". . . err, women. Um . . . ladies?" He looked at her, unsure where to stop.

I pushed him to the side and hugged Jennifer. I pulled back and gently punched him in the chest. "What's the new movie?"

The relief on Carl's face was precious. He really had no clear idea how to handle the situation. Back to the movies, though. That was the trick.

"We have a great script," he said, rushing over to a speaker stack and grabbing a thick printout. "You'll love it; it has all your favorite stuff . . ."

He flipped over a couple of pages and began quoting.

> *Burned-out cityscape, Jacob walks through a street lined with destroyed cars, swinging a crowbar and calling out.*

> "Come out, little children, the end of the world has come and gone."

> *Several misshapen creatures shuffle out from behind an overturned bread truck, their limbs twisted, their faces covered in weeping sores.*

> "Come to me, my children. Let me end your suffering."

> *The two mutants rush the tall man.*

Carl looked up. "Postholocaust, warrior, mutants . . . and . . ." he flipped a few pages deeper in. "Survivalist cheerleaders."

Jennifer laughed out loud, and Carl looked startled.

"Hey, we cut out the orgy scene," he said, his feelings clearly hurt.

"Thank heavens," I said, rolling my eyes. "Don't need too many costumes for orgies."

Jennifer sighed and took the script from him, handing it to me. "It's really good," she said. "We'll need you to read it, get some ideas together for setting and props."

I took the manuscript, flipped back to the front, and nearly swallowed my tongue. The names on the cover were Wendy Lawson and James J. Montgomery. "JJ?" I looked at them as if the world were ending. "Are you shitting me?"

"Give it a chance," Jennifer said, rushing over Carl's protests. "We had him tone a few scenes down, but the love story is excellent and the ending is very heartwarming."

I shook my head. Heartwarming and JJ did not go together.

"Who's Lisa Acres?" I asked.

"Friend of his," Jennifer said.

"Some sorority girl he's sleeping with," Carl said at the same time.

Jennifer was obviously exasperated. "The writing is good," she said, tapping the pages in my hand. "Just read it and trust me."

I folded the manuscript and saluted her with it. "I'm on it."

"Good," she said, all smiles again. "We have to finish blocking the first scene. You go take inventory."

I turned on my heel and walked to the back. We'd be doing some outside shooting, needing wrecked cars, maybe even blowing some things up. Carl had a buddy who did explosives, and I knew where we could get a couple of smashed-up choppers. Qindra would know where all the wreckage from this spring was stashed.

Although, going back inside that chopper where I'd rescued Katie may take more nerve than I was willing to muster.

The cage where I kept most of the props doubled as my personal domain in the movie world. The sound of the lock opening as I turned the key was homey. The smell of foam rubber, Handi Wipes, and cardboard greeted me like an old friend. I sat at my desk, dropped the script on top of a box of gauze I never used for the last movie, and sat in my duct-taped chair. It squeaked as I leaned back and groaned when I swiveled around to face the desk. It was good to be back.

An hour later I carried my official clipboard over to Carl's office. He and Jennifer were standing in front of a whiteboard laying out the cast and crew they'd need. *Elvis Versus the Goblins* had been a great experience, and I was ready for a new challenge.

"We're pretty thin after EVG," I said, sitting on the edge of his desk.

He looked at me like I punched his mom, and I stood up waving him down. "Don't get your knickers in a twist." I settled into a chair by the door and tapped my clipboard. No touching Carl's desk. I wondered if the rule held forth for Jennifer now that they were doing the nasty.

Maybe I didn't want to know.

Instead I asked, "When do we start shooting?"

Jennifer flipped open her planner and drew her finger down the page. "Casting call goes out tonight; we hope to have everyone in place in two weeks."

"Pretty sporty."

Carl shrugged. "We can rely on most of the same cast from EVG, I'd suspect. I know we'll have JJ and Sandra for the main roles."

"Who the hell is Sandra?"

Jennifer glanced at Carl, who rushed forward. "You remember, the way we recut the last few scenes, the blonde with the . . ." He held his hands in front of him, simulating very large breasts.

The dog, he was watching Jennifer's reaction as he did that, a grin on his face.

"He's a pig," she said, shaking her head. "He finally gets laid and he thinks it gives him a right to be vulgar."

The look on his face was priceless. I think I'd have given up my entire stake in Flight Test, Ltd. to have that on video.

He spluttered as he turned to her, "Aww, come on . . . I was . . . Jennn . . ." he practically whined. "You do the same thing."

"Jennifer," I said, in mock shock. "How scandalous."

"To be fair," she said, glaring at Carl. "It's okay if I notice."

Carl threw his hands up in the air. "She was topless for three weeks, how could I not notice?"

She crossed her arms and turned away from him.

"They aren't as cute as yours," he said, placing his hand on her shoulder.

That's it. I couldn't take it. "Eww . . ." I said, standing and dropping my clipboard on his desk. "Please, have sex, have a lot of sex, just don't talk about it in front of me."

They were both laughing as I walked out of the office. This had the potential to be a very long shoot.

I hoped I'd be around for the end of this one.

# Twenty-nine

I CALLED JULIE TO MAKE SURE SHE KNEW I WAS COMING HOME for dinner and got a list of things we needed from the grocery. I loved sharing life with another person—most of the time. It was very cool to have someone remind you when the milk was going to expire so you didn't slop a chunky mess on your last bowl of cereal when you were already late for work.

Katie could keep an eye on the milk as well as Julie. And the fringe benefits would be a billion times better, but something was holding me back. Fear? Duty? I owed Julie, that's for sure. She lost everything because of me. Katie had her life together: family, job, a place to call her own.

Julie just had me. How could I deny her that, after all that happened?

Katie understood, mostly.

There was a thrift store in the same plaza as my grocery, so I stopped there first and perused through the joint. Most of my costuming ideas came from shops like this. And postapocalypse was easy—just patch together old clothes in a very controlled yet haphazard fashion.

I noted several old suits and an old leather briefcase that would add a nice touch to a scene. I was getting fairly handy with a sewing machine, needle, and thread as part of the props-manager gig.

Mom would be proud if she knew. I hesitated a moment. Would she be proud of the life I'd made? I wanted to believe it was possible, but I couldn't remember the last time she'd shared in my dreams. Did she and Megan have that?

I grabbed the lot for just under fifty dollars. I tucked the receipt in my wallet, dropped the loot in the back of the Taurus, and headed to the grocery.

Didn't need much—some eggs, carrots, milk, and coffee. I added a six-pack of Belgian ale and headed to the checkout.

I loved this store. They had friendly staff and quick checkers. Everyone knew where those obscure items were that I could never remember and rarely asked for. They were open twenty-four hours and had a wide selection of beer and wine, including several brands of mead. You could only buy the hard stuff from a state-run, which kept very limited hours.

The evening was young still. The sun just beginning to set as I walked across the lot toward my car. It may have been the surreal aspects of the day, or the way the light looked so amazing at this time of twilight . . . either way, I totally missed the homeless guy squatting down behind the row of shopping carts near my car.

He didn't lunge at me, just stood up and gave me a little wave. I jumped about three feet into the air and nearly dropped my beer, which would have elicited a beating, then strode a wide path around him.

I used the key fob to open the trunk, pushed the lid upward with my hip far enough to leverage it with my loaded hands, and placed the bags inside.

He hadn't moved, just stood there, one hand out, like he wanted me to shake it or maybe give him some change. I closed the trunk and stood to face him across the ten or so feet.

"I'm right sorry to have startled you, ma'am," he said.

No slur, hell, better language than I usually used. "No worries," I said, giving him a smile. I noticed he had a dog with him, beagle mix, lying with its head and floppy ears resting on the guy's pack.

"Begging your pardon," he went on, obviously relieved I hadn't yelled at him, or dismissed him as most people would. I'd had bizarre experiences with odd homeless men that most people wouldn't understand.

"I have a message for you," he said, straightening and pulling a folded sheet of paper from his coat pocket.

"Message?"

He cleared his throat. "*Blood magic, blood ties,*" he looked up, with an odd twitch in his cheek. "*The time grows short, Dragon's Bane. You must wake from this slumber and rally the fearful.*"

The runes along my scalp flared, and I grabbed my head in my hands. It was as if my brains were trying to burn their way out of my skull.

"*The seas must boil, and vile intent will scorch, the very air burn, if you do not lance the World Tree with blade and cleansing flame.*"

His voice echoed in my head, mightier than this little man could muster. There was magic in his phonetical phrasing, power in the intonation and vibration—this mummer, this puppet, this mouthpiece of gods.

"*Skies will break and bones shall quake,*" he ranted, and thunderclaps echoed across the asphalt. Rain began to pelt down, and lightning flashed above the grocery, now the only point of light in a darkening world.

"*The kindred fail, the blood will flow, and an ancient rite renewed.*" He squatted down to me. "*They must not gain the mead.*"

I hadn't noticed I'd shrunk down, squatting behind my car with my hands tightly wrapped around my head.

"*The sword must waken, the blade must sing.*"

I looked up at him, my eyes throbbing with the echoes of

lightning. His face was huge, the stubble on his chin the rotting posts of some ancient ruins.

"*'Ware the bidders*," he whispered. "*Their schemes shall ensnare you, bind you with their lust.*"

"Who?" I squeaked, my throat thick and my voice raspy.

"*Take it, hide it, consume it,*" he paused, drawing in a ragged breath. "*Deny this to the scaled ones. They must not have this draft, this bloody brew.*"

Brew?

"*The ancient rites have begun, lifeblood has begun to flow. No time remains to save the skald; you must act now or the madness will be reborn.*"

His voice was urgent, panicked.

My heart was bounding in my chest. After everything I'd been through, I knew a message from Odin when I heard it. I felt the compulsion in the channeled voice, the power in the voice of the heavens.

I reached up and grabbed his shoulder with one hand to steady myself. "What must I do?"

His eyes were glazed, and he spoke without knowing his words. The paper in his hand shook, and drool ran down his chin.

"*Stop them!*" He began to shake, his teeth rattling against one another. The wind rose in a sudden roar and the skies opened like never before. For a moment, I saw a remembered dream: a broken tree and a crucified god.

"Where do I begin?" I asked, but he fell backward. Time slowed in that instant and his falling took a hundred years.

From one breath to the next, the eons flashed, and the world became undone, a blackened orb, diseased and rotten—plague, pestilence, war, and death.

He hit the ground with a thud, his arms flung out to his sides. His beagle barked, three staccato beats at the raging sky, and the bonds that had frozen me shattered.

I scrambled forward, holding his head in one hand, shielding his face from the rain with my body.

He continued to speak, but his voice was raspy and hoarse. *"The wheel is broken,"* he murmured. *"Free it from the shackle, let it turn again, or we are doomed."*

His eyes rolled up into the back of his head, and he began to shake. Seizures.

I looked up, across the parking lot. An old woman sat in her car across the lane, her fear-ridden face illuminated by the dome light in her car.

"Call an ambulance," I shouted to her. "Get help."

She shook her head, terrified, but she had a cell phone in her hand.

Lightning slashed down, lancing into a power pole across the parking lot.

Fire exploded into the sky.

"Help me," I screamed into the night as the man shuddered beneath me.

After a moment, his shuddering stopped, and as quickly as it had begun, the rain stopped. I sat on my heels, cradling his head. The rain had washed away most of the filth from his face, allowing his youth to show through.

He was my age, maybe a little younger, and so he would remain forever.

People began streaming out of the store, yelling and calling to one another.

Somewhere in time, an ambulance arrived and a nice man wrapped a coat around me, pulling me away from the augur—he who spoke with the voice of a mad god.

I sat against my car, soaked and weeping as the flashing lights of the emergency vehicles filled the lot. I had his message, wadded up in my fist. The paper was soaked, falling apart as I carefully peeled it open. The words inside were lost, the ink running in delicate smears. The only word I could read was *blood*.

Above the warbling of the sirens and the thrum of the crowd, the beagle began to howl his lament.

# Thirty

Somehow I found myself at home, cold, wet, and exhausted. Julie shepherded me into the shower, and afterward pressed a cup of hot cocoa into my hands, smothering me in blankets and concern.

I explained the evening, how the homeless guy had collapsed, keeping the bit about Odin out of the telling. My head throbbed with his echoed words, the runes a dull ache.

Odin warned of the bloody mead. That's what the dwarves wanted with Ari. That was the connection. Ari had been snatched to be used as part of this blood ritual, and I should have stopped it. Barring that, I now needed to find those who had him, stop them from killing him, or at the very least stop the ritual they were performing with his blood.

Which meant I had to go back to Vancouver, but I had no idea what to do or where to start.

Only, I did have a clue, and . . . I glanced at the clock on the wall . . . in just under two hours, I'd be having a little long-distance séance with someone who had a very good idea where Ari was being kept.

Otherwise, I could just go to Vancouver and wander around until someone took notice of my presence and attacked me. This didn't feel particularly productive.

I sipped my cocoa and watched the minutes tick by. Julie went to bed at eleven, only after I promised her I'd sleep soon and wake her if I had dreams or anything. Part of me missed the mothering.

Once she was in her room, with the door closed, I got out the mirror and set it against the coffee table. I got a bottle of glass cleaner and a roll of paper towels out from under the sink and set about cleaning the lipstick off the mirror.

The day had been exhausting. I let my head nod forward— sleep dancing along the back of my brain—when someone tapped me on my exposed foot.

I started awake. Skella was in the mirror, her hand inside my apartment, pulling back from where she'd touched me.

"How do you do that?" I asked her, pulling away from her. Not really my most pressing question, but her ability to travel through mirrors was damn annoying.

"We just do," she said. "Look, I'm really sorry about every-thing."

She wasn't in the same place she'd been the last time.

"Where are you?"

"Public bathroom near the bandstand," she said. "Harder to tell I've been here, there's so many people coming through here every day."

I looked at her. She was in the same goth getup, with the same shy smile and deep, haunted eyes.

"You can't have the sword," I told her. Might as well get down to business.

She nodded. "We had to try. It's too late now, anyway."

"Too late for what, and why did you have to try?"

She didn't want to tell me—I could see the shame on her face. Somehow she'd failed.

"They moved him tonight." She looked even more haunted. "Don't know details. Gletts is out right now trying to find where."

Of course she meant Ari. "Why tonight?"

"New moon, I think."

Made as much sense as anything else.

"They're gonna kill him soon, any day now."

Anger was boiling up into me again, and I was in no real mood to let it go. "You work for them, these dwarves who snatch kids?"

"You don't understand," she said.

Yeah, of course not. "So explain it to me."

"We wanted to help him, but we couldn't."

Fire licked at the back of my skull, pushing aside the fatigue. Adrenaline surged through me. "He was right there. I saw him the night you attacked us."

"I know," she growled.

That was new. Some backbone, perhaps?

"That's why we tried for the sword," she continued. "We're not evil, if that's what you think." She was getting angry as well. "They used special chains—iron and art. We couldn't touch them, much less break them. That's what the sword was for. We thought, if we could free him, get him out safely, the dwarves would be stymied."

Okay, that I didn't see coming. "Fuck me," I breathed. "Why didn't you just ask?"

"We . . ." She coughed and wiped her face. Her makeup was running, and I could see she had started to cry.

I wasn't sure, the lighting was bad, but it looked like some of those shadows under her eyes were bruises.

She rolled on. "After you tried to stop them, they came back here, angry and ready to kill. If it wasn't for the need to wait for the new moon, they would have killed him that night."

I got the impression she and Gletts had taken some of that anger. I didn't interrupt, just let her run on, sobs or no.

"Gletts was on guard that night, at the burrow, making sure

the eaters didn't get in, so I was at the compound, keeping the gate open as per our bargain."

"What gates? What are eaters?"

She sighed. "Gletts and I can open mirrors, use them to travel from one place to the next. The dwarves have used that for as long as I can remember to thwart Jean-Paul along with the local police."

"The dwarves have a fairly prosperous clan here. They have a few real smiths, makers who can work the old magic, but most of them are less skilled." She smiled, shrugging. "They get by, and we help them in exchange for their protection."

She was torn, I could tell. Her part in this wasn't sitting too well with her.

"They helped us keep the park clear, helped us have a home here when we couldn't get back to Alfheim. But now, things have changed. Without Jean-Paul to keep us all aligned, they've started branching out, demanding more."

I was starting to have some sympathy for her. Sounded like a raw deal.

"We kept the gates open, kept the eaters from coming through the sideways places, and in exchange, they helped us."

Eaters did not sound like puppies. "What are eaters?"

She gave a little shudder. "Think spider, only, you know, like big as a dog."

Okay, that I didn't need to know about. I slid back from the mirror, glancing at the edges.

This made her laugh. "You're safe," she said. "They are rare, more rare than the dwarves know." She got a wicked smile on her face. "We kind of embellish things so the dwarves respect us."

I smiled. Clever. "Okay, that's smart. But . . ." I eyed the mirror's edges again. "They do exist, right?"

"Oh, yes," she said, her face growing serious. "They are attracted to power. We don't use a lot to open the gates, but sometimes, when the dwarves are doing something big like blood magic, they attract more of the unsavory things out there. Working with the dwarves kept us safe, but sometimes the price is too high."

"So, let me get this straight." I tried taking deep breaths, thinking of cool water and soft colors. Red flames raged at the corners of my vision, and I could almost smell the cinders. "Did you know they were snatching Ari? Did you know what they wanted to do?"

She nodded once, looking at the floor. "What is the import of one individual in the grand scheme of our very survival?" she asked. "You must understand. When we found they were offering the brew to the scaled ones, we argued with them, tried to persuade them."

That would explain her bruises. I had a whole new hate on for those damn dwarves. Who was I to judge her? I didn't even know the dragons existed before this spring. She and her clan had been living under their bloody talons for their whole lives.

"The ends do not justify the means," I said finally, searching for a place to direct my righteous indignation.

"You are naïve," she said wearily. "You of all of your kind should understand the evil they are capable of. You have spoken with Òðr, greatest among the Æsir." She waited, expecting a response.

"Um, do you mean Odin?"

She nodded. "He and his ilk were betrayed from within and without. First Loki tricked Thor to lay aside his belt and gloves, allowing the Jötunn to slay him."

*Jötunn* I knew. Giants.

"Loki fell to the sword of Heimdall as he crossed the rainbow bridge, attempting to return to his father's home in Asgard."

Different from the myths I'd read. Not that I should be surprised. Besides, how trustworthy was she?

"Nidhogg had whispered from her place at the foot of the

World Tree, invading Heimdall's dreams, warning him of Loki's betrayal. It was the drakes, you see. The scaled ones who coveted the place of the gods. They had begun to move in the open then, hunting down the godlings."

"This part I've heard."

"Good," she said, rushing onward. She seemed to be fearful of the time, so I didn't elaborate.

". . . then, the terrible beast, Fenris, foul offspring of Loki, felled Heimdall at the great bridge, calling his mean brethren from the wastes of Midgard. But before the dire wolves of the northern wilds could ascend to Asgard, Heimdall blew such a note on his horn that the rainbow bridge was shattered, sending the fell beasts back to their darkling woods."

The storm rose again in the night, wind wailed around my apartment, and I hugged the blanket closer.

"What does this have to do with Ari, or the mead?" I asked.

"Indeed," she said, growing more desperate. "The Vanir and the Æsir had joined forces, and Kvasir had been born of their combined will."

"Clueless here," I said, feeling frustrated.

"Kvasir was a great skald, a god of wisdom and insight. It is due to him that the opposing factions became as one. But the dwarves killed him and took his blood. They brewed a bloody mead to give themselves power over the gods. This is what the dwarves here hope to re-create. With it they could command the hearts of men, sway the will of legions, undermine the rule of the scaled ones."

"Then why would they offer to auction it to the highest bidder?" I asked, confused.

She sighed heavily and rubbed her forehead. "Because dwarves are mean bastards who can seldom see beyond the thoughts of glory or gold."

I thought of Rolph and his schizophrenia around Gram. "They are fickle creatures."

"Crazed and drunk with their own worth," she spat. "They have taken my people hostage, killed a few, enslaved the rest."

"But if you can travel through mirrors, why don't you just lead them from their captivity?"

"Iron," she whispered. "We cannot abide it, and they line the way with tricks and traps. We are helpless to cross certain thresholds. Only Gletts and I have a sort of protection, as we are not true blood." This last bit seemed to cause her pain, this admission. "We are children of two worlds."

I tapped the edge of the mirror.

"Let me get this right. You befriended us, then poisoned us to get your hands on the sword. All to save Ari from becoming the new version of this magic mead. Only, you couldn't stop them, and now Odin's on the rampage and the dwarves are making deals with dragons?"

"Pretty much."

My head hurt. I wanted to go to sleep and pretend none of this mattered. "Why Ari?"

She looked thoughtful for a moment, almost sad. "He is strong in the ways of charisma and song," she said, finally. "There are many who could serve the same, but few have embraced the gifts as powerfully as he—sought out the glory, drawn the magic to him."

"He isn't one of the reborn, is he?" I held my breath. Surely not.

"No, definitely not. But the lineage of Kvasir is long and varied. While Kvasir's blood was the first used to make the mead, back in the days of the Elders, he was not the only man of charisma, wisdom, and beauty. There have been poets and kings, skalds, performers, politicians, and their ilk, who have chosen the path to glory."

Okay, this was hard to take. "He chose this? Chose to become powerful? You can do that?"

"Sarah," she said quietly. "Do you not feel you've had a hand in your own fate? Chosen certain paths, made certain decisions that have brought you here?"

Heady stuff, for true, and more than my sleep-deprived brain could handle at the moment.

"Okay, so the dwarves get wind of Ari, see his rising star, and snatch him. Where did they learn about the blood mead? I'm sure you can't just find a recipe on the Internet."

"How these dwarves knew of such a thing is a long and sordid tale," she said, her facing growing stony. "Living under Jean-Paul was a hard life. Some chose dark ways, learned forbidden secrets to survive." She paused, drawing a deep breath. "Don't misunderstand. Some drew from the knowledge held by Jean-Paul and his allies. He was more powerful and cruel than you can begin to imagine."

I wasn't so sure about that. I had a damn good imagination. "So, they made a deal with the devil?"

"You could say that."

"Let me get all this straight. The dwarves worked with Jean-Paul, or for him, I guess. Learning dark secrets, blood magics, and, in the end, happened to snatch Ari the night I was there?" Coincidence much?

"They had no idea you were here. If they'd known, I'm afraid they may have taken you and left Ari." The thought seemed to scare her even more. "I have no idea what kind of potion they would make from your blood." She shivered.

Good to know. Dwarves could want to kill me for my blood. What a fucked-up world. "I appreciate the four-one-one, but what, exactly, do you want with me?"

Now her face lit up—hope, perhaps. "I want you to come back to Vancouver. We need your help."

"Today? Right now?" Man, I did not want to drive there this tired.

She shook her head. "No, I needed to seek your forgiveness, first. We are not ready. I will alert you. Blood has been spilled, the first draft of the mead is made. They have only bled him a little." She glanced over her shoulder. "There is no use tipping our hand at this juncture. We are thinking when they are distracted with the auction, our people will be abandoned in their cells. This is when we'll need you to act."

I yawned hard, my jaws cracking and my ears popping. "Let me know," I said. "I'll do what I can."

"I told Gletts you would help us." She smiled broadly, looking as much weeping clown as angst-ridden goth child. "He said you would not forgive us."

I leaned forward, letting my face get within her grasp, if she chose to reach through the mirror. I bared my teeth in a wide smile but I felt no joy. "I will help you against these idiot dwarves and to prevent the dragons from gaining this mead. But do not mistake a common enemy as friendship. You attacked me and Katie, when all you needed to do was ask for help."

She made a wry mouth, nodding once. "It has been hard to trust anyone," she said. "I should have taken your deeds at face value, but I was fearful. This has been my grave error. I will accept your wrath and your judgment when the mead is secured and the dwarves punished for their crimes against my people."

"Get word to me," I said, yawning again. "I need to sleep now. I'll look for a sign from you to come north."

"You have my thanks, Sarah Jane Beauhall. You are a light in the darkness." Then she was gone.

I stared at my own reflection for a moment, and then slid the mirror, facedown, under the couch.

Christ on a crutch. This was out of control. I just wanted a normal life. How the hell was I supposed to take on a full clan of dwarves and rescue Ari? Maybe Skella could sneak me in, use a gate to travel north. Pretty neat trick. Of course, there were the eaters to consider. And to think, I used to be worried about silly things like bills and such. At least I didn't have to watch out for giant spiders every time I opened the freaking door.

But, even having killed Jean-Paul and faced down more than one dragon, I'm not a superhero. I'm just me. Berserker or not, I was not indestructible. And Odin was pissed, that much was obvious.

Damn it. I had a life to live. Obligations to meet. I just couldn't make a suicide run into the heart of dwarf country, not to mention the King of Vancouver and whatever madness he had cooking up. It was all just overwhelming.

Oh, god. And Anezka and Bub. My life was a carnival.

Time to pull out the hide-a-bed and catch some Zs. I just knew I was going to dream about this madness. Dinner Wednesday with Katie couldn't come too soon. I just wish she was here to cuddle with. I was getting sick of sleeping alone.

# Thirty-one

I MET ANEZKA OUT AT TRIPLE LOOP. ACTUALLY, SHE MET ME since I beat her there. It was nice, for once, not to be the straggler. I was inside talking with Mr. Culver when she pulled up in an old F150. Thing looked like hell, and sounded like it needed an engine overhaul, but she'd made it.

After introductions and some swapping of general gossip with Mr. Culver, Anezka and I headed out to the barn. The horses were ready to do some running by the look of them, so Mr. Culver let them out into the pasture while we worked on his two ponies. I liked working ponies as a general rule, but they were so damn short, it took more bending and was harder on the back.

Anezka dove right in, asking me a few questions, but really fell back into the rhythm of shoeing. The ponies were fairly placid and gave her no trouble.

The horses were another story. The little mare rolled her eyes and stomped, bucking and blowing. We couldn't get her under control until Anezka left the barn. She spent the rest of the day working on shoes for me to lay down.

I had a sneaking suspicion it was as much the aura of Bub, and his scaly stench, as Anezka that got them stirred up.

Gave me plenty of good practice, and Mr. Culver was quite relieved to be getting the herd tended. Later, as he was writing out a check, he confided in me he'd called around to see if anyone else would give him a quote.

"Hell, I even called Jude Brown over at Broken Axel Farm, and he said that if Mary Campbell over at the Circle Q spoke that highly of you, then I'd be better off waiting for you folks to get to me."

We hadn't even called Jude Brown. He only kept a couple mules he plowed with, no horses or ponies, so we didn't see him much. I'd have to give him a call.

"Well, with Julie laid up, and the smithy burned down," I said, shrugging, "it's been rough."

He grew solemn then, crossed himself and leaned in to speak away from Anezka. "You done right by my lot, but that woman is a little odd."

I smiled and nodded. "She's doing us a favor by helping out," I said. "Good to have someone with expertise along to make sure I toe the line."

He patted me on the shoulder. "You tell Julie we'd love to see her out as soon as she's able, but I'm more than fine with you coming out on your own."

I glanced at Anezka. She was packing the little propane forge we'd used to adjust the shoes I'd brought. If she heard or noticed, she didn't give any indication.

It was the first time I'd taken the money while someone else cleaned up. Felt good and awkward all at the same time. Like I was the big kid for once.

We'd driven down to the fence line and through the gate when Anezka waved me over.

"Wanna stop over at The County Line for a beer?" she asked, once Mr. Culver had closed the gate.

"Sure, could use something to knock down the dust."

We drove north toward Gold Bar and hit the wide spot in the

road that was The County Line. It was a real hole-in-the-wall that catered to bikers and farmhands. My ugly sedan stood out among the bikes and trucks.

We went inside and sat at the far end of the bar. Anezka bought the first round, boilermakers. A tall beer and a shot of whiskey each. We tossed back the whiskeys, smacked the bar, and picked up the beers. I can drink most girls under the table, but she beat me to the bottom of that glass. It was impressive.

She belched like she was about to explode and asked to be set up again. I opted for just a beer and trundled off to the bathroom.

By the time I got back, she was standing at the jukebox plugging in quarters. Soon Def Leppard was shouting about pouring some sugar, and Anezka was out on the floor shaking it for all she was worth.

I sat at the bar, nursing my beer and watching her. She threw herself into dancing like I did with fighting. Like I had that night with the cowboys. She was drawing some serious attention, and I was getting a bad feeling.

When the song ended, I scooted across the sawdust and tapped her on the shoulder.

"You wanna dance?" she asked me.

"Tempting," I said, smiling despite the eyes staring at us. "But I thought we should grab a seat and talk before things got too wild."

I could tell she didn't really want to stop dancing. She hadn't been out much since Justin left her. Who could blame her for wanting to cut loose? But I wasn't in the mood to be mauled by cowboys, and, while there was a part of me that wouldn't mind a bit of a tussle, punching someone would do bad things to my knuckles.

Instead, we landed in a booth with an order of nachos and two tall glasses of sweet tea. She wasn't too happy, but kept her party face on.

"Tell me about Bub," I said after the waitress left.

Anezka watched her walk away, whistling quietly. Pretty brazen, but I doubted those denims peeled off for just any cowgirl that strolled into the bar.

"Bub says you're one crazy bitch," she said, turning back to face me, laughing. "Didn't see a second of fear in you, and the way you kept jumping around Kelly's place, taunting him. You've earned his respect."

Good to know, though that wasn't exactly how I remembered it. "Glad he's not in the mood to kill me and eat me," I said, fishing through the chips for a jalapeño.

She nibbled, and sipped her tea, making a face. "If I wanted to be sober, I'd have stayed home."

"Don't want you getting into trouble."

She screwed her face up, gnawing on something sour. "You're harshing my buzz," she said. "Maybe I want to get hammered and go home with a couple of these young fellas—"

The waitress walked by again, her midriff showing with her T-shirt torn and tied under her breasts.

"—or she might make for a fun evening."

The waitress, Angie by her name tag, rolled her eyes and cleared the next booth over. When she bent over the table to wipe the far end, several of the patrons whooped and hollered—Anezka among them.

"Look," I said, pulling her back around to sit in the booth.

"Back off, Snow White," she said, standing up and stumbling toward the bar. "I'm a big girl."

*Snow White? What the fuck?* Of course, I just sat there while she lined up three shots and knocked them down one after another.

Next she was out on the dance floor having the time of her life.

I dropped some money on the table, slipped out of the bar, and called Katie. This night was not going to end well. Hell, I didn't want to sit around and watch her get hammered and nailed.

Katie said I wasn't responsible for her, that Anezka was a big girl. Maybe I should just head on home, let her live her life the way she wants.

I just had a very bad feeling.

# Thirty-two

FREDERICK SAWYER STOOD IN FRONT OF THE BANK OF WIN-
dows overlooking his city, holding a letter in the sunlight. An
opened box sat in the middle of his large desk, the Bubble Wrap
sticking above the edge of the open flap. "Surely you understand
what this means?" he asked, excitement coursing through him in
waves of fire. He glanced across the room to where Mr. Philips
stood. "If this is true, imagine the influence I could wield."

"Of course, sir," Mr. Philips said. "So you believe this is
true?"

Frederick looked down at the page again. There were two sets
of writing there, English and a language that resembled Old High
German. The letters were blocky and trended more toward runes,
but it was a language that tickled the back of Frederick's mind. "I
believe this is Dwarvish," he said, letting the glee rise in him.
"There is a legend among the ancient ones of a mead such as the
one described here. To own it would be invaluable."

Mr. Philips clasped his hands behind his back. "I find it interesting that this revolves around parties in Vancouver, but excludes
the self-proclaimed King."

"Quite right," Frederick said with a toothy grin. "All the more
reason to pursue this. Obviously this King does not have total

control over the city as it first appeared. Best to spread our efforts to all opportunities."

"We will require a testing of this brew," he said, not turning. "This mead gives the imbiber the voice of the gods, a power to move men's hearts and enthrall their minds."

"If I may be so bold . . ." Mr. Philips interjected. He looked at Frederick for permission to continue. Frederick nodded. "You have had your eye on the Montgomery lad for some time. Perhaps this potion, if authentic, could be used to boost his natural abilities, providing you a greater asset, regardless of the outcome of the auction for a superior vintage."

Frederick nodded. "I like the way you think, Mr. Philips. Let's invite Mr. Montgomery to dinner."

Mr. Philips turned to the computer and began tapping on the keys.

"Find him a suitable dinner companion as well," Frederick said, stroking his chin. "Someone buxom, and fawning."

The *click-clack* of the keys continued unabated for several minutes. Finally, Mr. Philips looked up. "Invitation has been sent, sir."

"And the girl?"

"Redhead, five-six. Bikini barista from that quaint little shop on Burnside."

Frederick nodded. "Excellent. She will do just fine."

She was a handsome lass, and not so intellectual as to intimidate young James.

*Yes, this would be delicious*, he thought.

"Invite some of the regulars," Frederick added. "Let's see if we can dazzle Mr. Montgomery."

Mr. Philips nodded and returned to his work. Frederick took a fat hand-rolled cigar from a humidor on his desk, snipped off the end, and settled down in his leather chair. He pulled a slender wooden shaving out of a different box and held it to his lips. With a breath he set the twig alight, then put the cigar in his mouth. Blue smoke rose around him as he sucked the flame into the tobacco.

"I love when things go my way."

# Thirty-three

I GATHERED MY IDEAS FOR PROPS, COSTUMES, SETS, AND AN estimated budget into a spreadsheet and e-mailed them to Jennifer. Julie had been sawing logs long before I went to unfold the couch.

My hand was hurting more than usual, so I broke out the knitting. I'd read about people who knitted with wire. I thought it would be cool to do, but I promised Katie I wouldn't do anything outrageous until I'd finished the scarf I was working on. I held it up. Foot and a half of crap. Somehow, about halfway through, I'd increased the width without really knowing how. Katie had offered to help me figure it out, but I just had to finish it my own way. It would suck, but I would own that suckage.

I checked the mirror periodically, hoping to catch some word from Skella, but the mirror never changed. After thirty minutes, I gave up . . . the mirror went back under the couch, knitting went into the satchel of shame, and I crawled under the blankets with Anezka in my mind's eye. While she wasn't a real looker, I got the impression she could have just about any man or woman she fancied. Not a bone of fear or doubt in her.

As I drifted to sleep, I thought of her at Burning Man, dancing naked around a bonfire, covered in body paint and shouting her joy at the cold stars.

The screams of joy mingled with screams of horror when I looked into the sky above the village.

Village? I spun around, confused. Where was I? Several of the thatched huts were burning, and the sound of crying filled my ears. There, on top of the long house, the dragon raised its long neck to the sky and roared, its great wings beating the flames that rolled across the roof.

"You have failed to give me tribute," the dragon roared.

I recognized that voice, something in its timbre reminded me of another I'd grown to loathe.

A large man with pale skin and a full, shaggy beard burst from one of the huts brandishing a long spear. His wild hair haloed his face as he skidded across the dust of the gathering circle, flinging the spear with a roar. He cursed as the dragon batted aside the spear with one of his great wings.

"You refuse me the tribute I am due," the great beast yelled, arching its neck down toward the now-weaponless man. "I only ask for one of your daughters to have as my own, dwarf. Not even the youngest; I leave it to you to pick."

"Die, wyrm!" the dwarf yelled. "You canna have another of mine."

"So be it," the dragon said, his voice a knife that cut through the wailing. In a blink he leapt from the roof of the long house and landed in the central square, crushing the well and snatching the dwarf from the ground in his great-toothed maw. Blood showered the square.

I couldn't move, couldn't run to this beast, to find a weapon to stop his murder. He knocked down a large hut, and one after another killed or ate the inhabitants. It was horrible beyond anything I'd seen. Even the battle with Jean-Paul had not been this matter-of-fact, this blatantly one-sided.

The next evening, as the fires faded with the final rays of the sun, a strapping young dwarf crawled out of the ruins of the smithy. That first night the boy buried the remains of his family, a piteously small task, and fell asleep in the ruins of the long house.

The following evening, he began to clear away the wreckage from the smithy. Once he had the forge cleared, he dug through the family's home, carrying out a box of intricate design.

For six nights he worked, beating the shattered fragments he pulled from that box into a recognizable shape. Every night, he tied the family bull to the ruined well, feeding and watering the great beast, singing to it songs of glory.

On the final night, as he fired the blade for one last time, he crooned to the bull, apologizing for what was to come, and calling on the gods to take the beast into the golden pasture. Then he stalked across the yard and plunged the glowing blade into the heart of the tethered bull. The great beast bucked and frothed as the blood boiled and ran steaming around the blade, filling the night once more with a coppery stench.

The bull shrieked as it died, a death I could not begin to imagine. After a moment the youth pulled the blade forth and held it toward the sky.

"Woden, One-Eye, You who have forsaken my family. I have reforged the blade you sundered. My father and his fathers before him kept the shards at the command of your son Thor, until such time as the world would have need of the blade again. I claim this in your name, to slay the great dragon who has hunted this land for far too long."

Of course I recognized the blade. How could I not, as the runes along the furrow glowed in the deepening night? Thunder rolled in the distance, and the boy crawled into the ruins of the lodge, away from the coming of the dawn.

In the distance, atop a rocky outcropping, I saw the dragon, watching the boy and laughing.

Then the dragon paused, turning his head toward me, and his laughing ceased.

"Smith? Is that you who haunts the dreams of my youth?" Frederick Sawyer asked. "Be gone from me, meddler. Mine is not for you to observe."

And I awoke to the sound of screaming.

# Thirty-four

WELL, NOT SCREAMING, BUT THE SOUND OF THE COFFEE grinder was enough to jerk me awake. Unfortunately, I wasn't in my bed. Every muscle in my body was cramped, and my neck hurt from being cocked in one position too long. The lingering mockery of Frederick's rebuke filled my head with anguish. I tried to raise up, but got tangled in something draped above me. I fought against it, struggling with the thick clothes that hung around me. My guttural cry of anger and frustration must have been what signaled Julie, because the next thing I saw was her opening the doorway, bathed in light.

That's about the time my brain finally kicked in. I was in the hall closet. I'd taken refuge there in the night and curled up on the floor with the boots and fallen scarves, single gloves and broken umbrellas.

"What the hell are you doing?" Julie barked at me. She leaned on her cane, clutching her chest. "You about gave me a heart attack. I thought you'd gone to Katie's."

I climbed out of the fallen coats and hangers, crawled over the assorted debris, and rolled out onto the floor, ending up flat on my back, spread-eagled.

"Pretty," Julie said, shaking her head and turning toward the kitchen. "Why don't you get dressed?"

I looked down. I had on a T-shirt, socks, and panties, but nothing else. Not exactly a graceful moment. How the hell had I ended up in the closet?

"I didn't mean to wake you," Julie said, putting the coffee grounds into a filter and assembling the coffeemaker she'd purchased, "but considering the fact you were in the closet . . . why was that again?" She glanced back at me. "Some metaphorical psychological experiment around your sexuality?"

Bitch . . . she was teasing, of course, but I was a little jittery.

"Nightmare," I said. "You know, the usual: dragon, sword . . . that type of thing."

"Sorry," she said. Julie had been through worse than me in the whole fiasco in the spring. Burned out by a dragon, mauled by trolls and giants, beaten, and eventually broken. Hell, at least I got to hunt the bastard down.

The jeans and bra I'd worn the night before lay crumpled in the floor by the hide-a-bed, and I shimmied into the jeans. "No worries," I said, zipping up the fly. "What time is it?"

"Four."

"Holy . . ." I paused, reaching for my bra. "In the morning?"

Julie took a coffee mug and saucer from the cabinet and set them both on the counter. "Yes, the morning. Like five hours after I went to bed."

Dawn was a good two hours away. Not a great way to start the day. But I was wired, the adrenaline was pumping, and my senses were aligned to "Danger Will Robinson" levels.

"By the way," I asked, as politely as I could through clenched teeth, "when did we get a coffee grinder?"

Julie shrugged. "Last week. Cheaper than going out for coffee every day."

True enough. Still . . . "I like Monkey Shines, though, and they have crullers."

The look she gave me was not sweet or pleasant. "One day, Sarah Jane Beauhall, you will be concerned about your weight and"—she opened the fridge and pulled out a huge grapefruit—"you'll be worried about what you eat."

I flipped the couch back together and sat down on it, pushing the overhanging blanket down between the arm and the cushion I was sitting on.

"Might as well head out to Anezka's place, see if she got home and all."

I looked up at the sound of a knife striking a cutting board. Julie had just cut her grapefruit in half, but the force was a little beyond expected parameters. Was she pissy about Anezka?

I stomped my feet into my Docs and tied them loosely. "You okay, boss?"

She just mumbled something and pulled the chair out, sitting down with her cup of coffee and her half a grapefruit.

There wasn't a better teacher than Julie. I'd tell anyone. Not only did she have me pegged on life issues, but she knew where I needed work, how the metal sang, and how the fire was to be wielded. She'd let me grow up, find my way, in a way no one else had ever done . . . well, no one but Sa Bum Nim Choi, but that was a totally different thing. I wasn't eleven anymore, and this wasn't Tae Kwon Do.

I sat at the table, flipped my hair out of my eyes, and pulled her coffee cup away from her reach.

"Hey," she said, looking up at me—definitely pissy and hurt.

"Julie . . ." Too proud, I saw then. Hurt, angry, and falling behind in the big game. "Anezka is a loose cannon—out of control—and horses shy away from her."

There was no budging there, just fatigue, almost . . . was it defeat?

"I was thinking about heading over to the U District tomorrow after work, seeing Gunther at his shop, maybe. Want to go with? Maybe get some Italian?"

She squinted at me, not quite up to full-on stink eye, but dubious all the same. "Dinner? You sure?"

"Oh, yeah. Definitely," I assured her. "Things have been crazy lately, and I'd love to get your take on a few of the more interesting items. Very weird items."

She reached over and took her coffee back. "I'll have to tell Mrs. Sorenson I can't make it over for rummy."

"I'd really appreciate it," I said honestly. "It's just not the same without you kicking my ass and giving me advice."

She harrumphed me, picking up her coffee. "You never showed up before nine in the morning. What's so damn exciting about Anezka's place that makes you want to head right over?"

"That's part of what I want to discuss." I got up, grabbed an apple from the basket on the table, and took a large bite. "She's not . . ." I chewed quickly, mumbling the words around the pulpy fruit, "half the farrier you are." I swallowed.

I looked down at the apple in my hand. It was the most delicious apple I'd ever eaten. "Oh my god, this is great. Where'd you get these?"

"Bought them from a guy on the corner, set up a stand with stuff from eastern Washington."

There was a crisp tartness there that I'd never experienced before. For a second my head swam and my vision wavered. "Kinda light-headed," I said, sitting down again. "Any chance these are poisoned?"

She grabbed the apple from my hand and took a bite, chewing thoughtfully. "Nope," she said finally, turning her attention to her grapefruit. "When was the last time you had a glass of water?"

Hydration. Check. "Too long," I admitted. Stupid of me.

"You smell like beer, too," she said, digging out a section of grapefruit.

It was my turn to give her a look. I pulled out the edge of my shirt and took a quick smell. She was right. Besides, I didn't have to get over the mountain this early. I wasn't even sure Anezka made it home last night.

"Fine," I said, standing and stripping my T-shirt over my head. Julie covered her face and groaned.

"I liked you better with body issues," she said.

I walked over to the bathroom, leaving a trail of T-shirt, boots, socks, and finally my jeans.

"You'll pick those things up, young lady," she called after me as I shut the door.

Yep, good to see her fighting back.

I turned the shower on full hot and let the steam fill the room before I stripped out of my delicates. Once the mirror was obscured I wrote in the steam, backward—"no peeking"—and climbed into the shower. Needed to get a better handle on my nutrition. Heck, my cardio wasn't doing great these days. Maybe I needed to go for a run later tonight. If I wasn't naked, and had thought of it, I should have gone for a run before showering. C'est la vie.

When I got out of the shower (wrapped in a towel, mind), Julie had on her iPod and was vacuuming the living room. She made a particular point of going around my clothes, which I thought was hilarious.

Not sure I remembered owning a vacuum, though.

I picked up my clothes, went into the bedroom, and dumped them into the hamper. Before Julie had a chance to finish, I was dressed once again and ready to start my day.

# Thirty-five

By seven I'd stopped at a coffee shop in Leavenworth and grabbed a couple vats of joe and some pastries. If Anezka was as hungover as I expected, she'd want some fortification. Hell, she might not even be there.

The road to Chumstick was devoid of any traffic, which was no surprise. I wasn't even sure anyone else lived there. I parked on the side of the road and crossed to her spread. Once again, I felt the pressure, the energy barrier, that surrounded her place.

She wasn't up, but her truck was parked around back, very close to one of the metal warriors. Not a real quality parking job, there. I took the coffees into the shop, grabbed an apron, and began cleaning up. The place was more filthy than I recalled, dust and metal shavings all over. Had I left it like this on Monday?

Things went well at first. I didn't snoop, open any of the lockers or anything. Then I knocked into a stack of steel rods, sending them clanging across the concrete floor. It sounded like the dragon sculpture had shaken off half its scales.

I was cleaning up the rods when Anezka came staggering out of her place, dressed in a pair of running shorts and a wifebeater and carrying a shotgun.

I sat back on my behind, holding my hands in the air . . . "Don't shoot."

She stumbled to a stop. "Fuck, Beauhall. What the hell's wrong with you?"

I grinned at her. "Just cleaning up."

The barrel of the shotgun wavered for a minute; then she lowered it, grunting and grabbing her head with her free hand. "Gawdawful hangover," she moaned.

"Glad you made it home last night," I said, standing up and brushing off my jeans.

She threw me an evil look. "Almost had company, too," she said indignantly. "But the damn bartender asked me if I'd give him my daughter's phone number." She pointed at me, and for a moment I thought she was going to shoot me. "Stupid country fuck." She turned back to the house, waving her empty hand in the air. "I'm going back to bed. If you wake me up again, I *will* shoot you."

She slammed the door, but I saw her wince when she did it. Been a while since I'd been that hungover, but not so long ago that my stomach didn't churn a little in sympathy.

To play it safe, I grabbed my coffee and walked cautiously out back leaving the iron pickup sticks where they'd fallen.

Now, I didn't flinch, nor did I lose control of my bladder or anything, but my heart about leapt out of my throat. Bub sat, hunched on the head of the dragon, eyeing me with those black, teardrop-shaped peepers. Tilting his head from one side to the other, he reminded me suddenly of Jean-Paul or Frederick and the way they watched their prey when in dragon form.

Da would name him demon, I was sure. Not convinced he wasn't. This world of dragons and gods confused the hell out of me. No doubt the fine folks who wrote the bits of the Bible about demons and devils had seen creepy little dudes like Bub.

"Sorry I smashed your skull," I said, feebly. "No hard feelings?"

He smiled, showing off very long, pointy teeth. "I'm sure I'll forgive you at some juncture," he said. Fine wisps of smoke escaped his mouth and nose. I guess he was excited to see me.

"You've been in Anezka's family for a long time, huh?" Keep the critter distracted . . . always a good idea.

He thought for a moment, then dropped from the dragon's head, landing on his hands and feet, like a cat. He reminded me of Gollum from the *Lord of the Rings*, only scaly and with better teeth.

"You seem to misunderstand the relationship," he said, his voice more singsong than I thought could come from a face like that.

I took a step away from him, turning to keep him squarely in my front defensive zone. Just wished I had a weapon better than a cup of weak coffee. "Misunderstand how?"

He stroked the dragon affectionately, worshipfully.

I noticed then that he smelled of cloves, if you can believe it. Like those cigarettes the kids smoked in college, when they weren't smoking dope.

"I serve the amulet. That has been my bond and my master for all the centuries since I was called from Múspell, the home of my hive mates."

The runes on my forehead stung—somehow I knew those words, a tickle of understanding like the words had been spoken in the past. I just couldn't place where, or by whom. *Múspell* meant fire, I thought. Something like that. I could see bits and pieces, like someone else's memory, maybe. Why was that so familiar? It had something to do with the tree, that tree that Odin had been crucified on in my dream. Something there clicked.

"Múspell is one of the seven worlds, right? One of the worlds that can be reached from the World Tree?" I knew it was true the minute the words left my mouth.

He eyed me, stroked the wiry whiskers on his chin, and laughed. "You know more than you pretend," he said gleefully.

World Tree was Yggdrasil, right? Nidhogg lived at the base of the World Tree in mythology—did that put it near here? Maybe she moved.

As I pondered, he picked his teeth with one razorlike talon.

I leaned against the hood of the truck all nonchalantly, wishing I'd thought to bring out one of those hammers. Would it be too conspicuous if I went back in and got one? Probably so.

Something in his attention shifted. He snapped his head around toward the house, toward Anezka. From the small window in the back, I could hear her vomiting. Nice.

"She is not well," he said, a touch of sadness in his voice. "There is a sickness in her belly. One I cannot understand."

"Cancer?" I asked, standing up straight, suddenly frightened for her.

"Not that form of malady," he offered. "Something else; her humors are out of balance. It is the fault of that bastard Justin. He took from her, and she has been wounded ever since."

"Heartbroke's my guess," I said. I also thought she could be pregnant. "When was the last time she'd been with a man?"

Bub growled low in his throat. "It has been five months, since the foul one was here last, tormenting her."

Foul one? "Justin?" I asked.

He nodded once.

"Maybe she's lonely. Needs companionship—a new lover, perhaps. Somehow she thinks it will make her feel whole again." It felt right to me, although I wasn't sure if I was projecting my own insecurities into the situation.

There was a small clap of sound, like a balloon popping. He vanished, only to appear again hunched on the shoulders of one of the warriors. "You are observant for one of your kind," he said, not unpleased. "I find you interesting and," he rubbed his hands together, "a little wicked."

Wicked? Where was that coming from? "I'm just me," I said with a shrug. "Don't know about wicked."

"She is drawn to you, drawn to the darkness that flows within you. That is her curse, to be pulled to it like a moth to the flame."

He made my head hurt. Moth? "She seems capable to me," I offered. "I don't see her coming unglued or anything."

The weariness in his body spoke of a different truth. "You do not hear her weeping, see her falling into despair," he confided in me finally. "You did not have the joy of seeing her rages, glorying in the pain."

Pain, rage . . . I was very familiar with those things, but glory? "What the hell are you talking about?"

"She is growing soft, weak," he said, and then vanished with a *pop-pop*. I turned to find him atop the cab of the truck, his long neck craned down the window, his body lowered between his knees. "You are not weak. I see the fire in you, feel the violence just under the surface. Your anger is delicious."

Fuck you very much. I stepped away from the truck and faced him square. "Pretty wacked, don't ya think?" I asked. "Anger, darkness . . . sounds like you aren't exactly on the side of the angels."

"Thank you," he said, bobbing his head. "Perhaps it is time . . ."

*Pop*—once again he vanished.

I spun around, looking for him, but didn't find him again. What the hell?

*Pop* . . . he reappeared back on top of the metal dragon's head. ". . . for you to take a firmer hand with our mistress."

With a final crack, he vanished. I imagined the sound he made when he moved was the sound of air collapsing into the spot he'd just vacated. Not like I had any evidence beyond my early exposure to Nightcrawler from the X-Men comics.

I waited a few minutes, but he did not reappear again. Finally, I went back into the shop, drank the last of my coffee, and considered the freak show my life had become. Later, I'd call over to Broken Switch Farm to confirm for tomorrow.

For the moment, I took down one of the three-pound hammers and sat on the edge of the table, toying with my cell phone, hammer in my lap. Couldn't promise to get through the day without smashing Bub's head in again. I didn't trust him as far as I could spit.

Instead I texted something smutty to Katie. She'd be at school already, but didn't start class until eight. I was really looking forward to seeing her later.

# Thirty-six

AROUND EIGHT THIRTY, I CALLED GUNTHER. I REALLY wanted to get his opinion on the Ducati. He didn't open the record shop until noon on Wednesdays and lived fairly close to Black Briar, so Chumstick wasn't all that far. I hoped.

"Hola, chica," he said with his rich tenor voice. It was like sorghum molasses. He spoke Spanish, several languages in fact, but Gunther was so Nordic, it said Viking on his driver's license.

"Hi, Gunther," I said, feeling my heart race. I had been avoiding them—him and Stuart. Guilty conscience, I knew, but with the two of them hanging with Jimmy out at Black Briar, they suffered by his company. Yes, I needed to address all that, but until Deidre was better, Jimmy would never forgive me.

I sighed heavily. This was so damn hard.

"Any chance I could ask a favor?" I ventured.

He laughed, a lovely sound that reminded me of sunnier days. "Sarah, you know I'd walk through fire for you. You need something, you just ask."

Tears pushed their way into my eyes, damn it. I hated that, but I'd missed him so much.

"Could you come out to Leavenworth? There's this motorcycle I'm thinking of buying and I'd like you to look at it."

"Interesting. I didn't figure you for being awake this early, much less already over the mountains," he said, the laughter still in his voice. "Buy me breakfast?"

"Deal!"

"Okay, I'll meet you at the Waffle Pantry in ninety minutes. Will that work?"

I smiled, feeling better than I had all morning. "That's excellent. I may have someone with me, but we'll need to go out to Chumstick to see the bike."

"Fair enough, see you in ninety. Oh, and I'll drive the truck, just in case."

He hung up, and I looked at my phone, amazed how that little effort had washed away a huge swath of angst. Maybe I should call Stuart next.

Seriously, but he was already at work. Couldn't bother him there. He didn't have his own place; he worked for the university. They frowned on too many personal calls. Besides, after what we'd been through in the spring, I think I wanted to chat him up face-to-face. Maybe I needed to ask him over to dinner. We could show off our scars and swap war stories. He'd been in the fight longer than Gunther, seen more of the death up close. Gunther had fallen early on—smashed hip. Stuart had walked the field, bringing in the wounded, marking the fallen.

And there I was getting all morose again. It would be good to see Gunther. He'd give me sound advice on the bike, and it wouldn't hurt to get his opinion on Anezka. I didn't have the experience to deal with someone like her, no matter what kind of inside knowledge she did or did not have about the world we lived in. I just couldn't figure out how blasé she was about it all. And I wasn't sure she and Gunther didn't already know each other. The circle of those in the know seemed fairly tiny. But then, what the hell did I know?

Later today, Anezka and I would discuss kobolds, dragon fire, and lost loves. She needed a friend more than I thought possible. Spending all her time with that creepy little monster would bring anyone down. Not like me to come to anyone's emotional rescue, but here was a place I could do some good.

I could hear her banging around in the house. She'd be out soon, and I'd see if she wanted to go with me into town. Might be good for her and Gunther to meet—she had said she didn't know him, come to think of it.

# Thirty-seven

Qindra woke with an urge to be on the road. She rose
from her bed and cast the runes, contemplating the dream that had
faded too quickly to capture. Something about blood and pain.
Likely related to the package they'd received, the vial of mead presented by the Dragon Liberation Front. Puzzling name, for sure.

The runes were awkward this morning, speaking of dire need
and shopping. Didn't make a lot of sense, but some days, you just
had to roll with it.

She dressed in a conservative yet comfortable outfit: slacks and
a blouse. Once dressed, she stopped at the kitchen and greeted the
staff with a warm smile and an approving nod. These were her
people. Perhaps she should take one of them shopping with her.
They rarely left the grounds.

But, alas, Nidhogg would forbid it, and it was not worth stirring her ire on a whim. Still, the company would have been welcome.

Qindra ate a piece of toast, and the cook handed her a very
large coffee to take. She thanked the old woman, complimenting
her work, and left the children to their oatmeal and juice.

Leavenworth, she thought. They'd be in the beginning stages of
Oktoberfest. Maybe she would look for some crystal. The mistress

would like that. It would be good to replace what had been shattered the last time Nidhogg had lost control.

She frowned. She couldn't bring back the children who'd been killed, but the crystal would be a distraction. Besides, the drive would give her a chance to think. Perhaps it was time to scry for Sarah Beauhall. She'd been disappearing lately.

# Thirty-eight

Anezka moaned the whole way into Leavenworth. She rode with her head against the window and rolled it down a couple of times as if she was gonna hurl. I wasn't at all sure breakfast was the best thing for her, but she assured me she was starving.

"Just a little green around the gills, that's all."

She seemed more chipper. I think getting out of that house, off that property, was a good thing for her. The place had some bad energy.

Gunther was in the lot when we arrived. He leaned against his big Dodge Ram, dressed like a cross between Neo from *The Matrix* and Malcolm Reynolds from *Firefly*. The cane stood out from his trench coat and heavy motorcycle boots, which were the major accent pieces to his black, straight-legged jeans and white muscle shirt. He had a big chest, broad and well muscled. His hair flowed down to his shoulders in great blond waves.

The fact he was in his forties didn't hurt him at all. I waved as we swung by, parking across the lot in the only open space, and Anezka practically unscrewed her neck craning around to look at him.

"Is that him?" she asked.

She pulled the visor down and began fussing with her hair, which was not helping in the least. If she wasn't so damn desperate it would be comical.

"Yeah, that's him," I said, patting her on the knee. "Take a breath."

He walked across the lot to meet us, the cane not slowing him down a bit. I climbed out of the car, shut the door with my hip, and waved at him. He grinned, strode toward me, and engulfed me in a huge bear hug.

"How the hell are you?" he rumbled.

I bit my cheek to keep from crying again. "Doing okay," I mumbled into his shoulder. He pushed me back, his hands on my arms, looking at me. He grabbed my right arm, holding it up, checking out the scars where I'd been burned to the bone by dragon fire, months earlier.

"Surprised, but very glad to see this has healed up so well," he said. His voice was a bit husky there. Pain and worry painted his face for a second; then he laughed and pulled me into a hug once again. "Katie tells us you decided on knitting to work the hand."

I grimaced and he smiled.

"Too girly for you?"

"I prefer fire and steel," I said, pouting.

He laughed, holding me there. After a second, we stepped apart, and he wiped at his eyes. "Stuart and I thought we may need to come out and beat your ass," he said, smiling. "When are you coming back to Black Briar?"

I must've grimaced, because he sighed and shook his head. "Stubborn as always," he said. He pulled me around, wrapping one arm across my shoulder, and walked us both around the car. We went a little slower than I expected. Maybe he did need that cane still.

Anezka stood there, flipping one stray hair out of her face, and shuffling from one foot to another.

"And this beauty must be Anezka."

What a charmer.

He dropped his arm from my shoulder, stepped forward, and held out his hand. When she reached out to shake his, he took hers, turned it over, bowed deeply, and kissed the back of her hand.

Fear and rapture flushed across her face for the briefest of moments, and then she giggled. He was grinning before he straightened up.

"Pleased to make your acquaintance," he said.

She curtsied, which should have looked ridiculous in her jeans and sweatshirt, but there was an innocence and a beauty there that shone through. They stared at one another for a long bit, and I finally cleared my throat loudly.

"I'm hungry," I said, overblown.

Gunther turned and held his elbow to Anezka. She winked at me, took his arm with both of hers, and strutted toward the restaurant, with a spring in her step that was nothing like the Anezka I'd come to know.

I rolled my eyes out of reflex and followed behind them. This was going to be a long breakfast.

Once inside, Gunther held out a chair for Anezka, then me. It was gallant and old-fashioned in a way that wasn't creepy. Under most circumstances I'd have given him crap about it, but Anezka was eating up the attention.

We ordered eggs, ham and bacon, pancakes, and plenty of hot coffee. By the time the food came, Gunther and Anezka were laughing like old friends.

I sipped my ice water and watched them, wondering if I should just find another table.

Once the food arrived, however, it was down to business.

"Sarah says you know your motorcycles," Anezka said as she poured hot sauce over her eggs.

Gunther shrugged. "Been riding since I was a kid, tinker around with them when I get a chance."

"He's being modest," I said. "He's good with engines and making things run."

"I like a man who is good with his hands," Anezka said, reaching for the salt and pepper.

Gunther winked at me as she dusted her eggs with pepper, and I almost choked. Totally soap-opera time. It was cute, though. Didn't think I'd need any syrup for my pancakes at this rate.

Not soon enough, our plates were empty and we were settling down to drink our coffee and chat. The earlier hangover seemed to have faded from Anezka and she appeared much more relaxed.

Gunther picked up the check. As he was paying, Anezka leaned over to me. "I should probably ride with him, show him how to get out to my place, don't you think?"

Oh, dear lord.

I smiled at her and patted her arm. "Good idea. The directions would be pretty iffy . . . what with that one sudden turn, right off of Highway 2 onto 209."

She giggled again, slapped at my hand, and stood up. "I'll go tell him," she said.

I drank my coffee and watched her walk up to him as he paid. He stood a good foot or more taller than Anezka, so she had to look up at him, but she had her serious flirt on. If he hadn't been so damn flirty himself, I'd feel sorry for him.

I'd never seen Gunther like this. Only time I really saw him was at Black Briar events, and most of those he was running with Stuart. "The twins," as we called the two of them, were the backbone of Black Briar. Jimmy led the group, sure, but the Twins were the dynamic force. Maggie and Susan Hirsch had been another pair of players equally as personable and supporting, but they'd been killed by the dragon, horrible deaths that still haunted my dreams.

Gunther and Anezka rolled back laughing, and it seemed disrespectful all of a sudden.

Gunther dropped two fives on the table and waved from me to the door. "Shall we?"

I stood up, drained the last of my coffee, and set the empty cup on the table.

"Good idea," I said, and headed to the door. There was definitely something dark in today's mood, despite the way they carried on. I could feel it.

He held the door for her as she climbed into his truck. They both waved at me as they started off, like I couldn't see them.

I followed them in the Taurus. At least Anezka sat against the door and not right up against Gunther, but she was turned toward him, talking and laughing the whole way. Maybe he'd put the cane in the seat between them, just to be safe. Made me smile.

Bub was going to have kittens.

# Thirty-nine

GUNTHER DID HAVE A DAY GIG THAT HE NEEDED TO GET TO, so we really and truly needed to just look at the motorcycle when we got back to Anezka's place. Keep it simple. No sweat, right?

I pulled up behind them in my traditional parking place across from her spread. Gunther stood beside his truck, leaning on his cane and eyeballing the place like it was haunted, though I don't think Anezka noticed at first. She was halfway across the road, rattling on about something or other, when she finally realized that Gunther had stopped dead in his tracks. He was sniffing the air when I got out of my car and walked over to him.

"You feel it, too?"

He glanced at me, straightened his jacket, and nodded.

"Starts about where she's standing," I said quietly, pointing at Anezka.

She stood there, crossing her arms and watching us. I didn't know if she felt it or not. I'd never asked her, which in hindsight seemed like a fairly dumbass move on my part.

Gunther walked forward slowly, setting the cane down with deliberate force, like he was afraid the road was slippery. He paused at the barrier and then pushed onward, carefully, like he was walking into the surf. I followed, felt the usual pressure as I crossed over into her domain, and let the uneasy feeling settle over me once again.

"First the bike," Gunther said, smiling despite his obvious worry. "Then I would like to discuss a couple of other things."

Anezka looked at him sideways, a petulant tilt to her smile. "Then, maybe we can discuss dinner sometime."

Gotta hand it to her. She swung for the fence.

Gunther's rich baritone laughter rolled over us, and the palpable malaise that surrounded the place faded measurably. "Deal," he said and walked into the carport.

I parked myself on one of the empty oil drums she hadn't cannibalized yet and watched as she unburied the bike. It looked like I remembered—long and sleek, with unexpected power and raw energy. Kinda like sex, only in red, black, and chrome. I had a serious hankering to open that beast up on the highway—let the wind wash over me at crazy speed— feel her purring between my thighs.

Man, was it just me, or did things get a little fuzzy there for a moment?

I may have moaned. Anezka and Gunther both looked at me, confused.

I cleared my throat. "Don't mind me."

The official inspection began with the fanfare one would expect of a Viking jazz mechanic: after much harrumphing and a few ah-has, Gunther slapped his big hands together and shook his head at us with a *tsking* reproach.

"Criminal," he admonished us, "to let a fine piece of machinery like this be so neglected." He walked across the driveway, turned back, and held one hand up. "Don't touch anything," he said. Then he hurried over to his truck and grabbed a box of tools and a charger. Obviously he had some practice, carrying the tools in one hand while he kept his balance with the cane, but I think he was just showing off.

He hooked up a battery charger and began tinkering with some valve or other, checked the oil, even tested the gas in the tank with a dipstick thingy he kept around for such purposes.

Anezka sidled over to me, leaned against my drum, and whispered sotto voce: "He's dreamy."

No way he didn't hear, but we all pretended.

"She's in pretty good shape," he announced after a final cursory inventory. "Needs some work, but I think I can get her humming pretty well."

This time, she waited until he was taking the tools back to his truck before she mentioned how he could make her hum anytime. I mean, seriously.

The charger did its job, and he cranked the bike over. It sputtered and coughed at first, but he revved the engine over and over until the idle smoothed out and the bike didn't actually rattle apart, despite early indications.

"Injectors are seriously clogged," he said, wiping his hands on a rag. "New battery, and I'll have to check out the chain drive, brakes, coolant, the whole nine yards."

The more he said, the worse I felt. "Bad?" I asked.

He laughed again. "Nothing critical at this point," he said, smiling at me. "She's a smoking hot ride."

I elbowed Anezka before she could say anything, but the way she choked, I could tell she was dying to.

"Anyhoo," he said, cutting off the engine, "I think I can have her up and running in a few days."

"So I should buy her?" I asked, glancing between him and Anezka.

"Depends on price," he said. "But I'd be willing to bet you'd get a good deal."

"Offer stands," Anezka said with a nod of her head. "Three hundred firm."

Gunther coughed. "Okay, that's seriously undervalued. What am I not seeing?"

Anezka shook her head. "Just friend's discount, that's all."

I looked at her—no use lying to Gunther. He knew there was more to the story. "Old lover, bad blood," I said, shrugging. "Don't want to inherit any bad karma, but it fits my budget."

"Can't argue with that," Gunther said, looking past us into the smithy. "What's his take on the whole deal?"

Anezka and I both turned at once. Bub sat on top of the brick forge, preening.

Gunther hadn't even batted an eye. Was the whole world in on the joke?

I mean, he'd seen the dragon, and the giants, trolls, ogres . . . hell, he knew about dwarves long before I did, but how could he be so unfazed by all of it?

"Bub lives here," Anezka said, making it a challenge—territorial all of a sudden.

The thing about protecting a territory is that you lock yourself in, by keeping everyone else out. That likely explained the barrier we felt crossing onto the property. Between her and Bub, they'd built such a wall around them that it had become physical.

"At least this one isn't a simpering git," Bub cawed from the other room.

"I assume he means me," Gunther said, amused.

I looked from one to another. Anezka was about three seconds from fleeing inside the house. Panic covered her face in scarlet blossoms.

Bub was arrogant and demonic, but that was how he always seemed.

"My, my," Gunther drawled, slipping his thumbs into his belt and stepping between Anezka and Bub. "So this is the beastie that's been hurting you for so long?"

Anezka opened her mouth but didn't say anything.

He stepped into the smithy, pressing in on Bub's domain. "Not quite what I expected under the circumstances, but I guess even the runt of the litter can find a home."

"Bite me, old man," Bub said, rising on his toes and snapping his jaws together with a *clack*. "You're not the boss of me."

Gunther flourished his left hand, his fingers crooked in a specific way I couldn't make out, and called in a booming voice: "Fljúg burt, þú eldskepna!"

There was a sonic implosion, and Bub vanished.

Anezka shrieked and swooned. I slid from the barrel and caught her before she hit the ground. What had happened?

"That won't keep him away for long," Gunther said, turning back to us. "But I'd rather not deal with his kind." He turned to Anezka and shook his head sadly. "How long have you suffered this creature's presence?"

She struggled upright, shaking. "Suffered?" she squalled. Anger rolled over her like a tidal wave. "What did you do to him? How dare you?"

She pushed away from me and threw a haymaker at Gunther's head.

He stepped back, deflected the blow, passing it in front of him, and channeled her energy away to the left.

She stumbled with the strength of her swing and nearly fell. He caught her under her arms and hoisted her back to her feet, being careful to step back when she had her feet under her.

And, of course, she spun around and swung at him again. This time she landed an uppercut to his midsection. It was hard enough that Gunther grunted and bent with the force of the blow. Anezka fell to her knees, holding her wrist.

"Oof," he said, rubbing his stomach. "Need to make a strong fist if you are going to hit someone, though." He held out a hand to her.

She slapped his hand away from her and stood on her own. For a second I thought she was going to hit him again. Instead, she stormed into the house crying.

He looked at me a moment and quirked his mouth into a grin. "That went well."

"You made her kobold disappear. How did you expect her to react?"

He shrugged. "He'll be back. She's got something here that is tying him to this place."

That I knew. "Amulet. In the house. Ancient family heirloom."

"That explains several things, actually," he said, stepping toward the house and watching the door like she might come out with a gun.

Which reminded me . . . "She has a shotgun."

"She's not gonna shoot me," he said, smiling. "I'd love to see that amulet sometime." He glanced over at me and sighed. "And we were getting along so well."

"Gee, ya think? Any more and I was gonna ask you two to get a room."

He laughed at that. "I'm sure she has a room here," he said, grinning. "But I don't know her that well yet. And," he waved his hand to take in the smithy, "there is the issue of the demon."

"Kobold," I corrected him. "Nothing particularly Christian about him."

"Interesting choice of words," he said. "Christians weren't the first to encounter such creatures. They've been around a lot longer than Jesus Christ and his ilk."

His ilk? Now, I didn't know a lot about Gunther's background. I knew he'd grown up in a Jesuit orphanage until middle school. Not much beyond that. "What did you say to him?"

"Just commanded him to leave. He's a minor beastie, after all. I couldn't ask one of his bigger cousins to just vanish without something to back it up."

"Pretty impressive," I said, leaning against my barrel and looking up into his wide face. "How come you're not bothered by this?"

"Bothered? Who said I'm not bothered? Holy lug nuts, this is freak city."

I looked around the place, trying to see what he saw. "Okay, besides Bub there, and the energy barrier which surrounds this place, what else?"

"See those beams?" He pointed up to the rough-hewn logs that made up the roof support of the carport. "They connect the smithy to the house."

I looked up. Hadn't really noticed them before. There were images carved there, runes and dancing figures. Demons, women, fire, mayhem.

"She goes to Burning Man a lot," I offered, as if that mattered.

"That doesn't surprise me," he said, walking back a few steps to look at the other side of one of the huge beams. "These are not too out of place with a fire wielder." He looked directly at me, a wicked gleam in his eye. "One who commands the flame to work the earth."

"Smithing, you mean?"

"Aye, and more. You are kindred spirits, I think."

I could see how we both had anger issues alike. We were both passionate about life, and other things. I thought back to the spring, when I'd gotten totally hammered and did that bit of dirty dancing with a couple of cowboys. Anezka wasn't the only one who let herself get out of control.

"Point taken."

"Some nice carving there," he said, pointing to an elaborate bacchanal depiction of drinking and debauchery. Caligula and orgies came to mind.

"So, yeah. That and . . ." He studied me a moment, then shrugged. "She's pretty damaged."

"Well, you were sure flirting hot and heavy there."

"She's striking. And totally reciprocating, if I'm not mistaken. Besides, I said she was damaged, not broken."

That pretty much described me, I thought. "So, she thinks, or thought—before you iced her buddy—that you two were gonna hook up."

He smiled, sheepishly. "She's a fascinating woman, that's for sure." He stared off into space for a moment, contemplating something, and I left him to his reverie. I couldn't tell what he was calculating, or what music was in his head, but after a few seconds he smiled at me, then turned around a full circle—taking in the smithy, the house, the detritus, and sculptures. "There is much here to understand."

"So, you taking her on as a project?" I wasn't sure how I felt about all this. My head was beginning to hurt, and the secrets were thick. "I have to work with her."

"Have to? Don't you have a choice in the matter? You are not without skills and means."

I narrowed my eyes, letting the heat flush my cheeks. "I'm just an apprentice. I can't work without a master. I have to do things right."

He didn't look convinced.

"There are rules, you know? Obligations to fulfill."

"I see." He tapped the cane on the ground three times, and then hobbled over to the back edge of the carport, looking out over the dragon statue. "We use the word *obligation* to define our debts to another."

The sun was high over the mountains by now, moving toward midday.

"These are scores kept in our hearts, and are of no consequence to anyone but ourselves."

*Uh-oh.* Now we were treading into different territory. I didn't want a lecture on Black Briar, or Julie, dragons, fear, fire . . . damn it. The list was long.

"Jimmy doesn't blame you," he said, his voice gentle and quiet. "He's hurting and scared. Hell, we all are. Sarah, you do not understand the magnitude of what you've done."

"So it's my fault!" *And* I was crying again. When the hell had this started? I think it was this place; the energy here sucked.

He turned from the view of the mountains and opened his arms to me.

I stepped forward and let him engulf me in a hug once again. It felt good to put my head on his shoulder. Made me miss my Da all of a sudden.

"No, you misunderstand," he said, making shushing sounds.

After a second, I pushed away from him, wiping my face. "I'm not sorry I killed Jean-Paul."

"No, and nor should you be. But you have opened yourself and others to a world that has been hidden from most of us for eons."

"I killed Bub once already, did you know that?" I asked, feeling hysteria huddling along the edges of my brain. "Bashed his head in with a fire extinguisher, and he came back to discuss it."

"You did what I did, really. Only with a little more force. He's not really here, not truly. If you saw his true form, it would likely drive you mad."

Here we were, discussing demons and dragons in Anezka's carport like we were still discussing the motorcycle. I couldn't take it.

"Gunther. You know I think the world of you, and Stuart . . . and . . ." I took a deep breath, keeping it together. "And Jimmy."

"But?"

"But I can't have this conversation here. It feels wrong."

"Can't argue with that."

"I need to see if Anezka's going to be okay. I need to get my work life back in order, get Julie out of my apartment, and try to have a normal life. Hell, I've run into freakier things than Bub in the past couple of weeks—things that would curl your short hairs."

"Maybe you should come to Black Briar and discuss it."

"Not today. Today, I need to fix this. Maybe salvage something, help her get on her feet."

"You take too much onto yourself, you know that, right?"

I sighed, letting the stress flow out of me like Sa Bum Nim Choi had taught me when I was a kid. Letting my shoulders sag, loosening the muscles in my back and neck. "Look. I'm in over my head."

"Amen to that," he said, smiling. "Sarah, the world is a chaotic place. The dragons are aroused—"

"Eww . . ."

He gave me a stern look, and I settled back on my heels, hands in my back pockets. That look could really burn a layer or two off the top.

"And the gods are stirring again," I offered.

"I think I'd be careful about what I discussed here," he said quietly. "Alliances are not always what they seem."

Bub claimed kinship to the dragons. Maybe Anezka felt that extended to her. I nodded. "She needs people, a way to connect to the real world. Might as well be me."

"She does amazing work," he said, pointing across the yard. "Very talented."

"You don't think Bub had anything to do with that?"

He considered it a minute. "He's a creature of fire. If anything, he could help inspire her, but the value would be offset by the volatility. Passion is a double-edged knife, as I'm sure you know."

Boy, howdy.

"I hope I never end up like this," I said. "Scares the hell out of me."

"You are young. Life is full of excitement, and . . ." he nodded past me. "Motorcycles. I'm sure Katie will be very impressed."

"You think so?" I asked. I hadn't considered that. Honest. Suddenly my head was filled with thoughts of her snuggled up behind me, holding on as we sped through the night. I smiled. That was a welcome fantasy.

"Tend to your friend," he said, laughing again. "But do not make her any promises, and don't be surprised if she is angry when I leave."

"What about the bike?"

"We'll load it into the truck, and I'll take it over to Black Briar to work on it. Maybe you can come by this week and pick it up?"

He had the ramps in the back of his truck already. Man came prepared. He rode the Ducati into his truck without much effort. It ran for shit, but it ran long enough to get up the incline. Man had guts; I was sure it was going to fall off.

"Ask her about the carvings," he said after he'd turned the truck around and was pointing toward town. "Her friend Bub didn't carve those. There's something else going on here."

I climbed up on the running board, hanging onto his mirror. "You betcha," I said, patting his arm. I leaned in and kissed his cheek.

"Ya'll play nice," he said.

I jumped down and waved as he drove away. Now to face Anezka and her craziness. I scuffed my boots as I crossed the road. Wonder how long it would take for Bub to get back this time?

# Forty

I LET MYSELF INTO THE HOUSE. I COULD HEAR HER IN ONE OF the back rooms, crying.

"Anezka? Are you okay?"

She grew quiet but didn't say anything. I listened intently for the sound of a cocking shotgun, but didn't hear it. I wandered down the hall, glancing in each room, looking for her.

Opposite the bathroom was the laundry room, jammed full of boxes, like someone who was halfway between moving . . . coming or going.

Past that were two rooms opposite one another. The door on the right was closed, but on the left, I could hear her. The door was slightly ajar, so I pushed it open with my foot.

She sat on the edge of the bed, the shotgun in her hands all right, but she was putting the muzzle in her mouth.

"Holy shit," I said, diving toward her. She had her shoes off, trying to reach for the trigger with her toes. I yanked her to the side, and the shotgun went off.

I couldn't hear anything for a minute, but I rolled off her and pushed the gun away. She lay on the ground, sobbing, her arms covering her head.

There was no blood. But she'd blown a serious hole in the side of her house.

"Are you out of your fucking mind?" I shouted, pushing myself back onto my heels. I held my hands against my ears. "Anezka, seriously."

She looked up at me, her face smeared with mascara, snot, and tears.

"Fuck you," she shouted and launched herself on me.

I fell back as she pummeled me with both fists, more a tantrum than actual fighting. Hurt like hell, though, and she was stronger than I was.

She tried to pin me beneath her. I rolled to the side, smashing against a dresser and hurting my hip. She knew what she was doing and had the element of surprise.

For a moment she was on top of me, in full control. I squirmed, trying to get my legs free of the dresser and her weight. There were several things she could do to me in that position, and most of them resulted in me with something broken or otherwise maimed.

"Get off!" I bucked, trying to dislodge her weight, but she flattened herself on top of me, dropping her full weight on my chest.

It knocked the wind right out of me. I saw stars for a second and loosened my grip on her arms. She moved like a trained fighter, getting one arm under my neck and grabbing her wrist with her other hand.

Any second now, she would slide her arm down my side and crank my neck into a very uncomfortable position. I kicked out, knocking several things off her dresser. She head-butted me.

I blacked out for a second, and things got really weird.

She let go. Just like that. One moment the anger and fire were so hot inside her that I could feel it all around me—an aura of hate and carnage. Then she went limp, whimpering, and rolled off me.

"What's happening?" she whispered, turning her head away from me.

I lay beside her, gasping for air, wondering when she was going to grab something really heavy and bash in my head.

When she didn't, I sat up, pushing away from her, and rocked against the dresser again. A bottle rolled to the edge and dropped off the side, pinging me on the head.

She ran out of the room. The next second I could hear her vomiting in the bathroom next door. I leveraged myself up, trying not to knock anything else off the dresser while keeping pressure on the throbbing pain in my head. I glanced around and saw a heavy perfume bottle on the floor. Mystery solved. Once I was steady on my feet, I looked in the mirror, which was askew. Of course I was bleeding. My hand and the hair under it were matted with blood. I reached out and touched the mirror with my bloody hand to straighten it, and the surface roiled like boiling water.

"Jesus H. Christ." I stepped back

"Pretty mouth," Gletts said, appearing in the mirror. "I thought we'd never find you."

I stumbled back as he and Skella climbed through the mirror.

This day just kept getting better.

# Forty-one

"We wondered where you disappeared to," Skella said, stepping to the doorway and hugging the side of the doorframe. Anezka was still puking.

Gletts bent over, one long finger out reaching for the shotgun. I pulled him back. "Don't touch that."

"Nasty bit of work, that one," he said. I glanced down and saw the stock was carved with fiery faces.

I pulled the blanket off Anezka's bed and tossed it over the shotgun. "Just leave it, okay?"

Gletts shrugged and sat down on the edge of the bed, away from the gun. He pulled a Rubik's Cube out of his fanny pack and started twisting the sides frenetically.

"What are you doing here?" I asked.

"We've been looking for you all day," he said, not looking up. "Skella insisted."

"How'd you find me?"

Skella glanced at Gletts furtively, but did not answer.

"Just thought you might be here," he said, again not looking up. "Been here before, back about a year ago. Dwarves had some business here."

"For the dragon," Skella said quietly. "But I couldn't find you in this place. It's blocked to me."

Gletts smiled. "You'll find it now that you've been here."

Skella let out a shuddering sigh. "Creeps me out."

I looked over at her. She smiled at me and turned back to the hall. The toilet flushed, and she scampered back into the room, ducking down beside the dresser. "Don't let her see us."

"Great."

I walked out to the hallway, pulling the bedroom door mostly closed, and tried to get a good angle view into the bathroom.

"Anezka? You okay?"

"No," she moaned.

I hurried to the bathroom and saw her lying on the floor by the tub. She was covered in blood.

"What did you do?" I cried, rushing in to her.

"Something's wrong with the baby," she said, sobbing.

Baby? She's pregnant?

What the fuck?

I grabbed a towel off the rack and reached for my cell phone. It wasn't in my pocket. Where the hell had I left it? Restaurant? No time. I handed her the towel. "Here."

She looked at me, confused, and took the towel.

"Don't move," I said, and I ran out into the living room. "Where's your damn phone?"

She had a phone, right?

I couldn't find one. We needed an ambulance.

Or, I could take her in my car? Not the best idea. An ambulance was the only way, with that much blood. And I knew who could get me one.

I ran back down the hall, stopping and kneeling by Anezka. "Hold on," I said, touching the side of her face. "I'll get help."

"Okay," she whispered. "I'm getting cold."

This was nuts.

"Skella!" I shouted.

"Who?" Anezka asked, looking around.

"Skella, get in here now!"

"Eep," Skella said, skidding around the doorframe and stopping when she saw us on the floor. "Oh, crap."

"I need you or Gletts to get an ambulance. Tell them she's pregnant and bleeding. You hear me?"

"We can't," she started, but I gave her a look that I hope scared her future children.

"Right," she said, and darted back out of the room.

"You'll be okay," I said to Anezka. "I'll make sure you're okay."

No promises, Gunther had said. What the hell else could I say?

Soon, Skella was back in the room, rinsing a washcloth in the sink and handing it to me. "Gletts has gone off to find help," she said sheepishly. "Sorry for how that works out."

I glanced up at her. "Meaning?"

She shrugged. "We can only see people in mirrors we know of, and can only travel to them if they are around one of them. He's at your apartment now. Your master, Julie. She knows where you are, right?"

Oh, jeebus. Great. "She should, but he knows to tell her I'm at Anezka's, right?"

"Well, he knows you are at a house, and it's full of pain," she said apologetically. "We don't know Anezka."

"I'm Anezka," Anezka growled from the floor. "Who the fuck are you, and when did you get here?"

Skella squeaked and scampered back toward the bedroom.

"Friend of yours?" Anezka asked through gritted teeth.

"It's complicated," I told her. "Just hold on."

It took the ambulance another thirty minutes to get out to the house. By the time they arrived, Anezka had slipped into unconsciousness.

When the volunteer firefighters pounded into the house, I was sitting on the bathroom floor with her head in my lap. We were both soaked in blood. She had a pulse, but it was weak.

I mentioned a baby and miscarriage, and they didn't ask any more questions.

By the time they got an IV in her and called in her vitals, the chopper arrived.

It was one of those medical jobbies. I shaded my eyes as it landed, stirring up gravel and dust in its rotor wash.

The firefighters loaded Anezka into the chopper and scurried back toward the house as it lifted off again. She'd be in Redmond in no time.

"She's stabilized," the middle-aged firefighter said as he set a kit on the porch beside me and bent over to look at my scalp. "But before they loaded her, she wanted me to tell you she expected you to keep an eye on things around here."

I looked at him. "She said that?"

He nodded. "She was quite insistent. Said you'd know what needed looking after. She got a cat or something?"

"Something," I mumbled. Great.

"Ya'll fight?" he asked as he poked at my head.

"You could say that," I said, wincing. "Could you tell them she tried to kill herself?"

He stood back, eyeing me. "Thought it was a miscarriage."

I nodded. "That's what she said, but before that I had to stop her from blowing her head off."

His partner walked over to us, and my guy stepped away. I caught a glimpse of his name sewn onto his shirt. Jerry. The other guy, about thirty and stocky, like a football player, was Mitch.

They talked a minute; then Mitch walked over to their truck and got on the radio. Jerry cleaned the cut on my head and closed the wound with two butterfly stitches.

"Keep that clean and dry for a few days," he said. "And you

should be fine. The cut wasn't too deep, but you might want to check with your doctor, just in case."

"Thanks." I touched the wound carefully. "I'm sure I'll be fine."

"Try not to touch it," he said, shaking his head. He watched me for a second. "I guess you are the new girl Anezka has working for her, huh?"

I looked at him, wondering who knew what in these parts. "Just for a while," I said. "My current gig is on hiatus."

"I remember you," he said, snapping his fingers. "You pulled those people from that fire in the spring. Out north of Gold Bar, where all those people died making that movie."

Great. Just what I needed, publicity. "Was a bad time."

"Yeah, for sure."

Mitch came up with a clipboard and asked me a few questions for their records. Then they packed up and headed back to Leavenworth.

I sat on her stoop and watched them drive away, my blood-soaked jeans congealing into a cold and nasty mess.

A nice hot shower and some clean clothes sounded like a good idea. I'd clean up her place, maybe patch the hole in her wall so critters and weather didn't get in. Then, I'd see about getting a hold of Julie, then Gunther, and eventually Katie. God, it felt like I hadn't seen her in a year.

I was across the road pulling my pack with my spare clothes out of the trunk when Skella started screaming.

What in the living hell was going on now?

# Forty-two

BUB WAS BACK. HE HAD SKELLA PINNED IN THE KITCHEN, snapping at her with his massive jaws. She was up on the table, about to throw a salt shaker at him, when I burst in the door.

"Don't bother," I said, storming into the kitchen. "He'll just eat it."

He turned to me, hissing and baring his bajillion teeth.

I swung my pack as hard as I could, catching him upside the head and flinging him across the room to smash into the refrigerator. Before he could rise, I stomped on his head. Squish, and Bub was dead again. He must be tired of this by now.

The little bastard managed to put a bite into the sole of my Doc Martens, though. Damn it all. I sat on the floor beside his already-bubbling corpse and pulled my boot off. They were soaked in blood as well, and the sole was ruined.

Good thing I had sneakers in my spare-clothes kit. But those were my favorite boots. This I was not going to forgive.

"Okay, now I know where you've been disappearing to lately," Skella said, looking over the edge of the table at Bub's frothing corpse. "There's some seriously dangerous magic around here."

"Gee, ya think?" I said, pulling off my other boot and climbing to my feet.

She slowly climbed down off the table and edged around the

room toward the door, keeping what remained of Bub in close view.

"Really weird shit," she mumbled and bolted across the living room and back to the bedroom.

I stood in the kitchen and stripped off my jeans. For the time being, I shoved them in the sink, along with my socks. Finally, I just said to hell with it, and stripped off my shirt, and added it to the stinking pile. My bra was unscathed, thankfully, so I left it on. After I washed my hands I'd take it off.

I padded across the living room, shut the front door, and went into the bathroom. I knew there was a washing machine somewhere here.

"Skella?"

"What," a frightened voice called from the bedroom.

I stepped out into the hall and down toward the bedroom. Skella was looking in the mirror. "You leaving?" I asked, annoyed.

"No," she said. "Looking for Gletts. He knows about blood magic. I don't like the dark stuff."

Blood magic. I glanced down at my soiled hands. How much trouble were we in? Pieces tumbled in my head, connections fell into place. "Is this related to the mead and Ari?"

She sat on the edge of the bed and dropped her hand in her lap. "Gletts is better able to talk about all this," she said with a sigh. "Some of the dwarves worked with the dragon. Their loyalty was rewarded; power was gained."

I could tell she was scared, but this rang in my head, a resonance with Odin's warnings. "Blood magic," a chill ran through me. The connection here, this place, Justin, Flora, Anezka . . . Was there some connection to the mead? "How did you find me here?" I asked. "You said you couldn't see me."

"It was Gletts," she said, studying her hands. "He knows some tricks."

"Tricks?"

For a minute, she looked embarrassed. "He did something the dwarves taught him, a little thing to help find someone. The more powerful they are, the easier it is."

"That explains a few things."

"But this place," she said, looking around. "This place is bad. He knew about it, was surprised you were here."

Coincidence? It made my brain hurt. I hated coincidences, and this was a big one. "Is Anezka connected to all this?"

"No, like I said, we don't know Anezka. It was the man. He's not here any longer."

"Justin?"

She shrugged. "Jean-Paul had dealings with him."

I staggered back. "Holy fuck."

She looked embarrassed. "It's something about this place. There is power here. Can't you feel the taint of it?"

I could. "Yes, it's palpable."

"I thought the world would be better after you killed Jean-Paul. But it's still just as big a mess."

I'd had a sheltered life compared to hers, Christ. And I thought my problems with Da were bad. "It's better. He's dead. Life goes on."

She didn't look convinced. "I just wish Gletts would hurry up."

"He'll be back." I was getting cold. "In the meantime, do you know how to operate a washing machine?"

She cocked her hip at me, turning for the first time and seeing me in nothing but my bra and panties. "Nice," she said, averting her eyes. "Do you have to be naked?"

"You and Gletts watched us in the shower, watched us making love," I said angrily. "So suck it up. I'm taking a shower. Do you think you could find the washing machine?"

"Fine," she said, keeping her eyes covered. "But if that thing comes back, I'm leaving."

"It will take him a while," I said, nearly laughing. "Besides, you came here for a reason, and I, for one, can't wait to find out what it is."

"Oh, right," she said, turning to me, nakedness forgotten. "They've taken my people to a new place. Someplace we didn't know existed. I'm pretty sure it was a prison for when some of the dwarves worked for the dragon."

"Crap."

"Yeah, and moved the boy as well."

"He's not dead?"

She shook her head. "No, they've been bleeding him, trying to use him like a blood bank. They've made a small batch of the potion for samples."

Damn. That was out of control. "Do you have any leads as to where they've gone?"

She just shook her head. I could tell how scared she was. I wanted to dislike her, but there was something about the way she was so earnest and vulnerable.

I felt like the queen of the island of misfit toys.

"Let me try and get the blood off the floor in the bathroom, take a shower, and dress in something that doesn't smell like death. You find the washer, and we'll try and salvage her towels."

"Okay, then we make a plan, right?"

I bobbed my head. "Right. A plan."

The bathroom wasn't that big, but there was a lot of blood on the floor. I used one of the already-soaked towels to mop up the floor, and then I rinsed it in the toilet. When you're covered in someone else, toilets aren't really that icky.

Once the blood was all off the floor, I climbed into the shower.

Later I'd find some bleach and mop the place, hit the walls and tub, toilet and sink. Right now, I just wanted it off my skin.

I shucked off my panties and bra, laid them across the back of the toilet, and climbed in the steaming hot shower.

The water ran cold long before I felt clean, but the blood had stopped running out of my hair and off my body. I'd have to check the butterfly stitches later, but I didn't think any of the blood was fresh.

Once I was done and dressed, Skella and I loaded up the washing machine with towels and ran it on heavy-duty load. Then we went into the living room and waited for someone to show up. Julie, Gletts, Bub, someone. Either way, I wasn't going anywhere until I got some answers.

# Forty-three

THING ABOUT WAITING IS, I CAN'T JUST SIT AND DO NOTH-ing. Within fifteen minutes, I had Skella mopping the bathroom and I was out in the smithy looking for boards and nails to cover the hole Anezka had blown in her bedroom wall.

She had everything I needed. I set up her ladder and was just finishing nailing a piece of plywood over the hole when Bub found his way back.

He was on the roof above my head, pissed and not taking any chances. Luckily he didn't consider pushing the ladder over.

"We need to talk," he said.

I looked up to find him sitting on the eave, his feet dangling over the edge.

"Seriously," he mewled. "And stop killing me."

I finished hammering in the last couple of nails and climbed back down the ladder. He followed me along the roof as I walked into the carport. Anezka had a huge roll of plastic sheeting in there, so I used a zip knife to cut off a good-sized square and picked up a heavy-duty staple gun off the shelf by her freezer. She likely did her own weatherproofing in the winter. Wind must be a bitch up here in the mountains.

"Will you talk to me if I promise not to hurt your prissy friend inside?" Bub asked, scampering along the roof as I walked back to the ladder.

I aimed the stapler at him and pulled the trigger. The staple flew at him with no more force than a light breeze. It didn't even make it to the edge of the roof.

"You ruined my favorite boots," I growled as I climbed up the ladder.

"Gee, and you keep smashing my head," he said, edging away from the ladder in general. "I think you bear the greater weight of sin."

I stapled the first corner of the plastic onto the side of the house and looked up at him. "Let's play a game, shall we?"

He twisted his head this way and that. "I'm listening."

I shot several more staples into the plastic, trying to create a tight seam. The eave would prevent most of the water from getting in, but I wanted to do a good job. At least until we could fix it up right.

"I'll ask a question, and you give me a straight answer."

He nodded, but before he could say anything, I fired six more staples into the house, closing off the top and left side.

"If you answer them to my satisfaction, we keep playing." *Pop-pop* went the staples. "If you piss me off, or lie to me, or in any way do something that I disagree with—"

I slammed the staple gun against the house with three loud staccato bursts.

"—then I send you back to Múspell with my regards."

He watched me but didn't say a word. I continued working on the plastic. When I finished, I climbed down the ladder, brought it down, and carried it and the staple gun back to the carport.

"Deal," he said, dropping off the roof and landing behind me. "But do you think I could get something to eat? It takes a lot out of me, this gruesome death and spectacular rebirth cycle."

I nodded toward the house. "Within reason."

"Can you cook something? Something greasy, maybe. Like a cheeseburger?"

I glared at him. "Last time you had a burger, you went a little crazy and tried to eat me."

"Good point," he said, slouching. "Maybe just a fried egg?"

"That we can accomplish . . . as long as she has eggs in her fridge."

As soon as I opened the side door from the carport, Skella came out of the bedroom. "Doesn't look bad from this side—" she was looking back over her shoulder, into the bedroom, and only turned toward us when the room was no longer in view. She stopped in her tracks and squeaked.

"Get a grip," I barked. "He just needs some food . . ."

She took a step back toward the bedroom, blanching.

"Oh, grow a pair," I said. "He's not going to eat you." I glared down at him. He seemed shorter, smaller in stature. "Right, Bub?"

He bobbed his head. "That is the deal."

I rolled my eyes at Skella and walked into the kitchen. Christ, I was surrounded by screwups and pansies.

I made fried egg sandwiches, which Skella refused to touch. Bub was good with that, eating hers and the entire jar of mayonnaise, jar included.

Once we cleaned up and were settled into the living room again, I found Anezka's phone. Or at least her cell phone. It was jammed into a ficus by the front door.

I called Katie. Time to get things straightened out. She didn't answer, but Julie did.

"Hey, we're in Katie's car heading to Evergreen."

Excellent. Good to have somebody see after Anezka while I took care of a few things here.

"How long until you get there?"

She covered the phone, and I heard Katie saying something in the background. She sounded pissed.

"About fifteen minutes. Katie wants to know if you're okay."

"I said she was fine," I heard Gletts say from inside the car.

"Sarah?" Katie yelled into the cell phone. Julie must've put it on speaker. "Are you hurt, or under any duress?"

"I'm fine. Things are a little nutso, but I'm here with Skella."

I looked over at Bub, who just shrugged.

"And a friend of Anezka's. Gunther's met him."

Bub hissed when I mentioned Gunther's name, but he didn't move.

"Can you meet us at the hospital, or do we need to come get you?"

Skella nodded, but Bub just shrugged. I covered the phone, "What?" I asked him.

"I'd rather not," he said.

"It's complicated," I said into the phone. "Give me thirty minutes and I'll head that way."

"Okay," Julie said. "If we don't see you in a couple of hours, we're coming out there."

"Any word on how Anezka is?"

"Melanie is already on it," Katie called into the phone. "She got a hold of the hospital. Chopper should be there already. She's checking with them to ferret out the deets."

"Thanks. I need to go take care of something here, take me a little bit to fix. Don't worry."

"Love you," Katie said.

"Us, too," Gletts called from the backseat, laughing.

I heard a smack and a grunt. One of them didn't think he was too funny.

"Be careful," Julie said, taking the phone off speaker. The sound of wind quieted. "You sure you're okay?"

"Yes, boss," I said, smiling. "Nothing I can't handle."

I gave Bub and Skella the evil eye.

"I'll see you in a few hours."

I shut off the cell phone, walked into the kitchen, pulled a Diet Coke from the fridge, and walked back into the living room. Neither of them had moved.

"You first," I said to Bub, sitting on the couch with my arms on the back. "What is going on with Anezka?"

He glanced at the amulet on the wall over the fireplace for a long moment, then back to me.

"What I am about to tell you has not been shared, even with Anezka."

Great. More secrets.

# Forty-four

Bᴜʙ sᴛᴏᴏᴅ ɪɴ ғʀᴏɴᴛ ᴏғ ᴛʜᴇ ғɪʀᴇᴘʟᴀᴄᴇ ᴡɪᴛʜ ʜɪs ᴄʟᴀᴡᴇᴅ hands behind his back. As he spoke he rocked back and forth on his heels like a schoolboy.

"I have served the amulet for one hundred and seventy-three generations," he began. "I was called from my hive mother by a powerful blacksmith and bound to this world." He looked at me, his huge eyes shining in the failing light. "In the earliest days of his youth, my first master—Völundr—had been bartered to a clan of dwarves. He grew unto them as a servant, but he proved a brilliant and quick-witted child. Before he stood as tall as me," he held one clawed hand to the top of his head, "they apprenticed him to their greatest blacksmith—Sindri. My master was a shadow to the mighty Sindri, learning through hard work and perseverance.

"One day, Sindri's brother Brock returned to the clan declaiming how the god Loki had insulted them all and how he swore to prove that Sindri was the greatest smith the gods of Æsir would ever know. My master, a human, had learned all he could from the dwarves by the time of this disagreement with the gods. His apprenticeship was long over, yet the dwarves would not release him. In a moment of jealousy, he stole a trinket, really—a bauble of the meanest sort. This he used as a basis, a seed, as it were, to create a new item."

He pointed to the amulet over the fireplace. "At the heart of that, my bond—my chain to this world—lies an older power, one I do not fully understand."

Skella sat on the big comfy chair with her knees pulled up to her chest and her eyes wide. The sun was setting, the last falling rays illuminating Bub like a spotlight.

"Once this trinket had been acquired, my first master used the power of the dwarves to take a bit of this and that—dribs and drabs of magic and leavings the dwarves felt were of no real consequence. From each of three powerful artifacts, he took a measure.

"As Brock and his brother Sindri went to Asgard to present ever greater gifts to the gods, my master hoarded his pilfered items. He utilized the magic he'd garnered from the dwarves and summoned me, binding me to this thing."

He waved his hands above his head, taking in the shadow box above the fireplace and the amulet that hung within.

"The three gifts of Sindri and Brock were presented to the gods: the forged boar, Golden Bristle, which could fly through the air and shed light from its many bristles; Draupnir, the Ring of Increase—an arm ring of gold that creates eight copies of itself every ninth night; and finally, Miölnir, the mighty hammer of Thor himself, the greatest weapon to be wielded by the ancient ones."

"Holy . . ." Skella gasped. "I have heard of these." She turned to me, practically bouncing in her chair. "The dragons collected or destroyed as many of the artifacts as they could find. But I've seen Draupnir!"

Bub and I both looked at her. A golden ring that could copy itself eight times every ninth night. That would seriously destroy the world gold market, if it got out.

"Where did you see this?" I asked Skella.

"At the concert," she said. "Was probably one of the copies. They aren't magical, right?" She turned to Bub for confirmation.

"Correct," he said, bowing slightly in her direction.

Skella smiled nervously and gave a quick nod in Bub's direction before she turned back to me. "I saw it at the concert. The leader of The Harpers wore it."

I remembered that armband. Thought it was cool. I'd have to ask Mr. Stone how he came by it. Did he know what he had?

I pointed above Bub's head. "When Anezka showed me the amulet, it had a reaction to me, seemed to change when I held it. Any idea what that was about?"

"Its allegiance is in question," he said matter-of-factly. "The amulet seeks a master who is both skilled in the ways of a maker, but also strong of will." He looked embarrassed. "I fear it will forsake the fair Anezka."

"I'm sorry, what?"

Worry painted Skella's face. "That's a problem."

I pressed my thumb against my forehead. The runes had begun to throb.

"You serve the amulet. Don't you understand how it works?"

"The creation occurred before he summoned me from my hive mother," he said. "I am sorry I do not fully understand. Please do not stomp on my head again."

He was a killing machine, and I think he was afraid of me. I studied him hard, not answering right away. Maybe not afraid, exactly, but intimidated somehow.

If he'd come to the amulet from his hive mother, he probably didn't know the rules for his kind. How much did his previous masters understand either?

"I believe you," I said, and Bub nodded his head once.

I stood up and walked to the fireplace. His behavior had started to shift. He was growing less erratic, calmer. I stepped forward, into his space. I wanted him to understand that I didn't fear him—that I was the alpha around here. I learned that from the Dog Whisperer. Don't tell.

As I expected, he stepped to the side. I opened the shadow box and pulled down the amulet. The chain was a nickel alloy, normal and plain. The amulet, on the other hand, vibrated with power.

I walked back to the couch and sat down. Neither Skella nor Bub had moved. I leaned forward with my elbows on my knees and looked at the amulet, dangling it from the chain in front of my face.

The runes looked the same, but it felt different. The power resonated with me, ebbed in time with my heartbeat. Had this been what tipped the scales with Anezka?

I held it out to Skella, but she tucked her hands under her arms and shook her head. "Nuh-uh," she said. "That's dark stuff. I don't want to touch it."

I rolled my eyes and sighed. Everyone was a wuss.

"Anezka doesn't understand how this works, does she?"

"No," Bub said emphatically. "She is too volatile, too erratic. When I've tried to give her hints, she has not understood."

"If I claim this," I said, grasping the amulet in my left fist, feeling the warm throbbing of the ceramic, gold, and steel against my flesh, "you would come to my calling?"

Bub nodded in the affirmative.

"And you would help keep the forge hot, the fires under control. Heat the metal evenly and generally manage the fire and flame?"

Again, he nodded.

"But, if there is no attempt to control things, you leak, allowing the passions to rise, is that correct? You enhance anger and passion, rage and . . ." I thought a moment. What else was ever described as fire? "Creativity?"

"You are correct," he said. "I cannot give you what you do not already possess, but I can call it forth, draw out the emotion, the warp and the weave. I enhance what already exists."

Interesting. He acted as an amplifier. No wonder Anezka ran so damn hot all the time. She couldn't help it. I bet she rocked Justin and Flora's world, though. No wonder Flora couldn't hang around. This place was a regular inferno of emotions.

"But there is more," he said quietly. "Something changed here, something unwholesome."

I watched him. "When?"

"It was that man, Justin," he said, the disdain in his voice. "I do not know, as I was banished to the forge for a period of time, but something happened in the spring, some great shift occurred here. Something that has broken Anezka."

"Wait . . . I thought Justin had been gone a year or more."

Bub shook his head. "He returned in the spring; he had something to show Anezka, something powerful."

"What was it?" Skella asked with a squeak.

He shook his head. "I am ashamed that I do not know. She cast him out, or so she claims. I was free to roam the grounds again, but things were different, tainted."

Things were pretty volatile around here. If they'd amped up recently, like in the spring, I wondered if they had anything to do with me reforging the sword. Could be a coincidence, but with Nidhogg being out of sorts, and the other dragons agitated, who knows? Whatever it was, things here were chaotic.

"Next time Anezka gets her panties in a twist, she's gonna succeed in killing herself," I said as bluntly as I could.

"That must not happen," Bub said.

I didn't think he even had tear ducts or anything to allow him to cry, but the thought seemed to make the little mouth breather sad.

"I like Anezka," I said, trying to sound reassuring. "But you're not helping her. All this chaos around here is making her more crazy than she'd be otherwise."

"Losing the baby won't help," Skella said.

Oy, she was right. I rubbed the spot on my forehead between my eyes.

"What baby?" Bub asked.

"She had a miscarriage," I said quietly. "She's off to the hospital."

He rushed forward, slamming his clawed hands onto the coffee table, cutting grooves into the wood. "She was not pregnant!"

"But she was bleeding," I said, looking over to Skella, who nodded in confirmation. "And you said she had something inside her, something that was sick."

"I would know a child," he said angrily. "Did I not witness her own birth? Was I not there the night her mother died bringing her into the world?"

What can you say to that, exactly. "Then what happened to her?"

"Perhaps." He turned and slumped to the floor. For a moment he looked like he did just after I'd crunched his head. "She is a maker, after all."

"Meaning what?" Skella asked, sliding to the edge of her seat.

"Meaning," he said, staring into the fireplace, "perhaps she has taken the anger and the hurt, the lost love and the fear and created a child in her womb." He turned halfway and pointed to the amulet in my hands. "Not a viable child, but something altogether different—using that."

I dropped the amulet onto the floor, where it rang a hollow sound.

"Is that possible?"

"A powerful maker can do many things," he said. "The dwarves could take a boar's skin and create a living creature of gold that could fly and give off light." He got up and turned to me, his elbow on the table. "I cannot see her die. Please help her."

"What if I just broke the amulet?" I asked, pushing it across the floor a few inches with my foot.

"No," he said, leaping to his feet.

I snatched the amulet from the floor, ready to command him to stop if he attacked. Instead, he wrung his head in his hands, scraping off scales under his thick black claws. He began to moan and pace.

What the hell? "Okay," I said. "I won't break it."

He slumped to the floor, and his moaning subsided.

"Would it be so awful to be free of this place, to go home to your hive mates?" I asked him.

He didn't move for a long time. I looked over to Skella, who just shrugged. "Maybe he's afraid," she whispered.

"I love her," he croaked. "If you break the amulet, I will have no hold in this world."

That wasn't awkward. What did this creature know of love? Hell, I barely understood the rudimentary aspects of it myself. On the other hand, he'd been around for roughly five thousand years. Maybe he knew it when he saw it.

"Okay, we find a way to keep Anezka from killing herself, allow Bub to stay around—within parameters." I glared at him, but he didn't even flinch.

"What about my people?" Skella asked. "We need a plan to rescue them, right?"

"The dwarves who have captured your people are all smiths, right?"

Skella shrugged. "Most of them have given up many of the old ways, but there are those who work with fire and steel, yes. They are the ones who forged the chains that bind the boy, and the bars that hold my people."

"Where there are smiths, there is flame." I looked over at Bub. "I think he may be able to assist us in our little adventure."

She eyed him dubiously. "I'm not so sure about him."

"I can help you," he said quickly. "While you may travel through mirrors, I can travel through flame."

I gave Skella a smug smile. "See, that's what I'm talking about."

She rolled her eyes, but she didn't argue.

First things first. We needed to get to Black Briar before they sent a search party after me.

"Okay, troops. Here's what we are going to do. Skella, you go around and batten down the hatches. Lock the doors, windows, et cetera. Hell, water the plants, too. We are going on a road trip."

"What shall I do?" Bub asked, standing up straight and tall.

"Give me a quick inventory," I said. "I know about the shotgun, but I don't understand the carvings on the stock or the carvings on the support beams in the carport."

"Flora did that work," he said. "She is an adept craftsperson but could not stand the situation here. It would have been better if she had stayed and that awful man had left, but life is full of missteps and incorrect choices."

Man, did I know for choices. I could fill a book with second guesses and missed chances. "Tell me about the gun, then. Is there something special about it?"

"It is very powerful," he said. "Flora had a way of collecting the energy here, focusing it and enhancing the items she worked. The protections on this house are a large part of her work. She channeled the power of the amulet into her work, and she didn't even know it."

Interesting. "Can I use that shotgun?"

He shrugged. "It is a weapon. There is no implied ownership. It will work for whomever wields it."

Maybe I'd take it with me to Vancouver. Couldn't hurt to have something besides the sword. Deidre used a shotgun in the battle with the giants—for a while anyway, before it failed with all the magic around. I bet this one was different.

I bundled the shotgun in a blanket and laid it in the trunk of my car. I transferred my dirty clothes into a garbage bag and added those in with the shotgun.

It was well after dark by the time I had the kids in the car. Bub called shotgun, ironically, so I made him ride in the trunk. Skella thought it was pretty hilarious.

I just didn't want to explain to anyone who he was.

Before I pulled the door to, I picked up the amulet and slipped it into my pocket. I felt like I was betraying Anezka, but I needed to find a way to fix all this. What I needed was some expert advice on this little wonder.

# Forty-five

WE DROVE DOWN TO EVERGREEN HOSPITAL. I HAD THE RA-
dio on, letting the tired DJs over at the metal station prattle into
the silence. Skella watched the traffic go by the window, and Bub
seemed to be singing a lullaby of some sort. I could hear him when
the DJs fell silent.

His song was sad and unnerving; I turned the radio down. Skella
cocked her head to the side, listening, and we rode into the night
serenaded by the lovesick eating machine in the trunk of my car.

It started raining before we cleared the pass, and the rhythmic
slap of the windshield wipers and the hum of the tires on wet
pavement accompanied Bub's surprisingly sweet voice.

When we pulled into the parking garage at Evergreen, I turned
the car off but did not get out.

"Gletts is with Katie and Julie," I said, looking at Skella. "I don't
think Katie's forgiven you, and I wouldn't push it tonight, okay?

"Sure," she said, continuing to look out the window. It took me
a moment to realize she'd been watching the wing mirror all this
time.

"Who are you watching?" I asked quietly.

"My grandmother," she said. "She is an old woman, not used to
the rough treatment of the dwarves."

I patted her on the knee. "We'll rescue them. I promise."

"I know," she said, turning to face me. "You killed the dragon that killed my parents. You wield the black blade. Your blood sings of battle and vengeance."

I watched her, cautious. "What do you see?"

"There are those among my people who have a gift," she said, turning to glance at the backseat and, by extension, Bub. "They have a way with animals and birds. One—an old man—older than my grandmother, he can call the fish from the sea." She looked back at me, her face filled with awe and wonder. "But you can control fire, bend metal, such as the mightiest of the dwarves I have seen." She paused, collecting a stray thought. "You will like my grandmother," she said finally. "If she lives long enough for us to find them again."

I watched her face, but she was lost in thought. I couldn't reassure her any more than I already had, so I turned to face the back of the car.

"Bub, can you hear me?"

"Yes," came his muffled reply.

"Please stay here. I'd rather no one saw you, if you understand."

"Of course," he called back.

I opened the door. "Come on, Skella. Let's go see what's going on."

The closing of the car doors echoed through the chilly parking structure. The rain muffled the sounds of traffic out on the main road, and it seemed as if we were in a separate world—a world of secrets and pain.

We dashed across the open space and ran along the side of the hospital to the emergency entrance.

Katie and Julie were sitting inside, huddled together, and Gletts sat several seats away watching the fish in a very large aquarium.

"Katie?"

God, she looked great. I hoped I never grew tired of being

surprised by her—how someone like her would be with someone like me.

She turned. Relief and worry warred on her face the second she saw me. She rose, walked hurriedly toward me, casting an ugly eye toward Skella.

"Hey," I said, stepping close to her.

She leaned into me. "Hey, yourself."

I put my hand on the back of her neck and she tilted her face up toward mine. I fell into her kiss. It was cautious at first, then for a second I forgot anyone else was there and pulled her to me, relishing the taste of her, breathing in her scent. We kissed until I forgot to breathe and we pulled apart with effort.

"I've missed you, too," she said breathlessly.

I hugged her for a long time, letting our hearts align, feeling her energy wash over me.

"Get a room," Julie called, laughing.

I turned with my arm over Katie's shoulder and waved my left hand. "Hey, boss."

"Glad to see you finally made it," she said, nodding at the clock. It was well after eight. I'd taken about two hours longer than I'd promised.

"I was giving you 'til eight thirty," Katie said, snuggling her arm around my waist. "Then I was calling out the troops."

"Sorry," I said, slipping out of her grasp and pulling her down into seats beside Julie, holding her hands in my lap. "How's Anezka?"

Katie looked down at our hands before answering. "She'll live," she said quietly. "Melanie was out a minute ago, said they had the bleeding stopped and that she was sleeping."

"Good. She needs to sleep."

"There was no baby," she said. "Something was wrong for sure, but no baby. Melanie said they were doing an emergency hyster-ectomy. Only real chance to save her."

"Shit." I leaned back against the hard plastic of the chair and covered my face with my hands. "That'll send her over the edge."

"Is she unstable?" Julie asked.

I lowered my hands, glanced at Katie first, and then looked at Julie. "Depression for sure, maybe bipolar."

"Treatable," she said, settling her hands on the head of her cane. "She's one of ours, you know. Blacksmith guild will look after her. Besides, she's in on the secret."

Katie kinda shrugged with her face—raising her eyebrows, tilting her head. She wasn't surprised.

"And what about those two?" Julie asked, pointing to where Skella and Gletts sat huddled together.

"Couple of scared kids way in over their heads," I said. "Long story that I'd rather tell with the Black Briar gang in tow."

"Okay," Katie said. She took out her cell phone and began punching numbers. "I need to let Jimmy know you're okay anyway."

"Not tonight," I said quickly, waving my hand at her. "I'd really rather wait for the light of day."

She nodded as she got up, cupped her hand over one ear, and spoke softly into the phone. I laid my head back against the wall and closed my eyes. Man, I hated hospitals.

"Smell drives me bat-shit," Julie said.

I cracked my eyes open and glanced at her.

"Hospitals are the suck," she said.

I laughed. "I was just thinking how much I hate these places."

She patted me on the shoulder and stood up, only leaning on her cane a little. "I'm going down to the cantina to get a soda. You want something?"

"Water, maybe?" I asked. "No caffeine; I'll have a hard enough time sleeping tonight."

She motioned over to Katie. "I'm sure she can think of something that would help you sleep."

I grinned at her. "Has your mind always been in the gutter?" I asked as she turned and walked away.

"Noneya," she said, waving one hand at me over her shoulder.

Yeah, yeah . . . noneya damn business. I shook my head and leaned forward, hands on my knees.

Just being here with Katie and Julie, even with the uneasy vibe from the hospital, made me more comfortable than I'd been in days. But I needed to settle one thing.

I walked over to where Skella was wringing her hands and chattering at Gletts in a language I didn't recognize. She wasn't happy.

"Everything okay here?"

Gletts turned his languid gaze at me and smiled. "You got a nice apartment," he said.

Skella looked over at me, a frown turning her mouth down. "He will not listen to reason."

I squatted down, putting myself more on their seated level. "What's the problem now?"

Gletts rolled his eyes. "She wants to go home, back to Vancouver and scout around, try and find out where those bastard dwarves took our family."

"Seems reasonable to me," I agreed.

Skella gave him a smug smile.

"I think, however, that we should just stay with you a few days, let things settle down."

Oh, great. Two angsty goth elves in my apartment along with Julie and the cabbage smell from Mrs. Sorenson. Fun times.

"He just wants to rummage through your things," Skella said, punching him in the shoulder.

"Not a good choice," I said, giving him a stern look. "You did a fair enough job rifling my things in Vancouver."

"Whatever," he said, standing up. "Fine, let's blow this place."

Skella stood hurriedly and gave me a guilty smile before crossing to her brother. "I'll contact you when we find out where they have taken them," she promised. "You'll have a plan, yes?"

"Sure," I said. "When you call me, I'll come up and kick some ass."

This seemed to reassure her, and she took Gletts's arm.

"Besides," Gletts said, "this place, this whole city, smells like death."

"And dragon," Skella said in a whisper.

Nidhogg stank over the whole city. Nice.

The two of them walked around behind the aquarium to a floor-to-ceiling mirror that ran along one wall.

One second they were there, the next they were gone, vanished back into the wilds of Stanley Park.

Gletts was a particular brand of teen I disliked, but Skella seemed sweet and earnest. I hope they stayed out of trouble. I watched the mirror, wondering when I'd stopped being the angry teenager. This made me laugh. Julie and Katie would totally disagree, but I thought my issues were beyond those I had ten years ago. Not really fair to Gletts and Skella I supposed. They'd spent their entire lives under the violent rule of a right sadistic bastard who happened to be a dragon. Not saying any of them were particularly lovely, but Jean-Paul liked to play with his food too much.

I made a warding sign and spit over my shoulder. May he rot in hell.

Katie, Julie, and I spent another hour in the emergency room waiting for Melanie to give us the lowdown. Anezka had indeed been rushed into emergency surgery. Once she was stable, she'd be in here for three or four days. I started to give the charge nurse my cell-phone number, but as I'd lost the phone, Katie stepped up and gave hers.

Later, we stood in the lobby, deciding our next moves. We were all exhausted.

"Why don't you come to my place tonight?" Katie asked. "Then we can go out to Black Briar in the morning together."

"Okay," I said, smiling. "I'd love to."

She kissed me quickly and went back over to the nurses' station to get some things straightened out with Melanie.

"Told you," Julie said, drinking the last dregs of her coffee. "I'll get a hold of Frank in the morning, let him know what happened and that she'll be okay."

"Good thinking," I agreed.

"One of you will have to take me home first," she said, grinning. "Think you can keep your clothes on long enough for that?"

"Nice," I said, shaking my head. "Maybe you need to get laid, mouth like that."

Julie laughed. I crossed my arms over my chest and watched Katie and Melanie talking head-to-head.

I'd gotten over my jealousy of Melanie, but we'd never really be close. Too much history. Well, between her and Katie. I wasn't sure I'd ever really feel okay around her. She was too perfect, too pretty, and too damn talented. I didn't think Katie would ever throw me over for her, but there were moments where that conviction wasn't as strong as it could be.

Katie headed home to clean up, and I took Julie back to our place.

On the way I hit a drive-thru. I got a chicken sandwich, but Julie looked at me strange when I ordered seven double cheeseburgers. She grew even more worried when I pulled out of the drive-thru and climbed out of the car with the burgers. I opened the trunk, dropped them into the back, and closed it again.

Once we were on the road a few minutes, a very large belch reverberated from the trunk of my car.

"Long story," I said.

She looked at me, squinting at the backseat. "And foul smelling."

"You don't know the half of it," I said, laughing. "Let me tell you about my new friend Bub."

Julie didn't ask too many questions, but the ride home was a most interesting conversation.

# Forty-six

I let Bub ride in the front seat on the way over to Katie's.

"Listen," I told him. "Anezka is going to be okay, but she'll need to be in the hospital a few days."

"Okay," he said, picking Styrofoam out of his teeth. "Can I see her?"

"Too many people, cameras, and such in there for you to visit," I said. "Besides, just being around the equipment could fry it—could put her in danger."

"Right, good thinking."

He couldn't see over the dashboard, and I hadn't insisted he put on the seat belt. Besides, it would hit him across the face, and that wouldn't be comfortable.

"I need you to stay in the car tonight; can you do that?"

"Sure," he agreed. "I'll sleep in the trunk."

I looked over at him. "So, you do sleep?"

"I'm not a machine," he said. "Different from you, but the same in many ways."

"Okay, I need to know you'll stay in the car, and that you'll be okay."

He grinned up at me, his rows of sharp, pointy teeth evoking the shark image again. "I can handle myself."

I rolled my eyes. "Just stay in the trunk, and in the morning I'll hit another drive-thru. How do you feel about breakfast burritos?"

"Intrigued," he said, licking his lips.

We pulled into the alley behind Katie's apartment. Elmer's Gun and Knife Emporium had long since repaired the broken window from the fight I had with the giants in the spring. The power lines had been restrung, and the landlords had repaired Katie's door. The alley looked just the same, and I half expected to see Joe digging around in the Dumpster, but I was sorely disappointed.

"Don't let anyone steal my car," I said with a grin as Bub climbed into the trunk.

"You said you hated this car," he squeaked as I pulled my pack out of the trunk.

I grabbed the garbage bag with my old bloody clothes as well. "That should give you more room."

"I'll be fine," he said, curling into a ball in the back.

"Sleep well, Bub."

"You as well, master," he said as I pushed the trunk closed.

Master? Man, this was getting complicated.

Katie buzzed me up as soon as I hit the intercom, and I bounded up the stairs two at a time. By the time I was on the second floor, she had the door to her apartment propped open with a shoe. I didn't have a copy of the new keys, not since they'd repaired the place. After the way things crashed and burned a few months earlier, I was keeping a modicum of distance there. A minor precaution, I knew. She'd be more than happy for me to move in, but not today, not at the moment.

We made love with abandon. I don't know if it was the proximity of Bub or the chaos of the last few days, but things were much, much more intense. There was a point where she was screaming so loudly, I thought someone would call the police. I'm fairly sure at one point I blacked out. It was crazy.

I lay awake after, listening to her sleep, thankful she'd said my name and no one else's.

I placed my hand on her stomach, feeling her breathing, her life force filling the room. We had a connection like nothing I'd ever experienced. It scared the hell out of me, but I craved it. I'd isolated myself for most of my life. Well, since I was nine or so, when things at home got odd, after Da decided to protect his little girl from the whole bad world. I missed them: Ma, Da, and Megan. Especially Megan, the little runt. Only she wasn't a runt any longer, she was tall and beautiful, suffering under the restrictions I fled. Things got hard there, and I left them, abandoned her, young and alone.

Then there was the Black Briar crew, who I'd made a point of distancing myself from after the fiasco in the spring. So many dead and wounded because of my hubris, my mistakes. I know the dragons weren't my fault, and the bastard Jean-Paul sure didn't play fair, but Jimmy was so angry and hurt, and I just couldn't face him.

I still dreamed of Susan and Maggie dying, Susan a broken doll under the claws of the dragon and Maggie riding toward him, a flaming comet on her dying horse, Dusk. I could see her crawling toward Susan, her body engulfed in dragon fire, reaching out to her one true love.

Katie moved, and I let my hand slide off her side. I loved her, I had no doubt, but did I love her like that? I'd gone after her, fought the dragon, but did I have it in me to crawl to her as my skin melted?

So, I avoided them all, avoided the land and the people. I realized I was a runner. Not a pattern I was proud of.

Time to step up, though. Going out to Black Briar would be good. Painful but good. Confronting Jimmy after five months of silence would be hard, but I faced a dragon. I'd let his sister get captured, let his wife get hurt. Jimmy was a pussycat compared to

Jean-Paul Duchamp, or even Frederick Sawyer, but I dreaded his disappointment and his wrath.

That reminded me of the real danger in the world: Qindra, Nidhogg, giants, and trolls. How had we ever built a civilization like this and never noticed all that going on right under our noses? And what of this King of Vancouver? Picking up the pieces of a city once ruined by a dragon. He was a brave one, taking that on. I can't imagine what the dragons will do with that power vacuum.

I'd like to meet him, figure out his angle. I just hope he wasn't worse than the dragons. They were nasty, but they stayed to themselves mostly.

Of course, if they were right under our noses, we'd have less luck with technology. Magic screwed up tech, that much I was understanding. Basic tools worked just fine, however. I would be trying Anezka's shotgun, if it came to that, but in the end, I trusted my hammers and Gram.

Gram.

Like a lover, that sword called to me. Just thinking of her sent a chill through me. There was a buzzing in the back of my brain. She slept, the black sword of mine, but her slumber was restless. She dreamed of battle. Tomorrow, I would find out what Jimmy did with Gram. There were too many secrets on that front.

And Bub. Now that I'd spent some time with him, I was growing to like the little flamer. I was fairly sure that it would be difficult to crush his head again, if he got out of line.

I glanced over to where my jeans lay crumpled by my tennis shoes. Inside was the amulet. I got out of bed, padded across the floor, and squatted down, fishing in the jeans for the amulet. The room was chilly, and I broke out in goose flesh. The light from the street lamps crept in around the blinds over Katie's windows, but it gave me enough light to see by.

I dangled the amulet by its chain, watching the gold and steel gleam in the dim light. After a moment, I realized that squatting in the middle of the bedroom floor, naked, fondling an ancient, runic artifact was too damn strange, even for me. I wrapped the amulet in a sock, stuffed it down into my shoe, and crawled back into bed.

Katie rolled over onto her side, pushing her backside against me. I snuggled close, throwing one arm over her, cupping a breast in my hand, and closed my eyes.

With the warmth radiating from her, and the smell of her, I was able to finally sleep.

# Forty-seven

By the time we'd gotten coffee for me and Katie and burritos for Bub, it was nearly nine. We drove out to Black Briar in Katie's new Miata. Bub rode in the trunk again, content to gnaw his wax-paper-wrapped tortillas, beef, cheese, and jalapeños. "Just don't make a mess in my new car," Katie had admonished me as I was dropping the bag o' food into the trunk.

"You heard the lady," I said

"Yes, boss," he agreed, bobbing his head and eyeing the bag. "If those taste like they smell, I may love them more than cheese-burgers."

"Let me know later," I said and shut the trunk.

They wouldn't last long enough for us to get out onto the main road.

Katie and I talked about Anezka, the new movie I'd be working on, her classroom's antics, and a few other things of no real consequence—anything to avoid answering any questions about Jimmy and the rest of Black Briar.

Obviously this meeting was going to be serious. She even adopted her best schoolmarm voice at one point when I was getting too persnickety.

By the time we pulled up the long drive toward Black Briar, a caravan of vehicles was parked all around the house.

Like I wanted a freaking audience. It *was* all about me . . . right?

I noticed a whole gaggle of people in armor out by the new barn as we got out of the car. Jimmy stood on the deck off the back of the house with his arms folded across his chest, and his best *don't fuck with me* look perched on his face. Katie bounded around the car and took my arm, guiding me to the house, like there was a chance I'd make a run for it.

It's happened before.

Gunther and Stuart were standing near the old ruined barn, on the opposite side of the yard from where we'd parked. It reminded me of a shattered rib cage—the image of a heart being ripped out of the farm was fresh in my mind. I must have started to stiffen because Katie squeezed my arm gently.

"It's okay," she said. "No ghosts here."

"Not yet," I offered. "We should double-check on Halloween."

That drew a laugh out of her, and I felt a little less tense.

Then someone screamed.

I looked around. Bub had appeared on top of Katie's car, carrying the shotgun. Okay, good to note. He teleported out of the trunk, carrying the gun with him. He had not brought the blanket.

I let go of Katie and held up my hands. "Hang on folks; he's with me." I cast a look at Gunther, who shrugged.

"You working with demons now, Beauhall?" It was the first thing Jimmy had said to me since the barn raising—the night Deidre had gotten out of the hospital. Not a stupendous moment.

"Why are there so many people here?" I asked.

"Drills," Katie said. "Gunther and Stuart are building a regular army."

That explained why we had such a broad audience. There in the crowd, I saw some of the survivors from the battle in the spring. Many wore swords at their hips, and I noticed a line of pikes leaning against the back of the house. I also saw a couple of hammers in the crowd, backup weapons by the rigging, but it did my heart good to see them. Learn from the enemy's weakness; survive to fight another battle. Ogres and their rocky hides wouldn't surprise them a second time.

I took a deep breath, steadying myself for what I had to do. These folks deserved to hear from me, deserved more than they'd gotten in the last five months. I walked toward the stairs, looking up at Jimmy. I didn't wait for him to act, just climbed the stairs and turned to face the silent crowd of people.

"I think it's time we cleared the air about a few things," I said, feeling the tightness in my chest.

I glanced at Jimmy out of the corner of my eye. He raised his eyebrows but didn't open his mouth. Neither did he uncross his arms. I scanned the faces of the Black Briar crew.

"I haven't been here for a few months—"

"No shit," someone called from the milling crowd.

I nodded, and continued. "Things have been broken here, since the spring." I tapped my chest twice, then my forehead. "Here, inside me—where the fear dwells and the anger makes its home." People stepped forward, moving closer to the porch. Bub crept up the stairs to stand behind me, holding the shotgun at parade rest. He was almost cute.

"I'm sorry," I said to the crowd. "Through my actions, people here died."

Jimmy scowled, and Katie started to protest, but I held up my hands to forestall them. "I don't take the blame for their deaths, but I know if I hadn't found the sword, if I hadn't reforged it, we may have never been bothered by the dragon and his army."

"Likely more would have died," a woman called from the crowd.

I looked at her, recognition dawning. Trisha. She'd been injured at the same time Gunther had. He'd saved her life just before I saved his. Her hair was cut really short, and she had a hard look to her. Not like the bouncy clerk I knew from before the battle. She'd have some wicked scars under her armor.

"We'll be ready for them next time," Trisha called from the crowd. "We ain't babies no more."

Stuart called out—"Hoo-rah," and half the crowd answered in kind. Gunther sang out as well, and what had to be his squad answered. For a full minute they called back and forth.

"Red Squad!"

"Blue Squad!"

Until Jimmy held up a hand.

They fell silent immediately.

I glanced down at Katie. "You were going to tell me this, when?"

She grinned. "When you managed to drag your cute but sorry ass back out here."

The crowd broke into chatter, several people wolf-whistled, and Gunther roared with laughter.

"I'm serious," I said, holding my arms in the air.

They fell silent once again.

I had tears in my eyes, and the crowd blurred. "Too many good people lost their lives here, and I need to make amends."

I heard a whirring sound, then the slamming of a screen door. I turned to see . . . holy god, Deidre. When did she get out of the nursing home? She rolled out of the house in a souped-up wheelchair—looked like a cross between a Harley and a Segway. "That's bullshit!" she bellowed, stopping long enough to snatch the shotgun out of Bub's hands. He looked surprised and backed away several steps, but he didn't react, didn't disappear.

"Those bastards took our kith and kin," she bellowed, cruising to the edge of the deck and pointing at Katie. Her voice carried over the crowd, which mumbled agreement. "We just did what we had to do to get them back."

She turned to me, her face stern, the anger obvious on it. "So, you can just cut the crap, Beauhall. No lingering guilt, no woulda-coulda-shoulda." Her face softened, and a smile broke over it like a rainbow. "You're a god-damned hero; suck it up and start acting like it."

I felt my heart leap into my throat. I stepped to her, bending over and hugging her, despite the shotgun. "I'm so sorry," I said into her shoulder.

She patted me on the head and made shushing noises as I cried.

"Oh, Deidre came home yesterday," Jimmy said, his voice thick with emotion.

"Thanks for telling me," I mumbled into Deidre's shoulder.

She squeezed me and laughed. "He's such a man."

After a minute, I straightened and faced Jimmy, rubbing the tears from my eyes. Okay, time to face this. "How's it hanging, Jim?"

Deidre laughed, and a little ice fell away from his face.

"You stirring up trouble again?" he asked frankly. "Gunther was just telling us about Anezka's place when Katie called us about a fight and blood and an air ambulance."

I looked around. "Been a crazy few weeks," I said. "Anezka ain't the half of it."

Jimmy glanced over at Bub. "Always good to see something . . . ," he hesitated a second, ". . . or someone new." He nodded at Bub, who nodded back.

"Bub promises to play nice." I looked at him steadily. "Right?"

"Yes, ma'am," he said with a little bow.

I jogged my head to the side, giving Bub the permission to escape Jimmy's gaze. He bowed a second time and wandered to the back of the deck and sat down against the house under a large window.

"And if that isn't enough," he said, "you've gone and lost your damn mind?"

"Huh?" That was a non sequitur.

"Gunther brought the bike here," Jimmy said. "Good-looking piece of equipment. You'll look pretty damn hot as they scrape you off the pavement."

Deidre waved her hand. "He's just flirting."

The crowd laughed and began to disperse out into smaller groups, now that it appeared Jimmy was not going to strangle me.

Relief washed over me. I needed to explain all this, but I didn't want to do it in front of the greater crowd.

"Just saying it's a nice bike," Jimmy said, flustered. That was something we didn't see too often.

I smiled. "Not gonna be mine if we don't get Anezka settled," I said. "She needs some serious looking after."

"If she's a friend, Black Briar can step in," he offered. "But we'll need the whole story, including the skinny on him." He pointed over my shoulder to where Bub sat on the deck, carving something into the wood with his claws.

"Bub, stop that," I barked.

He looked up, startled. "Sorry."

Like a four-year-old, I decided. Just a baby in most ways. I really needed to get a handle on all this.

"Can we talk, someplace quiet?" I asked Jimmy. "I don't mind a few folks, but it feels personal, especially where Anezka's concerned."

"I think we can arrange that," he said. He strode to the edge of the deck, squatted down, and spoke quickly to Gunther and Stuart. They both nodded and turned to the crowd.

They immediately had the mob formed into their two separate units, each armed with an assortment of weapons, including the pikes from the side of the house. They marched them out into the back of the yard just beyond the barn and set some sergeants to drilling them on their formations. Once that was going, they trotted back over to us. I noticed that Trisha had a squad of six. She handled her pike with strength and grace. Not quite a cash register, but she knew her stuff.

"They should be busy for an hour," Stuart said, smiling up at me.

"Hi, Stuart," I said.

He stormed up the stairs and threw his arms open wide. I melted into his hug. "Let that giant of a man hug you first," he groused. "I'm beginning to think you like him best."

I looked over his shoulder to Gunther, who stood at the bottom of the stairs and grinned. "Saved the best for last," I said and winked at Gunther.

Stuart squeezed me harder and stepped back, wiping his eyes. "You've stayed away all summer," he growled. "You are seriously behind in your training."

He turned and pointed out to the two squads drilling. "We've got a few new recruits and are working them into a more cohesive fighting corps. We can't have a repeat of this spring's massacre."

"And with your buddy there," Gunther added. "Those who were skeptical about what we've told them will be dancing to a different tune."

Stuart looked over at Bub and shook his head. "Gonna mean more questions, you mean."

Not something I'd thought about. Hell, I just assumed that since I was living in the land of the strange the rest of the world was up to my speed. Stupid on my part.

"No mind," Stuart said, brushing the subject aside. "When can we expect to see you swinging some rattan?"

I nodded, serious and attentive. "Soon," I said. "I'd love to start coming out here again, you know, depending . . ." I could feel the fear and shame rising in me, suddenly. Jimmy blamed me for Deidre's being hurt, for so many dead, for bringing the dragons down on all of us. My blood grew hot, and I felt the flush run up my neck. I glanced over at Jimmy. "If I'm welcome."

Jimmy stepped to Deidre's side and placed his arm over her shoulder. "It's been pointed out," he gave Deidre's shoulder a squeeze, "that there's a slight chance I've been a right grumpy bastard."

I started to open my mouth, but Deidre gave me a look that quelled that instinct. "Don't everyone rush in to correct me," he said with a smidge of crankitude.

"What he means to say," Deidre said, poking Jimmy in the side, "is that you're welcome here anytime, Sarah."

Jimmy cleared his throat. "Of course. We're all family here." He glanced down at Deidre, who shot him a look. He rolled his eyes, but a smile graced his face. "You've been gone too damn long."

And just like that, the anvil hanging over my head vanished. Katie came up the steps and people started cheering. The troops in the field had stopped marching and were shaking their pikes in the air. I'm not sure what the signal was that alerted them, but it was amazing. I lost my anger and my fury but let the love and acceptance of this crowd, this family I'd chosen, wash over me.

It was like losing ten pounds after a week of beer and chocolate. I kissed Katie again, just because I wanted to, and then waved out at the crowd with my arm around her. Here, if nowhere else, I was free to love who I wanted and could lay my own ghosts aside. Nice to have a place like that.

We settled in, the bunch of us: Katie, Julie, Jimmy, Deidre, Gunther, and Stuart. The twins tapped a keg of summer ale, and we raised a pint in remembrance of the fallen.

I gave them the 411 on all that had happened in the last few weeks, from the concert and kidnapping to the rumors of the

King of Vancouver, the mead, dwarves, elves, Skella, Gletts, Anezka, and finally Bub.

I pushed Jimmy for answers of my own. He didn't like talking
about it, but with all the things that had gone on, and with Deidre's prodding, I got some information out of him.

I learned about his parents, for example, and the fact that they
were members of a secret sect of scholars who'd been following
dragon lore for centuries.

Gunther shared his bit of history, the part where he was raised
for the first ten years in a monastery outside Beattyville, Ken-
tucky, before moving to the Northwest.

They answered every question I asked, even if they were evasive and shrouded in vagaries. Then we were back to Anezka, the
oddities of her place, Bub, and the amulet.

They asked a few questions, but in general just listened.
Gunther copied the runes from the amulet, but none of them
touched it.

Bub for his part sat quietly outside our ring, listening and
watching. When we were done, I asked him what he wanted to do.

"Go home," he said quietly. "Can we, please?"

I actually patted him on the head. "If you can appear here when
I call you, can you just pop home?"

"It's pretty far," he said. "I can come to the amulet, but going
the other direction is too hard."

"Okay," I said. "I'll get you home. Besides, someone has to watch
over the place."

He swelled up at that. Little eater just needed someone to look
after, something to do. With Anezka's mental state, he'd been
running wild for a long time.

We stayed around long enough for the twins to break out the
big grill and cook up a whole mess of burgers. The crowd was

fascinated with Bub and took turns tossing burgers at him, delighting in him catching them in his mouth and eating them whole.

Not sure why none of them considered the possibilities that he could eat them just as easily. Maybe I was being paranoid.

# Forty-eight

SARAH CAUGHT A RIDE BACK TO CIVILIZATION WITH TRISHA. Katie needed to spend some time on family business. Sarah would've stayed, but she had work the next morning. As it was, Katie was pissed. She sat with Jimmy and Deidre, so obviously fuming that the twins excused themselves, wanting no part in a family feud.

"There's more going on here than you're letting on," Katie said, rounding on Jimmy after the twins had gone. "All this, the dragons, Sarah's sword, Mom and Dad." Her voice cracked at the end, and she coughed in an attempt to cover it.

"What do you want from me?" Jimmy implored, placing his hands on the table, palms up. "They told me to protect you, told me to keep you from harm. How could I do any less?"

Deidre placed her hand on Jimmy's shoulder, squeezing. "She's a grown woman now, Jim. Maybe you need to stop protecting her, and start sharing things."

"I don't think that's a good idea," he said, shaking his head. "She can't be held responsible for what she doesn't know."

Katie laughed at that, a pained bark that opened the damn of tears. "Like when that fucking dragon snatched me? Like then, Jim?" She stood, slamming her chair against a cabinet. "Like when I watched Sarah in that hospital, burned by dragon fire. You saw her arm; it was horrible. And the battle? Were you going to protect us all from that as well?"

Jimmy hung his head. "I failed them," he said quietly. "Failed Black Briar and failed you and Deidre."

"You're not my father, Jim. I appreciate everything you and Deidre did for me after Mom and Dad disappeared, but you're my brother. You can't fail me, unless you stop loving me."

She reached out and squeezed his hand for a moment before drawing back. "But you know things about Mom and Dad. Things you have hidden from me. I deserve to know everything about them. I deserve to know why they disappeared."

"It's just not that simple," he said. "It's all muddled together— dragons and witches and all the rest." He looked up, peering into her face. "And Sarah, dear god. She's off the charts, Katie. I've talked it through with the twins; we can't figure out why she's here or who she represents."

"Who she represents?" Katie let her voice grow louder. "She's not one of your projects, Jim. Not something for you to catalog and hide from the world. She's a caring person, broken and beautiful. And whether you approve or not, someone I happen to love. How dare you try and categorize her?"

"I didn't mean . . . she's not . . . I know she's special."

"Special? Like short-bus special, Jim? One of those flawed heroines who can't get past her own baggage to save herself at the end of the movie?"

"This isn't a movie," he said quietly. "And, while she's seriously flawed, she's family."

Katie sat back at that, crossed her arms, and pulled a face. "I'm terrified I'm gonna lose her like I lost Mom and Dad. I love her, damn it. Love her so bad it aches inside."

They sat quietly for a long time.

"What's it gonna be, Jim?" Katie asked, her voice shaking. "When do I get to be a grown-up?"

He didn't answer, didn't look at her, just squeezed his hands into fists and raged silently.

"I'm tired of being left out," Katie said. "You can't protect me from the world."

She turned and stormed out of the kitchen, leaving him to his tears.

# Forty-nine

I spent the next week operating out of Anezka's place. Her truck was in such bad shape I had it towed to Black Briar. Some of the crew would fix it up. In the meantime, Jimmy loaned me his truck on a day-to-day basis. I'd hit Black Briar at o'dark thirty and swap my beast for his truck. I think he wanted to make sure I was out there every day, instead of being tied to Anezka's place where things tended to get weird. I had to go into town to get Internet. The electronics were getting worse at her place.

I spent some time on the intertubes, looking for information about blood magic, researching the news around Vancouver, looking for clues. Rolph was a big help, being on the ground there and knowing of the dwarven communities. No word about Odin, but Vancouver was rife with rumors of the mead and of dragons.

Rolph had been contacted by the King of Vancouver, who questioned his place in the community. So far, Rolph had remained neutral in all of it, but he said the King was right pissed about the dragon interference.

Every day I'd hit one of the local farms: Broken Switch, Tandem Rail, and Busted Modem (Microsoftees). The work was good, but harder than I was used to, going solo. Luckily, these were small farms, mainly hobbies for the luxuriously wealthy.

On Tuesday I met the gang out at Black Briar and sparred with

Stuart while Gunther worked on the Ducati. The bike was a dream, but the parts were hard to come by. Apparently they were produced by little old Italian women who only worked on alternate Wednesdays.

He said I'd have it by the weekend and loaned me a little Suzuki 550cc he kept around as a spare for when he was working on his Harley.

It was a sweet little bike, great on the city streets but not very powerful on the mountain pass. I rode it between Chumstick and Black Briar. It did okay, but I dreamed about tooling down the road with that Ducati humming between my thighs, Katie snuggled up against my back.

Helped while away the long hours back and forth to Anezka's place. Anezka'd be coming home on Saturday as well. Bub was thrilled like I wouldn't expect and asked me to get her a cake. Funny, the things he thought about. Of course, it did involve food.

Bub and I spent nights discussing smithing history as well as his recollection of dragons and the gods. His knowledge was sparse, having been tied to the amulet and its owner for so long. He spent years doing nothing more than keeping the hearth lit and the forge hot. I can't imagine how freaking boring that would be.

I had great plans to research more, dig into things, but by the time I got home each night, chatting with Bub was the last thing I could muster. The place drained me. I can't see how anyone lived here full-time. It was an energy sink. I slept on the couch and woke cranky nearly every morning. Bub was happy, though.

Julie was in hog heaven having the apartment to herself. I was afraid to ever go home again. I bet she'd have lace doilies inside the refrigerator by the time I got back. She was cruising around well enough on her cane. The docs said she could start driving an automatic soon. No stick shift for a while. I'd give her the Taurus, since I had the motorcycle now. Not what she needed to work, but she could start coming out to the farms, make a show of getting back in charge.

And Deidre was taking command of Black Briar. The house was hopping 24-7. Saturday we were having a planning meeting. They wanted to do some more building. A big surprise. I couldn't wait.

First thing Saturday morning, I arranged to pick up Julie and head over to the hospital. Anezka was coming home.

# Fifty

I drove the Taurus into town to get Julie and pick up a few things since I'd be staying out at Black Briar with Katie. Big shindig called for drinking and other things.

My place didn't quite scream frilly valentine yet, but I thought I'd need a corset soon just to hang around the kitchen. It amazed me how much of a girl Julie was at times.

I filled my pack with fresh underthings and tossed her the keys to the Taurus. She was gonna love it. I didn't quite run down the stairs, but between the doilies and the smell of cabbage, I barely recognized the place.

The ride over to Evergreen Hospital was more harrowing than I'd hoped. Julie hadn't driven in six months, and apparently the concepts of mirrors and large yellow concrete barriers were lost on her. I was sure the right rear quarter panel would pop right back out. Yep, that was the theory.

We made it to the hospital without any more mishaps and sat in the parking garage a few moments before going inside.

"I spoke with Frank," she said to me, slipping into her boss voice.

"Okay. How's Frank?"

She looked at me, thinking how best to tell me something hard, I'm sure.

"He says Anezka's good people, despite the crazy. She's been working for a benefactor for many years. Someone who pays her bills, keeps her flush, and in exchange she does work for them. She has really good insurance."

"Anyone we know?"

"He suggested it was a little iffy and that the last he'd heard, Anezka had fallen out with this benefactor over the sculpture she's currently working on."

"The dragon piece?"

Julie looked at me, startled. "He didn't say. But dragon artwork, Seattle benefactor, flush with insurance . . . Sound like anyone you recognize?"

Fuck . . . Nidhogg. Surely not. "Really?" I asked. Damn, I'd have to touch base with Qindra, see if it was true. Double damn. I hated being entwined with them.

"I think Anezka's upside down on the deal right now. Once that sculpture is finished, the final payment will be deposited in a trust fund of some sort."

"Well, I guess we need to help her get that set done then."

"Frank said it's bad blood, something Anezka won't discuss even with him, and they've known each other for twenty years or more. Ever since she first moved out here."

"I'll ask Bub about it, if she won't spill," I promised. "We look after our own, right?"

Julie nodded. "Aye. Oh, and Sarah?" She reached out and touched me on the arm. "I want you to know how much I appreciate everything you've done for me."

I looked at her and rolled my eyes. "Please," I said. "Like I'd let you off the hook that easy."

She looked at me, confused.

"I'm not done with my apprenticeship. You owe me another year, as far as I'm concerned."

She smiled and squeezed my arm. "Eighteen months, to be exact, but you're right. But we have an obligation that goes beyond master/apprentice. I think we're friends."

"Absolutely," I said. "Now let's go and get Anezka before you make me cry."

She laughed as she got out of the car. She barely leaned on the door as she got the cane out of the backseat. She'd be okay, I could tell. For the longest time, I thought the depression and the trauma would sink her, but with Anezka needing help, she seemed to be coming out of herself. Made me happy to see.

They brought Anezka down in a wheelchair—hospital protocol. We spent the better part of thirty minutes discussing various medications, follow-up appointments, et cetera; then I went out and got the car.

When I pulled up to the doors, Julie and Anezka were laughing and talking like old friends. I held the back door for Anezka, but she gave me a look. Sassy at least—that was a good sign. She climbed into the front, and Julie walked around and held her hand out for the keys. I handed them to her and climbed in the back. At least they didn't make me ride in the trunk.

As we rode over the pass, the chatter consisted mainly of the way certain doctors and nurses looked in their uniforms. I knew Julie was strictly into guys, but she had a good time discussing the various females that Anezka mentioned. It was funny to listen to. I stayed out of it, spent most of my time wishing I had my damn cell phone so I could text Katie. She'd think this was all hilarious.

I'd see her after we got Anezka settled in. Julie would drop me off at Black Briar, and we'd commence with the secret meeting. Julie was invited, but I think she and Mrs. Sorenson had a big gin rummy game planned. Honestly, how she put up with that was beyond me.

It broke my heart when we got to the house. From somewhere

Bub had found pink streamers. The entire house was wrapped in pink and white crepe paper, ribbons were tied around all the sculptures, and one of the warrior statues was standing in the middle of the carport, holding a dozen balloons.

Anezka did cry, and we let her head to the house on her own while we hung back, giving her space. Bub sat on the stoop, anxious and fidgety. For a moment, I wasn't sure what Anezka was going to do, but she passed right by him and walked into the carport to pluck the balloons from the statue.

"Have you lost your fucking mind?" She turned to Bub and held the balloons out, accusingly. "I told you to never touch the work," she ranted. "If you hurt them . . ."

I looked at Julie quickly. Holy crap. Was she losing *her* mind?

Bub blinked a few times, and then slunk off to the side of the house, his head down and his long arms dragging on the ground.

"Stop her," I said to Julie and ran after Bub. He was around the corner before I could catch him. I raced around the side along the back, but he was gone. Damn it.

I walked past the dragon statue and the rest of the warriors. None of them had been moved, other than the one in the carport. I heard a screen door slam as I entered the carport from the backyard. Anezka and Julie must have gone inside the house.

I examined the warrior who had been holding the balloons. Bub had cut a big smile into the otherwise blank sheet of steel that made up the face. It was sweet, if somewhat destructive to the piece.

Still, not an excuse to fly off the handle like that. I wandered into the house, and Anezka was seated at the kitchen table drinking a beer. Julie was getting a glass of water out of the tap.

"Don't start," Anezka said when I walked in. "You've made yourself at home here, but you don't get to defend him."

I glanced at Julie, who just shrugged.

I pulled out a chair and sat opposite Anezka. "Did it occur to you that Bub did all this?" I pointed out the window to where ribbons were hanging down. On the counter was a sheet cake that read WELCOME HOME. "It was his idea for the cake."

She watched me, her eyes hard while she took another long drink of beer. "What are you playing at?" she asked.

"I'm sorry?"

"You come in here, disrupt my life, steal from me, use my home like you own it." She waved her hand in the air, stabbing at me with clinched fingers. "You have no right; this is my place. You are a snake, a lowlife . . ."

I sat there, dumbfounded. What the hell was going on with her? She was happy and laughing in the car. Sure she was upset about the statue, but this was nuts.

Julie pulled a chair out and sat down at the end of the table. "Grow the fuck up," she said, slamming her water glass down on the table.

Anezka and I both jumped. Water sloshed from the glass and began to spread across the yellow Formica tabletop.

"Like I want to hear from a cripple," Anezka spat.

Julie picked up the glass and tossed the water onto her.

I stood quickly, knocking over the chair and holding my hands in the air, like a little water would make me melt.

Anezka sat there, blinking, her mouth open like a landed fish.

Julie walked to the sink and began refilling her water. I stood there, watching Anezka, who didn't move but just sat there while the water dripped off her face and hair.

Once Julie was seated again, she took a sip of the water and cleared her throat. "Frank Rodriguez speaks very highly of you," she said as if she and Anezka hadn't been cutting up for the last few hours. "But where I come from, we don't treat our friends," she motioned to me, "or our loved ones," she pointed out to the carport, where Bub had reappeared, taking the ribbons off the statue—"like scoundrels and villains."

"The little bastard . . ." Anezka growled, but stopped at the look Julie gave her.

"I don't know who you have in your life," Julie said matter-of-factly, "but that little guy out there has missed you as much as any friend or family member I've ever known."

"He's a menace," she said. "Those statues are important."

"I'll fix it," I said, leaning against the doorframe, my hands behind my back to bear the weight.

"That's not the point," she said. "Everything that's gone wrong here is because of him."

How easy that was, blame everything on the little demon dude. Yeah, he was odd, and could eat a truck, but he loved her, would kill for her, and she suddenly didn't give a shit about him. What happened?

"You know he'd take a bullet for you, right?"

"Justin told me you were running wild here. Said I should watch my back." She made a face and took a long pull on her beer. I wanted to smack her, shake her, knock some sense into her . . . I could feel the anger rising, the heat building, and realized it before I reacted. This place was a hot spot, and with her and Bub both hurt, doubly so. "You saw Justin?"

She laughed. "He called me, warned me about your meddling."

What the fuck? "You know he's screwing with you, right? Remember how he took your stuff, stole your designs?"

She stared at me a minute. "He said you'd be defensive, worried he'd see through your schemes."

"I've never met the bastard," I said, defensive. "But he was mixed up with Duchamp, dabbled in some nasty shit."

"You're just jealous of him," she said, sounding more and more like a lunatic. "You don't understand his genius."

Julie leaned forward. "This is the young man who hurt you?"

Anezka turned her head slowly toward Julie and shrugged. "Maybe you're right. He's not important."

"Look," I said. "You've been through a lot in the last week or so. Maybe you're just tired."

"Yeah, maybe," she said, pushing back from the table. She drained off the last of her beer and sat the bottle in the middle of the table. "But I need to get laid and drunk, not necessarily in that order."

Julie raised her eyebrows. "Don't look at me."

Anezka looked at me, and I winced. Seriously?

"Drunk it is," she said and turned to the fridge.

I crossed to the table and pushed the door closed before she could get it open. "I'm not sure beer and your meds go together too well."

She looked at me: hurt, anger, fear, and lust warred on her face. "Kiss me," she said. I stepped back, and she laughed, opening the fridge. She grabbed a beer and walked toward the back of the house.

Julie looked at me, stunned. "What the hell was that?"

I glanced around the room. "There's something seriously fucked up about this place, and it seems to be getting worse."

I knew what I had to do. I only knew one person with expertise in magic. I needed to call in the big guns. Best way to find out if Nidhogg was involved as well.

"I'll make a call."

Julie nodded at me, took her water, and walked into the living room.

Careful who you owe a favor to, huh? I hadn't talked to Qindra since the night of the Flight Test meeting. She'd been very personable at the bar afterward.

I reached for my cell phone, cursed colorfully since I didn't have it, damn it all. Who else had her number?

Jennifer . . . Flight Test had records for all board members. I walked to the back of the house. "Anezka, you okay?"

She came out of the bedroom, naked, and sat on the beanbag chair, drinking her beer.

"Lovely," Julie said.

"I'll be okay," Anezka said. "As soon as the acid kicks in."

And I didn't think this could get any worse.

"Can I use your cell phone?" I asked Julie, specifically avoiding looking at Anezka.

"Please," Julie agreed, fishing it out of her pocket. "Whoever you are calling, tell them to hurry."

I walked out the front door and to the carport, calling to Bub. He and I had to come to an agreement before I could call Qindra. Some things needed to be kept secret; I just had that feeling.

# Fifty-one

It took me three phone calls to track down Jennifer. Don't know why I didn't try Carl's place first. Silly me. They were so much in the goofy stage of lurve, it was hard to listen to. I only got off the phone by promising to bring Katie by for dinner sometime soon. Sheesh.

I called Qindra's number. She answered on the first ring and didn't even pretend to be a normal person. "Hello, Sarah," she said. "I see you are in need of something major."

That wasn't creepy, nope. Not one little bit. "Hello, Qindra. Yes, I need a favor."

"That makes two of us."

Awesome. I couldn't imagine a favor I could do for her. "Could I bother you to take a road trip?"

"Yes, well." She paused. "How far out?"

"Chumstick, out Highway 2, out past Leavenworth."

There was some movement on the other end, and I thought I heard glassware clinking. Crystals, maybe?

"I need to show you something anyway," she said. "Easy enough for me to come to you. Can you be more specific about exactly where you are?"

I told her, and we wrapped up. I had the strangest idea that she was put out that she didn't know where I was. Was she tracking me, somehow?

Next I needed to let Bub in on the game plan. I spent the next few minutes talking him off the roof of the house. "She's sick," I told him, "but I've called in some help."

He looked at me, alarmed. "If she is broken, who did you call?"

Another thing I hadn't considered. Who'd he know?

"Someone who can deal with magic and other odd things."

He shook his head from side to side. "No," he said, wringing his hands. "No, no, no . . ." He began pacing back and forth across the carport. "You cannot bring them here."

"Who do you think I mean?"

"Her . . ." he said, his voice quavering. "She who must be obeyed."

"Who?"

"The ancient one?" he asked, confused. "The Corpse Gnawer?"

Nidhogg . . . ah. Okay, he's heard of her.

"No, not her."

He relaxed visibly, slumping against the warrior statue, sliding to the ground, nearly deflating.

"But," I said, causing him to look up. "I called one of her people."

"The Eyes?"

I shook my head.

"Mouth?" He was panicked.

I nodded. Qindra had mentioned being the mouth of Nidhogg when we first met. I took it to mean she was her spokesmodel— the talking-head portion of the team. Nidhogg probably didn't get out much these days.

"She is hard, that one," he said. He turned once on the spot, sniffing the air. "I should not be here."

Before I could stop him, he vanished. I didn't know where he went in those moments, but it was damn unsettling.

I continued taking down streamers and crepe paper. It would be a mess once it started raining again, and for this area, that could be any second now. I shivered as a wind kicked up. It was definitely growing colder. May not be rain too much longer. This far into the mountains it would be snow, and likely lots of it.

I could see the appeal of the isolated life here, but it didn't seem to be serving Anezka very well these days, all this alone time. Maybe it was time for her to move into town. Not that she'd listen to me.

Qindra pulled onto the shoulder across from the house, looked at her map, and got out of her little Miata. She'd been close, I think. Probably in Leavenworth when she'd answered the phone. So, she was out looking for me. This just kept getting more interesting.

As she climbed out of her car, it struck me as a little creepy that she drove the same car as Katie. She looked around, appeared bewildered. I called to her, and she spun around, searching for my voice, but couldn't see me just across the road. Odd.

I dropped the last bunch of pink and white paper into the large burn barrel and crossed the yard. Once I was into the street, she spun in my direction, like she could sense me.

"Sarah?" she asked, a little shock and annoyance in her voice.

"Hey, Qindra." I waved, crossing the distance to her, and held out my hand.

She looked relieved as she took my hand. Her grip was firm enough, but her hands were soft. She did no physical labor, that's for sure. Oh, I had no doubt about her powers.

"What the hell's going on around here?" she asked.

I think she was not scared exactly but disconcerted, shaken.

"Part of why I called you," I said, stepping back and putting my hands in my pockets. I could feel the amulet there, tucked in behind my wallet in my front left pocket. I had my keys in the right,

along with my loose money. What has it gots in its pocketsses . . . ?
I laughed. This place definitely made me feel strange.

We stood at the car, and I explained a few of the recent events.
I kept Bub out of it, but she'd probably pick up his taint. Didn't
want to prejudice her on this. Let her come to her discoveries as
she could.

Besides, once I showed her the carvings, she'd pick up on the
aura of bat-shit crazy.

She listened intently. "Does this have anything to do with what
happened in the spring?"

I shrugged. "Not that I'm aware of, why? You think this is
dragon business?"

She jerked her head around to stare at me, choosing her next
words carefully. "This place is heavy with magic, protective charms,
and . . . ," she paused, touching her left temple, ". . . other things."

Her nails were not all painted like the time I'd seen her in the
past. They were plain, shiny with a clear coat, but no magic runes
adorned the nails. She was not prepared for battle or anything.
Well, as far as I could tell. I knew so little about her.

"How'd you get here so fast?" I asked.

"I was shopping in Leavenworth," she said, smiling. "Woke up
this morning jonesing for one of those fantastic gingerbread cakes
and a set of crystal glasses."

I gave her my best "Spock is confused" look. "Seriously?"

She shrugged. "I have a life."

"Now, for this place . . ." She drew a long wand out of her jacket
and wove an intricate rune in the air. It blossomed in front of her,
and I stepped beside her to see through it. It was like the magic
mirror on *Romper Room*. Who do I see in my magic mirror? She
glanced at me, her eyes questioning, but she did not stop me from
pressing my shoulder against hers to get a better view.

The rune expanded into a sphere about three feet across. It was like looking through a huge magnifying glass, only this one didn't make things bigger, just clearer.

"There is some distinctly distasteful power at work here," she said.

The buildings were there, just as you'd expect, but there was a red and black haze over everything. The carport was exceptionally bad, but the back corner of the house was freaky nightmareland. It was horrible, nauseating. There was a palpable evil there, something oozing and hungry, and there was a tendril drawn taut from the house to . . . I looked down . . . my midsection. I took a step back, and the tendril grew thinner but did not break. I looked back to the house, to the churning miasma of bruises and blood— the steady pulse that undulated against the gathering storm clouds. I felt a hitch in my stomach as the coffee I'd had earlier soured. I had to look away and concentrate real hard not to vomit. Holy shit.

"That what you asked me out here for?"

"Oh, god." A final glance through the rune set me off. I bent over, hands on my knees, and tried to breathe. My brain couldn't really describe what I saw. It was more a feeling, or a smell, but it was definitely nasty. Death, decay, evil. Grade-A evil, dude. Saliva flooded my mouth, and I knew what was next.

I stepped away from her and fell to my knees vomiting. My vision wavered, and I closed my eyes. My stomach heaved, and I heard the splatter of sick on concrete. I heaved a couple of times. There was nothing much in there beyond coffee, but I was thinking about tossing out a spleen. It hurt, the muscles spasming and my throat burning. For a second, I thought I would drown in it.

Then I felt Qindra's touch, and a coolness washed through me.

"You have been infected," she said. "This place is like a virus, a living thing looking to spread its hold onto anyone who is exposed."

When I raised my head again, the house looked normal, but I was terrified. "My friends are in there."

"They shouldn't be," she said matter-of-factly. "We should see what we can do to fix this."

She strode across the road, stopped briefly at the barrier, and said a few words, swishing her wand around like she was clearing away smoke. A gong sounded in my head, and a great moan reverberated from the house.

"Did you hear that?" I asked, but the look on her face told me she had.

The next moment, Julie slammed open the front door and hobbled out, looking over her shoulder at the house. "She's losing it," she called. "Better get in here."

The barrier was gone. We ran toward the house, and Anezka came out, covered in blood, screaming like a banshee and brandishing a large knife. Julie saw her at the last moment and dove sideways, swinging her cane up to block the knife as Anezka flung herself at her.

"Not prepared for this," Qindra said, looking over at me. "I'm not equipped."

Got it, no magic fingernails, nothing to stop a screaming psycho. Fuck.

I launched myself at Anezka, catching her in a full-body tackle and carrying both of us into a hedge. She was naked and bleeding; cuts crisscrossed her torso. Julie scrambled out of the way.

Anezka hadn't dropped the knife. I remembered enough of my martial-arts training to know I was screwed. I tried to block her knife hand, but she jerked back at the last second. I missed her wrist. The blade sliced the side of my hand, sending a flare of pain up my arm—hurt like hell.

I brought my knee up, catching Anezka in the breadbasket. She rolled to the side, swinging the knife. I saw it in slow motion. The blade was going to catch me in the thigh: I was trying to move, but a shrub tangled me.

Julie brought her cane down on Anezka's arm out of nowhere. Anezka screamed and dropped the knife. Julie swung the cane a second time and clocked Anezka in the side of the head, sending her back onto the lawn, stunned if not unconscious.

"Nobody move," Qindra called, and I looked up in time to see Bub. He'd appeared out of nowhere. He looked from me to Qindra, and finally to Anezka.

"Sorry," he mouthed. He lunged forward and grabbed Anezka. I tried to reach her, grab her by the leg if nothing else, but I was too late. Bub wrapped her in his thin, scaly arms and vanished, carrying her away with him.

Didn't see that coming.

I rolled onto my back, panting and holding my bleeding hand to my chest, looking up at the gathering clouds. Rain tonight, I thought. Storm likely.

Qindra leaned over me and held out her hand to help me up. "We should get that cleaned up and bandaged."

"Good idea," I said, taking her hand. My ass was going to hurt tomorrow. I'd hit the ground pretty hard on my left hip and butt.

Julie leaned on her cane pretty heavily, her breathing ragged and fast. "Not in as good a shape as I was before the . . . ," she looked over at Qindra, ". . . spring."

Qindra nodded and held the door as we both limped inside. She took the wand and drew a warding line around the door. The frame glowed blue for a long time after.

Blood was smeared across the kitchen cabinets, along one doorframe, and on the wall leading down the hall. There were swirls and glyphs painted in Anezka's blood.

"Lot of death here," Qindra said, eyeing the macabre artwork. "This could take a while."

She took out her cell phone and walked out onto the front porch. "I'm going to need some things."

Julie set an overturned kitchen chair upright and sat down with a grunt. "She went crazy just about the time Qindra got here," she said. "Was going for another beer when she grabbed the knife instead. Almost killed me, but thankfully she's still pretty weak . . . and fairly fucked up."

"Lucky, I guess."

She watched me for a minute and shook her head. "You're bleeding, Beauhall. Let's see how bad it is."

I winced. "Careful." Julie was good with cuts and such. Tended enough horses with minor wounds. I just gritted my teeth. No stitches, please. I hated stitches.

She stood, came to the sink where I was standing, and pulled my hand away from my chest. She ran it under cold water and clucked at the flap of skin that came off my palm partway.

"Stitches it is," she said. "We'll need to get you to a doctor. Unless there's stuff here?" She looked at me, expecting me to know everything. Hell, I hadn't snooped around, just slept on the couch and kept Bub company while Anezka was in the hospital.

We ransacked the bathroom and found a fairly empty emergency kit. There was gauze, but no tape. Nothing we needed for stitches. "She did some horse doctoring in her day," she said. "Might have some stuff out in the shop."

I shrugged. "She's got several lockers out there. Not sure what's in 'em."

"Guess we should go look," she said. "Just hope there's no bodies in there."

I shivered. Nothing had smelled when I was out there, but now that Qindra had broken the barrier that surrounded the house, I could smell an underlying odor of decay. Funny thing was, when the barrier fell, I didn't feel like I was being kept out, but that something had been unleashed.

As we crossed the carport, Qindra watched us and waved. Nothing too earth-shattering yet. I reached into my right pocket and felt the amulet. I bet I could call Bub back. Only, would he bring Anezka with him? She wasn't a bad person, Frank vouched for her, but she'd definitely lost her damn mind.

The lockers held junk, mostly. There were no med kits for horses or humans, but we did find a lot of collected crap: old work boots, coveralls, welding goggles, gloves. The typical stuff. No bodies, thank god. There was duct tape, however. We grabbed it and went back into the house. Iodine, clean gauze, and duct tape can make a pretty good field bandage. Was waterproof mostly and held together well. Nothing to do now but wait. The cut wasn't too deep, pretty shallow really but wide.

Qindra was still on the phone by the time I was bandaged, so I grabbed a couple of towels and mopped the water off the table from earlier. Once that was done, I took down a couple of clean glasses and got water for Julie and me.

"Qindra says the house is basically haunted. Bad juju," I said.

"That's a big duh," Julie said, taking the glass from me. "If this place was any more bizarre, I'd expect to see Bruce Campbell coming through the door."

I glanced at the door, just in case. No one came in. I could see Qindra out in the lawn talking on her cell and assessing the house. This was going to take a full-court press, apparently.

The blood came off the walls and counter reluctantly. Seemed like I was always cleaning up blood these days. Julie spent the next fifteen minutes dumping all the alcohol that she could find— seventeen beers, two bottles of tequila, and a pint of absinthe. That stuff would kill you.

I sat down and drank my water, toying with the amulet. Where were they? I scooted my chair around so my back was against the wall. I didn't want any surprises.

And so we waited for Qindra to finish or for Bub and Anezka to show back up. Was a helluva day so far.

# Fifty-two

QINDRA CAME BACK IN. I GAVE HER THE STORY AS I KNEW IT, putting the amulet on the table. She looked, but did not touch it. I flipped it over for her to examine the back, then slipped it back into my pocket.

"Old," she said. "I'll want to study it at some point, but not right now." She looked around the house, sensing, it appeared, trying to feel the way of things. "There is something old here, ancient, but the taint, the evil, that is here is newer, fresher." She stopped turning and looked at me, her eyes steely and full of anger. "There's been death here. Much death . . . and"—she paused, sniffed—"I taste pain in the air."

I gave her the grand tour of the joint, pointing out the wood carvings in the carport. I didn't take her to see the warriors and the dragon. Not yet. I wanted her to ask, to give a hint that she expected them to be there.

Once we'd made the circuit, she walked from room to room, casting runes and covering damn near every surface with little blue squiggles. They were readings, absorbing surrounding magic and glowing with intensity based on the amount present. The hallway grew brighter the closer we got to the back of the house. Like a freaking nuclear reactor in a cartoon.

"There's some serious power here," she said. "More than any

place I've been to, honestly. I wonder . . ." She trailed off, lost in thought. After a minute, she pulled out her phone and texted someone. "I'm willing to wager this house was built on a nexus," she said, smiling at me. "If that's true, we'll need some extra-strength haint remover."

"Nexus?" Julie asked from the couch.

"Haint?" I asked at the exact same time.

"*Haint* is a haunt, ghost, spirit, revenant. Really bad," Julie said, smiling.

"Oh." That made sense.

Qindra explained about the rarity of a nexus and how the dragons tried to keep track of any that formed. "They are not permanent, except in a few rare cases. We have the obvious spots like Stonehenge, Easter Island, several points along the Black Sea, and a few others I'd better not mention."

She talked about the known points of power and how they affected the areas around them. It was rather academic, actually, and I found myself losing interest—big blobs of untapped power. Excellent for almost no one.

I let Julie carry the conversation after a while. Waiting for Qindra's cavalry to arrive got me to thinking. It was spooky, wondering who was coming. Maybe I should even the odds and call in some Black Briar folks? But no, they were getting ready for the big event tonight and didn't need to be bothered. Besides, Nidhogg and her crew knew who I was. They didn't know all of Jimmy's folks. Keeping them anonymous was part of keeping them safe.

Still, I took Julie's cell phone and called Katie. Just to let her know what had happened, and to let her know we had things under control.

Man, she was pissed, but that's one of the things I love about her. Lot of passion in that woman. Protective and feisty. I'd been really looking forward to the party tonight. There was still a chance I'd make it, but I wasn't holding my breath. The day was getting on.

Qindra looked at my hand when I got back in and did something with her wand that made it tingle and itch. "Shouldn't need stitches," she said. "I could've fixed you up better if we'd had whiskey." She looked over at all the empties in the sink. "Not a whiskey kinda gal, I guess."

Julie dug through the fridge and made sandwiches from the supplies I'd laid in, and we each ate like we hadn't eaten in a week. Nothing like turkey and mayo to really hit the spot. The apples were the topper, though, sweet and crunchy. I loved how the flavor exploded in my mouth, clearing the final sour dregs from my earlier vomiting jag.

"Could I speak with you in private?" Qindra asked me after we'd eaten.

"Go on," Julie said, grabbing plates. "I'll clean this up."

"My thanks," Qindra said, bowing her head. "Sarah is lucky to have you for a mistress."

Julie watched us walk out, and I shrugged at her, smiling. The door closed behind us, and Qindra breathed into her hands. It was still early in the day, but it was growing colder. We walked past the abstract art, across the yard, and over to her car. Felt safer. Being in the yard felt like we were being watched—like someone or something was listening.

"With all the excitement, I'm not sure how to approach this." She looked down at her hands. Was she nervous? This must be the favor she wanted. "I know of your recent altercation in Vancouver."

I raised my eyebrows. I wasn't going to volunteer information.

"We have been contacted by someone." She paused. "Someone . . . unsavory."

"You?" I asked in mock surprise. "I thought you and the dragon types only hung out with the classiest sorts of people."

She rolled her eyes. "You are lucky I like you," she said. "There are those who fear to look at me, much less speak with such a familiar tone."

True enough, and I was asking her for a favor. But this place just made me reckless, more mouthy than normal, if that was possible.

"Before we get into the mystery of this place," she said, waving her hand across the street. "I need to ask you if you've encountered this so-called Dragon Liberation Front."

I blinked. "I'm sorry, what?"

She waved her hands. "Never mind who they are. They have contacted my mistress, offering an auction of a very interesting wine."

"Mead," I said without thinking.

She smiled and nodded slowly. "I had a feeling you knew something." She leaned back against the side of her car and crossed her arms. "My mistress desperately wants this . . . mead, as you point out. She believes it is imperative that she does not lose out to any of the other bidders."

"I'll play along," I said. "What other bidders?"

"That's a good question," she said, crossing her arms. "One would assume your dear friend Frederick Sawyer, but I have not confirmed that. We know there are four bidders. Considering Frederick as a likely candidate, and with Jean-Paul out of the picture, thanks to you—"

I bowed slightly, and she smiled.

"—that leaves two open slots. Are you aware of any further information in this matter?"

"Nope." Not sure I'd tell her the truth in any case, but being truthful was a good way to start. "I'm sure your mistress has the means to insure she wins this auction."

I don't know if it was the word *insure* or not, but she laughed. "She is not omnipotent," she said. "Her kind are powerful, granted, but they don't know everything."

"Thank god for small favors."

A cloudy look swept over her face. "It disturbs me, this place." She glanced from side to side, taking in the whole of the property. "This is in Nidhogg's dominion, and we had no idea of its existence."

"There's a lot of territory to cover," I said, being helpful.

"But I have never been to this place," she said, glancing back at the house. "There is powerful magic here. Something does not want to be seen, does not want to be scrutinized."

"So, you don't know Anezka?"

"I've never met the woman. Why do you ask?"

How should I play this? Bub knew her, or *of* her for sure, but was Qindra privy to all of Nidhogg's activities?

"Does your mistress fund much art?"

Now it was her turn to look confused. "Art? What do you mean?" She looked at the half a dozen sculptures in the yard and pointed. "Like those, you mean?"

I nodded. "Anezka was being funded by someone with power, someone who wanted her to make some things, commissioned the work in the back there. Sort of a diorama."

"I can inquire, but I doubt it has anything to do with Nidhogg. She does favor good dwarf-made items, but I've never known her to commission any art. Can you show me?"

"Sure." I motioned to the house, and we crossed back over. A thick layer of psychic filth settled over me once again as I crossed the road. How had I missed that? Maybe the house saw me as an enemy now, instead of an ally. Was it because of Anezka's crack-up? Or maybe she lost it because of the bad juju here? Or, it dawned on me: maybe it was because Qindra had broken the barrier.

We crossed through the carport, into the shop, and out the back door. Qindra stopped short, whistled softly, and took out her wand. "Beautiful work," she said. "The craftsmanship is stunning, but there is dark magic here." She stepped to one of the warriors, his arm held high, his sword ready to smite the dragon. "I don't understand how I missed the draw of this when I went through the house."

"Is it related?"

She glanced around, then pulled several small packets from her coat pocket. She bent one in half, and it cracked open. She spilled salt into her hand. They were from a fast-food restaurant.

"Seriously?" I asked, pointing. "You get your best magic supplies from drive-thrus?"

She laughed. "Salt is salt. It matters not where it is acquired." She paused. "Well, under most circumstances." She winked at me, the tramp, and began to sprinkle a pinch on each of the fighting men. They seemed to swell, gain stature, as it were, before settling back into their normal stances.

"Very interesting," she said. She looked at the salt in her palm, then to the huge dragon statue. "Definitely related," she said, and brushed the remainder of the salt from her palms, scattering it in the grass. "There is a connection, an umbilical of the same sort you were linked with. Each of these statues is linked to the house. Not the ones out front," she said quickly. "They are not the same. Here." She turned, drawing the rune from earlier in the air. "You can see for yourself."

There were strands from each of the warriors to the house—to the back room across from Anezka's bedroom. Had either of us been in there? Had Skella?

"Should we go look where those lead?" I asked, feeling sick to my stomach again. The turkey sandwich was starting to turn. Qindra must have noticed me turning green, because she touched me with her wand, flooding me with calm. With several strokes of her wand, the black tendrils fell away from me, disconnecting me from the house. I felt light, airy.

"You're like totally awesome for anxiety," I said, smiling. "You could make a fortune helping people."

She laughed at that. "My powers are not all that amazing," she said, walking back into the carport. "Parlor tricks, mostly."

"Uh-huh." I'd seen her call down lightning and make a Black Hawk helicopter explode. She was one dangerous woman. But maybe I'd caught her off her game. She'd been in Leavenworth when I'd called her. This side of the mountains. Not like she always traveled ready for combat. Hell, I didn't have my hammers or Gram. Not like I went around slaying dragons every day or anything. Maybe Qindra had a real life. Maybe she really just wanted to shop in Leavenworth today. But I didn't like the coincidence.

She refused to go into the back rooms until her help arrived. Made sense to me. Instead, we spent the next hour discussing the dragon statue and the differences in dragon anatomy. The dragon statue did not resemble any she'd seen before: not Frederick, Nidhogg, Jean-Paul, or any of the other six or seven she'd seen.

"This one is unknown to me," she said. "I'd like to know what my mistress would think of it."

"Well, someone commissioned the lot," I said, tapping one of the warriors with my tennies. "By the amount of money and magic involved, I can't see how it could be anything but dragon involvement."

She looked at me, assessing. "You are a child, Sarah Beauhall. There are many powers in the world, dragons and witches, true, but more unseemly things, and some more powerful than even Nidhogg."

"Powerful enough to cause this?" I pointed at the house.

"This seems like magic gone wrong, a combination of several things intermingled to form something worse."

I discussed the artists who'd lived here, the woman who carved, and the man whom they both loved.

"There has been death here," Qindra said. "Not quick death, but lingering—bloody and painful. Someone relished the pain they caused here, forged a bond between the house and the agony."

"Should we just burn the place down?"

She thought about it briefly, but shook her head. "No, I'm afraid we will need to spend time with stronger magic, digging around in the between places, looking for what has poisoned the ground."

Which brought me back to my little scaly buddy. "What do you know of Bub? Could he be involved?" Man, I hoped not. I was liking him. He seemed as much a victim here as Anezka.

She looked at me, considering her reply. "I assume you mean the scaly guy who snatched your friend, Anezka. I have never met one of his kind, but I have heard of them." She stepped through the doorway and crossed the carport to the driveway. I followed.

Qindra picked up a stone and squatted. I squatted down beside her, and she used the stone to draw on the concrete. "There are seven worlds, or so say the ancient ones."

"Beside Nidhogg, what other ancient ones do you know?"

"Only one other," she said, sketching. "But he disappeared before I was born. My mother met him." She looked over at me.

"Odd little man, more powerful than anyone my mother had ever met. Had no greater ambition than to sing on Broadway."

"Where did she meet this man?"

She finished drawing a large tree, with seven great branches. At the bottom, she drew a lounging dragon, and in the treetop, she drew a bird. "Buffalo," she said. "He played the vaudeville circuit. Dressed as a woman and sang the most haunting ballads."

"Ballads?"

For a moment, she was lost in thought; then she sang the first few lines of a sad song:

> *In a spot of land, where the rivers run*
> *and the Glori Mundi bloom*
> *I met a girl like the brightest star*
> *A peck of Gallen, like the kiss I craved*
> *Were not for such as me*

The tune was haunting, lyrical, and melancholy.

"I don't recognize all the words."

She drew several large globes hanging off the tree she'd drawn, smiling up at me. "Young Katie would know," she said.

I glared at her, and she laughed.

"Glori Mundi, and Gallen are apples. Teachers still get apples these days, do they not?"

Teacher . . . apples, yeah I got it.

"This tree," she said, tapping on each branch, "is Yggdrasil."

"Figured that when you said ancient ones," I said, annoyed. I didn't like that she knew Katie. Not one little bit. Oh, they'd met after the battle, but . . . I took a breath. Keep it under control. Just a quiet conversation about mythology. She's not a threat. Not yet, in any case.

"Your friend, Bub," she continued, tapping one of the left-side branches nearest the bottom of the tree. "He comes from Múspell, the land of fire."

"Yeah, that much I got," I said. "Of course, the World Tree is only a metaphor."

It was her turn to look smug. "There are those—my mistress among them—that believe this tree to exist. One of her greatest regrets is losing her way to Yggdrasil. Not since her youth has she gnawed its hoary roots."

"Sounds sexual to me."

Qindra laughed, falling back to sit on her rear. "I have considered my mistress in many circumstances." She had a bemused look on her face. "Like a parent, I guess, one does not consider them as sexual beings without trepidation."

"Jean-Paul was one of hers, was he not?"

She sobered then, nodding once. "Blood kin, child of her bones, but loathsome to her in memory."

Right evil bastard. May the devil drag his scaly carcass to hell before the good lord knows he's dead. Or something like that. I spit to the side and waved the warding sign I'd picked up from Katie over the last couple of years.

Qindra nodded appreciatively and stood, brushing the dirt from the back of her slacks. I jumped up, as much to put us on even footing as anything else. "So, that all you got about Bub? His hometown?"

She shrugged. "I am learned in many things, Sarah. But there are mysteries I have not plumbed."

"Fair enough." I slipped my hands back in my pockets, toying with the amulet. "Where do you think he goes when he teleports away?"

"Damn good question," she said and looked up sharply. "They are arriving."

I turned and looked down the road. Several vans came toward us.

"You should take your mistress and leave here," she said kindly, patting me on the shoulder. "What I have to do here will not be pleasant."

"What about Anezka . . . or Bub, for that matter?" I asked, feeling suddenly out of control. I had an obligation to this place, to Bub and Anezka.

"We will deal with them, when and if they reappear."

Julie came out onto the porch, wiping her hands on a paper towel. "Cavalry?" she asked.

I walked over to the house. "Yeah, scary, freaky exterminators," I said.

"More along the lines of energy-management crew," Qindra said, walking up to Julie. She held out her hand and shook it. "I would like to offer my condolences for your experiences of the spring," she said. "My mistress regrets that one of her valued citizens would suffer at the hands of her own."

Julie stiffened, but I shook my head. As if to say, *not now, don't get into it,* but she was savvy. "I thank you for your kind words," she said, giving Qindra's hand a final shake, before letting her hand drop back to the head of her cane.

This brought a smile to Qindra. "If you would like me to help with your hip . . ." She shrugged. "I may be able to ease the pain."

Julie looked at her, a long steady gaze. "No thank you," she said, as sweetly as can be. "Nothing personal."

Qindra bowed her head. "I assumed as much." Her smile was genuine.

She walked us to the Taurus while the vans pulled along the side of the road. They were each a nondescript white, fairly shiny, enough to draw attention if anyone came this way.

Not like that would happen. No one exited the vans, however. Awaiting Qindra's signal, no doubt.

Part of me was glad to be leaving the place. Since she'd broken the protective circle, I was feeling sicker and sicker being there.

"Oh, one more thing," Qindra said, holding up one hand to stall us. She opened her car and dug in the glove box for a moment. As she swung around and shut the door with her hip, I could see she had a small box and an envelope.

I took the envelope from her first, slid out the single handwritten sheet of parchment, and read it.

*Most Glorious Queen of the Night, Mightiest of the Mighty, She Who Must Be Obeyed,*

*We bring you tidings from the reaches of the far kingdoms. It is our great pleasure to offer you the nectar of the Gods. Not since the days of our most ancient fathers have the children of Durin provided such a wonder unto the world. The rumors of a mighty potion that sharpens the mind while allowing the voice to flow like honey are once again brought forth unto Migard by the humble yet crafty children of flame.*

*Please find the accompanying phial of this most excellent elixir. If it pleases you, we will auction the full vintage at a date and time to be disclosed upon final verification of your interest and ample time for fermentation.*

*Be advised, three of your estimable and worthy peers shall be included in this lively exchange. If it pleases you, follow the instructions that accompany the phial to contact us.*

> *Yours in bondage*
> *The Honorable Gentlemen of*
> *The Dragon Liberation Front*

Beneath the signature was a large stamp of a dragon rising above a fallen warrior. Reminded me of various woodcuts I'd seen in medieval texts we studied in college.

I handed the note to Julie and accepted the box from Qindra. Inside, ensconced in Bubble Wrap, was a test tube with a thick layer of wax over what I assumed was a cork plug. Qindra nodded at me as I grasped the vial. It slid out of the package easily. Handling it was tingly, like a slight current ran through it. She watched my face as I took it from the box.

"Interesting," I said, watching her watch me.

"You feel it, too, I guess."

I nodded and held it up to the sky. It glowed in the milky light of the failing afternoon. It was amber with a hint of red, but slightly cloudy.

I never brewed my own mead, but Katie was a huge fan. This would be fairly early for a fine mead. Probably still rather yeasty, not mellow at all. No way of knowing how long it had been fermenting before they added the blood. Ari had been kidnapped only a couple of weeks ago. He was alive according to Skella and Gletts. Skella had said they'd bled him to make a test batch. Not enough to kill him right away.

However the mead might taste, and I had no urge to open the cork, I could feel the energy radiating outward. Just holding it in my hand gave me a thrill, like a tickle along my back brain. It felt powerful, and a little dangerous, in a good way. Almost sexual . . . primal.

"You know what this is made from?" I asked.

Qindra nodded. "I have heard rumors of such a potion from deep in the past. And I have certain ways of categorizing the type of magic represented here."

Julie slid the letter into the envelope, handed it to Qindra, and held her hand out for the vial. I let her have it reluctantly. I wanted to keep it, to possess it. I couldn't imagine what a full tun of this would be like.

Julie eyed it, looking from me to Qindra, and shrugged. "I got nothing."

Qindra smiled, and I took the vial back from Julie.

"It is a subtle power," Qindra said. "It would take one who is very learned, or very sensitive, to detect it." She held the box out for me to return the potion.

I slid it back into the Bubble Wrap nest with a twinge of regret.

"We need to test this, of course," she said, closing the lid to the box, and holding it against her chest. "Blood magic is very old, very powerful." She pointed toward Anezka's place. "Not unlike what is unbalanced with your friend's home."

A shiver ran through me. I could feel something wild and chaotic swirling in the air, like the scent of a wounded beast.

Qindra seemed to sense it as well. She waved toward the vans, and they opened. Sixteen individuals climbed out of the four vans in full environmental suits, each carrying a pack, instrument, box, or, in two cases, caged animals: a cat and a large crow.

"I should see to this," she said, patting me on the arm. "You should be on the other side of the mountains before full dark. I'd rather there be distance between you and your new trinket . . . ," she pointed to my pocket, "and whatever is happening here."

I slid my hand into my pocket and felt the amulet. Was it part of the problem, or just tangled in its web?

"The amulet has claimed you, you realize," she said, her features set, her face stern. "I believe it switched its allegiance to you when Anezka first let you handle it. That is when things began to unravel here."

"Oh, great. So, part of this is my fault?"

Qindra shook her head. "Nay. Someone else is at play here. The amulet is a different issue. This place is a powder keg."

Julie waved the keys in the air, alerting me to her getting in the driver's seat.

"I need to know if Anezka or Bub comes back," I said. "I'd

rather they were safe and found shelter than . . ." I looked into her eyes, holding her gaze, ". . . otherwise."

"I will do what I can," Qindra said. There was a slight pause; then she bowed to me, a short dip that surprised me. I'd seen Mr. Philips bow like that, knew it as a way of showing respect. I bowed back, being careful to keep my eyes on hers. I had no intention of her believing I was less than her equal.

She grinned, and I knew she understood.

"Let me know," I said, opening the passenger-side door.

The cleaning crew was running police tape around the property, nearly out onto the road.

"What will the neighbors say?" I asked.

She shrugged. "They will believe what we tell them. Gas leak, something unobtrusive yet threatening enough to keep them away."

I shook my head. It was all about the words we believed, the words we told each other to make us behave in a certain way. The world was greased with the honeyed words of power brokers like Qindra and her mistress.

And they wanted the mead, the power to enhance their already-ill-bridled control over the populace.

She waved at us as we pulled away. I know she'd clean the place, or lock it down so none of Nidhogg's other thralls would be entangled in the decay and chaos. I just couldn't imagine what the payment for something like this would entail. Something I would be loathe to part with, I was sure.

I'd cross that bridge when the bill came due. In the meantime I had to do what I could for Anezka and even Bub, the little biter.

I closed my eyes as Julie did a three-point turn and left the space suits in our wake.

I'd be seeing Katie soon, be among friends. Didn't mean I'd

worry any less. Felt like running from a fight. It was a letdown, actually, a disquiet that I had abandoned my post.

Maybe being a grown-up was knowing when to take help and letting someone else clean up some of the messes.

Still tasted like failure to me.

# Fifty-three

THE DAY WAS STARTING TO FADE BY THE TIME WE PULLED
into Black Briar. There were a dozen cars and trucks in the yard
and a passel of folk. Gunther was directing a crowd to get a bonfire
set up. Made me think back to the battle in the spring, how the giants and dragon had scattered that bonfire, setting smaller fires in
the thick grass, making the battlefield that much more crazy.

I wandered over to the old barn while Julie hobbled into the
house to see Deidre. She'd leave soon, but for now she wanted to
be social.

I didn't see Katie's car. Stuart was helping a couple of young
guys carry out one of the newly built picnic tables that could seat
a dozen or more. They were lining them up along the side of the
new barn; two others were already in place. No one seemed to
notice me right away, so I stepped into the ruined barn.

Smells of damp and burned wood filled my nostrils. I'm not
sure anyone had crossed over the ruined threshold into the barn
proper since Maggie had ridden through the raging fire to attack
Jean-Paul in her suicide mission to try and save Susan—or join
her in death.

We knew the ground was tainted, so there could be no fires
anywhere the dragon had flamed or bled. Not until the ground
was purged clean. We'd lit candles just after the battle, and the

fires had roared a dozen feet into the sky, consuming the candles
and threatening to leap over to unscorched grass.

Not something we wanted to repeat.

I wandered out past the bonfire, along the north edge of the
fields, where the valley opened up and the ground fell away, toward a copse of trees I'd visited after the battle. I'd been brutally
wounded but was chasing Jean-Paul in his dragon form.

In that copse I'd found the winged horses of the Valkyrie—met
Gunnr, the stunningly beautiful and intoxicating warrior woman
who made me forget my own name for a moment . . . but not Katie's. I smiled at that. A kiss was her price to take her elegant steed
Meyja.

She'd told me to call her name and she'd come to me. I could
almost smell her for a moment, a shadow of leather and cloves.

I sat on the grass and took out the amulet, turned it over in my
hand and watched the valley below slide into shadow. Where are
you, Bub? Anezka was crazed, but still he stole her away, to save
her, I'm sure.

I hoped she didn't kill him, or herself. If Qindra could purge
the house, maybe Anezka could gain some sort of life back. She
*had* been stable. Not normal, but I didn't have a good barometer
for what passed for normal these days. Maybe Qindra was right. I
flipped the amulet over, saw that the runes were shadowed in the
palm of my hand. I concentrated for a moment, willing the damn
thing to chill. I didn't want it melding with me.

The runes glowed bright for a second, and I felt a flash of heat run
up my arm. Then it started to dim back to low glow. My hand was
free of marks. I straightened the chain against my leg, stroking the
twisted links, letting my mind wander over to the other problem.

Durin's folk, the mead, the dragons and their need to control
the world. And what of the things Qindra had mentioned? Things
worse than dragons.

Skella had been scared, but she'd gone with Gletts. Not that he seemed particularly bent one way or another about her. I took it on faith that he loved her, the sibling that she was. But he was wary, wild. There was something about him—a coldness that spoke of pain and fear. They'd grown up under the open aggression of dragons, suffered the demented whims of Jean-Paul and his cronies. The dwarves had helped the elves, sort of. They were only learning now what a deal with the devil that was.

I sat in the clearing, pulled a long blade of grass from the cool earth, and sucked the tender tip. It tasted clean, not like the sour smell that filled my head.

In the distance I heard more people arrive and music start up. I sat there, lost in the peace of the trees, the ocean of darkness that swallowed the valley below.

I'd flown over that valley, felt the brush of the first rays of dawn above the clouds. It had been a moment of freedom amidst the death and chaos of the night's battle. I yearned for that clarity, that moment of freedom when there was only one path, only one right thing.

I stood, turned from the valley, and looked back at the house. There were my family, my friends, and my lover. That was where I belonged, not out here away from the maelstrom of joy and love.

I let the slip of grass fall from my mouth and crossed back through the trees. I slipped the chain over my head, settling the amulet against my chest. It felt right there, warm and comforting.

Time to join the real world again. Maybe this time to solve a problem, instead of fleeing one.

# Fifty-four

As I walked back, music started and the crowd broke into a rowdy cheer. Katie was on the deck singing and playing her guitar, along with a couple of other folks. They were new: one was a young woman with an Autoharp, and the other a young man with a mandolin. Gunther sat on the edge of the stage, and Stuart stood next to the tapped keg with his arms crossed and his eyes sweeping the crowd. He looked vigilant.

I felt my heart soar. The music swelled, and Katie's voice washed over the crowd:

> *Blacksmith, warrior, giant-slayer, friend.*
> *Sarah flew across the gray of the dawn*
> *pursuing the bastard Duchamp*
> *carrying the battle to the North.*

She'd written a song about me. Was that the surprise she'd promised me? I couldn't breathe for a moment, overwhelmed with emotion. I didn't want this, didn't want to be part of a song or a tale. I just wanted to live my life, protect those I cared for.

The clan clapped and stomped, cheering the musicians on, and Katie's voice rose, filling the world with her song.

I slowed, afraid to approach the crowd. Maybe Katie thought to draw me back to the fold. That would be like her, the sneak. I smiled and took a deep breath. No use fighting it, I reckoned. She was gonna be who she was, and I had no desire to change her. Maybe it wouldn't be that bad.

You know the universe listens, right? Like, hey, she's happy and letting things slide. Let's kick her in the slats.

That's what ran through my mind in the next second.

On the other side of the yard, near the burned-out barn, I saw him. The one-eyed bum, Joe or Odin. Who was he tonight? I veered in his direction, the music a happy background, but the world tunneled toward him . . . only him.

"'Ware, smith," he said, and vanished.

I spun around, searching. He appeared near Stuart, squatting on the top of the long table with a wolf at his side.

"Folly and peril," he said.

The song played on in the background, and the crowd was singing along, clapping and stomping. I staggered through them, looking for the mad beggar. "No riddles," I shouted, and the people nearest me looked at me like I was crazy. They faltered in their revelry and followed me with their eyes, open-jawed and confused.

There near the stage, I saw him again. I began shouting, pushing. The people in front of me started to realize something was going on and began turning, anger and frustration breaking their joyous moment.

He watched me, his arms raised to the heavens, and he sang. I cannot tell you what he sang, but it seemed to be my name, maybe the song that Katie herself sang.

Then he was gone again. I was almost to the stage when he vanished. Had he been a figment of my imagination?

Bam! The power on the farm flashed out. Even the bonfire seemed to fade. The crowd shifted, allowing me to move through. Faces peered at me in wonder and fear.

A wolf leapt onto the stage, larger than a pony. The band didn't notice, but the crowd saw, faltered in their singing, their voices mingling into shouts and astonished gasps.

"The witch has fallen!" Odin's great voice issued from the wolf's throat. "Black blood rises to our doom!"

The voice was so loud that people fell to the ground, covering their heads with their hands. I ran to the house, pushing people out of my way, calling to Katie. The wolf sprang at Katie but vanished before reaching her. She spun around as if sensing the attack. The other band members fled into the crowd, and the noise returned—shouting and screams.

The old man reappeared behind me, on the picnic table.

"More than your love hangs in the balance, smith. Choose wisely." He crumbled into shadow, and two great crows leapt upward, pulling toward the sky.

Fuck! Odin showing up wasn't a good sign. Qindra was down? She wasn't half-bad as a person, but she was damn powerful. What was up with that damn house?

I ran across the barnyard, into the back of the crowd. It was then I finally noticed. Stuart wasn't lounging—he was on watch. His people were as well. There were warriors posted around the place, armored and armed. The farm had become an encampment. They were not playing games. Nothing was going to catch them by surprise again.

I sprinted past the barn. Stuart was directing two young women, pointing first at me, then at the barn. I couldn't tell what he was saying, but he didn't try to stop me.

"Katie?" I called, spinning about. She was nowhere to be seen. For a moment I panicked as chaos reigned. People were shouting, calling to friends and loved ones. Then, Gunther's strong voice rose above the din, shouting commands. The crowd parted, and I had a clear shot at the house. I leapt up the stairs onto the deck.

The band had scattered, the instruments were gone as well. I looked back into the crowd one final time and turned to the house.

The door stood open. Jimmy was waving a flashlight around, swearing. Deidre had been spilled out of her chair. He rushed over and knelt at her side.

She pointed at me, and Jimmy turned, his face flush with anger.

"The elf took her," he growled.

"Her? Katie?" It couldn't be happening, not again. "Where?"

I followed where Deidre was pointing at a large hall mirror. "Not Katie, Melanie," she said, gasping. "She was with me moments before the power went out, just before the voice shook the house."

"What about Katie?" I asked.

"She was with the band?" Deidre said, confused. "Who's fallen, Sarah?"

"Damn it, Beauhall," Jimmy said, his voice a dangerous step away from rage.

"Was it Gletts?" I asked.

They didn't respond.

"The boy? Was it the boy or the girl?"

"Boy," Deidre said, pushing herself up on her hands. Jimmy stood quickly, righted the chair, and bent to pick her up. She locked her arms around his neck and he melted a little, letting some of the anger fade.

Once she was settled again, he turned to me. "What do we do now?"

I was torn. Qindra was down, fallen to something or someone at Anezka's place. That was two hours away, and I owed her. Melanie had been snatched by Gletts. He probably wouldn't hurt her; he wanted me—or more to the point, he wanted Gram. So why Melanie?

"Where's Julie?" I asked.

Jimmy did a double-take, shaking his head. "Gone, before the band started up. Why?"

"I need wheels."

"Take the bike," Gunther said, coming into the house. Stuart was at his shoulder, holding a bundle.

"You'll want this," Stuart said, laying my chain on the kitchen table.

I turned to Jimmy. "Right." Ducati, armor . . . and . . . I looked into his eyes. Time to push him. "I need Gram."

He started to shake his head, but Deidre placed her hand on his arm. "Don't be an ass. The sword claimed her."

"Deidre," he started, but her look stopped him.

"I don't care what you and those two have been cooking up. That's her sword; she remade it and earned it with her blood, if you don't recall how all this went down."

He lowered his head, and I could hear his teeth grinding.

"I don't like it," he said, but he turned and stalked to the back of the house.

I started to follow, but Deidre held up her hand. "Just hang tight. He'll bring it."

One of Stuart's crew came in with my harness, and Kyle George handed me a holster with two hammers in it. The handle of one was stained dark. I had used it in the spring. The second was new, but a sister to the first.

"Thanks, Kyle."

He nodded, blushing. "Owe you for saving my life."

What do you say to that? Obligation, debt? Or just accept it as gratitude.

"Anytime." I held out my hand, and he grasped my wrist, shaking solemnly.

"You seen Katie?" I asked him.

He shook his head. "No, but I'll go look."

"Thanks."

I watched him push back out of the house. The squads were preparing, and the support staff was getting things in order. Battle lines, triage center, et cetera. Been a busy summer here. I turned to the task at hand.

The armor had been repaired and cleaned of any bloodstains. That made me feel better. The thick underarmor was new, however, as they'd cut the last off me. I slipped it on over my T-shirt and jeans, and then Stuart helped me with the chain shirt. By the time I had it belted and cinched just right, Gunther was back in the house with a motorcycle helmet.

"Was a present," he said, handing me the black helmet with wraparound face protection. There were crossed hammers painted on either side and a flaming sword across the top from nape to brow.

"That's hawt," I said, grinning.

He dangled the keys in front of me with a big grin. "She flies. Don't forget to touch the ground sometimes." He laid the keys in my hand, closing my fist in his hands. "Ride careful." He kissed me on the cheek and stepped back.

"Gotta run and see to the troops," Stuart said, stepping past Gunther to give me a quick hug. "Don't get killed." Then he dashed out the door.

Gunther tossed me a salute and followed, bellowing commands as he went.

"You are pretty scary," Deidre said, rolling her chair into the kitchen.

I nodded. "I'll be out at the bike, whenever Jimmy gets back."

"You think we'll be attacked again?"

I stopped, thinking. If I fucked up with Qindra, who knew? I wasn't even sure what I was facing. "Better safe than sorry," I said, smiling. "But hopefully I can catch this at the source."

"We could send folks with you."

I shook my head. "No. If they attack here, you want full strength. I'll stay out of trouble."

She rolled her eyes. "Liar."

I just grinned. What could I say?

"Just be careful, Sarah."

I hugged her quickly and fled out the door. I was not gonna start crying, not now.

The troops had hurricane lamps burning by the time I'd gotten back outside. They weren't messing around here. The first squad was still on the perimeter, watching for whatever may be coming, but Gunther's squad was in the barn, getting its act together.

The yard was empty except for the Ducati. I slowly climbed down the stairs and walked to it, expecting it to bite me. The leather was in good shape, and the light of the bonfire danced along the bottom of the chromed exhaust.

I grabbed the handlebars and stepped over the seat, settling onto the leather. I closed my eyes and let the feel of the machine settle into my legs. After three long breaths, I opened my eyes and slipped the key into the ignition.

"I think you'll be wanting this, too," Jimmy said, coming out onto the porch. He had my rig in one hand, with Gram snuggled inside her sheath and my helmet in his other hand. "You going off again, you'll want to keep your head protected. It's hard, but not that hard." He grinned at me, that old familiar smirk I was used to seeing. "They added some things to your saddlebags."

He tossed me the helmet, and I caught it in both hands. I stepped off the bike, set the helmet on the seat, and looked at the saddlebags. Inside were a change of clothing, some water, and PowerBars. The other side was empty. I stuck the holster and one hammer in the empty side and the other hammer in the full side, distributing the weight.

Jimmy handed me the rig, and I slipped it over my shoulders. Not as difficult as a bra, for what it's worth. I had the leather cinched tight, with Gram just above my right shoulder. I reached up, grasped the handle with my right hand, and pulled her clean.

I felt the amulet against my chest grow warm suddenly, and the runes along the blade burst into flames.

"Holy shite," Jimmy said, stepping forward.

I lowered the blade, turning it so he could get a look. "This is new."

"We'll talk about it when you get back. You going after Melanie?"

Good question. One I'd already decided, I realized.

"Going to Chumstick," I said.

Jimmy started to protest, but I slid Gram home into her sheath and held up my right hand.

"Whatever can take out Qindra and her cleaning crew is some fairly bad shit," I said. "Not something I want running around."

"What about Melanie?" He paused, squirming in his frustration. "And Katie?"

"What about Katie?" Katie called.

We both turned to see her striding out of the barn. She was dressed in a chain-mail shirt, and she had her guitar strapped over her shoulder, just like I had Gram. "What was that about Melanie?"

Oy. We spent the next few minutes sorting things out, and Deidre rolled out onto the deck.

"Don't forget this," she said, holding up the shotgun in a long holster. "Strap this to that damn infernal machine."

"I appreciate that," I said. "But I'm more comfortable with Gram here." I patted the pommel over my shoulder.

"I've been studying this, me and the twins," Jimmy said, stroking the stock, tracing the faces in the carved flames. "Powerful stuff, but not evil."

I looked at the shotgun in Deidre's hands. She looked pretty damn formidable.

"Why don't you keep that?" I asked. "In case somebody shows up here, ya know?"

Deidre started to protest, but Jimmy put his hand on her shoulder.

"Girl's right, Dee. I'd feel better if you had something that would work if anything funny happened again."

"I'm not helpless," she said, pulling a face. "But if you insist." She pumped the shotgun, slamming a shell into the chamber.

"I pity the next giant that steps in front of you," I said with a smile.

Deidre gave me a wicked grin, flipped the safety on, and dropped the barrel over her lap.

"What's coming?" Jimmy asked me for the second time. "Any ideas?"

"No idea," I said. "But I have a feeling if I don't get to Qindra now, we're screwed."

I turned to Katie, took her in my arms, and hugged her.

"Be careful," she said. She was upset, I could tell.

"Melanie will be okay," I said. "I just think whatever's taken Qindra is a bigger threat."

She shrugged a little, burrowing her shoulder against my chest. "We'll hold the fort," she said. "I just feel useless."

I tilted her face upward and kissed her. "You are far from useless."

"Yeah. Okay." She stepped back and smiled at me. "Go on. Time's a wasting."

I got on the Ducati, adjusted all the gear to make sure I could ride, and put on the helmet. I twisted the key, and the bike rumbled to life. Everyone stepped back as I turned the throttle, letting the engine growl. I waved at Katie, and the folks in the area waved back.

I eased the bike into first and shot down the driveway to the main road. At the end, just before it bent around the house, I stopped and looked back. Jimmy was with Deidre on the porch, and Gunther and Stuart had their troops getting ready for an unknown attack. The bonfire blazed in the middle of it all, and in front, standing alone, was Katie.

"Fuck it," I mumbled, popping the clutch, and gunned the bike with one foot firmly stamped onto the ground. The bike roared, the back tires spinning as we did a quick one eighty, slinging gravel out into the field away from the house.

Katie did not move except to let her hand drop as she waited for me to return.

I pulled up beside her, flipped up my helmet. "Get on!"

She didn't even hesitate, just hopped on the back and grabbed me around the waist. Jimmy yelled, people came running, but I gunned it, and we flew down the driveway.

She squeezed me hard, hanging on as we accelerated, her head against my left shoulder. I wasn't leaving her behind ever again.

# Fifty-five

It was freaking cold—let me tell you. After dark, October, going over the mountains. The amulet was warm on my chest, but my hands were freezing.

Then I heard her singing, felt her really, her face against my left shoulder. I didn't know what the words were, but a warmth spread through me, over me like a blanket. I knew she had her own power, but feeling it in this way was pretty new.

The time crawled. We stopped just on the other side of the pass at a rest area and got off the bike to walk around. There was a booth there where a local non-profit was giving out coffee and selling donuts. We got a cup and a couple sinkers. The young woman taking the money looked at me twice once she noticed the chain mail but didn't comment.

We stomped around while we filled up on hot sugar and caffeine. I was missing my boots. The tennis shoes were comfy but didn't hold up to the bike as well. Would be better to have the leather up over my ankle.

"We need to get you a helmet," I said as we sipped our coffee.

She smiled at me, slipped her arm around my waist, and squeezed. "Thanks for coming back for me."

I leaned my head over, kissing her on the ear. "I love you. I'd rather have you with me."

We hugged. I'd rather not have the chain mail between us, but it worked out. Later, when all this was over, I wanted to take her into a long, hot shower. Her singing was keeping the cold from being debilitating, but it was still not optimal.

"Your singing is powerful," I said as we walked back to the bike. "I guess I never realized how magical it is."

"Things are different," she said, serious. "I've noticed it since you reforged Gram. There is a change in the world. I feel powerful when I sing, like I can affect things like never before."

I kissed her. "You sing; I'll drive. When we get to Anezka's we'll reevaluate."

"Yeah," she said, climbing on the bike behind me, just as it began to drizzle.

And we were off again, the cold just tolerable. The rain was a cruel joke. We hunkered down and pushed onward, aware of the road conditions, the spray from trucks, and the creeping cold.

Coming out of the pass, I thought I saw things flashing past us, shadows against the darkness of the mountain. Above us, the clouds seemed to be moving in the same direction, fast and furious. Like all the bad weather was heading to Anezka's place.

Instead of going into Leavenworth first, I cut up 207 off Highway 2. Brought us to Chumstick from the north—felt safer.

The vans came into view first, glowing white in the drizzly night.

Once I saw the trucks, the house became apparent, a black hole in the otherwise black night. Shadow on shadow. I parked the bike beside Qindra's Miata.

Katie unslung her guitar and peeked in the trucks on one end, and I checked out the others. All empty.

I pulled the hammers from the saddlebags, strapped on the holster, and settled them into their loops. Their weight pulling against my jeans felt familiar, if a little breezy. We walked across the road to where the barrier had been and stopped. It was back, only far different.

I reached my hand out, and felt it, a bubble for sure, but thicker. Smoke swirled inside, black shadows. I pulled Gram from her sheath and the world brightened a touch. Here was power. She hummed in my hand as the runes flitted with flames. The amulet against my left breast vibrated in sympathy. There was definitely a connection. Relics made by the same hand, that's what it said to me. Hive-mates, Bub would have called it. Same maker, harmonious.

I took Katie's hand and stepped to the barrier again. It parted, reluctantly, and we stepped across. Inside the opaque dome was madness.

Things moved in the blackness, hungry things that wailed and shrieked as they flew around the house. The house glowed with a greenish light, like phosphorescent mushrooms, sickly and wan.

I looked over at Katie. "This could get ugly."

She nodded, squeezing my hand. "Let's see if we can get out again before we go forward."

"Good idea." I stepped back, felt the dome against my shoulders and turned, feeling along the curve upward. "They can get in but can't check out." I said with a grimace. "I think we need to find Qindra and see what the hell is going on."

"Okay, be careful."

Good thinking.

In the front of the house, the statues had been knocked around and the fence was collapsed in one place. We walked in that direction. Before we got too close, I could see where a body had landed on the fence. The white protective suit had been shredded and the helmet was cracked. I knelt down, pushed the helmet up. She had been a young woman, brown hair, pale eyes that stared upward into nothing. Her face was twisted in a grimace. She was very dead, but I saw no marks on her. I felt for a pulse just in case, but she was cold.

I looked up at the dome overhead and realized it blocked the rain. I couldn't see the cloudy sky, but I did see a wisp of smoke slip through the barrier with a small flash of energy. Once inside the dome, the shadow spun around and tried to leave again. It bounced along the inside of the field, shrieking as it tried to escape once more. After a second, it turned toward us, a presence of intelligence and malice. It fell toward us.

Katie yelled, pointing. I stepped forward as it sped in our direction, its banshee wail drawing other swirling entities to us. I waited until it was almost at me, then dove to the side, bringing Gram around in a cleaving arc. The shade, wraith, ghost—whatever you wanted to call it—wailed a final time and fell to the ground, dissolving into smoke.

I turned to Katie as several smaller spirit forms scrambled across the grounds to begin consuming the fallen banshee, absorbing the shadow and smoke, feeding on the fallen.

"What the hell is going on?" Katie asked, her voice shaking. "Are they eating that thing?"

I grabbed her by the arm and began walking us toward the house. "Looks that way. Let's keep moving while they're distracted."

The front door was thick with moving shapes, tentacles, web, something unpleasant. "Carport, then," I said, steering around.

As we stepped on the driveway, the warrior who'd been holding the balloons only this morning stood in the center of the carport. There was a body crumpled at its feet.

"What the hell?" I said, and it turned to me, holding up one arm.

It held a sword; I didn't remember it being armed. I also didn't remember it moving on its own. Katie took a step back, and I stepped forward. It swiveled its head toward me, and the grin was a cruel reminder of a sweet moment.

It lunged, swinging the sword downward. I brought Gram up. The blades clashed, sending sparks into the dark. It took another step, seemed confused as to which target to approach, and turned to Katie, avoiding me.

I stepped in front of it, holding Gram at the ready. "Back off," I growled at it.

It wavered, trying to go around me to get to Katie. It swung out its left arm, catching me in the side, and flung me across the carport into a stack of boxes. Old clothing, shoes, and other crap rained down on me. I'd been concentrating on the sword arm. That damn thing was strong. It lumbered at Katie, swinging the sword up in an overhead arc, and she scrambled backward.

The sword smashed into a stack of bins, scattering scrap metal across the carport.

By the time I'd climbed out of the debris, Katie was dodging and scrambling around the carport. She was getting winded but had avoided damage so far.

I ran forward and leapt into the air for a flying side kick. My foot connected with the statue's back, and it rocked forward, arms pinwheeling for balance.

I landed on my hands and feet, spun around, and kicked out, clipping it in the left knee. It buckled, dropping its sword, and fell to the side. I jumped up, brought Gram around, and sunk the blade in the neck, severing the metallic head.

The head flew through the air, bounced off a shelving unit, and rolled to land in front of Katie.

"Thanks," she said, climbing to her feet.

Black fluid leaked from the statue, steaming into the air. I reached over, dipped my finger in it, and brought it to my nose, sniffing.

Blood, coppery and rank. What the hell were these things?

It kicked once and tried to push itself upward. I brought Gram around and stabbed downward for all I was worth, throwing my entire body weight behind the blade, piercing the thick metal chest. It was like killing the Tin Man.

A shriek rose from the statue, and a great shadow emerged from it, shredding as it escaped around Gram. The wind whipped my hair, and the energy whistled for a few moments before it was gone. The statue stopped moving.

Katie walked over, holding out a hand to help me up. I took it, touched the side of her face, and gave her a quick kiss.

I pulled Gram from the statue and walked to the smithy. It was quiet, but there were several dead bodies there. Killed, no doubt, by mister happy over there.

We did a quick search, and besides blood and severed limbs, it was empty of anything new.

"What's out here?" Katie asked, opening the back door.

"Don't!" I called, but too late. Out in the yard, the other statues hunted, stalking about. Even the great dragon prowled. He was pitiable with his missing scales and wings, but there was no doubt he could kill us in a second.

The warriors turned toward us. Partially built and missing their weapons, they were still a threat.

"Time to go inside," I said, rushing over and shutting the door just as one of the warriors tried to cross the threshold.

The door from the yard to the shop wouldn't hold them, but it bought us a couple of seconds.

We made it to the kitchen door without another incident.

"You ready?" I asked as I reached for the door.

She only nodded, grasping my right arm above the elbow.

I grabbed the knob and twisted. The door swung inward without a noise, and we could see the inside was in shambles.

The kitchen was turned out, cabinets empty, the fridge fallen forward against the overturned table, the few contents strewn across the floor.

"I'd guess she's in the back by the bedroom," I said.

Katie just nodded and followed me, her eyes big but determined.

The living room had been destroyed. Something did not like furniture, as every stick and board was smashed. The fireplace mantel was broken, but a fire struggled in the grate. It was the only light in the house.

"See anything we can use for light?"

We both looked around, but there was nothing apparent. Maybe I should've had a flashlight in my saddlebags. Of course, they were out on the bike.

I looked back through the curtain on the door to the carport, and the statues were marching around. One had made its way around to the front and was fighting with the smaller shadows. Was going to be damn difficult fighting back through that mess.

"Do you hear something?" Katie asked as we looked around.

I stopped moving and listened. Something was dripping from the back of the house. "Water?" I asked.

"Blood, most likely," she said, making a face. "Where is everyone else?"

"I think I've seen this movie," I said, gripping Gram tighter. The flaming runes gave off some light, but barely enough to make out the overall shape of the room and the larger objects.

We crept down the hall. First room on the left was the bathroom. Laundry room was on the right.

There were four bodies in the bathroom. Tangled and broken, shoved into the tub. I pulled the door closed. Didn't need to worry about them at the moment.

There was only one person in the laundry room, and they'd been stuffed into the washer. Theirs had been a painful death. I could tell by the face that was pressed against the glass, desperate to get out.

Anezka's bedroom was at the far left, and the unknown room was on the right. If I had to guess, I'd say spare bedroom, but I'd never opened the door.

The door to Anezka's room was closed, but I heard something from the left.

"Fair before foul," Katie said, so we opened Anezka's bedroom. There was only one body in there. He'd been in his early fifties, I'd guess, but his face was purple and bloated. He swung from the light fixture, his feet several inches above the floor, an electrical cord around his neck.

At his feet were two cages. One held a very dead cat. It looked like she'd exploded inside her cage.

The crow, however, was unhurt. It squawked when we came in, fluttering its great wings.

"One survivor so far," Katie said.

I looked at her. Her face was panic-stricken, but there was a determination there that made me proud. I pushed the crow's cage to the side and grabbed the hanging man by his legs, swung him out, and cut the cord with Gram.

I let him crash down onto the floor. He was already dead, so I didn't try to ease him down. I just couldn't take him swinging like that.

"One more room," I said, turning away from the dead guy. "You ready?"

"Lovely," Katie said. "Wait. Let me try something."

She unslung her guitar, pulled a pick out of her pocket, and plucked a few notes. The crow settled right down. The tune she picked out was quick and lively, not a reel by any means but uplifting. The blackness pushed back, and the overwhelming sense of death faded a notch.

"Better," I said, winking at her.

Time to face the rest. I stepped across the hallway and opened the final door.

There was a room there, all right. But it was nearly empty. There was no furniture, only two high-set windows and Qindra.

She stood in the far side of the room, nose into the corner, mumbling quiet words.

"Qindra," I called to her. She didn't move. I glanced around, saw nothing to either side of the door, and crossed the room. Still she hadn't moved.

I placed my hand on her shoulder, and the world went black.

# Fifty-six

"SARAH?" KATIE ASKED. SOMETHING WAS DEFINITELY WRONG. She swung her guitar around to her back and quick-stepped across the empty room. Sarah had frozen, her hand on Qindra's shoulder.

Qindra, on the other hand, was fading in and out of visibility, her flesh becoming translucent one moment, with shadows swirling in the ether, and then solid the next. She did not appear to breathe, but she mumbled a continuous string of words, unintelligible and nearly silent.

Whatever had happened to her seemed to have caught Sarah as well. It was a trap of some sort.

Katie spun around, listening. There were noises in the walls. She glanced up at the windows; the black swirling mass of spirits continued to spiral down toward the house from the sky.

Whatever was happening here was drawing in the spirits from all around. Out of the corner of her eye, she saw spiders crawling from the walls. Eaters had breached the house. Masses of them were pouring through the windows then, flowing around Sarah and Qindra but coming right for Katie.

She ran.

Out in the hall, she bounced against the bedroom door. The dead man sat up, opened his eyes, and hissed at her. She fell back against the wall, ping-ponging down the hall, past the laundry, where the face spoke to her through the washer door.

Something scrambled across the tile of the bathroom, but it had not reached the door, and she ran on. In the living room, the glow of the fire seemed to keep the shadows at bay.

She paused there, grabbed a piece of the broken end table, and thrust it into the fire, followed by a large book on architecture that had once sat on top of the table.

The paper flared up, the slick pages curling and producing more smoke than flame. The finished wood of the table sputtered and did not seem to want to catch fire.

A shadow reached her, a tiny thing about the size of her thumb, and it bit her. The pain was sharp and quick, but there was no blood. She slapped the thing, and it vaporized into a wisp of smoke. There was a black smudge on her arm where it had dropped on her. More of the tiny biters were dropping from the ceiling, falling on her, biting her.

Katie swatted them from her, bumped back against the wall, her guitar making a god-awful twanging echo. The noise cut through the rising panic, gave her the moment of clarity she needed. She was a bard, after all. She had some budding powers.

She stumbled into the kitchen, which seemed to not have any smoke biters falling from the ceiling, and swung her guitar around to the front. As soon as her fingers found the strings, she opened her mouth and blasted a chord of both sound and light out into the room. Her panic settled as a wave of music pushed outward, dissolving the biters that leapt at her.

She sang the first chords of "White Rabbit," and the sphere around her swelled, glowing. They fell away, wisps of nothing. The bites on her skin faded, and her spirit soared.

Now she was getting somewhere.

She stepped into the living room, pushing aside the fear. Sarah needed her.

Three strides into the living room, however, the game turned.

A huge swell of smoke coalesced in the corner near the ceiling, taking shape. She sang louder, expanding the sphere. One of the dead shambled into the living room. It smashed into her shield and crumpled to the ground, a lifeless husk once more—the shadow that had animated it dissolving into smoke.

And still the mass of shadows grew in the corner between her and the hallway. All the shadows in the room were being sucked upward; even the smoke from the burning furniture rose to feed the mass.

*This is not good*, she thought, just as it took a shape.

"Hello, slut." The voice echoed across the room. *His voice.* She faltered, and the head of a dragon formed from the shadow, a head she recognized from her nightmares.

"Ready to play again?" His voice called to her. The dragon's head slammed forward, against the protective sphere. Katie flew into the kitchen, her guitar landed near the refrigerator, too far from her reach. She struggled to breathe as the shadow dragon loomed over her.

"This will be more fun than last time," he said, laughing. "I can hurt you oh so much more thoroughly."

It was Jean-Paul. Terror swept over her. He was dead. Sarah killed him.

Panic paralyzed her, and for a moment she was willing to do anything, including kill herself, rather than let him touch her again.

# Fifty-seven

I STUMBLED FORWARD INTO A ROOM LIKE A CATHEDRAL. Energy pulsed from all directions—like stepping inside a nuclear reactor.

Qindra sat in the middle of the room, a wash of energy flooding around her in great white sparkles. The energy sang with goodness and life. But a blackness swirled around her. Wraiths, ghosts, specters . . . I had no true name for the spirits that flew around her, diving headlong into the energy barrier, only to bounce away again. There were so many of them that I could barely tell where one began and the other ended, and they were flooding in with every breath.

Only I wasn't breathing. Of course. I looked down. I was there, but not there. I looked around. I'd been in the house with Katie, and I'd reached out to touch . . . I whirled, and the ghosties spun around Qindra, faster and faster. Their hunger was palpable.

"Qindra?"

She did not turn, did not move, but the energy field around her did not falter. She was a woman besieged. I had to help her.

Of course, I'd gone walkabout. Astral projection is the proper term, but somehow when I touched Qindra, I was sucked into this place.

I waded forward. Gram was solid in my grip. The blade moved

through the ghosts like cutting smoke. The first fell to the ground shrieking, and several of its friends broke away to consume the fallen.

The faster I cut them down, the more a few of them grew, until soon there were only a few, half a dozen of them at most, growing, blobs of negative energy. The total assault on Qindra had not slowed, only become more concentrated, and I could see cracks forming in her shield.

I had to do something different.

On the wall behind her I noticed an oblong object that floated just out of reach. I willed myself around Qindra and the energy well until I could get a better look.

It was a Valkyrie shield, tall and elegant but scarred with fire and talon. It was my shield, or rather it belonged to the Valkyrie Gunnr. She had given it to me when I went to face the dragon. How had it come to be here?

For a moment I was at the lake. Jean-Paul was charging toward me, flaming, and I was screaming, rushing forward, taking his flame on the shield as I stabbed with Gram.

I'd fallen then, burned and weakened nearly to my death. But the shield had fallen where I lay. Later, after the Valkyrie caught up with me, they helped me back onto the flying horse, Meyja, helped me fly home to Katie and Black Briar, but none of us had taken the shield.

Why was it here?

The shield floated in a stream of energy, clean energy that flowed through the shield and emerged black and tainted. This sickly power then shot upward into the world, under Anezka's house.

I was beneath the house. The shield was corrupting the power, poisoning the world above.

I reached out to take the shield, to pull it from the edge of the energy stream that roared from the ground like the natural gas flames I used in the forge. The moment I touched it pain and fear exploded inside me.

A vision unfolds, vivid and silent. A young man creeps along the shore of a battered lake as the Valkyrie and I fly over the tree line. He kneels at Jean-Paul's broken corpse and falls to his knees, wailing soundlessly. I watch, mesmerized, as he pulls his own hair out in great fistfuls, screeching to the heavens. After a moment, he rips off his shirt, and sops his hands in Jean-Paul's blood. I recognized this maddened figure from the picture Anezka had shown me—the three naked lovers at the Oregon Stone Henge. He was Anezka's lover, Justin. He paints his face and chest with great swirls of smoking black blood—scarring his face and torso.

Finally, he sees my shield lying to the side and drags Jean-Paul's body onto it, pulls a knife from his boot, and bleeds Jean-Paul onto the shield. Then he cuts Jean-Paul's heart from his broken chest. He holds the bleeding muscle to the sky, chanting wildly, and then bites into the heart.

Power erupts around him, tendrils of light weaving in with the blood and the shield. Finally, he uses his knife to cut deeply into his own abdomen and lies on the shield, allowing his blood to mingle with Jean-Paul's. The shield glows with a bright blue flare. Justin floats upward, spinning in the air, the remains of Jean-Paul's bloody heart held to the sky in one bloody fist.

He screams as his body smokes.

The wound in his abdomen closes, leaving behind a violent white scar. His hair is streaked white from where he ran his bloody hands through the locks. His face and torso are scarred with puckered pink handprints and smears. The scene fades into mist.

I jerked my hand from the shield and whirled around.

"You see?" Qindra asked.

The shield acted as a filter, polluting the energy flowing from the nexus. The power here was incredible. No wonder Anezka had grown erratic. Control of the amulet had shielded her at first, but with it switching allegiance, that no longer protected her. Once Qindra broke the shield that Flora had managed to create here, things went from bad to worse. The tainted flow was unimpeded. The broken things, shades and foul spirits, suddenly had a vibrant flame to flock to.

And here, in the flux and the chaos of the vortex, a great beast rose from the grave. I could taste his taint in the energy, feel his aura in the black power that coursed through this place.

"Jean-Paul," I screamed, and the eating things swung their great attention toward me.

"Come on," I called to them. "Come to your final death."

One of the great eaters spun away from Qindra and flew at me, but it was nothing compared to my fear and anger. I cut through it like it didn't exist. I was a mad woman, crazed and out of control. I yearned for the berserker, craved the mindless violence that would clear the horde that stood before me.

For the dragon was there. He fell from the house, a solid mass of shadow and smoke, beautiful and terrible. He turned his great gaze upon me. For a second he seemed disoriented, but his laughter echoed into the hall, and unfathomable hordes of nether creatures flew from his great form.

"Eat her; shred her," he called, laughing in his madness. The madness I had stilled once already, the voice I had sundered with this very blade.

I fought like a dervish, cutting through the monsters, fighting my way to Qindra. If I could free her, somehow, I had a chance.

Before long, I was covered in black welts and weeping sores. This was my spirit, I knew, but the pain was real, and the ice of the monsters' touch burned brighter than I had ever imagined.

Then, as suddenly as it started, I was free from them, free from the burning and the biting. I fell to my knees, weak and joyous. Gram clattered to the ground, and Qindra touched my forehead.

"Be healed," she said, her voice hoarse and raw.

I was inside the sphere, inside her protective circle.

"What the hell's going on?" I gasped.

"Hel is right," she said. "The dragons have killed the gods, down to the last dregs, and Hel has been closed for time out of mind. They," she waved at the black creatures that spun about the room, diving into the field, only to be broken and consumed by the others, "should go to the underworld; they have been trapped here on Migard for thousands of years."

"Um, ghosts?" I asked. "You'd think we would've heard about this sooner."

"Things have shifted, Sarah." I could see how tired she was. "You broke the covenant; you cracked the world, and this is what has come out to play."

I looked out to the swirling spirits as they fell upon one another. Jean-Paul reveled among them, consuming any that drew near him.

"I've tried to reinstate the barrier over the property," she said. "They cannot escape, but they are being drawn here every minute."

"And I saw Jean-Paul," I said, watching the energy rise into a fountain. She had diverted a thread from the nexus, pulled it to her. It bathed us, filling me with vigor.

Qindra watched me for a moment and shook her head. "It is seductive, this power," she said.

"What are we going to do?"

"I'm not sure," she offered. "Did any of my people get away?"

The look on my face told her all she needed. I could feel the sorrow bleeding from her, sending tiny cracks into the shield.

Qindra looked at me sadly. "We cannot leave," she said.

"Katie is out there," I said, grabbing her hand. "I've got to get back to her."

"It's taking everything I can muster to keep the barrier up," she said. "I cannot get you out of here. Your only hope is Katie, I'm afraid. If she can free you somehow, you may have a chance." She was earnest. "I just cannot risk letting this madness escape."

Well, that was a gut punch. Trapped here forever in a house of horrors. "I guess it's in Katie's hands then," I offered.

"I just don't understand how the shield came to be here."

"He brought it," I said. "The necromancer. He was Anezka's lover."

She twitched, sending a ripple into the air around us. The shield vibrated for a moment and a face appeared, young and lean. Justin floated above the shield. Words flowed through the ether, gibberish to me, but in a language that Qindra seemed to understand.

"He was a disciple of Jean-Paul's," she whispered. "He used Anezka to get access to the nexus. Used her and tortured her while all the time he worked for that bastard." She pointed across the cavern.

The dragon swirled in and out of focus, the great beast trying to hold its shape in the madness of the other creatures that flooded the room.

"When I killed Jean-Paul, he was there. At the lake. I saw it all when I touched the shield."

Qindra looked sickened, weak.

"The shield has been reforged in flame—imbued with both Jean-Paul's and Justin's essence, and their blood," I said.

"Aye," she said with a nod, "but it also contains your blood and some of your spirit." She looked up at me. "It holds Jean-Paul to this place. Ties his spirit to this world. But it also feeds this necromancer, gives him access to this energy."

Of course, that was the missing link. When he'd visited recently . . . what had Bub said? five months? Not long after I killed Jean-Paul. That's when he planted the shield. That's when the madness really began to overwhelm Anezka.

"What can we do?"

She shook her head. "I don't know. Not yet." She began chanting again. The sagging force-wall strengthened, and the spirits were thrown back. "But I must concentrate," she said, exhausted. "I must keep the monsters from being loosed upon the world."

I knelt down, brushed the hair from her eyes, and kissed her on the forehead. She was feverish, but strong. I willed some of my power to her.

"I broke the original seal," she said with a weak smile. "When you brought me here. The woman who carved the supports wove the field about this place." She pointed to Justin, whose image floated beyond Jean-Paul. "His first lover. She knew. She sensed all this. That is why the barrier was there, why the carvings are all through the house. You have not seen them all; they are powerful and frightening. All the better to hold the spirits here, to keep their dark yearnings confused and trapped." Her voice was growing fainter as her concentration grew stronger. "My fault," she said and then fell silent.

I picked up Gram and stood, waiting for the wall to fall, for the time when I would give my life to protect her.

Oh, my dear Katie. I hoped she was okay in the house. Might have been a bad idea to bring her after all. "Are you there?" I asked. "Can you see what I see?"

# Fifty-eight

KATIE TENSED FOR THE KILLING BLOW, BUT IT DID NOT COME. Jean-Paul drew back, shock on his fluid face. "*She* is here?" he bellowed. "This should hold you."

He lunged at Katie, opened his mouth, and breathed. Smoky blue flames erupted from his mouth.

Katie rolled across the floor. The flames smashed against the kitchen cabinet and splattered across the room. Blue slime covered Katie's shoulder and back as she scrabbled under the broken table, reaching for her guitar.

She had to save Sarah. Jean-Paul reared back once more and sucked in for another breath.

"No flame?" Jean-Paul roared, obviously confused.

Katie grabbed her guitar and pulled it to her chest. More shades were flowing into the house, but Jean-Paul turned at them, snapping them up. Each one seemed to bolster him, give him more density.

The blue ectoplasm began to smoke across the tile and up the cabinet. Katie felt a burning itch in her back. She rolled farther under the table, sliding the guitar to the side and pulling her jacket off. The sludge on her jacket was smoldering, like electric blue Jell-O made of battery acid.

Jean-Paul roared, thrashing about, and pulled his great forelegs through the ceiling, manifesting more of his bulk.

"Hide from me, little bug," he said, laughing. "I will deal with your lover first. You are not going anywhere."

With a sound like a sonic boom, Jean-Paul dove through the floor, leaving a scattering of crawling and biting things in his wake. They moved as one, flowing across the living room toward the kitchen. The first few that arrived smashed into the ectoplasm and flitted into vapor, but the next wave learned and moved around.

Katie looked around desperately. Taking her guitar, she began to strum, her hands shaking. A feeble light sprung from her, but it would not keep them all at bay. She was too weak, too afraid.

Then she saw it. She knew it from Sarah's description. The box that Qindra had shown her lay against the wall, spilled from the table when the room had been wrecked. She crawled to the back corner, grabbed the box, and ripped open the lid. The vial lay nestled in its Bubble Wrap home.

The first horrors reached her, scrambled up over her shoes. The first bite on her leg convinced her of her path. They were eating her, not her flesh, but the spirit. Each bite was a flash of pain like a burning ember.

She pulled the vial out, broke the wax seal, and wrenched the stopper out with her teeth. Without hesitation, she tilted the vial to her lips, drinking the harsh brew.

Harsh was not a strong enough word. The coppery taste of blood was overpowered by the yeast and alcohol. The mead was by no means fermented adequately, but from the moment the liquid touched her lips, she felt the power surge into her.

In an instant she knew exactly what to do.

She snatched her guitar from the floor, slamming out chords that Sarah would recognize. Heavy metal washed through the room. The vermin flew from her, washed into nothingness by the blast of song that rolled forth.

A bubble of golden light pushed outward, larger than before, more solid and strong. She stood, pushing the table to the side, righting the refrigerator and blasting away the ectoplasm dragon fire in a flash of gold.

> *I'm coming for you, lover mine*
> *The wolves will cower in their dens*
> *Raise your broadswords, stamp your feet*
> *Tonight we ride to victory!*

She strode from the kitchen, through the living room, and down the hall. The oozing walls and scrabbling spirits melted before the might of her song. Golden light washed away the foulness, leaving the walls and floors clean in her wake. Katie turned to the final room, pushed the door open with her hip, and strode to her lover.

As the light filled the room, destroying the shadows, Sarah moved.

In a blink she went from holding Qindra's shoulder to swinging around.

Katie stumbled back as Gram sliced the guitar from her hands.

The song faltered, and Sarah stumbled forward to her knees.

"Oh, god. It was him," she mumbled. "Jean-Paul. I was fighting him again."

Katie dropped the shards of the guitar and grabbed Sarah. "It's okay; we'll beat him together."

Sarah wrapped her arms around Katie and buried her head in her shoulder.

"We gotta move," she said. "Find a way out."

"What about Qindra?"

Sarah just shook her head. "She's holding the dome, keeping them contained."

The crow squawked from the other room, and Katie looked

around. The spirits were still coming to the house, drawn like moths to the flame. *The only other living creature in the place*, she thought. *Time to set him free.*

She stood, helping Sarah to her feet, and turned. Lyrics flowed from her as she began to sing again, about apples and love.

The glow that surrounded them was slighter without the guitar, but it was strong enough to allow them to see. They crossed the hall quickly. Sarah gasped, but Katie did not look back toward the living room. No time.

Once they were in the room, she opened the cage, never missing a note. The crow squawked once, hopped out of the cage, and flapped up, its mighty wings beating.

Sarah slammed the bedroom door shut. "Zombies!" she cried, moving the dresser over the door.

The crow flew up onto the dresser, squawking manically.

Mirror? "Sarah!" Katie shouted. "What about the mirror?"

Sarah turned from the door. "Damn, girl. You're a freaking genius."

Sarah grabbed the edge of the mirror and shouted, "Skella, for all that is holy, pay attention. Open the mirror!"

Something slammed against the bedroom door from the hall, and Katie began singing again.

Sarah shouted and smacked the mirror with her open palm. "Come on, damn it. Answer."

Then Skella was there. The room behind her was a maelstrom of activity.

"Sarah? Where are you? I can't see you."

"Never mind," Sarah said, "get us out of here."

"Okay," Skella said. "Hang on!"

Katie sang louder, letting the music overcome her fear. The pounding from the hall grew more insistent. Tendrils of smoke curled from under the door.

"You first," Sarah said to Katie, who shook her head no.

"This is our only shot," Sarah said.

"Okay," Skella shouted. "I've got it opened, but it's shaky; you'd better hurry."

Katie wasn't budging.

"Shit," Sarah swore, then sheathed Gram, jumped from the bed to the dresser, and dove through the opening.

# Fifty-nine

I ROLLED INTO THE NEW ROOM. IT WAS HUGE. FOOTBALL field in width, with a high domed ceiling. A dozen or more dwarves hustled about. In one corner I saw Melanie working on someone, and Gletts was nose to nose with a dwarf, yelling about crossing a line. I looked back, and the mirror had become opaque. Katie hadn't come through.

"Open it!" I shouted, rounding on Skella.

She leaned against the mirror, straining, tears running down her face. "It's too . . . ," she stammered, "hard . . . fighting me . . . too much."

"Katie!" I screamed, collapsing onto my knees in front of the mirror. My reflection shone back at me in the blackened glass.

# Sixty

FREDERICK SAT BACK, SMUG IN HIS VICTORY. YOUNG JAMES "JJ" Montgomery sat across from him, sipping his pinot noir and enjoying the company of the young barista Mr. Philips had scared up for the evening.

"I'm flattered," JJ said, setting his glass on the coffee table and looking around the huge room. "I like to think I could make it in Hollywood, but . . ." He shrugged. "You know. I'm no superstar."

The girl, Bridget, Bethany, something with a B, leaned in and kissed JJ on the cheek and squeezed his thigh. "I watched you in *Blood Brothers Two*. You rocked."

"Yeah," JJ said, beaming.

The girl leaned in, running her hand up his thigh and cupping his crotch. "Oh god, yes."

Frederick smiled. This was almost too easy. Of course the young man had talent, he'd seen it right away, but the speed at which he was so easily manipulated just added to his value. "Chance of a lifetime," he said over his glass.

"Your work in *Elvis Versus the Goblins* was spectacular," the young woman gushed.

JJ blushed. Brittany said something to him quietly, and he looked around, as if afraid Frederick had heard.

Frederick just smiled. The girl would bed him soon, perhaps

here on the leather sofa, if given a chance. He loved the little pushes he'd made throughout the evening. Dinner, wine, plenty of wine, promises of glory and sex. Not to mention his subtle charms, the heat he could instill in the willing. Delicious.

JJ drained the last of his wine, and Belinda kissed him, hands on either side of his face, holding him to her.

"A toast," Frederick declared.

Bonnie and JJ turned, seemingly having forgotten Frederick was in the room. They were both quite inebriated.

"I'm dry," JJ said, holding up his glass.

"I'm not," Betty said, giggling into the side of JJ's neck.

"I've been saving this," Frederick said, standing and plucking the glass from JJ's hand. "I think you'll find it amazing."

He walked to the bar, allowing the young ones a moment to grope. He took the mead from the cabinet where Mr. Philips had stored it earlier and poured it into the young buck's glass. He poured himself a scotch and turned back, clearing his throat.

Brenda paused, her hands obviously working the front of young Montgomery's trousers.

JJ's eyes were mostly glazed.

Frederick handed JJ the glass and held up his scotch.

Brandy took up her glass of pinot grigio and held her glass high. "A toast," she said.

"To the next George Clooney," Frederick said.

"Hell, yeah!" Becky said, draining her wine and lowering her head to JJ's crotch.

JJ looked at Frederick for a moment and then quaffed his mead in one long pull.

Frederick smiled, sipped his Talisker, and settled back into his chair.

Becky moaned loudly as she took him in her mouth. JJ tipped

his head backward, crying out, oblivious to Frederick's continued presence.

Neither of them noticed the glow that erupted around Montgomery, engulfing the two youngsters in a halo of gold.

# Sixty-one

Katie, for all that's holy. I smacked the mirror with my palm. Skella looked up at me, the strain obvious on her face.

"Don't," she murmured. "Don't break it."

"Open it," I shouted, and she strained harder. She battled Qindra's shield, I knew. I sat with my legs folded underneath me and held Gram on my lap. "Please," I whispered. "Let her be safe."

The dwarves were shouting. Two of them were arguing with such ferocity I expected to see them come to blows.

Gletts appeared at our side, sliding to his knees and placing his hands on the mirror opposite Skella's. He murmured an incantation, and Skella's voice rose to join his. They spoke in a language I half recognized, but the words were meaningless.

"Too hard," Skella said. "Nothing like I've ever felt."

He strained beside her, their breath coming in gasps.

Nothing happened.

"Katie," I whispered, reaching out to touch the glass, gently this time. "I need you."

Golden light burst from the mirror, and Katie flew through, slamming into me, knocking me onto my back.

She was bleeding, but laughing. There were cuts on her arms and face, but she leaned in and kissed me.

We'd escaped. For half a second I was giddy, light-headed with joy, then a deafening roar echoed through the room.

Katie lifted her head, looking back, and I peered over her shoulder. Gletts and Skella were thrown backward as Jean-Paul burst through the mirror, followed by a few thousand of the little uglies.

"Incoming," one of the dwarves bellowed, and they scattered.

Melanie screamed, and Katie rolled off me, scrambling to her feet and looking around.

I rolled the opposite way, bringing Gram around to shred a lumbering shadow creature that was within reach. A second one, which looked like a cross between a T. rex and a very ugly chicken, was snapping up the littler shadows as fast as it could.

But the big daddy in the room was Jean-Paul—or rather, his spirit form. Damn, I hated that I had to kill him again.

He scattered the dwarves, bowling several over before snapping his great smoky head down and biting one of the fallen. The dwarf screamed, and Jean-Paul reared back, tearing the dwarf's spirit from him. The body shook, a broken automaton winding down as the dragon threw his head back and swallowed the spirit in one gulp.

His laughter echoed across the great hall.

Some of the dwarves had taken up weapons and were battling the shadows.

Gletts was helping Skella to her feet. She leaned against him, exhausted.

"Sorry," she said. "I didn't mean for them to follow."

I laughed, the blood rising in me, the cry of battle and glory. "You brought Katie through," I yelled. "You have redeemed yourself as far as I'm concerned."

Gletts gave me an odd look, but Skella smiled.

"Katie?" I called.

Gletts pointed around the edge of the room, toward a large central altar. Katie was running to Melanie. She sang, bless her, sang as she ran, with her head held high. Golden energy flowed from her, forming a wall between the baddies and her friends. She was a rock star!

"They've been bleeding him," Gletts said, the disdain clear in his voice. "They wouldn't listen. They thought to keep him as a never-ending source of potion and wealth." He turned his head, looked at Skella, and grimaced. "When they'd gone too far, I went for help. They didn't expect me to turn against them," he said, a blush covering his cheeks.

"He's a good boy," Skella said in his defense. "He just learns the hard way sometimes."

I was all over that. My motto was "The hard way or no way," at least if you asked anyone who knew me.

"It doesn't matter," I said finally. "We all make mistakes. Can you get Katie, Ari, and Melanie out of here?" I looked at the mirror. I had a sense we weren't going back through that. "Is there another mirror?"

Gletts nodded and pointed across the great hall. Roughly two hundred yards away, with Jean-Paul and a dwindling supply of spirit monsters between us, was another mirror. "Okay," I said, picking my first target between me and the ones I loved. "We make our way to Katie. Once we hook up with them, we make our way to the other mirror."

They both nodded.

We were able to avoid those creatures who were feeding on their smaller brethren. They were gaining on Jean-Paul in size but were more interested in the easy pickings. Jean-Paul was reveling in his slaughter of the dwarves. Already I saw four or five fallen. Three groups had banded together and were making a stand. They were armed, most of them anyway, but not all the weapons seemed to have an effect. A few were successfully hurting the baddies.

I cut down a long serpentine critter that was taking its time eating a large elephant-sized spirit. I lopped off its head and sliced it down the middle.

Unfortunately this allowed the elephantine creature as well as several smaller, recently consumed biters to flood out.

"Get to the mirror," I called, and Skella and Gletts pushed on.

I yelled a battle cry and sprang into the middle of the rushing mob.

Gram cut through them like smoke. They gave no resistance to her blazing arc, but it was exhausting hacking up shadows. I kept expecting to feel resistance, something to slow the blade, and it was screwing with my timing.

And they got in, stabbing, biting, clawing. It hurt like hell. I watched the elephantine monstrosity fading at my feet when I noticed a small group of dwarves rushing through Katie's group carrying an urn. Melanie was knocked aside, and they dropped Ari. Gletts was yelling at the dwarves, and Katie did something, sang something different, changed chords. I couldn't tell, but suddenly the T. rex–looking critter changed targets and dropped on the escaping dwarves. Two fell, chomped by his ghostly bite. The urn hit the ground, black blood splashing across the rocky floor. I bet that was the blood they'd captured, bastards.

The two dwarf torturers and blood-letters made their way around the room, ignoring their fallen, and dashed down a corridor just short of the other mirror, followed hotly by several of the bigger beasties.

I cut across the room at a shallow angle, avoiding Jean-Paul for the moment, taking out smaller targets, trying to angle an intercept for Katie and company.

"Ho, ho," Jean-Paul's voice rang out, echoing across the cavern.

"You betrayed me in life, and now you reap your reward." He scattered one of the final groups of dwarves, sending several flying across the room to smash into the wall. One limped away, but the others lay still.

Jean-Paul swooped down on one of the fallen and ripped his spirit out, eating noisily. He'd consumed a huge quantity of spirit, fair and foul, and was massive. He was nearly twice as big as he'd been in real life. When he reared back on his hind legs and roared, rocks crashed down from the ceiling and those of us on our feet were knocked to the ground.

Time to take him down a few pegs, if I could. I rolled to the side, attacked a spirit that was within reach, and angled my attack toward Jean-Paul. He fell back onto all fours and stuck his long neck down the corridor where the lead dwarves had fled with the blood.

"No," Skella shrieked as Jean-Paul began to laugh maniacally.

"Canned food," he said, and lunged to the side. There was a cell there—I could just make it out—and one of Skella and Gletts's people was trapped inside. The elf prisoner fought the great beast with his bare hands to no avail.

Jean-Paul killed the unknown elf with a snap of his jaws, shredding the man's spirit and dragging it back through the iron bars leaving the body untouched.

Okay, enough of that. I dispatched two froglike spirits, who were attacking a fallen dwarf, rending his spirit with their long, wispy tongues. I held a hand out to the dwarf, who accepted it with surprise. He scrambled away toward a group of his brethren, loping with a pained gait.

I ran forward and swung Gram through the thick, smoky shadow of Jean-Paul's tail.

He reared back, smashing his head in the rock ceiling above the passage, and fell back. Before I knew what had happened, the head emerged from the back of his great bulk where his tail had been. Nice trick, bastard.

"Die," he screamed, and lunged at me.

I dove to the side, keeping an eye out for his wing tip. I remembered his tricks. The wing passed over my head, and his jaws snapped shut where I'd just been standing.

"Nice try, loser," I called, rolling to my feet. "You fought better last time."

He spun his head around and smashed into me, the great scales of his head shredding gouts of my spirit loose, sending it splattering across the floor like blobs of white glue.

God, that hurt. That was part of me, and it hurt having it ripped away. I did a reverse sweep with the sword, and he pulled his head back, narrowly avoiding my blade.

"Bastard," I shouted. "Afraid of a girl, still."

"I will kill you this time," he bellowed, rearing back to breathe fire on me. I recognized the move. I did what he didn't expect and charged him. The flame shot over my head and struck the fleeing dwarf in the back. It wasn't flame, exactly, but some form of glowing blue ectoplasm. I think I saw that in a movie once. The dwarf, however, was not merely slimed, but slimed with something that burned. Acid wash. I grimaced on his behalf as he fell to the ground, melting.

Okay, not fire, but very, very bad.

"Much better," Jean-Paul said. "I'm stronger than I've ever been. When I kill you, I will consume everyone here and break out of this cage to hunt once again."

Like in real life, he talked too much.

A tumble-bug spirit rolled by, and Jean-Paul swiveled to snatch it up. I dodged to the right and in under his wing. My blade whipped through what would have been the meat of his shoulder, but he felt it all the same.

He roared, losing his meal, which rolled on to catch its own prey.

"You'll pay for that," he screamed, kicking out with his front leg. I ran forward and launched myself into a roll, narrowly avoiding the smashing foot.

Shoulder rolls are not as effective on stone floors as they were back in my training days on mats, but the armor helped absorb some of the impact.

His wound closed, and he swung the wing tip around to smash a dwarf to the ground. They were harassing him from his right, and another group had dispatched the last of the beasties in their quadrant and were moving to his left.

Maybe with all of us, we could take him down, despite his unknown power.

We wore at him, weaving and attacking. The dwarves used hammers and swords, spears and axes.

I pulled out a hammer, the bloodied one, and gave it a whirl in my right hand. Two weapons were better than one. I felt more balanced. The hammer, steeped in blood and power from my first battle with him, seemed to have an effect on Jean-Paul and his ilk.

The dwindling number of spirits kept crossing our paths, and we fought them as well. It was horrible.

My blood was up; the battle lust flooded my mind. Thinking beyond the dance and carnage was growing difficult. I kept pace with my sudden allies, the orbit of the villains, and the great monster we harassed.

Katie, Gletts, Skella, and Melanie were carrying Ari by his arms and legs, shambling along like one of the multiheaded ghosties that hunted the room. They were nearly to the mirror when the T. rex saw them.

"Katie!" I shouted. "Look out!"

She turned her head just as the great monstrosity charged. He scattered them like bowling pins.

Gletts was the first back on his feet. He ran to a fallen dwarf, snatching up a blade. "Go," he shouted and charged the fifteen-foot-tall dino-ghost.

Stupid kid. Earned a few points with me, but he was outclassed.

Thing was, we weren't winning. They were whittling us down. It occurred to me that they were not dwindling; something was feeding them, and not just the fallen dwarves.

They were dragging Ari now, Skella and Melanie. Katie stood her ground, singing louder than I'd ever heard her sing. Her voice washed through me, clearing the battle fog, giving me something . . . made a connection with . . .

The mirror. That was it. I whirled around. There was a connection between the first mirror and the spirits. They were connected, all of them, back through the mirror to the nexus. No wonder they weren't really falling. Only Gram seemed to be destroying them, and I was way too outgunned.

I was halfway across the room, but I saw it clearly. Dozens of black threads running back through the first mirror, the mirror to the house. I took a deep breath, letting Katie's sweet voice fill me with her song, and threw the hammer.

It arced across the room, blazing with golden light. It was as if I was a conduit for her voice. The hammer struck the mirror with an explosion of energy and glass.

The spirits faltered, several falling to the ground. The dwarves swarmed forward, hacking those nearest, and the ghosts splashed across the floor like bloody urine, the colors of disease and death.

Okay, now we were talking.

Skella was at the second mirror, holding it open. I could see Evergreen Hospital through on the other side, only because I'd stood there, behind the wooden planters, watching them leave all those days ago.

I managed to kill a scuttling spider thing, slicing off its legs on one side, and then stabbing it in the main body as it fell to the side. It made a sad squishing sound as it dissolved.

Two more dwarves fell screaming beneath Jean-Paul's rending claws, and a third flew through the air, batted by his mighty wings, but the rest were hurting him. His roar was a constant now, echoing inside the hall and inside my skull.

He breathed his ectoplasm acid at a scattering crowd. Two dwarves went down. Those with viable weapons swarmed forward, hacking and smashing. Those without were dragging back the wounded, forming back on Katie, behind her protective sphere. She was glorious.

The sphere around Katie continued to grow. Melanie, Skella, and Ari vanished through the mirror. For a second I thought they'd managed to escape unscathed.

Gletts fell.

It happened quickly. I was ducking under Jean-Paul's mighty tail, coming in close to slice at his back legs, and the T. rex smashed Gletts to the ground. He slid across the room and crashed against the wall, unmoving.

Rage flooded through me. I swung through, cutting the hamstring on Jean-Paul's rear right leg. He crumbled to his knee, shrieking. Gouts of ghostly blood sprayed the surrounding area, and the dwarves to my right sent up a cheer.

I ducked under the wing on that side and ran for the T. rex. It was nearly as large as Jean-Paul was the first time I'd killed him. It had eaten so many of the other ghosts that it was having trouble keeping its form. A second head emerged, fighting the first, as some malevolent spirit attempted to wrest control of the greater whole.

The moment of confusion was good enough for me. I unsheathed my second hammer and spun into a whirlwind of smashing and slicing. The beast was gaining density, as had all of the ghosties since I'd shattered the mirror. Now that they were separated from the nexus, severed from their power line, they were succumbing to physical laws once again.

And still Katie sang a sphere of protection around the fallen.

The T. rex fell, and I ran to Gletts. He had no outward sign of injury, but he was not moving. I grabbed his arm and began dragging him toward Katie. A dwarf, tall and shaggy, ran out of the sphere to meet me, took him, and lifted him to his wide chest.

"Go, warrior. I will see to him."

I nodded and watched a moment as he ran back to the place Katie protected. Enemy of my enemy and all that. Gletts looked very small in his arms.

The dwarves had pulled down the last of the great shadow creatures, and Jean-Paul was staggering. He leaked oozing fluid from dozens of wounds, and he had no room to flee. He had grown so huge that he could not flee down the corridor, and he raged with a mindless abandon.

I flew back into the fray, dodging and weaving his wild strokes, cutting him whenever an opportunity arose. He was weakening and everyone knew it. The dwarves pressed onward, becoming more valiant in their attacks. Jean-Paul could not protect himself from all corners. He fell onto his great chest, his wings beating madly, knocking the dwarves aside.

I ran forward, throwing the hammer at him. He rolled, taking the hammer in his chest. While his left wing was pinned I jumped over one of the less-fortunate dwarves and brought Gram down with both hands. I landed on Jean-Paul, blade first, sinking it to the hilt in his chest.

He thrashed in his dying, rolling over the dwarves on his left and flinging me across the room. I managed to keep hold of Gram in my flight. I skidded to a halt near the place where the dwarves had been bleeding Ari and staggered to my feet.

Jean-Paul was melting. A fountain of fetid life force spewed from his chest. The dwarves fell back, away from his flailing limbs, his beating wings. He was dangerous still, deadly. He snapped at the dwarves, biting at them.

One was too slow, too elated by our apparent victory. Jean-Paul snapped his jaws closed on him, wrenching his broken spirit from his body. The wound began to close. The breach in his chest closed, and he rose up on his front feet, crawling to the cages in the hall, toward the helpless elves.

I climbed to my feet and ran forward. My right shoulder throbbed from where I'd slammed into the altar, and my muscles trembled from overuse. If he reached the elves, helpless as they were, he'd feed and be further healed.

The screaming was unbearable as he smashed into the first cell. Two elves died beneath his rending maw, and the wounds on his body closed.

A wail went up from the dwarves. Exhausted as they most assuredly were, they dashed forward again. We could not take him down again, not if he healed himself.

He smashed me to the side with his wing, a lucky blow on his part, as he was only paying attention to the food, the healing spirits he needed to consume.

I rolled with the blow, feeling my body giving up, betrayed by exhaustion and physical limitation.

Then Katie's song changed. In a moment's breath, she shifted from calm and succor to vengeance and rage. The song washed over me like a current. The runes on my leg burned white-hot, and I leapt upward, flying farther than I'd ever flown before. I swung Gram down with both hands, using every iota of energy I could summon. The blade connected with the side of Jean-Paul's neck, sliced through the thickening scales and the flesh beneath.

I smashed into the ground, Gram falling from my grip with an echoing ring. For a moment, I lay there, breathing, gasping. Then the great beast shuddered and fell.

A cheer rose from the dwarves and elves alike. I had severed his great neck.

The biting head smashed to the ground, his long neck thrashing from side to side. Black, viscous ichor sprayed from his severed neck—an oily blood like what poured from the statue I'd defeated. The essence of those sacrificed to tie him to this world.

Katie was at my side in a moment. Her song an echo in my mind.

"You did it," she said, pulling me into her lap. "You killed him."

I smiled at her, forgetting all else for a moment. "It was you," I said. "Your song, your love. That's what gave me the strength."

She cupped my face and cried, holding me to her as the dragon melted into the earth.

# Sixty-two

THE AFTERMATH WAS WORSE THAN I THOUGHT—TWENTY-seven dwarves down, six elves. Gletts was not dead so much, but his spirit was broken somehow.

Katie helped the surviving dwarves tend to their wounded, and I took Gram into the hall to free the elves. Many were hurt from the battle, but, beyond that, the dwarves had only been holding them hostage, not torturing them or anything.

I limped down the hall, Gram in my hand, ready to cut the doors open, though the thought of smashing through dwarven-forged steel locks didn't really appeal to me. I took a deep breath and raised the sword, but a cry from the hall stopped me.

One of the dwarves was running in my direction, jangling a large key ring. I lowered the sword. That would definitely make things a lot simpler. He apologized, said his name was Borimber, and bowed in my direction until I took the keys from his out-stretched hand.

I opened the cages as fast as I could. It seems no one else was going to do it, not even the winded Borimber.

The elves were quiet, watching me open their doors, following me as I worked my way down the hall and back. An ancient old woman with a long gray braid down the length of her back and a demeanor that shouted wisdom and control stepped forward, holding her hand out to me. "My name is Unun," she said, smiling at me. "I believe you know my granddaughter."

I took her hand and bowed my head. "We have met," I answered warily.

She laughed. "You are a mighty warrior," she said. "But you wear your feelings on your shirt."

I glanced down, but realized she didn't mean it literally.

"Skella is a willful child, quick to action, slower to learn."

What could I say? "Your grandson is wounded," I said. "I cannot help him."

Her face grew grave, and she waved at her people. They emerged from their cells, moving as one to the hall.

She went first, regal and stern. She would be a formidable friend . . . or enemy.

We spent the greater part of the night seeing to the wounded. A few of the elves had first-aid training, and they worked on the wounded.

Unun sat with her grandson's head in her lap, stroking his forehead and chanting "Come home to me, little one. Let me light your way," over and over.

The dwarves tended their own, separate from the elves, and I could see that some of them were shamed by the way they'd treated the elves.

Borimber brought us water but would not approach the elves.

Finally, one dwarf, a grizzled old man with a thinning beard and a broken arm, stepped to the elves. One of the elves, a large man by the name of Jara, stepped in front of him, his arms crossed over his chest, preventing the dwarf from reaching Unun.

The dwarf drew a long, thin sword. I sat up, ready to jump in, but the dwarf turned the blade around, offering the pommel to Jara. He went down on one knee, bowing his head, exposing his neck.

"I offer my life to you, Jara, in payment for the blood debt my clan owes yours."

Jara took the blade and glanced back at Unun, who did not respond but continued to croon to Gletts. He turned back and raised the sword, and the dwarves bowed their heads or looked away. The blade whistled down, and I turned my head. There was a meaty thud, and the dwarf's head hit the ground seconds before his body.

Katie cried out and looked away. These were not our people, not our ways, but I felt violated, confused. What kind of world was this?

"I declare blood truce," Jara said, stepping away from the decapitated body. "Let Krevag's sacrifice bind this peace."

The elves murmured behind him but didn't raise any objection. After a moment two younger dwarves came forward and dragged Krevag's body back to where they were grouped. Jara waited as another dwarf approached, then he turned the blade around and handed it to the dwarf, pommel first.

"It is so," the dwarf said. "My father's blood will seal this bargain." He bowed at Jara and stooped to pick up his father's bloody head.

"Can we go home?" Katie asked.

"Sooner the better," I said, watching them in horror. But I needed to check something first.

I approached Krevag's son. "I need a word."

He stopped. "I know of you," he whispered. "You who killed the great beast, not once, but twice."

"And I know of you," I said, letting the anger bleed into my voice. "You kidnap kids and bleed them, using blood magic to make mead."

His shoulders sagged. "It was not I, but Kraken and his brother,

Bruden. They are the weavers of spells. I am a simple craftsman, no more."

He looked at me, his father's head dangling from his fist.

"I need to know it's done, over."

He pointed to two of the dwarven dead who had been separated from the others. "There lay your villains."

The two that the T. rex had taken down. They were sprawled, untouched, in a pool of black blood.

It scared me, them soaking in the blood like that. I'd seen some pretty freaky stuff at Anezka's with similar-looking muck.

"We will burn them," he said. "Send their ashes to the great mother. Their spirits are shorn and cannot even beg to enter Hel."

Harsh.

"So be it," I said. "I want this to end."

He glanced over his shoulder, his face wracked with pain. "You are rash to judge, young one. You do not fully appreciate our lives."

"No, I don't. But we are judged by how we act in bad times as well as good."

He nodded. "Fair enough."

I turned to go back to my friends, and he stopped me. "Smith," he said quietly, "your name was brought to me by your friend, my brethren Rolph Brokkrson."

I stopped midstep and turned. "Yeah?"

"He says you serve the blade." It was definitely not a question.

I touched Gram in her sheath over my shoulder. "She is unsettled," I said. "Things are changing."

He smiled. "Life is change. I am sorry for our part in your pain," he continued. "I owe you a debt."

"Lot of debt around here," I said. "I've seen how that works with you folks. I'd rather not," I pointed to his father's head, dripping blood on the stone floor.

He bowed.

I turned away again, and paused.

"There is one thing," I said. "Who got the other samples of mead?"

# Sixty-three

TURNED OUT WE WERE DEEP UNDERNEATH A BASKETBALL stadium in the north end of Vancouver. The dwarves' stronghold had been delved into the earth long before the stadium and the surrounding park had been built.

Once we were escorted out through a tunnel that led to a river, Katie and I went with the elves, while the dwarves went back inside to tend to their fallen.

Jara knew people and went to a bank of pay phones and made a call. Within thirty minutes a bus arrived, one of those private tour coaches. The guy who drove looked at Katie and me as we climbed aboard with our armor, my hammers, and, of course, Gram.

"You're her," he whispered as I stepped up the stairs.

"Yes," Katie said, ushering me past the wide-eyed young man. "And she's very tired."

I almost laughed, letting her maneuver me to the back. They'd let us enter first, let us have our choice of seats.

Gletts they carried onboard, setting him in the back near us. The fallen elves they carried one at a time, laying them gently in the cargo area beneath the bus. A fine line separated the dead from the merely—I looked at Gletts—What was he? Lost? Wandering? Unun seemed convinced he would return somehow. I was waiting to be surprised.

The bus dropped us off inside Stanley Park.

I followed Unun and the elves as they carried their wounded and their dead into the forest. Dawn was just breaking over the horizon, but there was little joy in the returning light.

The fact that they lived in a heavily visited park and almost no one knew they were there would have surprised me a year ago. Now I just wondered at the magic used to conceal them.

Gletts and Skella lived with Unun; they had since their parents were killed by Jean-Paul's minions a decade ago. They took Gletts to a central building along with the others to be tended to. If Gletts wasn't exactly dead, maybe the rest of them were not beyond saving. All I knew was I was bone tired and could eat the bark off one of the surrounding trees.

Jara brought us food and water, settled us in a spare room in Unun's house, and left us.

Katie and I talked quietly as we ate the food offered: nuts, berries, bread, and cheese. They brought us wine and water, both of which were heavenly.

"I have a list," I told her as we ate.

"Of?"

"Where the potions went. They sent out four. Frederick got one, and Nidhogg. We know hers is in the house with Qindra."

"And the others?"

"Just addresses," I said, rubbing my forehead. "Memphis and Dublin."

"More dragons?"

"Not sure," I told her. "I would think so, but he was evasive."

She leaned into me, putting her head on my shoulder. "I'm very tired."

It must have been the exhaustion, but there was something different about Katie. I couldn't put my finger on it, but she seemed larger somehow, more in the now, if that makes any kind of sense.

We took turns cleaning our wounds and fell asleep in each other's arms.

When I woke, it was nearly dark again. I was stiff and sore. I stretched, trying to work out the kinks. Katie still slept, but she'd been awake earlier in the day. She had changed clothes, bathed somewhere. A bath sounded heavenly.

Unun sat in the main room knitting when I came out.

"How's Gletts?" I asked.

She didn't pause in her knitting, but looked up at me with a smile. "He's a strong boy. A good boy. He'll find his way home eventually."

I sat in a chair next to her, crossed my hands over my knees, and watched her work.

"Where's Skella?"

She nodded. "She's over with Gletts now. She looked in on you, but you were still sleeping. She and your Katie went down to the showers at the golf course. Katie said you would like to do the same when you woke."

Golf course? Seemed inconvenient, but I guess they bathed on a different schedule than I was used to.

"We could draw you a bath," she said, as if she knew what I was thinking, "but Katie said you'd balk at all the fuss."

That was my Katie. "She knows me too well."

"She loves you very much."

I let that just settle over me, the glory of it. She loved me. What else could I ever need?

I sat there in silence, just soaking in the nothing. Peace ruled this house, quiet contemplation and . . . I looked around at all the pictures, the artwork and crafts that filled every corner. This house was full of love.

"We'll need to get back, check on things. Let people know we are okay."

Unun nodded. "Always in a rush, your kind. Burn the brighter for it." She smiled, and I found no judgment there, no condemnation. Just a statement of fact.

She was right. I was itching to move, to get back home.

Katie woke soon after. She took me over to the meeting hall, where the fallen were laid out. Skella sat with Gletts, holding his hand and reading to him from a book of fairy tales.

She looked up as we approached and called one of the other women over to sit with Gletts. First she hugged me, crying. Then she escorted us over to the golf course. She hadn't said anything to me, just sat and chatted with Katie quietly in the locker room while I showered.

The water was hot and all my cuts stung, but the heat helped ease some of the stiffness and aches. Katie whistled when I came out in a towel, smiling at me and smirking. Skella handed me a set of clothes folded neatly. I stepped behind a row of lockers and dropped the towel.

The shirt looked familiar, as did the other things. I got into the panties and bra, pulled the jeans off the stack, and knew for a fact these were mine.

"Hey," I called, stepping around the lockers, one leg in the jeans, hopping to get the other in, "where'd you get my clothes?"

Katie and Skella shared a look, and Katie began to laugh. "Oh, dear," she said when she could talk. "You are in for quite the surprise."

Skella looked stricken.

Once I was dressed, including a concert T-shirt I'd lost a couple of months ago, I trudged back into the woods, fuming.

I didn't like being on the outs of something funny. Made me feel like I was being made fun of. Katie kept snickering every time I'd look at her, and I gave her a look.

She wrapped her arm over my shoulder and squeezed. "You will understand in a minute. Just be patient, Cranky."

We went past the little village and deeper into the woods. There, in the side of a hill, we walked toward a cave.

"Not more dwarves?" I asked.

"No," Skella said. "Not dwarves. Just something of Gletts's you should see."

We had to stoop going through the entrance, but, once we were inside, the cave opened up. There were several mirrors stationed around, and as we walked past them, Skella touched each one. They flared to life for a brief moment, each showing a different place I recognized.

My apartment, which surprised me, since I'd slid the mirror behind the couch. Apparently Julie thought it better to be out now.

Jimmy's bathroom, showers at the YMCA I went to sometimes, Monkey Shines, though it took Katie to point out it was the coffee shop. The mirror really just looked in on the hallway. Once I had context, the symbols on the bathroom doors made sense—high heel for women and hammer for men. Someone's idea of a funny gender designation that had always pissed me off.

On the far wall was a shrine. There was no other way around it. Several dozen pictures of me, in various states of undress, I might add, were stuck up on the wall. On a table beneath the pictures were several things I recognized.

There were the keys from my old Civic, which had been smashed in the battle with the dragon and the giants; another bra; some socks; an old pair of sneakers; several shards of metal that looked like waste from making horseshoes; my cell phone (dead); the charger I couldn't find during our Vancouver trip; three paperbacks (one smutty); and a bottle of Bimbo Limbo nail polish.

I sat down on a chair by the shrine with an oomph. "He's been stealing from me?" I asked, looking over at Skella. "Stalking me, stealing my underwear."

"He seems to have quite the crush," Katie said, taking one of the pictures down. It showed me in the shower doing something I never really wanted photographed. "I'll just keep this one," she said, winking at me.

I rolled my eyes. "Perv."

"You don't understand," Skella went on, specifically avoiding the pictures on the wall. "We've never known anyone who stood up to them. When we'd heard what you did, that he was finally gone . . ." She shuddered. "He idolized you."

"Uh-huh." I looked at her. She meant it, the earnestness in her face. She loved him, didn't want this to be a bad thing.

Stupid kids. I picked up my cell phone and charger, shoved them into my pocket, and then took down the pictures that showed more of me than I was comfortable with. Those I just handed to Katie, who smiled wickedly.

"This is creepy, you know that, right?"

Skella looked at me, imploringly. "Don't hate him. Please?"

"Okay, fine. But no more nudity. No more spying on me, you understand?"

"Yes," she said, nodding. "I'll explain it all to him."

If he ever woke up again. Life was tough all around.

"Friends?" Katie asked, looking at me with wide-open eyes.

I shook my head. "Why not?"

"Excellent," she said, clapping. "Wait until I tell Deidre I've got real elves for friends."

Lord preserve us. I glanced at Skella, who looked more relieved but still very worried. "You don't know any wizards, do you? Rangers or hobbits?"

Katie gave me a look, sticking out her tongue, but Skella was confused. "Park rangers visit us here from time to time, but only the ones we trust."

"Never mind," I said. "Katie can loan you the books."

I glanced across the mirrors. "Can we get word home, for starters? Let Jimmy and Julie know we are safe?"

"Did that already," Katie said, nodding. "While you were sleeping."

"But I could do more," Skella said. "Shall we contact anyone else?"

I thought for a minute; there were two I was most worried about.

"Yes, can you see the house? Can you see Qindra?"

Skella looked scared for a moment but shook her head. "I can try. I'm not sure."

"Try."

She used the mirror that showed Monkey Shines. It was a transient image, following me to places I went to regularly but were more public.

The mirror clouded, then cleared for a moment. The dresser had been knocked over. The dead guy lay on the floor by the bed, and the sky outside the window was black.

"It's hard," Skella said, straining. "The connection is tenuous."

The bedroom scene shifted as I moved around the mirror. I could see the hallway and partway into the room Qindra stood in, but I could not see her. The place was full of pain, though. I could see it in the air; the shades had not all died in the dwarven caverns. Some remained in the house, and I'd guess more were drawn there each day.

The scene shifted, rolling like watching the porn channels without paying to unlock them. I could hear strange noises, see shards of images, but nothing intelligible.

Finally the mirror blanked, and Skella stumbled. Katie caught her and helped her to the ground. "Too hard," she said.

"Could we travel through that?"

"No," she said, flatly. "No chance. I couldn't keep a strong enough connection. You'd be lost."

Lost in the mirror world sounded like a bad idea. Not something I wanted to explore.

We left the shrine and headed back to Unun. We needed to say good-bye and head home.

"Your place or Black Briar?" Skella asked us when we stood in her home again.

I knew what we should do. "Black Briar, I think."

Katie nodded at me. "Jimmy's worried."

"Okay, I can call Julie from there."

"What about Gletts?" Katie asked. "Will he be okay?"

"Gran thinks he'll come home when he wants," Skella said with hope. "He just has to realize the fight's over and he's safe again. Just need to lure him back."

"I have an idea," I said. "Let's go see him."

The room was solemn, lit only by the light from the windows, and deep shadows filled the odd places. Gletts was lying on a table that reminded me of a bier more than anything.

I walked over and stroked the hair off his forehead. He looked so small there, but I remembered him charging into battle to protect my friends and his sister. "Gletts," I said, sitting beside him on a long bench. "I need you to come home. Unun and Skella need you here. They need to tell you how brave you were."

Skella was crying. Katie stood behind her with her hands on the young elf's shoulders.

I pulled the sleeve of my T-shirt, tucking my arm back inside, and took off my bra under the shirt.

"Here," I said, draping the bra across his folded hands. "A to-ken of my approval. Thank you for helping them. Thank you for being brave."

I leaned over, kissed him on the cheek, and stood up, clapping my hands together. "Home now?"

Skella was astonished, and Katie began to laugh. "You have changed Beauhall, that's for sure."

I stepped close to her and kissed her on the nose. "Life is change. Let's get out of here."

# Sixty-four

THINGS WERE A LITTLE WILD AT BLACK BRIAR. ONCE THE attack they expected didn't come, they'd camped out for the night. Now that it was the end of the next day, folks were heading home. We just missed the twins, but Melanie was there with Jimmy and Deidre.

Ari would live, but his throat was pretty messed up. If he could talk again, he'd have a gravelly voice. He'd never sing again. Beats being dead all to hell.

We exchanged stories over dinner. Nothing happened at Black Briar, but there was some very funny meteorological activity in the area. Dark clouds streaking over the mountains, intense lightning, storms.

As soon as we were settled, I plugged in my cell phone. There was a call I needed to make. I looked around at the folks here at Black Briar, the family I'd chosen, and thought back to the one I'd inherited.

Qindra was trapped, just like Megan. Had I abandoned her to a similar fate? Had I escaped, only to never look back? I was a shit. I lay awake longer than I wanted, thinking about all the mistakes in my life, as well as what I needed to do to fix things. Maybe I needed to do some bridge building.

After breakfast the next morning, while Katie and I slept, Jimmy,

Gunther, Stuart, and half a dozen others had driven out to Anezka's place. Without knowing exactly where it was, they couldn't find it. Something in the way Qindra had shielded it was stronger than the original seal that Flora had worked into the beams and structure. You drove right by it, seeing only an empty field.

They'd picked up the Ducati when they figured they couldn't find a way onto the property and spent the better part of the day contemplating how they could break through the barrier.

Melanie had already filled them in on the ghosts, how Jean-Paul had come back, and the battle with the dwarves from her point of view.

Katie and I filled in the rest, about Qindra, the house, the nexus, and even the shield, which surprised everyone.

"I hate that she's trapped in there," I said after we'd run out of stories to tell.

"She works for the other side," Jimmy said. "Not like she'd cry over us."

Deidre threw a pillow at him. "Weren't you listening? She did it to protect all of us."

He shrugged, stoic. He had a hard time seeing shades of gray. Everything with him was black and white.

"And what about Anezka and your imp friend?" Deidre asked.

I pulled the amulet from out of my shirt and slipped the chain over my head. "Not sure," I said. "I could call him, but I'm not sure he'd come."

"Why don't you give it a try? We can handle Anezka if she gets crazy."

Was worth a shot. "Okay."

I stood up, walked into the living room, and stood in front of the fireplace. With a fire burning, it might make him more comfortable. I sat cross-legged in front of the flames and held the amulet in my hands.

"Bub," I said quietly. "I need you."

Nothing.

Jimmy snorted. "That was disappointing."

I thought about it, considering all I knew of the little pisher.

"Hey, do we have any burritos or cheeseburgers?"

Jimmy strolled into the kitchen and opened the freezer. "Couple of microwave burritos in here," he said. "Both are bean."

"Nuke those puppies and let's try this again."

In three and a half minutes, I had a steaming plate with burritos on it, covered in hot sauce. I held the amulet over the steam for a minute, and then whispered to it, holding it close.

"Bub, I have burritos. Can you bring Anezka home now?"

Again nothing. Deidre wheeled her chair back into the kitchen, and Jimmy slumped against the doorframe. Katie and Melanie were sitting on the couch chatting. They all assumed we were done.

"Come on, Bub. We aren't going to hurt her. Let us help. Don't make me eat these burritos without you."

*Crack.* The air imploded, and Anezka crashed onto the coffee table, shaking, rambling incoherently, and naked.

Katie and Melanie jumped up onto the couch, and Jimmy ran into the room.

"Hang on," I said. "Let's be calm here."

Bub looked ready to fight. He was angry, smoking with the flames. I stayed seated, reached over, and slid the plate toward him. "Here, big guy. Eat something. Let the doctor see to Anezka."

He looked from me to the burritos, then to Anezka, pain on his scaly face. "Don't hurt her," he said quietly.

"Promise," I said with a smile. "We okay?"

He nodded, and I turned to Anezka. She was totally out of it, past anything I'd seen from her.

"Shock," Melanie said, going to work. Jimmy grabbed a pack from behind the couch and handed it to Melanie. They kept serious medical equipment on-site ever since the big battle.

Melanie got an IV into Anezka, and they lifted her onto the couch. Katie stood beside the couch, holding the IV bag while Jimmy went and pulled a stand out of the back room.

"Let me sedate her," Melanie said. "Then let's get her to the back room."

"I can carry her," Jimmy offered, and I looked over at Bub.

"We okay?" I asked again.

He nodded, still not touching the food.

Once we had Anezka settled in the spare room, Bub ate the food. Then he told us how the moment he'd taken her from the house, she'd just collapsed like a rag doll.

"Where do you go?" I asked. "Where did you take her?"

"Sideways," he said with a shrug. "Not the most pleasant place, but it's not here."

"Maybe you can take me sometime," I said, patting him on the claw.

He looked at me, his eyes narrowed. I pulled my hand back and laughed. "Only if it's okay with you."

He ate the plate before I could stop him, but then he agreed to stick with regular food after that.

We arranged for him to stay here, sleeping in Anezka's room for the time being. Melanie would arrange a nurse to come out and stay with them while she came around.

"We'll evaluate things then," she said. "But I'm keeping her sedated for a day or so. She needs sleep as much as anything. Her numbers are good. Can't vouch for her mental state, though."

"I got it," Jimmy said. "She won't hurt herself or anyone else."

"We should call Gunther," I said. "He'll want to be here when she wakes up."

408                    J. A. PITTS

Jimmy raised his eyebrows, sharing a look with Deidre. "That's interesting."

"She likes him, is all. Maybe she'd consider him a friendly face, not a stranger."

"And how's your friend Bub feel about him?"

"He's an honorable man," Bub said from the hallway. "I would not begrudge his company, as long as he has her best interest at heart."

"Well, there you go," Deidre said, smiling.

"I've never thought of Gunther having a girl," Katie said. "This could be life changing."

"Can you stay the night?" Jimmy asked.

"I need to work tomorrow," Katie said. "Kids need a teacher. They won't understand all this."

"Can't you get a sub?" Jimmy asked.

She shook her head. "I need something normal."

I totally understood what she meant.

"Sarah," Katie said, pulling me out onto the porch. "Don't go home. Stay with me tonight. Come to my place."

"Sounds good to me," I said, hugging her to me. "But I need to make a stop. I'll follow on the bike. You head home."

"Can't it wait?"

"No. Not this."

She kissed me and went back into the house to say her good-byes. I grabbed my cell phone, helmet, and keys, and headed out.

# Sixty-five

ONCE I CROSSED OVER ONTO 522, I PULLED OVER TO THE breakdown lane and turned off the bike.

I pulled out my cell phone and cycled through the numbers. There was one I'd only called once, back in the spring, but it was critical.

It rang three times, and a young woman answered. "This is a private line. Who is this?"

I explained who I was, got directions, and headed back onto the highway. There was something I needed to do, and I had to do it in person.

After a twenty-minute ride, I pulled up to the gate and flipped up my faceplate. A guard stepped from the little shack and asked to see my ID. I showed my license, and he opened the gate.

The bike ticked in the cold as I walked up the steps and knocked on the door.

A young child, no more than six or seven, answered, bowing at me without saying a word, and turned to walk away.

I followed quickly, making sure to shut the door. The place was huge. It had a giant marbled foyer with dark-paneled walls with paintings and statues every few feet. Great plants sat in the corners, and three women hurried away, their heads bowed.

The waif escorted me to the end of the great entryway and

stopped in front of two ornately carved doors. She knocked once, and then pushed the left door open, stepping inside.

I followed.

The room was dimly lit, not dank or dark, but quiet and calm.

In one corner three women sat doing needlework, and a boy stood by a door that led to a veranda. An old woman sat in a rocker against the far wall. The room was larger than Jimmy's house. Large enough for a dragon.

"I know you," the old woman said, her voice weak and shaky.

I bowed. "Yes. We've spoken on the phone."

"Sit, child killer. What brings you to my home?"

I could feel the power emanating from her. Despite her age, this was a formidable woman, a power to be reckoned with on many levels.

"I bring you news," I said, trying to keep my voice steady. Inside, my brain was screaming *DRAGON! RUN!* but I kept it together.

"You are either very foolish or very desperate to come here," Nidhogg said. "Which is it?

"Heartsick," I said. "I bear you news of Qindra."

Everyone in the room froze. I didn't move my head but glanced around as far as I could see without moving. They were terrified. Would she rage like Jean-Paul had, killing his own troops? I had a feeling it had happened here before.

"What do you know of my wayward servant?" Nidhogg asked. She was a paragon of calm, but I avoided looking into her eyes. That way lay madness.

"She is alive," I said quietly.

As one, those in the room released their breath.

"But in grave peril."

I spent the next hour answering questions, telling her the truth of the matter. I couldn't lie to her. As soon as I opened my mouth,

I knew she could smell deception. Besides, I'd come here to relay this news.

"I see," she said when I'd finished. She rocked for several long minutes; the only sound in the room was the clicking of knitting needles. My fingers itched, thinking of the rhythm. The young girl who had led me here sat at Nidhogg's left, knitting. It reminded me of Unun, who waited for her grandson to return home.

"And what do you propose?" Nidhogg asked.

Here was a test. One that would let me walk away, or die at her feet.

"I give you my word," I said quietly, looking up into her face for the first time. "I will find a way to free her."

Nidhogg captured my eyes in her own and looked into me. I saw ancient sorrow there, pain and frustration. She was unfathomably ancient, yet a searing intelligence burned in her. And there were tears. Tears for Qindra.

"I accept," she said, nodding once. "Your life for hers. If you bring her home to me, I will consider your debt to me assuaged. If you fail, you and yours are forfeit unto me."

I bowed my head. "So mote it be."

Without another word, the young girl laid her knitting aside and led me back out of the house. I breathed the night air gratefully, as one does when the act had been given up as a lost cause.

I climbed on the bike and drove through the opened gate.

Maybe I'd stop and buy a bottle of mead. Something to celebrate with. Katie would love it.

As I drove across the floating bridge to the eastside, I thought of what I wanted in life. How those quiet moments of talking to one another were the best moments, how we accomplished so much more with words than with swords.

The dwarves had sent forth four bottles of mead. One lay trapped in the house with Qindra. Another went to Frederick. And the last two had gone to Dublin and Memphis. Why did I have a feeling they would come back to haunt me?

That was a puzzle for another time. My heart was full of pain, and all I wanted was to get home to Katie and fall into bed.

Tomorrow, maybe, I'd call my mother. If she had one tenth the sorrow I'd seen in Nidhogg, it would take a lifetime of work to assuage it all.

That felt right. Mending those rifts. Gave me hope that I'd be a grown-up someday. And, if I was going to grow all the way up, I'd have to accept some other things.

I'd give up my apartment. Julie could take over the lease until she got on her feet. Katie and I could find our own place. Someplace that was neither hers nor mine, but ours.

And that seemed like the best thing in the world.